SHADES OF MERCY

ALSO BY BRUCE BORGOS

The Bitter Past

SHADES
OF
MERCY

A PORTER BECK MYSTERY

BRUCE BORGOS

MINOTAUR
BOOKS
NEW YORK

First published in the United States by Minotaur Books, an imprint of St. Martin's Publishing Group

SHADES OF MERCY. Copyright © 2024 by Bruce Borgos. All rights reserved. Printed in the United States of America. For information, address St. Martin's Publishing Group, 120 Broadway, New York, NY 10271.

www.minotaurbooks.com

The Library of Congress Cataloging-in-Publication Data is available upon request.

ISBN 978-1-250-84809-3 (hardcover)
ISBN 978-1-250-84810-9 (ebook)

Our books may be purchased in bulk for promotional, educational, or business use. Please contact your local bookseller or the Macmillan Corporate and Premium Sales Department at 1-800-221-7945, extension 5442, or by email at MacmillanSpecialMarkets@macmillan.com.

First Edition: 2024

10 9 8 7 6 5 4 3 2 1

To all the kids in my life who have allowed me to enter their imaginations and make-believe worlds with my own tall tales. You have made all this possible.

SHADES OF MERCY

CHAPTER 1

At 92,000 feet, the Vulture suddenly developed a mind of its own. It dove like the hunter it was, screaming down through the stratosphere, looking for something to eat. Fifty miles away, from his chair in the control center at Groom Lake, a white rectangular box about the length of a shipping container, the remote pilot saw the first sign that something was amiss. The attitude indicator, the instrument that provided him the aircraft's orientation relative to the earth's horizon, pitched forty degrees to the right, a severe turn northeast. The control station was state of the art, featuring six twenty-four-inch touchscreen displays for each operator. The three topmost screens, arranged side by side, displayed the aircraft's various camera feeds. As his eyes moved to the top portion of the screen directly in front of him, the pilot saw the altimeter numbers falling rapidly.

"Uh, problem here."

His sensor operator looked up from her half-completed checklist. "What?"

"We're diving."

She shot him a sideways glance. "Stop screwing around, Sam."

The pilot moved his right hand from the keyboard and placed it on the control stick, pressing the button on the far left and taking the Vulture out of auto-mode. When he moved the stick toward him, nothing happened. "No joke. Vehicle is no longer on flight plan. Bearing is zero-eight-seven, and I have LOS."

The loss-of-signal indication was all the sensor operator needed to hear. She typed a command into her keyboard. "Sending lost link now."

The command was a fail-safe, one that instructed the Vulture's navigation system to begin flying in predetermined loops until they could regain control. It should have worked instantaneously. "No response," the pilot said. "Still descending, passing sixty thousand and decreasing speed. Better get on the phone."

The sensor operator punched a button on the hands-free base next to her that connected her to the RPA communications unit and began speaking into her headset. "Uh, guys, are you seeing this? Vulture is not responding." She listened intently for a few seconds. "Uh-huh," she finally responded. "Roger that."

"What?" asked the pilot.

"As usual, they don't have a clue. Going to call us back."

"Great."

"Did you do an instruments check?"

"Not an instrument failure. Everything is in the green." The pilot pressed several keys on his terminal and tried moving the control stick again. "She just won't respond. Someone else is flying her." He was ex-Navy, an aviator with twenty-two years of actual flight experience who had once landed on an aircraft carrier with a broken tail hook. "No response on signal reboot."

They both watched as the Vulture turned around just before the Utah border, sailing above the mostly barren desert on a flight path that would, in minutes, bring it back over the secret test range, or over Los Angeles in less than an hour. The sensor operator heard a ring in her headset. She listened. "Roger. Initiating patience timer countdown now." It was the auto self-destruct timer that could be activated in a worst-case scenario.

Twenty seconds later the patience timer expired. What should have happened next was a shutdown of the Vulture's engine resulting in a quarter rotation of the wings so the aircraft would spiral benignly to the desert floor.

The pilot grimaced. "Patience timer malfunction. Heading is now south-southwest at two-zero-two, altitude approaching twenty-seven thousand and—"

Letters suddenly began appearing on the monitors in front of them. They spelled out: "Apologies. Have this badass bird back to you in a few minutes. Please stand by."

The sensor operator rose from her chair. "NFW," she said. It wasn't a military acronym.

The pilot depressed a button on his console and spoke into his headset. "Flight Term One, Ops."

From high up on a mountain to the north, the reply was instantaneous. "Go for Flight Term One."

"Stand by to issue the command destruct signal on my mark. Do you copy?"

"Ops, Flight Term One copies all and is standing by."

"Terminate, terminate, terminate."

"Roger. Flight Term One is transmitting on four two eight megahertz at a thousand watts."

There was a lot of redundancy built into the flight operations of RPAs. If the patience timer wasn't working, the transmission of this signal should activate it. The pilot watched and waited for it to do just that. "Flight Term One, Ops, are you sure you're transmitting? No response from the article."

A different voice, this one female, controlled and unemotional, streamed into the pilot's ear. "Ops, Flight Term Two, we see Flight

Term One's signal. It's likely that the flight termination receiver has been disabled."

Before the pilot could respond, he saw the indicator for weapons system activation flash green. "Mother of God, the weapons system is arming."

Twenty-three thousand feet below, Shiloah Roy's seventeenth birthday party was moving into high gear. The celebration at the Double J Ranch was beautifully decorated, as was Shiloah herself, sparkling in her turquoise and gold gown, the skirt of which billowed in layers from her tiny waist to her knees and ended in a hem that was the same strawberry blonde color as the hair that flowed down her back in big, thick curls. She looked every bit the million bucks her father had intended, despite her pleadings for a normal birthday party with just a small group of friends. This was to be her formal coming-out, he told her, and people, important people, needed to see her. Shiloah wasn't stupid. She knew this party was more about him than her. It was a business meeting.

It was 8:30 P.M. The molten-colored sun descended through the haze of wildfire smoke, leaving only the thousand bulbs strung over the dance floor to shine on Shiloah and her friends. Jesse Roy watched his daughter from the extravagant barbecue pit adjacent to the ranch house he had already spent a fortune remodeling. She was everything. And though she seemed ebullient tonight, she had become distant, even combative these last several months, seemingly unappreciative of all the things he had provided, including the elite St. Paul's School in New Hampshire she attended. Yes, their ranch was in the middle of nowhere, and she had only a few friends nearby, but she had the finest horses to ride and every electronic gadget she could possibly want. Was it drugs, he wondered, a boyfriend back east she was missing? Was it her mother? After eight years, was Shiloah resenting him for her death? If only she would talk to him.

The margaritas and beer were flowing, and the smoke from the Cohiba Esplendidos he and the other men were puffing almost equaled what was coming from the caterer's grill. As the song faded into its last notes, Jesse Roy walked across the grass to the expensive Las Vegas DJ and took the microphone from him.

"My friends, please join me out here on this beautiful lawn," he said in a voice bursting with pride. Tall and slender, he was bedecked in a summer beige suit that contrasted nicely with his Kemo Sabe lizard skin boots. At forty-six, especially with his full, pomaded black hair, Jesse looked like the poster boy for what hard work and sweat could win you in life.

More than a hundred guests, about half from south of the U.S. border and the rest Shiloah's St. Paul's classmates and their super-affluent parents, stepped onto the grass. They formed two lines facing each other, and they watched as Shiloah walked slowly between them toward her father.

Jesse reached out and took his daughter's hand. "Shiloah, you are as beautiful as your mother." Choking up, he made the sign of the cross, an act of sanctification he normally reserved for a big bet at Santa Anita or Churchill Downs, and managed, "May God rest her soul."

Tears welled in Shiloah's brown eyes, and with his thumb and forefinger, Jesse squeezed the water out of his own. "I love that you were born on the Fourth of July, as you are a child of this great country and everything it stands for. Independence. That's you in a nutshell, Shiloah. And it means we have two reasons for fireworks every year." Everyone cheered. Jesse had paid a king's ransom for the Zambini Brothers' eight-minute pyrotechnics show, and he would be damned if he was going to let some county prohibition keep him and his guests from seeing it. Besides, the Double J was nestled in the heart of Dry Valley, surrounded by hills and miles off the highway. No one but Jesse Roy's guests were likely to see the illegal display. Still, he had a full complement of young men and water hoses standing by in case it sparked on the ground.

Jesse raised a hand into the air and spoke loudly into the microphone again. "Maestro, if you please?"

From the large oval horse arena a hundred yards to the west, the music started again, loud and heavy with drums. Suddenly, a thousand brilliantly colored lights shot into the now dark sky. The laser beams danced across the heavens in every direction, and from behind them came long strings of rockets and a cacophony of explosions and color that rivaled anything on the Las Vegas Strip. It was so loud the people on the ground couldn't hear each other gasp. Minutes later, it ended in a spectacular burst of red, white, and blue streamers arcing over the ranch and the heads of the party attendees. Bodies and eyes turned to follow the fading rockets, only to find another fireball, much higher and much brighter, coming toward them, leaving a white streak behind it for miles.

Shiloah turned to her father. "Daddy?" she asked, pointing. "Is that for me?"

Jesse Roy and his guests watched in awe as the streaking fireball suddenly seemed to divide. It was an explosion of light, the second fireball glowing even brighter and moving at a much greater speed as it pitched toward the ranch, its fiery propellant illuminating everything below it. Other than the Zambini Brothers crew, Jesse was the only one who knew this was not part of the fireworks he had paid to see. At the last second, he dove on top of Shiloah, covering her with his body.

The screen on the small laptop was gray, and the few glowing heat signatures that dotted it slowly moved out of view, only to be replaced by more. The hand guiding the Vulture was steady now, its new pilot learning quickly the micro-adjustments that turned the aircraft, made it climb or dive, or altered its speed. The hacker had studied, prepared. Practiced. Approaching the GPS coordinates that were now keyed into the RPA's navigation, the screen began filling with multiple heat sources. Dozens of them. Then hundreds. The operator slowed the Vulture even more, found the target that had been provided, and fired. The R9X, the missile known in the armed forces as the flying Ginsu, dove toward the ground.

In the command trailer eighty miles to the west, the RPA's pilot shot to his feet. "Jesus, what the hell did we just blow up?"

Much closer to the Double J, the Vulture's hijacker typed out an email. It was addressed to nuhaigottome997@gmail.com, and read, "Hey babe, amazing sunset tonight. Did you happen to catch it?"

The reply came thirty-four minutes later. "I did. So amazing. Happy Independence Day."

CHAPTER 2

Why Porter Beck was behind the wheel would be the topic of some heated discussions later, with lots of angry partici- pants, but it was an overdose call, and it was a friend. Had the rest of his dozen officers not been assisting with wildfires or patrolling the county for illegal fireworks, he could have sent one of them, but being shorthanded was a fact of life in Lincoln County, and despite being a daylight man, he was still sheriff.

The EMS team was still fifteen minutes away treating a drunken cowboy who had tried celebrating the Fourth by shooting a dozen roman candles out of his butt crack. So it was down to Beck and Bo to respond to the 9-1-1 call.

The Sheriff's Department sat literally across the highway from the Pioneer Hotel, probably no more than a half mile as the crow flew, but it seemed an order of magnitude farther to Beck as he steered his F-150 Police Interceptor like a student driver out for his first lesson. It wasn't mechanical issues that caused him to weave all over the road. It was because he was impaired, his vi- sion narrowed to a tiny tunnel. The disease had come on quickly, though it had been hiding in his DNA for the first forty years of his life. While he could see almost normally when the sun was up or internal lighting was strong, his eyesight after sundown retreated faster than the British at Dunkirk.

He had come to dread the night.

Right now, it was almost 8:30 P.M., the sun already behind Highland Peak to the west and the sky a fading pinkish hue from all the wildfire smoke. Inside the cab of the truck, Beck's newest officer, Frank Columbo, was holding on for dear life.

"You might want to buckle up, pard," said Beck as the truck shot over the 93, siren blaring. He sensed his deputy's unease, could hear it in his voice. "Doing the best I can. Your patience is appreciated." Columbo was growing on Beck, partly because he had a cool name for a cop, was quiet, paid attention most of the time, and loved a good cup of coffee. Mostly though, Beck liked him because he was a dog.

The night vision goggles were helping some. No doctor had prescribed them, and Beck was unaware of any studies that had tested their value for people with retinitis pigmentosa. All he knew was that they allowed him to see better than if he didn't have them on, sensing the smallest amounts of infrared light reflected off objects and then electrically amplifying that light into some kind of glowing green image. It wasn't nearly as clear as it would be for a person with normal vision, but the goggles allowed him to see most obstacles.

Heading up Main Street, the truck swerving, Beck jumped the curb and took out a stand of shrubs that lined the southern border of the LDS church parking lot. Bo yelped.

"A few bushes," he assured him, silently hoping that was true. "Pretty sure, anyway. God won't mind." An agonizingly long minute later, they careened to a stop in front of the Pioneer, and Beck could make out a glowing green form in front of the old building, arms waving. He knew it must be Josie Conrad. She was a wisp of a woman, in her seventies now, and after sliding to a stop, Beck had trouble keeping up with her as he ran, med kit under his arm, up the steep staircase to the second floor.

The Conrads had owned the hotel for more than thirty years. It had about ten rooms, all with their own western theme, and had originally been a saloon as well. Now it was only the hotel and a small restaurant.

As he and Columbo made the brightly lit second-floor landing, Beck tore off the night vision goggles. Down the long hallway, he could see Byron Conrad, Cash's dad, straddled over his son's thighs and performing chest compressions too slow to be effective.

"Sheriff's here," Josie yelled as she reached the room.

Beck came through the door a second behind her. Byron rolled off his son, gasping for air and crying. "He's not waking up, Beck. I can't get him to wake up!"

Beck gazed down at his oldest friend, on his back, shirtless, his face and lips blue. Not breathing. But it was the lifeless body of the family dog, an ancient golden retriever named Lillibelle, lying next to Cash that told Beck everything he needed to know.

He seized Byron under both arms, hauling him out of the room and into the hallway. "Stay out here, both of you," he told Josie.

He pointed down at Columbo. "Stay, Bo." The dog sat on command. Overdoses are not good places for canine officers, especially if there is fentanyl in the room. One wrong sniff of the stuff and that's it for the dog. No doubt Lillibelle had entered the room with Byron, had inhaled some of the ultrafine powder floating invisibly in the air, and had died almost instantly.

A young couple with worried faces came out of their room a few doors down. "Get back!" Beck yelled. "Everyone, back. Go to the end of the hallway." There wasn't much risk of fentanyl exposure to human first responders, he knew, but he wasn't taking any chances. He reentered the room and dropped to the carpeted floor, confirming Cash's condition in three quick measurements: pulse, pupils, and body temperature. He had no pulse. His pupils were the size of pinpoints, and his body, a shadow of its former self, was cold.

"Damn it, Cash!" Beck yelled. "Don't go on me like this!" He pulled the naloxone nasal spray out of his bag, popped the two yellow caps off the injector, attached the atomizer on one end, and screwed the vial into the injector. Then he shot the mist into Cash's nose. If it would work at all at this point, the drug might take a couple of minutes. But for that to happen, he had to get him breathing again. He rose to his knees and brought his hands, one over the other, firmly down over his friend's breastbone. He started compressions, aiming for two inches in depth, counting each one out loud. "Five, six, seven . . ."

From behind him in the hallway, Bo barked, helping with crowd control. "Twelve, thirteen . . ." Beck heard the awful crack, knowing he had broken one of Cash's ribs, but continued without a pause. "Fifteen, sixteen, seventeen. Come on, Cash! Not like this. Twenty-two, twenty-three . . ."

As he continued the chest compressions for several minutes, Beck slowly accepted the futility of his efforts. The naloxone wasn't working, and there wasn't the slightest hint of Cash's heart restarting. Finally, Beck yanked a blanket off a nearby sofa and covered his friend's face and chest with it. Watching from the hallway, Josie screamed. Beck got up and staggered to the door, looking down at Cash's parents. "I'm so sorry," he said, shaking his head. "He's gone."

With that, he closed the door, leaving him alone in the hotel room. On a small end table next to the couch above Cash's body, Beck saw a bottle of whiskey and a plastic dinner plate with some pills crushed mostly into powder. One pill was still whole, and Beck recognized it as a counterfeit M30 immediately. He had seen enough of them over the last few years to know the difference. Made to look like prescription oxycodone, these were Mexican Blues, smuggled up from Mexico like heroin and everything else. He moved the plate to the kitchenette's sink and scraped its contents into a Ziploc bag, sealing it. Then he ran some water over the plate, rinsed his hands in the warm water, and splashed some on his face.

The memories came flooding back. Beck had known Cash Conrad pretty much his entire life, had been to elementary, middle, and high school with him, had played Little League with him. Along with Jesse Roy, the three of them had been almost inseparable.

The nightmare had begun in their junior year at Lincoln County High. So much like his dad in physical appearance and athleticism, Cash had already received scholarship offers to play football at Southern Utah as well as a small school in Washington state. He had his ticket out, and the sky was the limit. He was an Eagle Scout and a good Mormon boy, a great kid all around. And then in the Homecoming game in October, he took a hard shot from a helmet to his lower back.

The vertebral fracture wasn't that severe. It didn't paralyze him. It healed without surgery. In a month, he was doing physical therapy and recovering nicely. But the lingering pain was unlike anything he had ever experienced.

It lasted for almost thirty years.

The back surgeries seemed to make everything worse. When the prescriptions dried up, heroin and morphine were readily available. It was a brutal cycle of rehab and relapse. Nothing was strong enough, not even the helping hand Beck extended when he returned home from the Army. By that point, Cash had made other friends. Their names were Jim Beam and Johnnie Walker.

As he dried his face, Beck realized that Cash's death made six already this year. In a population of 6,000. Last time he checked, they were close to leading the nation in overdoses per 1,000 residents.

The EMS guys eventually arrived, checked Byron and Josie for any potential fentanyl exposure, and told them they would be fine. Beck knew that would never be the case. They would forever feel as if they had failed their son. Once Cash and Lillibelle were sealed in tombs of thick plastic with a zipper down the front, they were transported to the medical center. Beck watched as they were driven away, then climbed back into the cab with Bo. He waited for the bar crowd that had gathered out front to dissolve before he let the tears come. Bo stepped over the console between them and nuzzled his way onto Beck's lap with an empathetic whine. He stroked the dog's big red ears and asked God to take care of his friend.

Through the windshield, he thought he saw a light streak across the sky, a fuzzy fireball moving at tremendous speed. He wondered if it might be his friend's soul speeding like a missile to heaven.

"Goodbye, Cash," he said.

CHAPTER 3

Beck slept about as well as a deer during hunting season. Images of Cash's lifeless body floated behind his eyes, and Columbo's restless legs syndrome didn't help. It also didn't help that he was sharing the small sofa in the break room with the new deputy. Around two in the morning, he gave up and walked back into his office. He sat down behind his desk in the old leather chair the last sheriff had ceded him, the springs screaming like a piglet stuck under a fence, and pulled up his email to check for any recent wildfire updates. There was nothing new from Esther Ellingboe, the Bureau of Land Management's district manager up in Ely, and no news was good news as far as Beck was concerned. He turned to the large map of the county on the wall to his right, the one with thirty-five colored pushpins clumped in various locations. Each pin constituted a wildfire, each color-coded to indicate a particular status. Green pins were for fires already extinguished. There were fourteen of those, spread throughout the mountains mostly to the east and south close to the Utah border. Eight yellow pins indicated fires under control but which were still active. Most of that was up north. Then there were twelve red pins designating more than 32,000 acres of woodland and high desert vegetation that were currently burning out of control.

He rose from the chair and placed a new red pin at the top of Highland Peak. He doubted there had ever been thirteen red pins in the map this early in fire season, certainly not in the few years since he returned home. This year, there had been little snow in the higher elevations, and by the end of April it was pretty much gone, and with it any hope of holding the devil at bay.

As a result, Beck's tiny force was spread out over the county's 11,000 square miles, assisting the Forest Service and BLM in evacuating residents and blocking roads into fire areas.

"That's a lot of fire, my friend," he told Bo.

Columbo rose from his position on the floor and began moving in circles before settling into a ball on the floor. The dog scratched one ear furiously, then clamped his big black eyes shut.

"Am I boring you?"

His cell phone pinged. Beck sat back down and noticed the new email at the top of his continually expanding inbox on his oversized computer screen. He thought it was some kind of spam and dangled the cursor over the delete button. But then the subject line caught his eye: RE: *Hello, Lisa1957*.

He leaned closer to the screen, hoping he had misread it, wondering for half a second if the retinitis pigmentosa was starting to screw with his inside-the-office vision, a progression of the disease he knew was coming someday. But he was reading it clearly. *Can't be a coincidence.* To the best of his knowledge, there were only three people in the world who had knowledge of and might possibly understand the meaning of the name Lisa and 1957 when they were combined. He was one of them.

He looked at the sender address, 0DayMei@proton.me. The name meant nothing to Beck except that Mei was a common Chinese name for girls. He could ignore the message, delete it even, but he knew it would be at his own peril. His fingers moved to his face and his perpetual two-day stubble, an absent-minded habit he engaged in when pondering a problem. He felt the creases at the corners of his light blue eyes, burrowing trails of time, like the gray popping up in his otherwise brown hair, still thick but beginning its grudging retreat at the top. He was officially middle-aged now, approaching forty-six and feeling it, and mysterious emails in the middle of the night weren't likely to help with his chronic lack of quality sleep.

Beck gazed at the screen once again. *Hello, Lisa1957.* He clicked on the message. It was brief: *And so it begins, Sheriff. I hope this note finds you well. I have done a lot of homework on you, and I hope my instincts about you prove true because I have a feeling I am going to need your help very soon.*

Beck cradled his chin in his folded hands. *Done a lot of homework on you? Going to need your help? And so* what *begins?*

There was no valediction, no name beneath the message. Was Mei O'Day the sender's name? That would be an odd combination but possible. He decided to let Google decide, but when he got no hits, he examined the name again, this time more carefully. It wasn't O'Day with an O. It was a zero. Zero Day Mei. He Googled that. It returned a number of hits on two Chinese pandas named Mei at the Atlanta Zoo as well as a story about a computer hack of some kind. Nothing immediately useful.

He hit reply and typed out *Who is this?* Then he waited twenty-five long minutes before summoning the courage to click send. Immediately, another email arrived in his inbox. *Delivery Status Notification (Failure).*

The communication was meant to be one-way.

CHAPTER 4

It was warm already when Beck finally got home shortly after 7 A.M. Setting up the obstacle course out in back of the house, he knew the mercury would probably top a hundred degrees by day's end. Once he and Bo got started, the only thing rising faster than the earth's temperature was Beck's temper. The dog had him tripping over every gas can and railroad tie on the course. "Stop!" he yelled, reaching down and grabbing his shin, tearing off the blindfold with the other hand. "Enough already. Which one of us is the blind guy here?"

Columbo stared back with uncertain eyes. He was a beauty, Beck had to admit. At twenty months, the fox red English Lab was about sixty pounds, a little on the low side for his age, but stout enough to pull his master to the ground if he saw a squirrel or, God forbid, someone with food in their hand.

Originally trained as a sniffer, Columbo had washed out of the Washoe County Sheriff Department's K-9 Drug Academy. His dream of rooting out narcotics at the airport quashed, he went next to the Guns and Ammo class. Didn't graduate. *Unable to stay focused*, his evaluation said. Slated to be sold, Beck spotted him in a kennel while attending the Sheriff's Association semi-annual meeting and got an idea. All he had to do was karaoke "I Shot the Sheriff" at the bar the Nevada lawmen found themselves at later that night. It was a horrible rendition, but for his effort they awarded him Columbo. Beck even slipped him into the department's budget as an officer-in-training, hoping he could teach him to be his eyes in the dark. With no guide dog training schools nearby, it was videos and books for Beck and Columbo.

After colliding with a bench in the grass, Beck peeled the bandana from his eyes again and stared down at his deputy with dismay. "Do you remember *any* of the videos we watched?" He bent down, tightening the dog's K9 Ballistics vest that had somehow slipped sideways over his trunk.

It didn't help that Pop was on the porch laughing his ass off. "I think he's doing it on purpose," the old lawman said. "Fine-looking animal, but I'm not sure he's cut out to lead you around in the dark, Porter." Only his dad and his adopted sister, Brinley, called him Porter. It was Beck to everyone else. "Might be you should get *his* vision checked."

"Well, stop feeding him those table scraps," Beck growled. "All that fat is clogging his brain." He made a mental note to have the vet check the dog's eyesight and looked up as his ears caught the sound of a helicopter approaching in the smoky summer sky. Sort of approaching. The pilot, like Columbo, seemed to be unsure of where he was going.

His phone rang. It was Tuffy Scruggs, his best officer and newly promoted lieutenant. "Yeah, Tuff."

"Hey, Beck, did I wake you?"

"Nope. I'm out back getting my skin slowly scraped away by my best buddy."

She laughed. "You're such a DIY guy, boss. You know they have schools for this, right?"

He looked down at the dog. "It's doubtful Columbo's delicate ego could handle flunking out again. What's up?"

"Sorry to bother you, but I wanted to let you know I had the NHP guys test the drugs that killed Cash Conrad. Definitely fentanyl. The most powerful stuff they've ever seen apparently."

Beck kicked at the ground and spoke quietly so Pop wouldn't hear. "Well, fuck."

"Yeah. Also, there's some government guy heading your way in a helo. Stopped by expecting you to be in on a Saturday, I guess. I gave him directions. Has he found you yet?"

Given the size of the county, even street addresses weren't easy to find, especially ones off the beaten path. Lost Meadows, the plot of land Pop purchased almost fifty years earlier, was even more difficult to locate from the air. Beck looked up into the sky again. "Not yet, but he's in the general area. What makes you think he's government?"

"Well, he didn't ID himself. No markings on the helo. Plainclothes, very official-looking, short hair. Goofball smile."

"Okay, you're describing the president. Is it the president?"

He hung up as Pearl Askins came out the screen door onto the back porch holding two glasses of orange juice. Beck had hired her a few weeks ago because Pop's dementia had gotten to the point where it would have been dangerous for him to wander off on his own. The retired sheriff was physically shrinking too, the memory loss sometimes causing him to forget to eat. Beck and Brinley had gone through three other caregivers before finding Pearl. Nothing wrong with the others, it was simply that Pop didn't think he needed to be cared for. But he had a crush on Pearl. She was twenty years younger and a widow. She handed them each a glass and Pop a breakfast burrito.

"Jesus," Pearl said, "it's only the first flush of morning, and it's already hotter out here than a whorehouse on nickel night." She was a fetching woman for being almost seventy, with long gray hair sometimes braided down her back, and she squinted up into the midday sun. "And what the hell is with that whirlybird?"

"Looks like he's getting ready to crash the thing," Pop said, pulling his long frame from his wicker lounger. He rubbed at the deep half-moon scar that extended from just below his right eye to the middle of his cheek, something Beck noticed he did now whenever he was trying to remember something. "Where's Little Joe, anyway? Don't want him anywhere near wherever this idiot sets down."

Beck set his juice on the rail, wondering if Joe Beck could even recall how he came by that scar. "He passed away, Pop. Remember? A few months back now."

Pop's eyes suddenly moistened, and he turned away. Little Joe had been their giant Leonberger, a full hundred pounds bigger than Columbo, a dog with a lion's mane but all the ferociousness of a field mouse. That was the ugly reality of Pop's dementia. Every day he lost his buddy all over again.

Beck got tired of watching the helo pilot crossing over the property multiple times and finally waved his arms until he saw it bank left. Reflected in the morning sunlight, he could see it clearly now. It was small, dark gray, nondescript. A minute later, the flying eggbeater landed in a small field of red brome a hundred yards away. A man scrambled out, and Beck noticed the pilot kept the rotors turning.

Living next door to the most secret military testing area in the country, if not the world, these kinds of visits were not out of the ordinary. It was likely that the guy approaching him now was going to read him the riot act for not patrolling a hundred-plus miles of bordering land with his contingent of twelve officers. Maybe somebody climbed a fence. Or maybe it was about last night. Beck knew there had been some reports of strange lights in the sky—he had even seen one himself—but it was the Fourth of July, so he chalked those up to errant fireworks. He hadn't gotten any calls about new fires yet, which meant this visit was probably about something else.

"I'm looking for Sheriff Beck," the man with the carefully combed black hair said as Columbo sniffed him up and down.

He was a younger version of Beck, by a dozen years or so, and he had the reedy physique that comes with a higher metabolism. His eyes were light brown and closely set, with pupils that were almost vertical, like a cat's, and they were covered with dark-rimmed glasses. Deep dimples in both cheeks accented a broad, welcoming smile. With the brown sport coat and tan chinos, though, he was definitely government. Hair length indicated the military.

"Old or new?" Beck asked. "You got both here."

The visitor's gaze passed between the two sheriffs. "Current, I guess." He opened his wallet, displaying a round, gold badge with dark blue lettering. "Special Agent Ed Maddox. Office of Special Investigations."

His accent was southeastern New England, maybe Massachusetts or Rhode Island, Beck wasn't sure yet. Before he could say anything, Pop jumped in. "Wait. Your name is Special Ed?"

Beck glared at the old man. "I'm the current sheriff, Porter Beck. The mean guy up there on the porch is my father, Joe."

He recalled what he knew of the OSI, the Air Force's equivalent of the Army's Criminal Investigation Department. It was composed mainly of younger career officers, which meant that Maddox was probably a captain—most of their senior agents were—but an older captain and probably not on an upward career trajectory if he hadn't been rotated out yet. Beck had some experience with military cops, spending twenty years bouncing all over the world as an Army Foreign Area Officer, and he figured

Maddox was probably out of Nellis Air Force Base, a little northeast of Las Vegas. Yet the helo he arrived in had no Air Force markings, and that was strange. "What brings you all the way out here?"

The OSI man glanced at the senior citizen with the horrible scar sipping his O.J. on the porch next to a woman he guessed was the old-timer's wife. "Could we speak in private, Sheriff?"

Pop laughed. "Trust me, Chief. Your secrets are safe with me. If I'm lucky, I'll forget you were even here in a few minutes. If that won't work for you, get the hell off my property." Pop had recently begun calling people "Chief" if he couldn't remember their name. That included Beck at times.

Having no such credentials in law enforcement or mental decline, Pearl scowled and started for the back door. "Damn, I was hoping to make this part of my podcast today." She slipped back into the house.

"That's Pearl," said Beck. "She does stand-up twice a week." He looked down at Columbo, who was sitting on his rump with his ears standing straight up. "We're all ears, Maddox."

That goofball grin retreated now. "Very well. We had a little trouble with one of our aircraft last night, and we lost a piece of it in your county. I would appreciate it if you could take a ride with me since I'm not familiar with the area."

Beck recalled the fuzzy streak of light in the sky he'd seen last night. "That's vague. Which piece exactly did you lose?"

Maddox turned and headed toward the chopper, as if it were a fait accompli that Beck would follow. "I'm afraid I can't say."

"Where in my county?"

"Tell you on the way."

Beck's last trip in a helicopter had been five months earlier. It had been a nasty evening, replete with death and deceit. He called out, "Why don't we drive instead?"

"Think of it as a flying car," Maddox yelled back.

He left Columbo with Pop. Once they were in the air, Maddox signaled to Beck to put on the radio headset. "Pioche is an interesting name for a town. Is it French?"

In no mood for small talk, the sheriff simply nodded. Maddox stared back until the history buff in Beck was forced to come out. "Named after a Frenchman who bought the town in the 1860s. Of course, the land belonged to the Southern Paiute at that time, who were somewhat surprised and disappointed by the news it was no longer theirs."

Maddox had the eager innocence of a ten-year-old. "I haven't spent much time in the west. From Rhode Island originally. Everything out here is so different. So big."

"*So* incredible," Beck said, rolling his eyes and already regretting his decision to come along. "You stationed at Nellis?"

Maddox laughed. "For now. Talk about a crazy place. Vegas, I mean. Did you know that it gets so hot there that you can fry an egg on the asphalt?"

Beck looked out his window, his thoughts drawn to Cash once more, his ability to chitchat waning quickly. "Yeah, how's that taste?" That shut down the conversation for a few minutes until the helo banked left and he could see where they were headed. *Of all the places.*

"What do you know about the Double J Ranch?" Maddox asked, staring down at a map.

As soon as he heard the name, Beck felt the pinch of regret in his chest. "Used to be the Roy Ranch, owned by Justin Roy. After he died, his son Jesse inherited the land. Renamed it, I guess."

Maddox cocked his head to one side. "What's the second J for?"

Beck chuckled. "James. His name is Jesse James Roy."

"Like the bank robber?"

"I suppose," Beck muttered, looking down at the place. "Is that where you lost part of your aircraft?"

Maddox didn't respond, which got Beck wondering why the Air Force would send out its version of a detective to chase down something that fell off one of its planes. The OSI investigated crimes, and this didn't sound like one. It made him even more curious about what had accidentally dropped out of the sky.

"This happened last night?"

Maddox gave a quick head bob.

"No one called us to secure the site. How come?"

Maddox sat there looking like the kid in class who never knew the answer to anything. "Don't know, but I wouldn't want to be the guy that dicked that up."

That didn't sound right. The military was exceptionally OCD about notifying and working with civilian law enforcement to secure an accident site. And there had been no report of property damage or injury from Jesse Roy. Still, in a county where cactus outnumbered people by about a million to one, Jesse might not even be aware something had fallen onto his very sizable piece of it.

They landed in a field north of the ranch entrance, a few hundred yards from where the main house used to be and where a spectacular Spanish fort was now being erected. Where there was once a flimsy swinging gate made from aluminum poles, two elaborately carved massive wooden bull heads now stood, their gnarled sharp white horns bearing down, colliding in the middle of two ornate wrought-iron panels. Over the massive beasts, the ranch's brand, J^J, was centered in a circle. The gate cost more than Beck made in a year. Or two. The size and weight of it made him wonder about the physics of how it even opened.

As he and Maddox approached on foot, he saw a college-age Latin male, another surprise. Not the man's ethnicity. Beck had just never seen a ranch entrance that was manned. The bull heads parted, swinging outward, and three identical black SUVs with darkly tinted windows drove out, the young guard waving happily to the occupants.

Beck showed the man the star on his hip and told him he would like to speak to Mr. Roy.

"Is there a problem, Sheriff?" he asked. The kid had a pretty heavy accent, but his syntax and politeness were better than Beck was used to.

"Well, for starters this gate is way too big and much too expensive. Might be a code violation of some sort." The kid stared back at him blankly. "Tell him it's Porter Beck." *Yesterday it was Cash. Today, it's Jesse. My two oldest friends in the world.* It struck him that Jesse would have no way of knowing what had happened at the Pioneer last night, and that he would have to break the horrible news once again.

The guard speed-dialed a number and whispered a few sentences. Beck didn't speak Spanish. Not yet. He was a polyglot, fluent in Russian, German, French, and Korean, all because of his stations in the Army. His aptitude was unintentional but remarkable; he simply remembered everything he heard and could parrot it back like a native. Understanding the words came later. He didn't need a lesson, though, to understand what the young man was saying. It took only a few moments, and then the guard motioned them inside. As they walked toward the sprawling ranch house in the distance, another man came down the dirt road in a rust-colored Jeep. He was a little older, maybe thirty, also Latin, which Beck found interesting. Hispanics composed about 5 percent of the county's 6,000 residents. In all the time he had spent at the Roys' in his youth, he couldn't recall ever seeing any nonwhite workers. Jesse's father didn't trust them. It was nice to see the son hadn't inherited the same bias.

Maddox and Beck climbed into the Jeep and were informed

Mr. Roy was up with the herd. They drove a quarter mile before entering a pasture that was so green it looked like someone had dropped a golf course down in the middle of the desert. Beck was sure there were a thousand head of cattle getting fat out there on the back nine. He could see a line of at least thirty portable sprinkler carts for watering pastures, and beyond them, a number of solar-powered pumps. Water rights in Nevada weren't the easiest to obtain, and well drilling was strictly regulated, and with the natural springs in the area drying up like good ideas in Congress, Beck wondered how Jesse could afford to create such a verdant landscape.

Far to the east, he saw an airstrip, smooth and dusty with a nice airplane sitting on the south end. Beck recognized it as a Beechcraft Baron G58. Not cheap. Not easy for a cattleman. Forget about irrigation costs. That particular bird went for about 1.5 million.

The driver stopped on the north end of the pasture and pointed. Beck and Maddox got out and walked into the middle of the herd toward two men on horseback atop a small hill a hundred yards away. The cattle looked to be a mix of mostly coal-black Angus, but Beck noted a few snow-white Charolais, as well as a couple hundred red and white Herefords sprinkled in. That constituted almost all his knowledge of cattle. These looked to be in extremely good shape for western cattle, especially drought-plagued Nevada cattle. In an era when livestock operations in the state were mostly shrinking, Jesse Roy's was somehow expanding.

Beck recognized Jesse instantly, despite him being on a horse and facing in the other direction. "License and registration, please," he said.

Holding a handkerchief over his mouth, Jesse Roy swiveled in his saddle and met Beck's gaze. A second later he was on the ground, his right cheek puffy with tobacco and an expensive white Resistol covering his crown. He walked down the hill to the sheriff. "Good God, look what the dog dug up. How the hell are you?"

The scent of rotting meat now entered Beck's nostrils. "Heard you were back, Jesse," he said, offering his hand. "Meant to come out and see you sooner."

Jesse took it, a wide grin opening on his face. "Well, that's mud in the fire. It's a big county, and we're a little off the beaten path. Been back for two months now, but the new house has been under construction for almost a year. These damn carpenters move slower than a herd of snails through peanut butter. Did you see it?"

Beck shook his head. "I saw that bigger version of the Alamo down there."

The lanky cattleman laughed. "Yeah, it's big, I know." He stuffed his hands in the pockets of his jeans. "Heard you finally left the Army and took your pop's old job. Been meaning to stop in and say hi. Got too busy, I guess, what with getting this place up and running again."

Beck glanced over at Maddox, whose surprise was evident, and thought he saw a trace of hope, hope that this meeting might go easier than expected. "Sounds like we're even, then. It's good to see you."

A few uncomfortable seconds later, Jesse said, "God, look at you. Soldier and now sheriff. Still looking out for everybody else." He raised an eyebrow, looking over his old friend. "What, no uniform? How does anybody even know you're the sheriff? Your pop must be rolling in his grave."

Beck adjusted his LCSD ball cap. The distance between him and Jesse had grown substantially since their teens. It was hard keeping a friendship when you never saw each other, and Jesse's marriage to Willa had made that even harder. He couldn't blame Jesse for making an educated guess about Pop. "Pop's still alive," he said with a tiny catch in his throat. "He's mostly rolling around the house now." He gestured to Maddox. "Jesse, this is Special Agent Ed Maddox with the United States Air Force's Office of Special Investigations."

Jesse reached out and took the OSI man's hand. "Special Ed, this man up in the saddle is my associate, César. I imagine you guys are going to explain to me what the hell happened here last night."

Beck took in the heavyset man whose hands gripped the pommel as if he were expecting the animal to bolt at any moment. He wore gray Wrangler Wranchers that were too tight and too dressy for sitting a horse, a khaki cowboy shirt with a floral pattern on the breast, and Black Jack alligator boots straight from the bayou that Beck knew fetched about five grand. The silver and red TAG Heuer on César's significant wrist brought the ensemble to easily more than $10,000. It was an ostentatious, if impractical, wardrobe for riding the range.

Jesse motioned Beck and Maddox to follow him up the hill. Looking down the other side, both men saw a crater about a foot deep but easily ten feet in diameter with the remains of what must have been a very large animal. Pieces of horns, parts of the hide in chunks, like it had all been put in a salad spinner. Dried blood caked the crater and the surrounding grass. And the flies were feasting. Two giant crows sat on a nearby dune, impatiently waiting for the men to leave. Metal fragments protruded from the ground as well, a few of which looked like pieces of blades.

Beck glared at Maddox. This was not the result of something *falling* from the sky. He cleared his dry throat. "Yes, Agent Maddox, by all means, please explain what happened here last night."

Maddox put his best face on, despite the smell. "Quite simply,

Mr. Roy, we had an aircraft malfunction. It was a test we were conducting, and one of the fuel tanks fell off."

Beck's forehead furrowed like a plow line in the dirt. There were no burn marks in the crater, no sign of combusted fuel. Jesse's narrowing eyes revealed a healthy level of skepticism as well. The rancher removed his hat and scratched his scalp. "Did you say *fell*, Ed? Because if something fell, even with my limited understanding of gravity, wouldn't it fall relatively straight down?"

Maddox shook his head. "Not really, sir. When things fall from planes—in this case a fuel tank—it follows a trajectory similar to a parabola with a forward speed equal to the aircraft's speed, and a downward speed starting at zero but increasing because of gravity."

No one said anything for a moment, and Maddox seemed quite pleased with his Wikipedian lesson on the laws of motion. Jesse waved his hat over the big hole in the ground. "Uh-huh. Well, whatever it was crossed a good portion of the sky before it blew up my prized bull. Out of all the cattle you see here in this pasture, you clowns managed to take out my best investment."

Before Maddox could respond, Jesse stepped right into his face. "Do you know what I do here, Ed?"

Sheepishly, Maddox adjusted his eyeglasses and glanced around the pasture. "I assume you raise cattle."

"I breed steaks. The best steaks for the finest restaurants from Arizona to Canada. That prized Angus bull you blew up was a semen machine."

Beck didn't doubt it. Unlike his father's operation, Jesse seemed to have the best of everything. *How* was the question. Out here, a really good cattle rancher might earn a nice living, but it was a tough life, and profitability was dependent upon a number of factors. From year to year, it could be a crap shoot. Especially when you factored in the drought over the last several years.

Maddox either didn't know or didn't care about any of that. "Again, I'm very sorry, Mr. Roy. The government is prepared to cover your loss."

Sure, Beck thought. After months or even a year of haggling before an eventual wire transfer that wouldn't come close to fair market value. But then he saw Maddox pull a large checkbook out of the inner pocket of his sport coat.

Jesse looked over his shoulder to César. "Oh, everything is going to be okay now, César. He's prepared to write me a check to cover my loss." Jesse turned back to the crater now, stuffed his hands in his pockets, and looked sorrowfully down on the remains of his steak-maker. "How much?"

Maddox didn't hesitate. "Full replacement cost, of course."

Jesse Roy whipped his head around. "Do you have any idea how much this bull was worth?" Maddox's expression indicated he did not. "I'm asking for a number, Agent Maddox. Give me a number."

Maddox looked to Beck for help, and getting none, offered, "Five . . . thousand?"

Jesse looked to Beck. "You want to tell him?"

Porter Beck was not a rancher, but he'd been around them a good chunk of his life. "For a breeder like the one you describe," he said, "and based on the quality of the cows I can see here, I'd say you paid north of fifty." Maddox's eyes ballooned.

"Ding, ding!" Jesse announced. "We have a winner. Very good, old friend." He turned back to Maddox. "I paid eighty thousand for that animal, sir. That's an eight with four zeros."

The Air Force investigator gulped a great lungful of air. "That much? I didn't know an animal could cost—"

Jesse held a finger up to the shorter man's face. "Eighty thousand is what I paid for the bull. He was in his prime breeding years. Now, some breeders might work their bulls six, eight, maybe even ten years. But prime breeding is maybe four to five. So, let's say five years, because I'm in a forgiving mood."

Beck could see the blood draining from Maddox's face.

"Five years of breeding seasons, and on the low side that's forty calves a season. That's a minimum of two hundred calves, which then get good and fat and which I sell for about three thousand dollars on average."

Strangely, Beck felt in the mood for a good steak now. With some eggs, maybe. Jesse waited impatiently while Maddox did the math, but Beck was pretty sure the man's brain had exploded already.

"Beck?"

"Six million."

"Six million," Jesse said, shaking his head. "That's a lot of fucking inconvenience, Ed."

Maddox took a step back. "Mr. Roy, I'm authorized to pay you up to twenty-five thousand dollars right now. Provided you can supply a copy of the bill of sale, I'm sure we can expedite the balance of the replacement cost in the next few days."

Days? Beck was astonished.

Jesse glared down at him. "I have insurance on the bull, Ed. They'll cover the replacement cost."

The OSI man raised an eyebrow. "The United States Air Force would prefer you do *not* contact your carrier, sir."

Interesting.

Jesse's eyebrow lifted. "You want to keep what happened here between us."

"We do, sir."

Jesse winked at Beck. "No problem. Then it's a hundred thousand dollars."

When Maddox looked to him for help, Beck grinned and looked away. "A hundred thousand?"

Jesse shook his head. "I can't drive down to the Quickie Mart and buy another bull like this, Agent Maddox. I have to locate one just as good. That takes time, and it's a major inconvenience. I have to have it tested and physically examined. I have to ship it. You want me to go quietly, it's one hundred thousand dollars, and you can consider yourself lucky."

Beck smirked. He was well aware the government occasionally had to reimburse civilians for losses they sustained due to the military's mistakes, especially unintended damages during a war. Across the west, it was still paying out up to $50,000 to people who lived downwind of the test site and qualified under the Radiation Exposure Compensation Act. It was a pittance for what they had suffered during the dawn of the atomic age, and getting compensation from the feds was never easy. He fully expected Maddox to balk.

"That seems reasonable," the OSI agent responded. "Of course, I don't work for the people who make the final decision in these sorts of cases, but I believe that's doable."

Beck nearly fell over. There was no way Maddox had the authority to say such a thing. Something was not right here.

"Very good, Agent Maddox. Very good. Let's go someplace we can sit down and complete whatever paperwork you have." Jesse draped an arm over Maddox's shoulder, and they walked down the hill and across the immense pasture toward the Jeep. César followed uncomfortably with the horses.

Beck mentioned to Jesse that he seemed to be taking the ordeal in stride.

"It's all about perspective, Beck, and here mine comes now." He pointed toward the road, where a young woman was loping toward them on a shimmering black Friesian, easily sixteen hands and muscular. *Probably another 30K*, Beck thought.

"Gentlemen," Jesse said, as she came to a stop across the road.

"This is my daughter, Shiloah." He introduced Maddox and Beck. "The sheriff and I used to hang out back in the day."

"Very nice to meet you both," she said.

The sight of her up close literally took Beck's breath. She was her mother. She was Willa. The same reddish blond hair and blue eyes, the same light and freckled complexion. He gave the gelding a rub on his head and reached up, taking the young woman's hand, holding it. "I knew your mom, Shiloah, and was very sorry to hear of her passing."

Her smile revealed well-to-do straight white teeth gently sweeping back into the contrasting dark corners of her mouth. "Were you sweet on her, Sheriff?"

So sweet it scared me away. "Everyone was," he said. "How do you like it here so far?"

"Oh, I absolutely hate it," she said, scanning the horizon. "It's not as pretty as Arizona, and there's nothing to do here."

Beck laughed. "I had similar feelings when I was your age."

She leaned toward him. "What did you do about it?"

"I skedaddled for a couple decades."

Shiloah nodded disapprovingly at her father.

"Last night," Jesse said, "we were celebrating my ungrateful daughter's seventeenth birthday." He pointed to the house a half mile in the distance. "We were all over there getting ready to set off some fireworks, and guess what happened?"

Jesus, Beck thought. *The Air Force nearly cooked a birthday party. No wonder Maddox is in a hurry to settle.*

Maddox knew it too and bit his lip. "I'm sorry, miss. I hope we didn't ruin your party."

Shiloah laughed, glaring down at her father. "Are you kidding? Best fireworks ever."

"Apparently it was a fuel tank from an airplane, Shiloah," he told her. "Now go back to the house, please."

She trotted off with a laugh but not in the direction of the house. Beck guessed she wanted to see the bull.

"Do you have kids, Beck?" Jesse asked.

"I'll check with my accountant, but I don't believe so."

Jesse laughed. "Half the time it's the greatest experience of your life."

"And the other half?"

He turned and looked back at his daughter riding away. "Makes you wonder if you truly understand what a great experience is."

Willa had always wanted a big family, wanted to start right out of high school. Couldn't wait to be married. At eighteen, Beck found that prospect frightening. Now he found himself wondering if he was somehow the reason Shiloah was an only child. Maybe that was the height of conceit. Maybe Willa couldn't have more. "She looks so much like her," he said, turning for a final glance at the girl on the horse.

"God, don't I know it. It makes me shudder sometimes, how much she does," Jesse said, putting a hand on his shoulder. "It was an aneurysm that killed her. Fired off in her head one day. Eight years now."

Beck stopped walking. "Can I ask you something, Jesse?"

"Sure, buddy." Jesse had always been affable, easy to like. At first.

"You didn't call my office to report what happened to your bull. I'm wondering why."

He stared into Beck's eyes for a second too long. "It was late. And dark. There was no fire. And I had guests. I was going to do that very thing after we looked over the . . . *damage* this morning. And now you've saved me the trouble."

Beck had learned to read faces over the years. Russians had the best poker faces. Jesse Roy did not. Something falls out of the sky, kills your best bull, and comes close to killing you and yours, and you don't call 9–1–1? He decided to let it go and instead pointed to the dirt airstrip to the east. "You fly that thing?"

Jesse grimaced, his right cheek tucking up under his eye. "Expensive hobby. Like owning a boat. My biggest vice really. You fly?"

"Not since we tied those cardboard wings to our arms and jumped off the Moon Caves in the third grade."

Jesse clapped him on the shoulder. "God, we were stupid kids. How did we ever survive?"

"We were made of rubber."

While Jesse was completing the government's lengthy claims form down by the barn, Beck marveled at the size of the new, nearly complete main house, noting that all the construction workers were Latino. Their trucks had logos from some outfit in Arizona. Maddox finally handed Jesse Roy a down payment for his bull, and the four men walked to the main gate. Beck decided it was a good place to pose for a picture for old times' sake and asked Jesse and César to join him. He handed Maddox his cell phone. After some coaxing, César reluctantly took a spot off Beck's right shoulder, and Maddox snapped off five or six photos. "Man," Beck said, taking the phone back, "the place is a lot bigger than I remember, Jesse. Your dad would have been proud, I bet."

Jesse nudged the Resistol higher up on his forehead. "I'd take that bet," he said and spat a stream of tobacco juice onto the ground. "The man never said a kind word to me after my mom died."

Like Beck's mother, Jesse's had succumbed to cancer at an early age, the probable by-product of having grown up downwind of all those atomic tests in the 1950s. Beck asked Maddox to give him a minute. Jesse did the same to César.

"No easy way to tell you this," Beck said. "Cash Conrad died last night."

Jesse's chin dropped to his chest, his eyes welling up. "His liver give out?"

"Drug overdose. Pain pills laced with fentanyl."

"Well, fuck," Jesse answered, turning away and spitting again.

Beck nodded. "Yeah, that's what I said."

Jesse looked into the face of his old friend. "He never could get that monkey off his back, I guess."

"Not a lot of people can."

"We drifted, didn't we, Beck? The three of us?"

"Like the continents. I should have been better about keeping in touch."

"I didn't make much of an effort either. Only saw Cash once since we got back." He shook his head. "Let's not wait years this time, old buddy. Will you let me know about any arrangements? If his folks need any help with the service, I'm happy to take care of it."

"I'll pass that along, Jesse. I'm sure they'll appreciate it."

Jesse turned to go. "Come by any evening. We'll do cigars and brandy. I'll take you up in that expensive toy of mine. We'll talk about Cash."

"That sounds nice," Beck said. But it didn't. It sounded like pain and regret and time he couldn't get back. It sounded like trying to jump-start a friendship that had run out of juice a long way back. As he walked to the chopper, he looked over his shoulder at the immensity of the Double J. Something was very wrong here. All this green in a parched valley, all this wealth in a weathless county. An old friend dead. Another whose prized bull had been blown away by a missile. People were lying.

He looked up at the mountains, swirled in smoke and forests crackling in flame, fighting to survive. July was going to be a bad month.

CHAPTER 5

As the helicopter rose into the sky, Beck gazed down at the ranch in its entirety, so different from the one he remembered. He had grown up the child of a cop, had learned to think like one, to see things with a critical eye, and had honed those instincts as an intelligence specialist in the Army. What he saw below him now didn't pass the smell test.

He asked the pilot to take him to his office rather than back home. Then he leaned toward Maddox, who was typing something into his phone, and spoke again through the radio headset. "You want to fill me in on what happened down there?"

Maddox set the phone on his lap, face down. "The United States government partially reimbursed a citizen for a loss to an animal caused by a fuel tank falling off an aircraft last night."

"I've seen missile debris before, Maddox."

The younger man's eyebrows waggled. "I have no idea what you're talking about, Sheriff."

Beck understood the world of military secrecy. About eighty percent of the land in Nevada was owned by the federal government, a good deal of it kept secret from the public, so it wasn't rare that he dealt with people and agencies that were habitual liars. But as sheriff he had a responsibility for public safety. Right now, he had two concerns. The first was that a missile had come very close to killing a bunch of civilians in his county, and the second was that the Double J was not on the border of the government's test range, it was a good eighty miles away.

"I'm ex-Army," he told Maddox. "I understand the position you're in. But it wouldn't be in your best interests to conceal information from me. You're an Air Force cop, not a claims adjuster. And there are hundreds of cattle out in that pasture but only one big steak-breeding bull that cost eighty thousand dollars. So, before the shit gets deep enough in here to crash your helicopter, why don't you tell me why someone targeted that bull."

Maddox removed his eyeglasses and cleaned them with one of those microfiber cloths. "You're overthinking this, Sheriff. Sometimes the simplest explanation is the best."

Beck had to give it to the guy. He was a polite slave to duty, could lie without guilt. On the one hand, Beck didn't have much to investigate. There was no real crime in the demolition of Jesse Roy's bull, and compensation had been offered and accepted. On the other hand, he knew from experience that when the government tells you not to worry, that's the time to worry.

He watched as the OSI man went back to his phone, waiting for him to make a different decision. When he didn't, Beck reached over and grabbed the device from him. A second later, he was dangling it between two fingers out the open door. "We should probably start again, Ed. I spent twenty-plus years in and around Army intelligence. I know quite a lot about aircraft and their capabilities and what is and is not possible. I know about fuel tanks and what happens when they hit the ground. I also know about things like air-to-ground missiles and enough to know the odds of anything *accidentally* hitting that bull are about the same as you being able to cut a check for twenty-five grand without calling a general somewhere in the Pentagon."

Maddox was a man perfectly in control. Not surprised or angered. He pointed toward his phone. "You know that's government property? You could get in trouble for that. I'm not kidding, Sheriff."

"Have it your way, Ed," Beck said, tossing it into the air.

"Wait!" yelled Maddox, watching Beck catch it with the same hand. "I wasn't aware of your background. I apologize."

Beck handed the phone back. "Don't apologize. Just level with me."

Maddox peered out his window for a few seconds. Finally, he swiveled in his seat to face the Lincoln County sheriff. "You're familiar with RPAs?"

Beck nodded. "Remotely piloted aircraft."

"One of ours was hijacked last night."

"I'm sorry?"

Maddox set his mobile down on the seat and leaned forward again. "Hijacked. Hacked, taken over, stolen."

Beck sat up straight. "You're serious?"

"Yeah."

"I've heard of that happening in the Middle East. Iran hacked a few of our birds, as I recall."

It wasn't a question, so Maddox didn't reply.

Beck was already thinking through the logistics. "The test range is a long way from Jesse Roy's ranch. How would someone else even have known the RPA was being flown last night, let alone have the tools and skills to hijack it?"

"Who said it came from the test range?"

Beck glared at him. "Come on, Maddox. You pick me up at my home in an unmarked helo. Nobody from Nellis or anywhere else called to ask us to secure the site. This was some black technology you guys were flying, which means you came from the place that stuff gets hidden from the rest of the world."

"You see my problem," Maddox said, nodding.

Beck was beginning to. The Nevada desert was not a combat operations theater, where an enemy would be aware of and could possibly detect and counter the flight operations of the other side. The Nevada desert was a secret place.

Maddox could see Beck's mental gears turning and anticipated the next question. "We have no idea," he said. "Once the missile was fired, the RPA returned to our control."

Beck rolled his eyes. "You're telling me the person who did this hacked the data link, the satellite that was controlling your aircraft?"

"No, I'm not. It would be against every rule in the book for me to tell you that, Sheriff." He paused a moment, searching for the right words. "It sounds like you have a fair understanding of the technology, however."

They were approaching Beck's office, and the chopper rocked in the heat waves coming up from the ground as it settled on the parking lot. Beck reached for the door handle, then looked back at Maddox. "But why target Jesse Roy's bull? I mean, you've got control of a flying killer robot. Why not pick a real target?"

"That's what I need to find out," said Maddox. "And I need to do it fast. You think 9/11 was bad? Think about this hacker pumping a missile up the president's ass."

Beck shook his head. That was the problem with drones. They were a gateway technology, opening the door for any country or any bad actor to weaponize artificial intelligence and execute lethal force while eating ice cream from the comfort of a recliner.

The pilot killed the engines. Beck took off his headphones and stepped out onto the pavement. Maddox followed him out. "Listen, Sheriff, everything I've told you is classified." They moved away from the still spinning rotor blades. "That said, I could use your help."

Beck turned, saw the concern in the man's eyes. "You think there's going to be more."

Maddox looked into the sky. "Honestly, I have no idea. It's hard to believe that the person who pulled that off last night was simply taking the thing for a joyride. It might have been a test. At this point, we don't know if it's a civilian or a foreign power. We don't know if it was a onetime thing or a prelude of something much worse. And if it is something worse, is it going to take place here or Los Angeles or Washington or halfway across the world? The only thing we do know is that Jesse Roy's bull was removed from the planet. Maybe there's a connection. It's thin, I know."

It wasn't thin in Beck's mind. "I'll dig into it."

Maddox reached into his sport coat and pulled out a business card. "I don't have to tell you. There are going to be people crawling all over this place by the end of the day. All the spook groups. You know the drill."

He did, unfortunately. They shook hands, and Beck started toward the building.

Maddox called after him. "Sheriff? What was it Mr. Roy said to you? Mud in the fire? What does that mean?"

Beck turned. "It's an old saying. It means we can't change the past."

CHAPTER 6

Beck wasn't quite sure where to begin. Jesse had lost a prized bull yet seemed no more concerned than if someone had dinged his car. The only crime that had been committed was federal—the theft of the drone—and didn't touch his jurisdictional authority. Part of his brain said to leave it alone.

But something was wrong. As wrong as liver and onions. And Beck felt for the Air Force cop and the unenviable position in which he had been placed. Military careers were made or quietly put to death by such assignments. While it was fresh in his mind, then, the first thing he did upon entering the main station was to pull Tuffy and Severo Velasco into his office.

"I see you went for a ride with the government guy," Tuffy observed. "What did he want?"

Tuffy was in her midthirties, with a pixie-cut head of sandy hair along with sand-colored doe eyes that were anything but innocent. She had seen a lot in her ten years in the department, could think on her feet, and could subdue a suspect with any number of wrestling holds she had learned in her youth.

"He took me out to Jesse Roy's place," Beck answered.

"The big spread out north of Caliente where they've been doing all the construction?" She pronounced the town's name *Calient,* without the *e* on the end, like most locals.

"Yeah, it seems that light in the sky last night was a missile fired by an Air Force drone, and it blew up Jesse's very expensive bull. The guy in the helo is OSI."

Tuffy shifted her weight to the other leg, so Sev translated. "Office of Special Investigations. Air Force cops," he said with a wink.

"I know who the damned OSI is, Velasco. I'm wondering why they would send a cop out for something like that."

"Me too," Beck said. He and Velasco had served in Germany together. The ex-soldier was a sliver over five and a half feet, but at forty still had one of those MMA bodies and the martial arts training to go with it. His uniform fit him like he had it tailored in Italy. Having grown up on the streets of Compton, California, the oldest of five siblings and a member of the West Side Pirus gang since he was nine, Sev Velasco learned very quickly how to handle firearms of every kind, but his real skills were studying tactics and sniffing out intelligence on other gangs, two things he parlayed into an excellent career in the Army. After the death of his most senior deputy, Beck recruited him. The weapons and tactics expert sailed through the training academy in Carson City and had been on the job all of six weeks now.

Sev folded his Popeye arms across his chest. "What kind of debris did you see?"

"Not a lot but a few pieces of what looked like metal blades sticking out of what remained of the bull."

"Hop up." Beck got out of his chair and Sev sat down and started typing. "Crater?"

"Not huge, not deep, but the animal was obliterated."

"So, no explosives. Inert warhead." Moments later, he showed the images of missiles to Tuffy and Beck, clicking on one after another. "Could be this. They call it the Ginsu. It's a modified Hellfire missile. Chops the target up finer than a Samurai flipping sushi at a Japanese restaurant but minimizes damage to the surroundings. Casing fragments?"

"Not that I saw," said Beck. "But I didn't get a good look."

Sev's fingers danced on the keyboard again. He was in his element. He had a German wife, Lina, and twin girls who were getting ready to start kindergarten in the fall, girls who would never have to join any gang except the Lincoln County Girl Scouts. "Okay, checking further."

"And not for public consumption, guys," Beck added, "but the drone was hacked. The OSI is looking for the hacker."

Sev looked up from the screen. "That doesn't sound right. Hackers maybe. Would be tough for one person. These things are normally flown with a pilot and a sensor or payload operator."

Beck shrugged. "Regardless, we can expect the whole alphabet to be on the ground here shortly."

"What's the alphabet?" Tuffy asked.

"CIA, FBI, NSA, DHS," Sev responded with another wink.

"Wink at me one more time, Velasco," she snarled and turned to Beck. "Where do we fit in? Since it's a fed case, I mean."

Beck pulled out his cell phone and showed them both the photos he took of Jesse Roy and the man named César. "Jesse and I go back. We were pretty close through high school, and I spent some of my summers working cows with him and his dad. I heard he was doing well, but what he's done with that ranch would blow your mind. Let's start there."

"You think someone is targeting him?" Sev asked. "A vendetta, some kind of business feud?"

Beck chewed on one side of his cheek for a second. "Not sure. All I can tell you is that when I knew him, the last thing he ever wanted to be was a cattleman. Now here he is running what is probably the biggest cattle operation in the state and someone appears to be sending him a very strong message."

"I don't like the looks of this guy," Tuffy said, pointing to the other man in the photos and winking at Sev. "The Latino."

The new deputy rolled his dark eyes. "Blatant racial insensitivity. Where's HR when you need them?"

Tuffy stuck out her hand. "Nice to meet you. I'm Sandra Scruggs, head of HR."

"Yeah, the other guy is a fish out of water," Beck said. "I wonder what he's doing on a ranch in Lincoln County. Could be Jesse's into something he shouldn't be. He was always looking for the easy score, the get-rich-quick kind of thing. Quite the scammer back in the day."

"Juvenile record?" Sev asked.

Beck shook his head. "I think he got popped for shoplifting beer once, but that's about it. Charges got dropped as I recall but his old man kicked his ass for it. I'll check with Pop to see if he remembers anything else."

"I'll see if the FBI in Vegas can run our Latino friend through facial rec. We'll put it together for you."

It was a Hail Mary. There were no shortcuts in police investigations, nothing like you might see on television where the cops or FBI could instantly identify a suspect by his photo, track his movements by a million traffic cameras, or access his phone number to determine his location in seconds. Especially out here. Police work was grunt work, much like the military, and it took people with initiative and patience to see it through. Tuffy had both qualities. She didn't have to be told what to do. It was the chief reason she would be his first choice to run the department when he left. That time, he knew, was coming. His declining sight would see to that.

Sev exited, leaving Tuffy behind in Beck's office. "How's every-thing else?" he asked her.

Tuffy sighed. "The Jolly Greens are running from fire to fire doing traffic and helping with evacuations if needed. The rest are taking their shifts here or down south. Other than a bar fight last night and a stolen tractor, it's pretty quiet all over the county. I think everybody's getting nervous about another wildfire starting up. Gotta hope that doesn't happen. We're going to need all hands next weekend."

Johnny and Jimmy Green, mostly known as the Jolly Greens but sometimes referred to as the Twin Peaks, were towering twin brothers in their midtwenties who were so identical Beck was still getting them mixed up. Tuffy, Arshal, and now Sev rounded out his contingent of real police officers while the rest were primarily paper filers and such. And Columbo.

Beck looked up. "What's next weekend?"

Tuffy raised both hands in disbelief. "Alien Independence Day. That event all the UFO nuts are coming in for."

Beck remembered now. It had been organized by some online groups who thought it was high time the American people found out what was going on inside Area 51. The plan was that, with enough people, they could storm the place. Beck laughed at the notion. Anyone who tried would be met by an army of highly trained, heavily armed security personnel. "Christ. I was hoping that was going to dissolve on its own."

"Nope," Tuffy said. "They're coming. It's not going to be any-where as big as they hoped, but I've been keeping up online, and I'd bet we see a few thousand down at Rachel. Maybe more. People are already coming in. Arshal says there's been a steady stream of camp trailers heading that way."

Arshal Jessup was his oldest officer, one of the first cops Pop hired. "That's all we need," Beck said. "All those people camping out there in the desert. I see a huge brush fire in our future. Where's Arshal anyway?"

"Fishing in Eagle Valley but on standby if we need him. He's downshifting to three days a week now, but if anything heats up before he gets back, we can pull one of the Twin Peaks down there."

"And how's Sev doing?"

Tuffy took a quick look behind her to make sure Sev wasn't standing there. "What can I say? The guy has two master's degrees. Knows more than Google. I hate him."

Beck laughed. "He'll make a good number two for you someday, Tuff."

Her face flushed with color, and she tried not to smile. "Why don't you go home, Beck? Take the day."

"Going to. Have to run down to Snow Canyon with Pop. Got a few things to zip up first."

He grabbed some hot coffee and returned to his desk, signed some purchase orders Tuffy had left for him and lingered over some emails, anything he could find to avoid making the phone call he had been considering since leaving Jesse Roy's place. The call to an intelligence officer named Sana Locke. She had helped him on a case last year and despite some challenges early on, they ended up getting along just fine, especially when they were twisted up like pretzels in the *Kama Sutra*. Professionally, Sana was one of those rare people with multiple skill sets, including the aforementioned physical dexterity, and Beck was thinking she might be able to help with the mystery of the exploding bull. He wasn't quite sure why. *Maybe because I want to hear her voice again.*

It's a bad idea, he told himself. *We parted uncomfortably. She helped me out. I helped her out. Leave it at that.* His finger was hovering above her number in his cell phone contacts when Sev walked in. "Something?"

"I think so. I sent the picture of Jesse Roy and his pal over to a friend of mine in the old neighborhood."

"That was fast."

"My guy has been around, did time for dealing when we were younger, but he made it out. Got a vocation. He's a sociology professor now."

"So, a communist?"

Sev laughed. "Pretty much." He took Beck's phone and found the photo. "My buddy says the guy on your right looks an awful lot like someone he knew from back in the day, a bandito from Mexico named Luís Trujillo."

"Bandito. Sounds serious."

"Gangs mostly. Very violent."

Beck took a few sips of coffee. "Okay, so instead of using any number of national databases, the facial recognition software you employed is a guy you spent your misspent youth with?"

"Best software is the human brain," Sev answered. "You and I both know that."

"And your guy thinks the man in the picture next to Jesse Roy may be somebody named Luís who was a street thug. Do I have that right?"

The lines in Sev's forehead were quite something to behold when he was annoyed. Beck had seen them many times over the years. They resembled the tributaries of a river coming together before a waterfall. "Would I bring you something that thin? I was about to hang up on my buddy because a guy named Luís doesn't really help us. Then he says Luís was his name, but the guy went by another name, something he told other people to call him because he was going to be a king someday. An emperor."

Beck's eyes opened wide. "César."

Sev took a bow. "César. Can't be a coincidence, boss."

It could be a coincidence but Beck's shaking head said he

doubted it. "Does your communist friend know what became of the man who would be king?"

Sev shook his head. "He does not. But he's looking into it."

Beck decided not to call Sana Locke. Right now, there was a movie he had to see.

CHAPTER 7

Jesse Roy's eyes followed the gooseneck livestock trailer as it pulled through the entrance to his ranch at the same time Porter Beck and the government agent lifted off in the helicopter. Dark gray snouts pressed into air holes on the sides of the double-decker, snouts that were connected to some of the best black Angus heifers anywhere in the world. The truck crawled east of the main house, passing a number of outbuildings. The first held a big front-end loader, a smaller Cat 259D, some spare cattle pens, and other essential ranch equipment. The second was a long red and white calving barn, and the third was a rectangular garage with automatic doors on both ends. As one of the doors rose, six Mexican cowboys walked out into the sunlight.

"What do you think?" César asked in his thick Sonoran accent as he and Jesse Roy followed the trailer.

Jesse removed his hat and wiped the sweat from his brow on the sleeve of his white shirt. "I think I've got a shitload of breeding heifers here and no good pizzles to put in them. That's what I think."

César's brow knitted. "*Cómo?* Pizzles?"

Jesse looked at the man and laughed. "Dicks. I lost my best bull, César."

César shook his head. "I mean what do you think about this man, Maddox?"

"Well, he cut me a check for twenty-five thousand without blinking, so I'm inclined to think the government would like us to carry on as if nothing ever happened."

César lit up a cancer stick and blew a long trail of blue smoke into the hot air. "I'm not sure Mr. Cordero would agree. Which is why I am still here and not on my way back to Mexico with Marta and my children."

From the back of his trousers, Jesse removed a can of Red Man and rolled it like a big poker chip between his long fingers. If Cordero was concerned enough about last night's incident to leave César behind, it would be wise to take this morning's visit by the American military more seriously. He opened the lid and set a pinch of the black dip into the right side of his mouth. "Yeah, I don't really believe in accidents either. Maybe someone is sending us a message."

"Who? The government? Does that happen here?"

Jesse shrugged. "Not that I've ever seen."

"And the sheriff?" asked César.

"Well, he's a do-gooder, that one," Jesse answered, rubbing his thumb over his lower lip. "Has a bleeding heart. But in this case, he seems to be playing tour guide for the Air Force."

"He made a point of taking our photo."

"Yeah . . . that was as phony as your wife's jewelry, and he wanted me to know it. But it won't lead him anywhere."

They watched as the driver expertly maneuvered the rig, backing it up to a long system of metal fencing and rails that ran mazelike through the dirt and ended in a cattle cage that would clamp its metal sides around the first heifer in line and every one thereafter, where the animals would be branded, vaccinated, and ear-tagged. There were a dozen in this shipment, all about eighteen months old and close to 75 percent of their mature weight, perfect for breeding. Once the cattle pot's rear doors opened, the ranch hands began feeding them into the queue.

"Any problems?" Jesse asked as the driver stepped down from the truck.

He was Caucasian, in his forties, and with his thick blond beard, the classic picture of a long-haul trucker. "Not a one, boss. Smooth sailing the whole way."

Nodding, Jesse said, "All right, let's see what we got."

As the first heifer was clamped into the cage, one man stood nearby with his hand twirling a branding iron in a long propane heater that roared with the infusion of gas and yellow and blue flame. When the cowboy determined it had reached the optimal temperature, he pulled it from the heater, and the J^J wrapped in a circle glowed cherry red. He pushed it into the animal's flank and rocked it firmly against the hide for about five seconds. The heifer tried to move but couldn't, trapped as it was in the cage, but it did voice its concerns until the cowboy withdrew the iron.

"He doesn't like that," César said with a laugh. "Can you imagine what that would do to your skin?"

Jesse glared at him and spat a dark stream of tobacco on the ground that splashed on César's expensive alligator boots. "First of all, César, that's a *female*. And second, you need to get yourself a pair of real working boots, 'cause you look like you're heading to a dude ranch in that outfit."

César reached down and carefully wiped the dark droplets from his boots with a black handkerchief. "That is very rude, my friend."

Jesse's eyes had already moved back to the branding cage and the next heifer inside it. "Uh-huh."

They watched until the others had been marked, and then they walked inside the large garage where the cattle hauler had been moved. Jesse hit the button on the near wall, lowering the rolling garage door and sealing them in from any prying eyes. Inside the trailer, the driver and his man each took a long metal pole with a hook on the end and began lifting up the metal floorboards, revealing a hidden compartment approximately ten inches deep.

"God bless the Second Amendment," Jesse said, peering down at the semiautomatic rifles, more than twenty of them lining the center of the trailer's real floor. Bordering those were a wide assortment of revolvers and semiautomatic pistols. Enough to start a war somewhere. Or feed a current one.

"Ammunition?" Jesse asked.

"You're standing on it," the driver said. "Let me show you."

Jesse moved off the metal floorboard and watched as the driver lifted it away. Tucked neatly into one side of the truck's bottom were many boxes of ammunition. Jesse dropped into a crouch to better see the manufacturer names along with various caliber indicators. He looked up at his associate from Sonora. "Legal commerce, César. Nothing wrong with legal commerce."

César didn't respond. Instead, he informed the men they would be hauling a load of steers and guns back to Mexico this afternoon.

"I think we'll wait on that," Jesse said, rubbing his chin.

"The boss is waiting, Jesse. Our men in Caborca need these weapons."

Jesse motioned César to follow him, and the two men returned to the floor of the garage and out of earshot of the driver and his man. "I'm not crazy about moving anything until we know who blew up my bull last night and why my old friend Porter Beck suspects something. Let's take a day or two."

César glared at him. "I thought you said the sheriff was a tour guide."

Jesse's face screwed tight and grew red. "Who's calling the fucking shots here, César?"

Sweating through all his western finery, César lowered his gaze respectfully. "Until such a time as it becomes a problem for us, you are."

"Goddamned right," Jesse said. "We wait."

CHAPTER 8

Snow Canyon was not named after the white stuff that occasionally drapes its higher climes but rather the two Mormon brothers who were among the first to settle that part of the territory. Pop and Columbo were excited passengers, both of them hanging their heads out the truck's windows and looking at the massive farms with their circular pivots of grass hay and alfalfa, and the mountains that gradually changed from forest to rock and sandstone. The farther south they drove, the hotter it got, and when they finally reached the state park around 4:00 P.M., the temperature gauge inside Beck's truck said it was 108 degrees outside.

There was no movie theater in Snow Canyon but there was a movie being made, and none other than Brinley Cummings was acting as the weapons master on the shoot. His adopted sister knew more about guns and shooting than anyone Beck had ever met, and that included ex-hoodlum and current deputy Severo Velasco. Guns were how she made her living, teaching people, mostly Hollywood celebrities and other rich people, how to use them without killing themselves. She had her own website, her own merchandise line. And she made a lot of money. A lot more than Beck made.

Beck had served with soldiers all over the world, only a small portion of whom he would want covering his six in a dark alley or a midnight recon mission. He would pick Brin before any of them. She was a survivor of an unimaginable upbringing, her father an abusive lunatic who lived in the mountains and sometimes chained her to the nearest tree. She was almost feral when Pop rescued her, and when he formally adopted her, so did Beck. Their relationship was not sibling-typical. It was stronger than that.

It was a quarter-mile walk from the parking area to the set, a sci-fi western type of thing by the looks of it, and Beck and his dad took it slowly over the uneven ground. More and more, Pop was becoming unsteady on his feet, and he hated when Beck would take his arm, which his son tried to do now.

"I've been walking since FDR's first term, thanks very much," he barked.

The movie people had erected a number of buildings, mostly log cabins, a livery stable, and a saloon, and on one end of the make-believe town was a shiny silver metal thing that looked similar to the spinning tops kids used to play with, only it was about two stories tall and was made to look as if it were partially embedded in the red clay rock of Snow Canyon, crashed and crumpled against the mountain.

Makes no sense, Beck thought. *You're from an advanced civilization. You've traveled light-years to get here. But you can't manage a simple landing?*

There were about a dozen trailers nearby Beck assumed were for the actors when they needed to change wardrobe or wanted to escape the sun. Lots of people were milling about, but he had no idea what any of them were doing. Some were in costumes that were certainly never worn in the American West, so maybe the

film was more science fiction than western. A pudgy uniformed security guard with dreads held up a hand to indicate they couldn't
go any farther.

"Sorry, gents," he said in London Cockney. "Closed set, I'm
afraid. Lots of other stuff to do in the park today, however. Have
a good day, then."

"Check your sheet, Bob Marley," Pop said, rebuffing him. "My
daughter, Brinley Cummings, is working on your damned movie.
I'm Butch Cassidy and the sketchy gentleman next to me is the
Sundance Kid."

A smile tugged at the corners of Beck's mouth. *He still knows
Bob Marley.* While the guard was checking his list of approved
visitors, Beck heard gunshots on the far side of the set, toward the
red marbled sandstone cliffs that made up some of the prettiest
landscape anywhere in the world. The scent of gunpowder caught
Columbo's nose, and suddenly he was off to the races.

"Good dog," Beck called after him. "You're actually supposed
to wait for my command, but you go on ahead. I like initiative."

Pop snickered. "Listens real good, doesn't he? Remind you of
anyone?"

Beck's eyes quickly found Brinley coming around a large rock
formation. She was in her element, with lots of people looking
on, including some really famous actress who Beck recalled had
been married three or four times before she turned thirty. Brin
was zigzagging through a maze of rocks, shooting on the run
at some guys dressed in black, while the movie star observed
her movements, mimicking her shooting crouches and how she
ejected and replaced the magazine from her pistol as she ran.
Beck wondered how many times a director had told Brinley *she*
could be the movie star. She had the physical beauty, even when
covered in dust. She was wearing camo pants and a black tank

top, and her caramel-colored hair spilled out of the back of her baseball cap, trailing down over her sleek, toned shoulders to the center of her spine.

Columbo remembered enough of his training to sit when he found a stash of guns and ammunition out in the open, and Beck found him doing exactly that on top of a folding table next to a couple of ammo boxes, all labeled *5-in-1*, the blanks they use on movie sets. They had the pop and the flash but didn't have an actual projectile. As soon as the gunfire stopped, he whispered to Columbo, "Find Brin."

Bo looked up, spotted her immediately, leapt off the table and covered the fifty yards in three seconds. The onlookers and special effects crew had no idea what was happening and collectively gasped as the vest-wearing police dog tore through the air in the direction of their weapons specialist. It wasn't until he knocked her down and smothered her with kisses that everyone breathed again. After a minute, Brin climbed to her feet, gave some final instructions to her trainee, and walked over to her family.

"You came," she said to Beck, removing her dark shades and looking right at him with those emerald-green eyes.

"Said we would."

She gave Pop a hug and kiss on the cheek and then wrapped Beck in her arms. "How did you manage to get Pop away from Pearl?"

Beck laughed. "She gave me some of those homemade dog treats he likes so much." They watched for a few minutes as the main actress ran the course, shooting and stumbling a few times before getting it right. Brin offered a lot of encouragement and instruction, and it dawned on Beck that this was the first time he had ever seen her doing her job. While he watched, a potbellied man stepped next to him. It was a pot Beck would recognize anywhere.

"What brings you down here, Greg?" he asked without looking.

Greg Knutson, the man known in Lincoln County as X-Files, was an ex-investigative journalist, an unkempt wreck of his former self with ratty brownish gray hair and an almost visible cloud of bourbon that followed him everywhere. He'd fallen into some disrepute a few years back, going off the rails about UFOs, alien abductions, and the government conspiracies covering it all up. The alcohol abuse didn't help sell his crazy theories. But Beck found that the old reporter had also uncovered a good many truths about what went on in the secret corners of the state, and they had a semi-cordial relationship going.

"The director is an old friend of mine. The film is about aliens coming here in the year 2070 after we've pretty much destroyed the planet. Turns out they thrive on all the greenhouse gases."

"Always nice helping others. But why did they crash? Pilot error?"

"I don't believe that's a major plot point," X-Files replied, belching into his hand.

"And you're providing some expert consultation?"

He smirked. "Funny man. But I seem to recall you needing my expert consultation last winter."

"Relax, Greg, you still have your Get Out of Jail Free card." Since he still had a murdered bull on his mind, Beck decided to pick the man's brain. "Hey, let me ask you something. What do you know about the technology needed to hack an RPA?"

X-Files was transfixed, watching Brinley adjusting the shooting stance of the actress she was working with. "God, that woman is hot. Not the movie star. She's okay, but the firearms lady. Hot."

"That's my sister, Greg."

"Smokin' hot," he said, dragging his gaze to Beck. "I know quite a lot, as you may have guessed. Otherwise, you wouldn't have asked me the question."

Beck's eyes rolled back in his head. "Does your arm ever get tired from patting yourself on the back?"

The old reporter scratched his heavily veined nose. "It's happened on a number of occasions already. RPAs are no different than any other computer, really. Sounds like you're talking about a military drone, though, which is slightly more complicated. Depending on the aircraft, it might be controlled remotely by a pilot on the ground or it might also be receiving targeting and GPS information from a satellite. A few years ago, some university kids in Texas managed to hack a Homeland Security drone by scrambling its GPS signals and feeding it false location data. The idiots at DHS didn't believe them until the kids actually showed them how easy it was. We've lost several to the Iranians as well. Drones use programming languages like any computer. Those programs have known vulnerabilities that hackers can exploit. But it doesn't have to be a drone. It could also be an aircraft with a pilot in the cockpit that gets hacked. Or a car."

Beck looked up into the sky. "But is it possible for a hacker to take over the weapons system as well? Even fire a missile?"

X-Files's eyes bulged, and he rubbed his hands together vigorously. "Was that our light in the sky last night?"

"Keep it in your pants, Greg. I'm just asking a question."

"Sure, the weapons system is another program, really."

So far everything the discredited journalist told him corroborated what Maddox had said. "What kind of equipment would you need?"

X-Files coughed a few times, wiping some nasty sputum onto his shirtsleeve. "Oh, I don't know. A laptop, some kind of joystick controller you see the gamers use. Probably wouldn't even need that."

"That's it?"

He jiggled his head. "Welcome to the brave new world, Sheriff.

The wars of the future will be fought by robots, and some of those robots will be taken over by the enemy and used against us."

Beck had no doubt that was true. He half-listened as X-Files went off on one of his pet alien conspiracies, namely that extraterrestrials occasionally traveled many light-years to Earth to suck the blood out of cows. Before Beck could stop him, he launched into the story of an Oregon cow that was left deflated on the ground like a dead balloon, though no blood was found and no cuts or injuries were identified on the animal's carcass. Not at all similar to what had happened to Jesse Roy's bull. "I'm sure we'll find some of that technology when we storm Area 51 next weekend."

He should have known X-Files would be neck-deep in the crazies getting ready to flood Lincoln County. "I think what you'll find, Greg, is that a lot of people are simply going to be arrested. I don't suppose I could convince you to stay away?"

The grin on X-Files's face was a mile wide. "Not a chance, Sheriff. It's time the American people found out what we're hiding behind those fences. And if I happen to get arrested, I'll give you a call, per our arrangement, of course."

"Uh-huh." Beck shifted his focus to Brinley, then checked his watch. "Well, thanks," he said, walking away. "It's been . . . educational." He wandered the set for a while before joining Pop and Columbo to admire more of Brinley's work. They watched her for another hour until it was approaching dinnertime. It was a ninety-minute drive home, and he didn't want to get caught out in the dark. Between shooting rehearsals, Beck motioned to Brin that they were heading out.

"Taking off?" she asked, sweating and out of breath. "Going to turn into a blind pumpkin?"

"Smart-ass." To punish her for the dig, Beck remarked that a lot of John Wayne's *The Conqueror*, quite possibly the worst movie ever made, was filmed on the very spot where she was now standing, and about 40 percent of the crew developed cancer as a result.

"Operation Teapot," Pop blurted out, as if he were giving a speech at the Rotary. "1955. Fourteen atomic tests in the first six months of the year. All that radiation came right through here."

Brin and Beck both looked at him. He had these moments of clarity when recalling the distant past, so they always tuned in closely, encouraging him to continue. Most of the time he wouldn't.

She gave her brother a big hug. "Thanks for the history lesson, professor. Tomorrow is our last day on location, so I'll be home for the next few weeks. Any big cases I can help with?"

Beck laughed. "Got a big one." He filled her in on Jesse Roy's bull and that it happened in the middle of his daughter's seventeenth birthday party.

"Shiloah Roy?"

"Yep. You know her?"

"She volunteers at the Youth Center in the commissary and library a couple days a week. Summer internship thing, I guess. Super-sweet girl."

In her spare time, Brin was a counselor at the Lincoln County Youth Center where they sent delinquents from all over the state. Beck had no doubt that, given her past, the kids found her easy to relate to. Some of them had similar horror stories.

Beck's interest was piqued. "What do you know about her?"

"Not much. She goes to some snobby boarding school back east. She's a bit of a loner, keeps pretty much to herself but seems to be friends with a girl named Mercy there, a real whiz kid."

"Another volunteer?"

She shook her head. "No, one of the members."

"Members?"

"We don't refer to them as inmates or prisoners."

"The girl's name is Mercy?"

Brin held up three fingers and then laid them across his lips. "Scout's honor. That's her name. Mercy Vaughn. Might be the smartest kid I've ever met."

CHAPTER 9

It was while Beck was feverishly consuming his Monday morning egg sandwich with hot sauce that he looked out his office window and noticed two dark SUVs pulling into the lot. In addition to Special Agent Maddox, five passengers stepped out onto the pavement. Four men, one woman.

You spend enough time in the military and you develop some habits that aren't much good to you in the real world. Striding with purpose is one. You learn to walk fast and in straight lines. Everywhere. To the latrine or to the movies with a date. The destination doesn't matter. Civilians can never keep up and hate you for it. In the mess hall, you learn to eat fast because you can be called away at any moment. At home, you tend to be done with your meal before the rest of the family has even finished their salad. You put hot sauce on everything because military chow has no taste. You also learn to obey without question, to treat subordinates as subhuman slaves, and to drink as if your life may be over tomorrow.

If you stay in long enough, you develop a keen eye for identifying someone's military occupational specialty (MOS).

The woman standing close to Maddox was on the cusp of thirty, un-smartly dressed in a black business suit. Her blond hair was pulled back tightly with a band, revealing even more of her perspiring pale complexion and a serious vitamin D deficiency. She was obviously from some government lair back east where wearing black in the summer sun didn't kill you. Her suit was close-fitting, indicating she was not carrying a weapon. The SUV's air-conditioning clearly wasn't cool enough for her. Beck decided she was NSA.

The other four passengers constituted a kill squad. The most elite killers on the planet. Nobody had an M4 rifle slung over his chest, but their bearing and wolfpack awareness gave them away. Beck had known lots of them over the years, in places far away and from operations that would never be revealed to the public. While only two of them sported beards, each of them was wearing lightly colored loose, breathable cotton, making the heat more tolerable and easier to conceal their favorite handgun. Dark shades on all. Guys who had spent serious time in the desert.

Beck watched as they huddled near the vehicles for a moment, Maddox communicating something to them. The kill squad remained outside while Maddox and the woman crossed the lot and entered the building.

"Someplace we can talk, Sheriff?" Maddox asked before Beck could even say hello.

He led them into the break room, motioning Tuffy to join them. "Sorry, we don't have a conference room here. Have a seat." He looked at the woman, fanning herself with a hand. "Something cold to drink?"

"God, yes, please," she answered.

"You're not used to the heat."

She laughed. "Is anyone?"

Beck opened the small refrigerator in the corner and extracted two bottles of water. Tuffy walked in and grabbed a chair. Beck started to introduce his second-in-command, but Maddox quickly interrupted. "We met briefly the other day. Shall we skip the introductions, Sheriff?"

"No offense taken," Tuffy said with a glare that could melt iron.

Maddox didn't notice or pretended not to. "I mentioned to you that the incident involving the RPA and the potential for more serious attacks was bound to attract other agencies. My colleague here is—"

The blond woman held up a hand. "Who I am or where I work is unimportant, Agent Maddox. Let's get to the business at hand, please. If I may?" Maddox stiffened but nodded for her to continue. "Sheriff Beck, what we are about to discuss has been designated classified information and must be kept in the strictest confidence. You understand? Do you both understand that?"

Beck and Tuffy strapped on their serious faces, and then Beck leaned across the table. "Are you requesting the Cone of Silence?"

She sat back, crossed her arms over her chest, and turned to Maddox.

"He's joking, for God's sake," Maddox said with a snort. "They understand what classified information is. Can we move on, please?"

Her eyes seemed to treat Maddox like so much lint, which signaled to Beck that she outranked the OSI agent, maybe not in the military but in the world that mattered, the world where information was power. Finally, she turned her attention back to Beck. "We need some information, Sheriff. And we believe you're in a unique position to help us get it."

Her accent was midwestern, somewhere in the Bob Evans breakfast belt. Beck didn't respond, only raised an eyebrow.

"We've been able to analyze the data from the flight of our aircraft the other night," she said, "and concluded that the RPA was indeed hacked. What we need to find out is who in your county would have the capability to do that kind of thing, fly it, and assume control of its weapon system."

Beck tapped the table with his fingers. "Why somebody in my county? I mean, you don't need line of sight to do this, as I understand it. It could be done from anywhere. What makes you think it's somebody here?"

"A couple of things, actually. You are correct that technically this could have been done from anywhere, but the telemetry analysis of the flight shows the RPA came directly east from the test range, and when it reached the Utah border it made a sharp turn southwest. It descended quickly—I can't get into the specific altitude, mind you—at which time its weapons and targeting systems were activated. It searched for the largest heat signature in that pasture before it fired."

"You're suggesting that this was an assassination."

Maddox chuckled. "It sounds silly when you say it, but yes. There's no question Mr. Roy's bull was the target."

That made sense to Beck, despite how crazy it sounded when he heard it out loud. "You said there were a couple of things. What's the other one?"

The blond woman took another gulp of water and removed a piece of paper from her black notebook. "After the missile was fired and the RPA returned to our control, the flight controllers on the ground received this message from the hacker." She pushed the paper across the table to Beck.

He read it silently and slid it over to Tuffy. She looked at him strangely, then read it aloud. "Please give my regards to Sheriff Beck. And sorry for the inconvenience."

Beck got up, refilled his coffee mug, added a splash of creamer, stirred it a few times. Said nothing.

"Sheriff?" asked Maddox. "Can you shed some light on this? This person obviously knows you."

"Or knows who I am." He sat back down, blew lightly on his coffee, and took a sip. "I don't know any hackers, guys, but I get your point about why he's probably in my county." While he spoke, his mind refocused on the email he had received the other day, the one with the subject line that read *Hello, Lisa1957*. He decided not to mention it for now. He also decided to delete that email at his first opportunity, because if the woman across from him was NSA, her people would be prowling his inbox in no time. Deleting it wouldn't slow them down much. Nothing was ever really gone in cyberspace.

"No one comes to mind?" the woman asked. "Nobody you've arrested, sent to prison? No one from your time in the Army?"

Beck scrolled through the names and faces in his mental Rolodex. "You're asking if I have any enemies?"

She shook her head. "Not necessarily. Could be a friend. That message was clearly meant to find its way to you, Sheriff, so I guess I'm asking why in the hell that might possibly be. I mean, you happen to know both the victim and perhaps the hacker as well. That's strange, don't you think?"

Beck noticed Maddox studying him, searching for clues. He was, after all, a cop in his own right. Beck's mind raced back to the events of last winter. Was there a connection to this hacker? Was Jesse Roy's bull some kind of warning? His eyes turned back to the blonde. "A friend would most likely reach out to me directly. Either way, to the best of my knowledge, I don't know anyone with these capabilities." He looked at Tuffy. "Have we ever run across somebody like this?"

"It's not like we're Silicon Valley here," she answered. "Not a bunch of computer nerds running around."

Maddox sat back in his chair. "Okay, maybe you don't know him, but like you said, he knows you. What is he trying to tell you?"

Beck shrugged. "At this point, maybe he's trying to tell me he doesn't think much of Jesse Roy."

The woman leaned in. "Mr. Roy is an old friend, yes?"

Christ. They're probably already into my Army file and everything else. "Yes, and as I told Agent Maddox the other day, we're looking into him."

"As are we, Sheriff," Maddox said. "But we need to look fast. We can't afford for this to happen again, and it's drawing all the worst kinds of attention, if you get my drift." He and the NSA woman stood up from the table.

Beck stared up at them. "We could have had this discussion over the phone, Ed. Why come all the way out here?"

"I needed to see your face," the blonde said, answering for him.

Beck took a moment before getting to his feet. "And what did my face tell you?"

She examined it again, his face. "You know more than you're saying."

"Well," said Beck, the corners of his mouth expanding outward. "Nobody likes a chatterbox." They would be looking for points of intersection between him and Jesse Roy and would not be above making them up if they weren't self-evident. "It's a big county," he told them. "We'll work as quickly as we can. Meantime, can you give us any information on the RPA, anything that might help us determine who the hacker might be?"

The blonde shook her head. "I'm afraid we can't."

Tuffy got out of her chair. "Not big on team sports?"

"The data suggests," said Maddox, "it was someone within a twenty-mile radius of the Roy ranch."

Beck's head tilted. "A twenty-mile radius is oddly specific. Are you referring to radar data?"

"No," the blonde said, rebuking Maddox with her eyes.

Beck frowned. This was about as easy as trying to pick fly shit out of pepper. He had been out of the Army for a few years now, and sometimes he forgot how arduous conversations could be when classified things were being discussed. "So, stealth drone. No radar track."

Maddox looked at the NSA lady, then back to Beck. "No comment."

Beck set his eyes on the woman. "Since the NSA is involved, can you at least confirm this incident involved breaching one of our satellites for GPS or other targeting information?"

"We cannot," she answered. "And nobody said I was with the NSA."

Beck chuckled. "And Al Pacino is not the brother of cappuccino." He shrugged. "Some things are obvious."

As they walked through the office, Beck scanned his brain for possible suspects. There was the kid at the County Clerk's office who helped them identify a penetration of the voter system last year, but he wasn't a hacker. X-Files might have some contacts in the hacker community, but it was unlikely any of them were working out of Lincoln County or would know Jesse Roy. *If only I could ask 0DayMei.*

He followed them out. Before they reached the government SUVs and the squad of special operators, Maddox turned to him. "Honestly, Sheriff, I don't know what any of this means, but as you can see, it's already getting the attention of some people very high up on the food chain. Whatever you can do to help us identify this person would be much appreciated. The alternative, I'm afraid, isn't good."

That was Maddox's way of confirming they were looking into him. The government would start pulling his life apart, piece by piece, looking for the thinnest tendril that might stretch far enough to wrap itself around a hacker. He could see the sympathy in Maddox's expression, and Beck decided he was too nice a guy for this job. And way too nice to be a cop. This case might be the end of him. Of both of them if Beck couldn't figure it out. "What's the alternative?"

"That it happens again. If it does, these people in your parking lot will turn this county upside down. It will get ugly. Fast."

"Can't you ground your drones until you figure this out?"

"You know it's not that simple. These birds are flying all over the world. Technically, the satellites can be hacked from anywhere."

Now Beck appreciated why the kill squad was here. Someone in the Pentagon, probably a whole room of people, were shitting their britches right now. Special Ops was here to find the hacker and shut him down, quickly and quietly. He decided to ask Maddox the same question he asked X-Files. "What kind of equipment would a person need to do this?"

"I'm told he would need a laptop."

Beck called after Maddox as he approached the vehicles and their trained assassin occupants. "This is my jurisdiction, Ed. If you find whomever is responsible for this before I do, you need to call me before you—or *they*—take any action. Are we clear?"

Maddox held out his hand. "Crystal, Sheriff. And I trust I'll be your first call should you locate him before we do."

"That door only swings one way," Beck said as they shook. "But you'll definitely be on my short list."

CHAPTER 10

Beck drove so fast he didn't even notice the silver Hyundai coming the other way, or the Asian man behind the wheel. When he pulled onto Hansen Street in Panaca and the home of Albert and Ellen Berg, the EMS guys had covered the body already and were about to load it.

He toggled the siren off. "Sit tight," he told Columbo, with a quick glance in the rearview mirror. The dog wasn't there. Beck twisted around and found him curled into a ball on the floor, somehow sleeping again. He left his narcoleptic deputy in peace and got out of the truck, signaling Stan Leavitt, the senior EMT, to hold up.

"Which one?" he asked, coming around to the rear of the ambulance.

Stan always had a toothpick twirling in his mouth. "Hey, Sheriff. Ellen Berg, God help her. Only forty-eight years old."

Beck didn't know the Bergs well, which was to say he didn't know if they had kids, didn't know where they vacationed or what card games they liked to play. He knew they ran the Panaca

Market a block away, but that was it. He motioned for the senior EMT to unzip the body bag. "Overdose?"

"Looks like. Neighbors said they saw her outside wandering around in a stupor in her underwear like she was drunk. Then she collapsed in the road. Cyanosis, respiratory failure, all the signs of opioids."

Stan drew back the sheet from Ellen Berg's round and swollen face, bloodied from colliding with the pavement. Beck stepped up next to her. "Fentanyl?"

"Good bet, considering how fast she went down. We got here ten minutes later. One of them tried to do CPR. He didn't know what he was doing, but he tried. Probably didn't matter. We took over but it was too late. Gave her the Narcan, but that was *no bueno*. No sign of what she took. She didn't have anything on her."

Beck turned sharply around, didn't want to look at her anymore. "Mr. Berg?"

Stan motioned toward the house. "Someone called him at the market. He's inside with Arshal." He and the junior EMT then lifted the gurney and slid it into the patient compartment of the ambulance.

"Thanks, Stan."

Beck walked into the house, the expansive entryway adorned with crosses, paintings, figurines, and other Christian symbols. He found Mr. Berg sitting on the sofa in the living room, crying and being comforted by a woman of similar age, probably a neighbor. Arshal Jessup came in from a hallway and motioned for Beck to follow. In the kitchen, the silver-haired deputy showed him two empty pill bottles.

"Old prescriptions," he said, his gravelly voice the result of three separate battles with thyroid cancer. "Both for Vicodin, both empty. Husband says she hasn't been on the stuff for six months or so because she couldn't get it from the doc anymore. She told him she had weened herself off and was only taking Tylenol now."

It was a common refrain. "Old injury?"

Arshal had been on the job for forty years, had worked for Pop for thirty. He was tall and lean and mean-looking, and he had Beck's undying respect. "From a car accident three years ago down near Ash Meadows. She got rear-ended by a semi in a construction zone. Guy didn't slow down fast enough. I handled the call at the time. She was lucky to make it. Fire Department had to use one of those big can openers to pry her out of the car."

"Jaws of Life?"

The old cowboy slid his bifocals down the long bridge of his nose and glowered at his boss. "That's what I said, isn't it?"

"How was Eagle Valley? Catch anything?"

Arshal's face lit up. "Couple of nice rainbows, some really nice largemouth bass."

"Good," Beck said. "Fish fry at your house. So where are the drugs?"

"I've checked here. Nothing. Was about to ask Albert if I could check the bedroom, but he's pretty torn up. They were high school sweethearts, married right after, two grown kids, two grandkids."

That news was like a swift kick in the genitals, making Beck sick and furious at the same time. A minute after getting Albert's permission, they were searching the main bedroom. Beck eventually found what he was looking for inside the bedroom closet, stuffed into the toe of one of the deceased's many pairs of snakeskin boots. The pills were in a Ziploc bag, and there were seven of them left. They were stamped with the same M30 markings he'd seen a few nights earlier. "Weapons of mass destruction. Same stuff I found in Cash's room."

Arshal walked over and took the bag from his boss, holding it by a corner and placing it inside a clear evidence bag. "Probably a long shot, but we'll dust it for prints anyway. Maybe we'll get lucky." When they walked back into the living room, Arshal didn't show Albert Berg the pills they had found, and Beck understood why. It would serve no purpose.

Beck was holding a laptop computer he had also found in the bedroom. "Albert? Did Mrs. Berg use this computer?"

Albert dabbed at his tears. "More than me. She was always on the Facebook," he said with a quick laugh. "I only used it to keep the store's books."

"Would you mind if I had someone look it over? Maybe she was communicating with the person who sold her . . . whatever she was taking."

Albert's shoulders rose toward his ears. "Take it. I don't care. I don't want to run the damn market without her, anyway."

"Is there a password?"

"TheLordismyShepherd," he replied. "Uppercase T, L, and S."

Beck felt the rage in his chest, searching like bad heartburn for a way out. A wife, mother, and grandmother wiped out in a single moment. He and the old deputy moved outside. "Arshal, I want everybody on this. We need to get the word out. Maybe put an announcement in the paper. We need to find out who is selling this stuff. Someone in this county has to know. Knock on every door. Tell people if they're buying any kind of pills off the street, there's a good chance they are going to die from it."

"You want me to take that?" asked Arshal, pointing to the laptop in Beck's hands.

He shook his head. "I'll take it. Got an idea." Back in the truck, he called Brinley on her cell. "Where are you?"

"The Youth Center," she said.

"You mentioned this kid the other day who's locked up there. Mercy, I think. Said she was gifted. Gifted in what way?"

"Huge tech freak."

"Like in computers?"

"No," she laughed. "Like in LEGOs."

"I'm on my way. Don't go anywhere, and tell Dan I need to speak to her."

"Okay," she said, "but you're taking me to lunch after."

CHAPTER 11

Beck had been to the Lincoln County Youth Center a few times and mostly knew the superintendent, Dan Whiteside, from their Saturday softball league. He liked the scenery of the place, sprawling over many acres on mountain foothills and gentle slopes, a calming setting for some of the state's most troubled children. The center housed about a hundred and forty kids from twelve to eighteen years of age, boys and girls. The man who ran it was a retired state trooper, and like many state employees, Dan jumped agencies when he needed a change that wouldn't take him out of Nevada's retirement system. He'd actually played two years with the Denver Broncos as a defensive back before tearing up his knees but had always struck Beck as more of a teddy bear than someone whose job it was to kill a wide receiver.

Brinley was waiting for Beck between the two sets of glass doors at the entrance to the administration building, but it was Columbo she traded kisses with. Beck only got a lanyard with a visitor's badge over his head. The receptionist buzzed them in and two more doors opened automatically. They entered a long hallway. "Are you going to tell me what's going on?" she asked.

"We had another overdose death. Ellen Berg in Panaca."

Brinley stopped in her tracks and bent over at the waist. "Ellen from the market? Albert's wife?"

Beck thought for a moment that she was going to be sick. "Same pills Cash Conrad was taking. Pretty sure anyway." He held up the leather satchel carrying the Bergs' laptop computer. "Hoping your whiz kid can get something off this thing that can tell me who she was buying from."

Brinley stood up and hugged herself. "The market supplies our food here. Did you know that?"

Beck pulled her in close and spoke quietly into her ear. "I had no idea. Sorry."

The hallway emptied into a foyer that resembled a nurse's station in a hospital, with offices arrayed behind it in a semicircle. The one on the far left belonged to Dan, and as they entered, they found the superintendent carefully placing potato chips inside his roast beef sandwich.

"Hey, Beck," he said, getting up from his chair and wiping his hand on his slacks. They shook. Dan noticed Columbo, his face brightening. "Who's this?"

"Name's Columbo. Bo, say hi to Dan." The dog obeyed without hesitation, moving around the desk and placing his forelegs over Dan's thighs.

"Wow," Dan said. "He likes me."

Columbo lifted up higher, rising on his haunches, his long nose passing over the top of the desk. "He likes potato chips," Beck said. "And sleep, apparently."

Dan could see Brinley was visibly upset. "Hey, what's going on? You okay?"

"Dan, Ellen Berg died this morning," she said.

Dan grabbed both sides of his face and looked at Beck, who told him about the overdose and Cash Conrad, and the fact that fentanyl was making the opioid crisis that much worse in Lincoln County. "I'll get out to see Albert after we're done," he told Beck, shaking his head. "Fucking opioids, excuse my French. Half the kids here used to be addicted to them. But Ellen Berg? She's been working with the center since before I got here. I can't believe it. I didn't even know she had a problem."

"Neither did her husband," said Beck. "At least, he thought she was over it."

"Is that why you're here? I thought you wanted to speak to one of our members."

Having smelled the entirety of Dan's office, Columbo came over and sat down on Brin's feet.

"I do, Dan," Beck said, pulling the laptop out of the bag. "I'm in need of some technical support, and Brinley tells me you've got somebody here who's a savant with these things."

Dan rocked back in his top-of-the-line office chair, built to support his 250 pounds, and ran his thumbs under his waistline. Then he bobbed his colossal noggin. "Mercy Vaughn. She's definitely a savant, but I'm afraid we restrict her access to computers. It's why she's here, Beck."

Beck shook his head slightly. "I'm in a bind, Dan. I need to know how Ellen Berg was getting her drugs. Can you at least tell me about this girl?"

The big man shifted his jaw back and forth several times, framing his response carefully. "Well, she's a special circumstance. She's sixteen and brilliant. And I mean *brilliant*. Tests off the charts. Been here about seven months, a model citizen really, no disciplinary issues, which is rare." He looked to Brinley and then back to Beck. "She comes from a single-parent family that was broken from the word *go*. Her mom was an addict, a convicted felon who disappeared when Mercy was eight years old. The term *at risk* doesn't begin to cover it."

Beck had seen this picture a hundred times, mostly from runaways who found their way to Lincoln County. "Eight years old. So, she was in the system after that."

Dan pushed his plate to one side of the desk. "One foster family after another. You can do the math. She did some things, got sent here. Does that help?"

"Too soon to tell. Just how good is she with computers?"

"When she was about twelve, she started committing online theft. Picked up the skills in school apparently and even used their computers. Started with credit cards. She figured out how to get them fraudulently over the internet and then used them to purchase things. Graduated quickly to more serious cybercrimes. Began selling the passwords of online games and their licenses to other kids, which is apparently a lucrative business. Moved on to creating fake IDs which were so good you couldn't tell the difference between them and the real ones. She was fourteen when she got caught, and that was only because a competitor ratted her out. But she kept going. It escalated from there."

"To what?"

The ex-Bronco crossed his big arms over his chest. "I'm sorry, that's all I can say. Other than the fact she has a problem with impulse control, as most cybercriminals do. She's here for another two years."

Beck sat up straight. "Two years? That's an awfully long sentence for white-collar crime, especially for a juvenile."

"Not my call," Dan replied. "I hold them as long as they tell me to."

"I'd like her to take a look at this laptop."

Dan leaned across the desk like he was getting ready to blitz. "I'm inclined to say no, Beck. I understand your need, but letting her tinker with that thing would be like putting a blackjack table in front of a gambling addict."

Beck rubbed his eyes. "Please, Dan. If I send this down to Vegas, it could be weeks before I get some answers. We've already had two overdoses in the last three days."

Whiteside looked down at the silver laptop for several seconds. Beck sensed he was weighing his options and took the time to give Bo a good ear rub. "Keep it brief," Dan finally said.

"I'll get Mercy," Brinley said. "Meet you in the library?"

A minute later, they were heading toward the other side of the campus. Dan took Beck around the large circular pods that served as housing units for the kids. There were seven, five for the boys and two for the girls, set out in a grassy area on the north side of the facility. From the outside, it was all very nice, sedate even. There were no guard towers or razor wire, only normal fencing, and the guards Beck could see were carrying pepper spray, handcuffs, and a radio, nothing more.

He noticed some boys heading across the lawn, marching single file, each in a plain blue T-shirt with jeans, each with an arm tucked behind the middle of his back. "Do you ever have a kid go missing?"

"It's happened," Dan replied. "But we recover them quickly. It's not like we're in a city and they can hop on a bus. There's nowhere to go, and they know that. And they know when we catch them, it'll mean more time."

Yep, Beck thought, miles and miles of nowhere to go. Dan opened the door into the gymnasium where some of the boys were running the court or doing passing drills with a basketball, most of them heavy and out of shape and moving at the speed of molasses in a blizzard. "Idle minds are the devil's workshop. That's especially true here. We keep them busy, even during the summer."

They made their way into the small library and took a seat while they waited for Mercy to be brought in. He turned his attention to Dan. "I understand Mercy is friends with one of your interns? Shiloah Roy?"

The question caught Whiteside off guard. "Shiloah? Well, Brinley would know more about that than me. Why do you ask?"

He was about to answer when the door opened and Brinley escorted a girl into the library. T-shirt and jeans, hair straight and short, the color of winter wheat and parted slightly left of center. Average height but slight of build. At first glance, she was forgettable, nondescript, easy to miss. A typical American teenager. But her gait had purpose and confidence. *No*, Beck thought. *Grace. Like a dancer.* As she drew closer and under better light, he assessed her other features. Skin a whiter shade of pale, and almond-shaped eyes with an epicanthic fold of the upper eyelid that covered the inner corner, not something you see a lot of in this part of the world. Those eyes were alert, constantly assimilating information, with large irises the color of moss floating in milky white scleras, and her nose was broad and flattened out near the bottom.

It was an unusual face, and it bothered him for a reason that strangled in his brain before he could understand it. What was clear was that she could easily pass for twentysomething. In different clothes, in different surroundings. In disguise.

And since the moment she walked in, those eyes had never once left Beck's. She didn't acknowledge Dan Whiteside, didn't look down or back to Brinley. Without breaking that contact, she raised her right leg over the back of the chair and slowly lowered her thin frame into it. Beck kept up the staring match, reaching down to the floor and pulling the laptop from the tired leather satchel. He set the magical box lightly down on the table, keeping it closed, the silver metal cover reflecting the light above, and it was only then that Mercy's eyes moved, and even then it was the smallest of movements. The corners of her mouth moved outward ever so slightly, not nearly a smile but as much as she was willing to give. Under the fluorescent light, Beck now got a better look at those eyes, with bits of brown and green and gold in them, changing in different conditions, exactly what a chameleon needs to blend into its surroundings. It was in that moment, without a word having passed between them, that Beck decided Mercy Vaughn might be able to help him with something more than online drug transactions.

"Mercy Vaughn," Brin said, "this is Sheriff Beck."

She said nothing, refusing to look away and lose the upper hand, a life skill Beck knew wasn't easy, not even for some trained interrogators. Finally, her hand opened, her fingers uncurling to reveal a die of some kind which had many more sides than the six of a normal die, all equilateral triangles. It was deep blue with numbers on each side and it pulled his gaze away from hers for a moment. When he looked up again, she was smiling. Like she had won.

"I am very pleased to meet you, Sheriff. What exactly may I do to help you?" Her voice was like the warm, gentle breeze of a summer evening in the tropics.

Beck snuck a quick peek at Brin, who was stroking Columbo's head and grinning. "It's very nice meeting you as well, Mercy. I don't know that I've ever met anyone with that name before."

The smile ran from her face, leaving only two perfectly pursed lips. "I am quite certain you do know, Sheriff. You do not strike me as a man who forgets much." She glanced at Columbo. "I like your dog. He suits you. Not so much as a partner but as a friend."

It was as if there was a cloud of power around her, and Beck had to remind himself that he wasn't at a palm reading. "I'm investigating an incident that occurred on the Fourth of July."

No reaction, not the slightest twitch of a muscle. She simply passed the blue die slowly between her fingers. She was an actress, he decided, and a good one. She had been taught by someone, learned how to carry herself in the most confident, yet inconspicuous manner. Learned how to disarm.

She watched him watching her. "Brinley informed me you need some assistance with a computer."

It was the die. It was special to her. A keepsake maybe. "I do. But let me ask about something else first. I understand you and Shiloah Roy are friends, is that right?"

Finally, Mercy pulled those chameleon eyes from him and moved them to Brinley.

"Nobody is looking to stitch you up, Mercy," Brin said. "You can trust him. He's actually my brother."

Mercy studied the two of them, her gaze moving from one to the other. "But not by blood, I think." She set the die down on the tabletop and ran the flat of her hand over it, rolling it, feeling its many edges against her palm, rolling it again, this time letting it go. The number fifteen came up. She glanced at it. "Yes, Shiloah and I are friends. She volunteers here. She has been here a couple of months now, I think. But you said you wanted to ask me about an incident?"

"Yes, at her father's ranch. How did you two meet?"

Mercy's eyes flitted to Dan Whiteside. "Well, I am incarcerated here, and—"

"I'm sorry," Whiteside interrupted, "but what does this have to do with Ellen Berg's computer?"

"Give me a minute, please, Dan," Beck replied, his gaze never leaving Mercy's. "Did you and Shiloah meet before she came to work here? Online maybe?"

Her eyes narrowed to tiny slits. "I am not from here, Sheriff, which I believe you already know. How would I have become acquainted with her before she began working here?"

There were cues, verbal and nonverbal, to help tell when people were lying, and Beck had studied them all. Most people were horrible liars. Either he was losing his touch or this girl was very good. "Do you know anything about what occurred at the Roy ranch on that night?"

"I am sure I do not," she answered with a short laugh. "Would you like to tell me what happened?"

She's interviewing me now. Calmly. Methodically. Like a seasoned cop. "Do you know Jesse Roy, Shiloah's father?"

Another tiny laugh escaped her lips. "Sheriff, I do not know anyone outside this facility. You know this already." It was a polite scolding, like a shrink admonishing him for avoiding a question. Her diction was as perfect as any professor of English, her intonations as calming as a hypnotist, not at all what he expected, which he had assumed would be the clipped and coded vernacular of a teenage computer nerd.

"Okay, let's talk about you. Tell me why you're here."

Dan interrupted again. "I'm sorry, Beck. I don't see how any of this is relevant to the reason *you're* here."

Beck's hand shot forward and snatched the die before Mercy could close her fingers around it. "Then let's get relevant, by all means. Mercy, do you have any idea how someone could hack into a military drone and initiate its weapons systems?" Without the die in her hand, he could see the smallest, almost undetectable flinch in those eyes.

She took a slow breath, letting her chest rise and fall. "Sheriff, I believe the girl you are looking for lives in Sweden."

Beck's jaw flopped open. "Sweden?"

Her eyes widened. "Yes. And she has a big dragon tattoo on her back."

Brinley brought a hand to her mouth, stifling a laugh. Beck's expression remained impassive. "Something tells me this is entirely within your wheelhouse."

She curled some hair around an ear. "Drones are boy toys. I

have heard it can be done, yes, but it is not something that interests me. I do know that it has happened a number of times already. Mostly in the Middle East theater."

Theater. It was a word from his world, not hers. A slip. He watched her clench her teeth ever so lightly, handed her back the die. A reward. "If it did interest you, how would you do it?"

He could see her relax again, her shoulders drop, her almost perfect composure returning. "I would not," she answered. "Like I said, boy stuff. And dangerous, reckless."

"How would someone *else* do it?"

Mercy made the briefest eye contact with the superintendent. "I would have to . . . study the situation."

Beck leaned forward and flashed the smile his mother gave him. "Would you do that for me, Mercy? It's important."

She considered him again, like a scientist peering into a microscope, the way she had been trained. "Let me see if I understand you correctly, Sheriff. An incident occurs on the night of July Fourth at a ranch near here, the ranch where Shiloah lives. This incident involves the hacking of a remotely piloted aircraft, and it occurs to you that you somehow might gain insight into this situation by coming here to interview me?"

"Remotely piloted aircraft? I didn't use that term. I said drone."

Mercy fidgeted in her seat. "I am familiar with the most current vernacular, Sheriff. Apparently you are not."

Starting to come undone. With a shrug of his shoulders, he let it go. "My mistake. Would you study the situation for me? And I have another favor." He pushed the laptop across the table toward her.

She covered her grin with a few fingers and exhaled. "Ah, finally. I have gotten into some trouble with computers, Sheriff, as I am sure the superintendent has explained to you. Not allowed to play in that particular sandbox."

Beck opened the laptop. "I understand that. This is about

something else." He paused, sensing that for Mercy, cracking open the computer wasn't, as Dan had suggested, like tempting a gambling addict. It was her Bible, her Quran, the place she found the answers to life's questions. "Mercy, I've just come from the home of a woman named Ellen Berg. You may have seen her here. She and her husband run the corner market in Panaca. They supply the food for the center."

"A great many people come and go here. I do not know them all."

Beck started to speak but had to stop, the words choking in his throat. "She died from a drug overdose. An old friend of mine also died the other day. It's been happening here a lot. You can't get these drugs at the pharmacy, and our normal efforts to interdict narcotics coming into the county haven't been showing much results lately. I know it's possible to get what they took on the internet now, but I don't know how. Whoever is distributing these fake opiates is very careful, very good. Not your typical drug dealers. This is Mrs. Berg's computer. I was hoping you—"

She rolled the die again, and it came up a twelve. "Certainly. Sounds like dark web stuff. You would like me to take a look." It wasn't a question.

"I have the password. Don't need you to break into it."

Mercy opened the laptop, tapped a key. "Fire away, Sheriff." She looked up at him. "Sorry, figure of speech."

A smile danced on Beck's lips. "TheLordismyShepherd. Caps on the T, L, and S."

"Let us hope He is," she said, "for Mrs. Berg, at least," her fingers tapping the keys like a concert pianist. Beck and Brinley exchanged a quick glance.

"I was thinking you might start with her emails," Beck said quietly, afraid he was interrupting the recital.

"I am already into her directory," Mercy responded, scanning the screen and typing at the same time. "Here it is. She has Tor downloaded."

"Tor?"

"It is one of the web browsers you can use to access the dark web, the most widely used, in fact. Like Safari or Firefox but for all things anonymous. Let's see if Ellen used a different password on her dark web emails." She tapped out a burst of letters, the corners of her mouth turning down. "She did not." After a few seconds, she leaned closer to the screen. "Oh, Ellen, what do we have here?"

They waited. "She has made two . . . no, three orders for something called M thirty in the last four months."

That fit with the time line Albert Berg had provided. Ellen had been cut off by her doctor about six months ago. "Can you tell me who she was buying from?"

Mercy stopped typing and looked up, her back straightening in the chair. "Quick lesson on the dark web. It is designed to allow people to procure any number of things, drugs, weapons, you name it, all anonymously. Drugs are a small but growing part of internet commerce. Tor routes this traffic through many computers, with layers of encryption, making the transactions almost impossible to trace. Buyers and sellers find each other using email providers not unlike Gmail or Yahoo but which are more secure, and they use crypto instead of hard currency for payment."

Beck was used to drug dealers working out of a van or a stash house, not online. He held up a hand. "But how do the drugs come to someone like Ellen? How did she get them?"

"That is the beauty of it. The drugs typically ship via USPS with mailing labels printed to make them look legitimate. The buyer and seller never meet."

Beck interrupted. "But if they're coming to her house—"

Mercy shook her head. "What would you know? The return

address is fake. There is nothing to trace. The seller is most likely using a number of post offices, none of which will be close to home. Ellen, if she was smart and wanted to hide them from her husband, might not have even had them sent to her house. She might have rented a P.O. box under a different name or had the drugs sent somewhere she could pick them up without being noticed, like the market she and her husband operate. It is practically foolproof."

"Jesus," Brinley said.

"Dear God," Dan added.

Beck felt his chest tightening, so much so he almost forgot why he was there. "Mercy, how do you know so much about the internet drug trade? From what I understand, it's not really your area."

She was looking at the screen again, typing furiously. "It is all my area, Sheriff. This is where I live."

Beck glanced at Dan and Brinley. "I really appreciate your help on this, Mercy. It gives me a starting point at least."

She bowed her head slightly. "I am very sorry about the loss of your friend, and I hope you can find the people doing this."

Beck reached over and pulled the laptop back. "Would you think about the drone hacking thing, and let me know how it might be done?" He pulled a card out of his shirt pocket and handed it to her. "Dan, would you mind if she called me?"

Dan looked at her. "Just schedule it, Mercy, like you do with your attorney."

"Noted." She stood and reached out her hand. "Perhaps one day you will be able to help me, Sheriff?"

Almost the exact words in my mysterious email. He took her hand, their eyes meeting again. "One last question?"

She squeezed his fingers. "Hmm?"

"That die in your hand. What is it?"

She looked down into her other palm, revealing the blue die

again. "It's a D twenty. Dungeons and Dragons. A silly game I play."

"Ah," he said, finally withdrawing his hand, feeling that he had somehow laid himself open to this girl, like she had figured out his password and was already hacking his life.

CHAPTER 12

After Mercy left the library, Beck sketched out the basics of what had occurred a few nights earlier. Dan shook his head. "That's amazing and interesting, but it couldn't be Mercy."

"You say she's locked down with no access to computers outside of her classes. Could she have accessed the computer lab that night?"

Dan shook his head. "She would have had to get out of her room first and past our guards, both of which are impossible."

"Well, it was the Fourth. Were all your members in their rooms the whole night?"

"No, we had our own fireworks show. Very small and safe. Everyone was outside."

"What time?"

"We had a barbecue for dinner, and then everyone was in the quad until about eight. Do you think—"

Beck was already moving toward the door. "I'm guessing you have security footage?"

A short trip down three hallways and they were in the main security room where two of the center's guards were watching a bank of approximately twenty monitors arrayed in an arc in front of them. Dan asked them to pull up the feed for the quad from the Fourth. One of the guards, a woman, typed a few commands into her keyboard and the view of the quad appeared on the larger central screen. "What time?" she asked.

"Go to 5:30 P.M. and run it from there," Dan replied. "We're looking for Mercy Vaughn."

"She was definitely out there," the male guard said. "I saw her. She helped serve the food. And I saw her afterward when we took them all back to their rooms."

Dan turned to Beck. "All of our video is backed up to the cloud. No tapes. No discs. State of the art." The playback forwarded, and Beck could see people setting up for the evening's festivities in fast motion. Then came the barbecue buffet. All normal. But at 7:23, the screen went black.

"I don't understand," the female guard said. "Give me a sec." She adjusted the controls. Nothing. Only blackness. Dan asked what the problem was. "I don't know," she answered. "It's very odd."

Beck asked if they had a camera covering the computer lab. A few seconds later, it appeared on the central screen, the camera covering the large room with a wide angle lens. With the date and time stamp at the bottom of the video, they could see the days advancing. The light in the room changed quickly as the sun moved in and out of frame through the west-facing windows. The playback speed changed to three times normal. At 7:23 P.M. it also went black.

"Did we have a power issue on the Fourth?" Dan demanded. Both guards turned to him and shook their heads. "Find whoever was working that night and get them in here. And check every camera. I want to know how many had this problem."

Having some experience with surveillance cameras, Beck put a hand on his shoulder. "Dan, it's not the cameras, it's your backup. It's gone. Wiped." Whiteside was still shaking his head when the three of them left the security office. Beck asked if they ever had issues with the backup before.

"Not to my knowledge. But we seldom have reason to check it."

"You should contact whoever provides your cloud services and have them look into this."

Dan took a step back. "There's no way she could have done any of this, Beck. Even if she could have slipped away at some point during the night, those cameras are running around the clock. And she has no key card to access anything here. She can't even get in her room without a guard opening it. How would she take down our cloud backup?"

Beck told him he didn't have a clue at this point and then asked if Mercy had access to a phone.

"We have one landline that members can use for one ten-minute call every seven days, and that has to be approved in advance. She can't possibly have been involved in what happened at the Roy ranch."

"Visitors?" he asked, ignoring Dan's obvious irritation.

"She has no family, but visitors, like phone calls, have to be approved in advance. I'm pretty sure her only visitor has been her attorney."

"Can you double-check that for me, Dan?"

"Why?"

"Humor me."

Dan promised to get him the information and walked him and Brinley out to the parking lot. "So why is she really here, Dan?" Beck asked. "And I'm not buying that it's the white-collar crap in her file."

Whiteside could see Beck wasn't leaving without more answers. "She hacked into the Federal Reserve and stole almost a billion dollars."

Beck's jaw almost hit the pavement. He turned to Brinley. "Did you know this?"

"No one knows," said Dan. "Almost no one, anyway."

"A billion dollars?" Something about that figure struck a chord in Beck's brain. "Wait, this isn't the case from last year where a bunch of money got sent in error to someplace in Asia? Was it the Philippines? I read something about it."

"Yeah, that's the one. But it was no error. It was a hack. More sophisticated than any of the bank's experts had ever seen, apparently. They didn't notice until it was too late."

Beck had to laugh. "And she thought hacking a drone was dangerous and reckless? I seem to recall the actual transfers were far less than a billion, that only about seventy or eighty million was actually taken."

"Correct," Dan said. "I don't understand most of it, but yeah, if they hadn't realized what was happening and turned off the spigot, the whole billion would have been gone."

"What happened to the money she did steal?"

"Hell if I know. She got caught, got tripped up somehow. And they couldn't let her walk, obviously." He paused for a moment, folding his big hands together in front of him. "Does that help?"

Beck scratched his head. "Probably. Maybe. I don't know." It did better explain the two-plus-year sentence. He thought about what Maddox had told him earlier in the day. If someone could hijack an RPA and engage its weapons systems, what couldn't they do?

"You actually think Mercy hijacked that drone," Brinley said as they drove away from the Youth Center.

Beck cranked the wheel to the right, heading north on the 93. "I'm sure of it."

Brin set her bare feet on the dash. "But Porter, she doesn't have a computer, and you saw the security."

Beck looked over at her. "She did it, Brin. She was practically bragging about it. There are only two questions: why, and did she have help?"

"Bragging about it? Was I watching a different interview? The girl is incarcerated. She doesn't fit inside whatever nice little box you're putting together."

Beck turned his eyes from the road and put them squarely on his sister. "No," he said. "She doesn't fit. There's something very wrong about her, isn't there?"

She could tell he was really speaking to himself, not her. Thinking out loud. "There's nothing wrong with her. She's a kid who found a way to survive. Trust me on this, brother. I know what that's like."

He nodded. If anyone knew about survival, about desperation and need, it was Brin. "And yet," he said, "she hacked that bird and blew up Jesse Roy's bull. Why did she need to do that to survive?"

Brinley stared at him incredulously. "Are you hearing yourself?"

He thought about the strange email again. "She's not done, Brin. And that train's coming in pretty quick, I think. Meantime, I might know someone who can help." He pulled out his cell phone and punched in the number Maddox had given him. "I may have a lead on our hacker," he told him, filling in the details. "Can you do some digging for me?"

CHAPTER 13

Twenty hours before Beck and Brinley left the Youth Center, a South Korean man named Dal Cho was enjoying his overpriced beer in the right-field arcade section of Oracle Park in San Francisco. He loved sitting in this section since it was where left-handed hitters' home runs would often land, if they didn't sail all the way over the railing and into McCovey Cove. It was a warm day at the ballpark, midseventies and blissfully still, which was a relief for Cho and the fans whose backs were to the water and often subject to the chilling winds that blew in off the bay. Cho loved baseball, had played it extensively as a child, and had been a huge fan of the Lotte Giants in Busan for as long as he could remember. If he could have been anything else in life, he would have been a professional baseball player. But as things turned out, he was better at being a spy.

Strange, he thought, how his life path had brought him to this place. He was thirty-two, had come to America to study at Berkeley when he was eighteen. He'd never left, except for short trips home every once in a while, and had forged a career as a political consultant in California after graduation. It wasn't baseball, but it allowed him to hobnob with the policy makers and shakers of the state that represented the fifth largest economy in the world.

It was the seventh inning stretch, and none other than Tony Bennett was singing "Take Me Out to the Ball Game." Cho's cell phone buzzed in his pocket. It was a simple text, benign and friendly. "Hoping you'll come on Friday," the message read. Cho read the blurb in half a second and stuffed the phone back into his pocket. He rose immediately and walked to the nearest restroom. The text was an order to immediately find a private place and stand by for a larger message.

He stood in the bathroom stall and waited, knowing that the new message would be coming from almost 6,000 miles to the west, in the offices of the Hainan State Security Department (HSSD), a provincial arm of China's Ministry of State Security. In fact, Dal Cho was not South Korean, but he had lived with the name and the legend for so long now that he had all but forgotten who he really was.

He passed the time by keeping up with the game on his ESPN app. Finally, his phone pinged. Cho pressed two buttons on the keypad, a command to decrypt the text. What he read in the next thirty seconds both disturbed and excited him.

The tech nerds in HSSD had been poring over the emails of the senior executives at America's Minos Defense Systems, emails they were reading in real time, thanks to Dal Cho. A tiny piece of malicious code, inserted via a thumb drive in the laptop of a beautiful Minos systems engineer, provided a backdoor into the defense contractor's systems and the credentials of the entire operations team, the corporate officers, and the company's board members. It had been easy work for Cho. He had done it a hundred times on a hundred different laptops.

To any credentialed user, everything appeared completely normal. Files could be executed, transferred, and archived, and that was because the malware had already identified any antivirus programs that might detect it. After the malware went live, the HSSD tech team simply issued itself new credentials and administrator privileges, such as access to employee emails. The hack was quickly becoming a treasure trove of classified information.

The email on Cho's screen had been flagged and routed to senior HSSD officers because it had been sent by someone named BlueTiger in the U.S. Air Force, and it was received by the CEO of Minos. Three other corporate officers were copied. The subject line read: *Incident of 4 July.* It went on to describe that top U.S. intelligence experts had analyzed the code used to hack a classified next-generation remotely piloted aircraft as it flew over Nevada's secret desert test range and believed it to be similar in complexity to the one used to blow up an operation two years in the making, a hack designed to steal a billion dollars from the New York Federal Reserve Bank.

That last piece struck a deep, painful chord in Cho. He had worked for months on his contact at the Fed's San Francisco office, listening to her bleat like a goat during sex, revolted by her noxious body odor and hairy arms and legs. She loved his taut body, and the way he selflessly pleasured her for an hour before satisfying himself. Afterward, her comalike sleep provided Cho an opportunity to peer into her computer and glean more about the bank's processes and procedures. Eventually, the plan came together in his head, and Beijing had been thrilled. The theft had been executed flawlessly, over a long holiday weekend that provided cover for the financial transfers, moving the money in increments that would eventually total almost a billion dollars from Bangladesh accounts in New York to several places in the Philippines. But then, after $81,000,000 in transfers, the money was suddenly gone, transferred again, this time to accounts untraceable. The remaining $900,000,000 in transfers were interdicted before they could be executed. The hack had been hacked, not by the U.S. government but by some unknown cyber-assailant. But now there was a lead on the thief, this drone hacker perhaps, and the Ministry of State Security directed Cho to run it down. *Locate and secure,* his orders read. A flight reservation had been made, a car rental too. Directions were given for meeting a contact at the Las Vegas airport. Why the HSSD believed the hacker was in Nevada instead of anywhere else in the world was something Cho hoped would be explained once he landed.

He left the ballpark immediately. As he walked from the Willie Mays Gate to the Uber pickup on Third Street north of Townsend, he wondered how Western countries could produce individuals with the intelligence and capabilities needed to commit the most sophisticated computer crimes yet be so inept at finding them. In China, children were screened early in life, technical abilities assessed and graded, so that by the time they reached their teens, their online movements were meticulously tracked. The more competent went to work for Cho's employer, the Chinese government. Those that elected a different path were hunted down and imprisoned.

There was no need to take a gun on his flight to Las Vegas. The weapon arrived via a handoff in the restroom off the baggage claim area, inside a black duffel bag identical to the one Cho brought with him on the plane. It was almost midnight when the shuttle dropped him at the rental car center south of the airport. He went directly into the garage and the nondescript silver Hyundai Sonata reserved for him. As soon as he was in, he flipped on the overhead light and turned the air conditioner to max. The outside temperature in Sin City was still 95 degrees, without a trace of humidity but still oven hot. Next, he opened the duffel bag and extracted the manila envelope containing his instructions.

In the time since he had left the baseball game, the geek squad at HSSD had gleaned little additional intelligence. However, it had surmised that because the drone hijacked on the night of the Fourth had fired a missile, destroying some expensive livestock, the hacker might be acquainted in some way with the owner, a cattle rancher named Jesse Roy.

In addition, there were two individuals leading the efforts to locate and detain the drone's hijacker. One was an underperforming OSI agent by the name of Maddox. The second was the local sheriff, a man named Porter Beck. Profiles, each about a page long, were included on all three men but without any preconceived judgments. Cho would draw his own conclusions, having learned the hard way to rely on what his eyes told him, what he witnessed firsthand.

Also included were topographical and street maps of Lincoln County to the north. Like everyone in America, he had a smart phone with multiple GPS applications, but redundancy was key in intelligence operations. There was no telling when you might get separated from technology, and a paper map had once saved Cho's life. Additionally, Cho found a laptop in the bag, one he knew would be encrypted, a small police scanner that could attach to one of the car's USB ports, and a thin metal square hardly bigger than Cho's thumb with a circle touchpad in the center. Cho pressed the circle, turning the tracking device on to make sure it worked. Inside a concealed pouch, his fingers spread over the grip of a QSZ-92 pistol, his personal favorite and the gun favored by the People's Liberation Army, along with two spare fifteen-round magazines loaded with 5.8 millimeter ammunition and a short suppressor, black and an inch longer than the barrel of the pistol. Cho ran his hand over the bottom of the bag. In another hidden sleeve carefully sewn into the fabric, he found two syringes, both capped and full of fluid, one to kill, one to render the recipient unconscious. Like trusted old friends, he had relied on both more than once.

Sleep was something he neither coveted nor needed in any great quantity, so he drove in light traffic and under a full moon until the four lanes of interstate turned into two lanes of rural highway, and then for two hours more, until he parked behind a boarded-up gas station well off the road, plugged in the police scanner, and allowed himself finally to shut his eyelids and drift into the slightest of slumbers.

He spent most of Monday driving the roads around the Lincoln County Youth Center. Now he was waiting for his moment.

CHAPTER 14

By 4:00, Beck and Brinley were in Lund, a tract of land given to the Church of Jesus Christ of Latter-day Saints back in 1898 by the U.S. government. The population had peaked more than a century ago and had been tailing off like the mines around it ever since. In ten years, it would likely be another shuttered, tumbleweed town. For now, though, there remained the tiniest of post offices, and when Beck pulled into the empty parking lot, he was afraid the postmaster had gone fishing.

Brin's blood sugar was low, and she was in a foul mood. They had skipped lunch altogether, bypassing Pioche and driving north into White Pine County. Beck had promised her a big ribeye at Jake's in Ely, but this wasn't Jake's, and there were no steaks in sight. "What now?" she grumbled.

Beck climbed out of the truck. "Give me a sec, okay? Play with the dog. I'll be right back." And he was. He didn't say anything, didn't start the engine. After a minute, he said, "Do you remember what Mercy was saying about how people ship drugs out of post offices now? Well, I asked the old guy in there if he remembered anyone picking up or dropping off packages who wasn't from around here. I mean, he knows everyone in this town, right?"

"Sure."

"He says there's a woman who comes in every month or two with a number of small parcels that she ships all over the country."

"And he doesn't know her?"

Beck raised an eyebrow. "He sort of does. Says she works at one of the brothels in Ely."

Brinley grinned. "And he would know this because . . . ?"

He started the engine. "I believe his exact words were 'Because I ain't dead yet and fancy a nice bordello from time to time.'"

"Does he have any idea what's in the packages she's mailing?"

"He does not. Said the boxes are always sealed and addressed ahead of time. Preprinted mailing labels. They only need postage. But he said he asked her once, and she told him she makes jewelry and has her own website. Gets customers from all over."

"Which doesn't explain why she comes down here to Lund to mail them."

Beck shook his head and turned back onto the highway. "No, it does not. There's a post office right there in Ely."

"Could be anything in those boxes, you know. Could even be jewelry."

"Could be pills too." He paused for a moment. "But here's the weird thing, Brin. I had my guys dig into Jesse Roy's life. There was a lot of it I missed while I was in the Army."

Brinley spun in her seat to face him. "Wait, you think Jesse Roy is the one dealing drugs?"

"I'm beginning to. There was a guy at the ranch the other day who we believe has a very shady past. And Jesse seems to have way too much money for a guy running cattle. You should see his place. And his airplane. He owns a number of other—"

"You sound jealous of him, Porter," Brinley commented.

He looked at her, head tilted. "I probably am. But apparently Jesse frequents the same brothel in Ely where our mysterious jewelry maker works."

"Well, that's a little more coincidence than we like, isn't it?"

"I think it is."

"In that case," she said with a grin, "if you're taking me to a whorehouse, I'd like dinner first, please."

More than a hundred miles to the south, Dal Cho was munching on a Clif Bar and watching a group of teenagers picking up trash along the highway. They sported bright orange vests, the kind road workers wear for high visibility, and they were on the west side of the highway, across from the hot springs, roughly where his latest intel suggested they would be. The geek squad back in Beijing had determined two things from a number of intercepted emails. The first was that the local sheriff had interviewed a sixteen-year-old female inmate named Mercy Vaughn at the local Youth Center about the hacking of the military drone. She had been incarcerated there for almost seven months. The second was that Mercy Vaughn was scheduled to be on a road cleanup crew this very afternoon. The emails had come from the OSI agent assigned to the case and were sent to BlueTiger in the Pentagon. The Air Force, and no doubt the combined cyber resources of the American intelligence community, were working feverishly to determine if this girl could be the culprit.

If true, this could be the only opportunity Cho would get to grab her. From the tree-lined wash on the east side of the road, he took another look at the digital photo on his phone and peered through his small bird-watching binoculars. A caravan of fifty or more vehicles arrived then, clogging the highway and moving slower than his mother's Tai Chi class, most of them decorated with drawings of what appeared to be Hollywood-like green-skinned aliens. Colorful placards hung from windows or were affixed to the front and sides, all touting messages about Area 51 and saving E.T. from the government. They were honking their horns and playing loud music as if on parade. And they were blocking Cho's view. He cursed the stupid Americans under his breath, willing them to move faster. But then, through a small break in the caravan, he picked Mercy out of the group of delinquents. She was wearing a red ball cap that fit awkwardly, her eyes intense and alert.

He recognized those eyes, older now but . . . He told himself it couldn't be. He couldn't be that lucky. That girl had vanished four years ago. His own eyes were playing tricks! But then she removed her baseball hat and wiped the sweat from her forehead, and that's when Cho became certain. *Four years I've been looking for you!*

The parade came to a brief halt, allowing the dozen boys and girls to cross the highway, their guards, one very overweight man and one woman, driving the two pickup trucks carrying the bags of collected refuse behind them. The band of trash pickers began to spread out in the dense vegetation fed by the natural hot springs. Cho could not believe his luck. Mercy Vaughn was moving quicker, putting more distance between herself and the rest of her group. Cho's car was only thirty feet away, and he could pop the trunk with his key fob. As she approached, he crouched in the tall bush, watching and waiting for the right moment as the alien hunters streamed past again, one of the vehicles blaring the song "Aliens Exist" by Blink-182. Cho smiled. The noise and the spectacle were the perfect cover. Like a cheetah, he crept through the bush, withdrawing the syringe from his pocket.

CHAPTER 15

The hostess at Jake's Steak said to come back in a half hour, so Beck suggested to Brinley that they try to find the jewelry-selling prostitute while they waited. They walked the short block up Fifth Street and turned right onto "Bronc Alley," the west end of which housed Ely's three legal brothels. The sale of sex had been a part of the town since the 1880s, its establishments having changed ownership and names many times, surviving mostly because of mining and remoteness of location. In the only state allowing legalized prostitution, their importance to the community could be gauged by comparing their number to other local institutions, of which there were currently twelve churches, eight gas stations, and one movie theater, the latter evidence of how the city of 4,000 ranked its entertainment.

The Moondust Ranch was the newest of the three brothels and was sixty years old. It had a bright neon marquee, resembling an orange sun setting over the Pacific, and a large BIKERS WELCOME sign tacked to the wooden slats that served as the front of the building.

Beck had never been inside, though he was having some difficulty convincing Brinley of it, and was expecting more the seedy opium den setting of the Far East than the well-lit, pleasantly perfumed atmosphere of the Moondust. It had a long cherrywood bar and even video gaming for customers. Off to one side was a smaller reception area with couches and chairs and the busy carpeting you might find in any casino. There were seven women within his field of view, all in flimsy gowns, four in the reception area competing for their next customers and three in the bar warming up what were probably regulars for a night that would leave those men precious little money for groceries.

Brinley was watching them too, her lips parting, her jaw falling, fascinated and disturbed at the same time.

"Not what you expected?" Beck asked.

"I was thinking that the world has changed a lot since people started painting pictures in caves. And here we are all this time later, and not much has changed between men and women."

There was no emotion in her words. They were as dispassionate as if she were describing water droplets and the physics of dew. But he could see the pain in her eyes, knew what she must be thinking. He didn't need to hear her describe it. He heard it in the screams of her recurring nightmares. And he saw it in her face when she would suddenly withdraw from him and Pop for days at a time. He couldn't imagine the power of those demons and suspected they were the reason she had armed herself with every gun imaginable.

As they moved to the bar, Beck noticed the women's eyes following Brinley, all probably wondering if this woman who looked like one of those super-toned fitness instructors was here to apply for work, a result that would surely cut a wide swath into their earnings. The old guy who looked like somebody's grandpa behind the bar was mixing drinks and asked if they saw anything they liked.

That got a laugh out of Brin. Beck lowered his voice and slid his badge onto the bar. "We're just here for some information."

"Little out of your jurisdiction, aren't you, Sheriff?" he asked, leaning toward them. "Last time I checked, Lincoln County was south of here."

"It hasn't gone anywhere. Are you the proprietor?"

He popped a dish towel inside a beer glass and twirled it around with his fingers. "The wife and me."

"Oh, good, a family business." Beck pulled out his phone and located the shots of Jesse Roy and his man César. "I understand the man on the left comes in here occasionally."

The old-timer motioned them down to the end of the bar where it was a little darker and there was a modicum of privacy. "We don't talk about our clientele, Sheriff. Unless you got a warrant."

"I appreciate the need for discretion," Beck said. Though buying sex was legal here, no doubt a good many of the patrons were married. "I'm trying to figure out why someone might want to hurt him in some way. He doesn't owe you money, does he?"

The old guy laughed, tapping a lung nail out of the pack and lighting it. "The opposite. He's more than generous. You can ask Mona. She—damn, I've said too much already."

"Her name is *Moan-a*?" Brinley asked, the pitch of her voice higher than usual. Beck felt her hand on his now, squeezing. He turned to her, his eyes asking if she was okay. She nodded.

He handed her the truck's key fob and turned back to the bartender. "Mona working tonight?" She was with a client, so Beck ordered two beers. When the suds arrived, he reached for a bowl of nuts, but tipped the side, spilling them over the bar.

Brinley rescued what was left and placed the bowl in front of him. "Are they getting worse? Your eyes, I mean?"

"About the same. I don't know. Still see plenty good in sunlight, but nighttime . . ." He looked around, could see almost nothing. "And in places like this."

She reached out and set her hand on his. He wished he could stare into her eyes right now. "I don't want you to worry, Brin. I'm not going to have you taking care of Pop and me both. That's not going to happen."

She could see into his eyes just fine. He was her protector, had been since she was a young girl. Yes, it had been Pop who rescued her up in the mountains, but it was Beck who made sure she was never again touched against her will. At her insistence, they spent countless hours sparring, with Beck teaching her arm bars and leg locks, along with how to attack vital areas. They were still sparring, whenever she was home, and she loved him for it. "You're going to figure it out. We'll figure it out together. And I'll tell you what's not going to happen, Porter. I'm never going to be out of your life. Even after you finally find a nice woman to marry, someone who can put up with you racing through your food like a Formula One driver.

"Listen," she added. "I know you're convinced Mercy hacked the drone, but even if she somehow found a way to wipe the security camera backup, she would need a computer, and like X-Files and Maddox both told you, probably some sort of joystick thing-amajig to fly it. You've seen the Center. That stuff isn't available outside of a class setting. It would have been physically impossible for her."

"That's a fair point, but I'm still convinced. Here's why: a wealthy cattle rancher is celebrating his daughter's birthday when a rocket screams out of the sky and blows up an eighty-thousand-dollar bull. Roy's daughter happens to be friends with a girl named Mercy who is so good at hacking she stole a billion dollars from the Federal Reserve." Beck paused, downed the rest of his beer. "And the place Mercy is confined has a video surveillance system, but the backup for it, the only way to prove she's the hacker, has mysteriously gone missing."

Brinley listened, motioning to the bartender for a refill. "Speaking of missing things, aren't you missing a motive? And are you suggesting that Shiloah is using Mercy to hurt her father?"

Living with a cop for most of her life, Brinley had picked up some solid police instincts. Beck drained his glass, recalling the almost gleeful look Shiloah had the morning after her dad's prized bull had been obliterated by a missile. "The question is, *why* does she want to hurt him?"

They met in an outdoor area in back of the building that butted up against a steep hill. Brinley had retreated to the truck, so Beck and Mona sat at a picnic table that had lost its color next to an old whiskey bar set up on the gray gravel. It was almost 7:00, and the sun had another hour in its trip west, but it was still hot and low enough in the sky to be a bother, so Mona cranked open an umbrella above the table.

She was no more than thirty and quite pretty, Beck thought. Her hair was lush, artificially blond with orange highlights, and her blue eyes were naturally attractive. Still, he had never interviewed a sex worker and found it difficult to maintain eye contact. Mona seemed to sense his discomfort and put him right at ease by complimenting his smile.

"Thanks," he said. "It was my mom's."

"Is she still around?"

Beck shook his head. "Not for a long time now."

"I'm so sorry." He had to give it to her. She would have made a good cop. But it was time to flip the tables, so he asked her about Jesse Roy.

She immediately stiffened. "Yeah, he comes in once every two or three months, usually when he's buying or selling steers at auction. He's very nice, very generous. Is he all right?"

Her concern seemed genuine enough. "He's fine. Somebody killed one of his bulls the other night, and I'm trying to figure out who might be holding a grudge or want to hurt the man, that's all. We're old friends, Jesse and I."

She shook her head. "Funny, he's never mentioned you. But I have no idea. He really is the nicest man. Very professional. Always treats me like a lady. Takes me to dinner before . . . you know."

"And no enemies that you're aware of?"

Her fingers played with one of the large loop earrings dangling from a lobe, and her lips parted seductively. "Well, that's the thing, Sheriff. I wouldn't know. But I doubt it. Every time we're out somewhere, people seem to like him."

She wasn't lying. That was Jesse Roy. Fun-loving. Always smiling. Likable. "Has he ever asked you to do anything for him outside of town?"

She frowned. "Like?"

He shrugged. "Mail a package or two. I know you've been down to Lund a few times to mail boxes of something. I'm wondering if you're doing that for Jesse."

The blood rushed to her face, covering her normal milky complexion, but she kept her eyes on him. "I have a custom jewelry business on the side. Sometimes I mail from there, sure. But that's *my* business, not Jesse's. And not yours."

She lied for a living, stroking her clients' egos, but unlike Mercy, she wasn't very good at it. Didn't have to be, he guessed. "I'd love to see what you make."

Her eyes dropped to the table. "I don't have any inventory right now, I'm afraid. I've sold all my recent pieces."

Beck beamed. "Congrats. Good for you, Mona. I thought you might be shipping drugs, which would be a federal crime and very serious. You could get twenty years. I'm glad to hear you're not doing that."

Mona looked up, meeting his eyes. On quivering lips, she tried to smile.

When Beck got back to the truck, Brinley was in the driver's seat, Bo curled next to her with his big head in her lap. He filled her in on his conversation with Mona.

"You know she's going to call him, right?"

"I hope so," he answered. "Didn't come all this way for nothing."

"So, you're looking to rile the man."

He grinned. "That's generally when people fuck up, after a good riling. Now, let's get that steak."

"Call from Dan Whiteside," the lady that lived in his cell phone announced. Beck put the call on speaker. "Dan, I've got Brinley with me. What's up?"

"It's Mercy. She's gone."

Beck shook his head. "Gone mad? Gone wild? Dead and gone?"

"She was out on a road cleanup crew late this afternoon. And she disappeared."

"What road?" Brinley asked.

"Main highway. Right by the hot springs."

"Dan," Beck said, "is she the only one who went missing?"

"Yep. We had four of the girls and eight of the boys out there, and all of them are accounted for except her." Beck could hear a little panic in the man's voice.

"How many people do you have out looking for her?"

"The two guards who were with the kids on the road crew,

and two more, but they've been looking for about ninety minutes already. We need some help."

Brinley was already backing the police pickup out of its spot. "Did you call NHP?" Beck asked. It was a question of jurisdiction. The state Highway Patrol was primary in this case since the Youth Center was a state institution.

"My next call. But your people are a lot closer."

Brinley mashed the gas pedal and flipped on the light bar and siren. "We're on it," Beck assured him. "Dan, after we left today, did Mercy receive or make any phone calls?"

"Hold on, let me check." A few seconds later, "One call. From her attorney. Right before they left for the road cleanup."

Beck asked him to text the attorney's contact information. "Any news on the issue with your video backup?"

"Oh yeah. They called a few minutes ago. They were hacked and didn't even know it. That's how good it was, apparently. I guess you were right about Mercy. I'm sorry, Beck."

Beck didn't say anything but gave Brin the "I told you so" look.

"Call me back," Dan said. "If you find her."

"Hang on. One more thing. The attorney. Man or woman?"

"Uh, man, I think. One sec."

Beck moved his finger rapidly in a circle, motioning to Brinley to go faster. The sun was going down now, his vision pulling back with every passing minute. "Yep, a man," Dan said. "Sandy Barnes-Nobler. Is that important?"

"Might be. Thanks, Dan."

Beck clicked off, ending the call. After he speed-dialed Tuffy and got his troops moving, Brinley looked over at him. "It still doesn't make sense to me. How could she hack a military drone from the Youth Center?"

Beck grinned. "You said it yourself, Brin. She's the smartest person you've ever met. These people exist."

"But not sixteen-year-old girls."

"While I was waiting for Mona to finish up with her customer back at the Moondust, I started Googling teenage hackers. There was this kid, Jonathan James, sixteen years old back in '99 when he got caught breaking into the computers of the Defense Threat Reduction Agency."

"What's that?"

"It's a division of the DOD, and its primary function is to analyze potential threats to the United States. But here's the kicker. Turns out he installed some kind of backdoor in a computer server somewhere in Virginia, which allowed him to do all sorts of things like read people's emails, see their passwords, stuff like that. But what he got his hands on was the International Space Station's source code."

"Oh, please, no," Brin said softly, as if she were listening to a ghost story.

"Oh, yes. If he wanted to, he could have shut down the life support system on the station."

Brinley took her eyes from the road, glancing over at Beck. "What happened to him?"

"They locked him up. He was the first juvenile incarcerated for cybercrime."

"Like Mercy."

"Let's hope she doesn't end like he did."

"How was that?"

Beck gazed out his window into the darkness. "He shot himself a few years later."

They drove in silence for a minute before Beck pulled up his recent calls and hit the number next to Maddox's name, holding the phone to his ear. He answered after the first ring. "Maddox. Beck here. Did you snatch her?"

"Who?"

"Don't bullshit me. The girl. Mercy Vaughn. The one I told you about at the Youth Center. Did you take her?"

Maddox was apoplectic. "I only got her file an hour ago. Are you telling me she's gone? What the hell happened?"

Beck glanced over to Brinley. "She was out on a road cleanup detail. Walked off or someone picked her up. It wasn't you and your guys from the Army of Northern Virginia?"

It wasn't a reference to Robert E. Lee's army but rather a name that many in the service used to describe the special operators attached to the U.S. intelligence community and its associated agencies, many of whom lived in Virginia.

Dead silence on the other end of the line. Finally, "How did you let that happen, Sheriff? Why wasn't she in your custody?"

Beck felt his internal temperature rising. "That's not how custody works, Maddox. Mercy belongs to the State. I'm the local guy. I couldn't have gotten her out of there if I'd wanted to."

"Shit, shit, shit!" Maddox screamed into the phone. Brinley winced and Beck gave the OSI man a minute to regain his composure. "What do we do now?"

"We're out looking for her. We'll find her."

Maddox didn't hesitate. "We'll be back out in the morning, Sheriff. To *help* you find her. Any other good news?"

His brain flashed on the email he'd gotten the night of the Fourth. "Nope, but I've got a question for you."

"Go ahead."

"What's a zero day?"

Ten seconds went by before Maddox answered. "It's a previously unknown software vulnerability or bug that can be exploited. Zero day is the day that vulnerability becomes known, because whoever made that software still doesn't know about it. The hacker that found this flaw writes some code that instructs a buyer—which is often the software developer itself—how that vulnerability can be used to exploit and subvert the software. Why do you ask?"

"No real reason. Came up in conversation. Thanks. I'll keep you posted."

After he ended the call, Brinley moved her eyes from the road to Beck. "Why did you ask him that?"

He removed his cap and scratched his scalp. "I'm not sure. But it's interesting that an Air Force cop knew the answer."

CHAPTER 16

They searched for Mercy all night. *They*, of course, meant anyone with working eyeballs. But there was still no trace of her. According to the other kids on the detail, she had been there one second and gone the next. Beck was more than a little worried. Maddox and his people were hunting her, and they had the resources and license to take her down. She had no shield outside the Youth Center, and a twenty-sided die would not help her.

Come morning, there were three possibilities bouncing around Beck's brain. The first was that Maddox was lying and had grabbed Mercy. Without a lawful warrant to remove her from the Youth Center, that was kidnapping. Not unprecedented for the forces of the United States government, but hardly commonplace, and hardly necessary. The second was that someone else had taken her. Beck was certain Mercy had hacked the drone and destroyed Jesse's prize bull, and he wondered now if Jesse could have also made that connection. He couldn't see how. Even if he did, he would have had no way of knowing Mercy would be out on a work detail or what she even looked like. That left a final explanation: she was running. If she was, it was likely she was still in Lincoln County. From where she disappeared from the work detail, Mercy was smack in the middle of the county along a north to south line. There were three small towns that dotted this axis along Highway 93, Caliente to the south, Panaca and Pioche to the north. East were mountains too high to climb for someone not properly outfitted, and to the west there was nothing but inhospitable desert for a hundred miles. Could she have hitched a ride with a trucker or someone else? With her charm, sure. But hitchhiking takes time, and someone would have seen her. No one had.

Two cups of coffee did nothing to render a clearer picture in Beck's head. He spent some time on the phone with Esther Ellingboe discussing the fire situation again, which was growing worse by the day, and wondered how long it would be before there was no more timber to burn and all the forests were gone. It wasn't a problem he could solve, so when the clock struck eight, he gathered his keys and aspiring Seeing Eye dog and headed for the door. The next step in locating Mercy was to have a talk with Shiloah Roy.

But in the front lobby, he found a woman of Native American descent dressed pretty much like him, with blue jeans, well-worn tactical boots, a plaid long-sleeved shirt, and a tactical drop-leg holster with a Colt 1911 semiautomatic pistol strapped to her right thigh. She held up her Department of Public Safety detective shield. "Looking for Sheriff Beck."

Columbo moved quickly around the high counter and gave her a good sniff-over. She immediately bent down and swallowed him in her arms. This was a woman who had dogs.

"That's me," Beck replied. "The guy with the poor manners here is Columbo."

Standing back up, she stuck out her hand. "Charlie Blue Horse. Nice meeting you both."

She had nice hands. "Charlie?"

"It's really Charlotte, but Dad always called me Charlie."

She was attractive, in a rugged nature-girl sort of way, with wonderful dark eyes and hair the color of raven wings that stretched past her shoulders. "You're Paiute, I'm guessing?"

She nodded. "Good eye. Walker River. I'm a bit of a mutt, actually." She looked him over. "But isn't almost everyone these days?"

Beck laughed. His own genetic history was a mix he was only now getting comfortable with. "Sorry, bad habit. You're here about Mercy Vaughn. I figured someone from the state would be here today." He could see she was groggy. "You must have driven all night."

She yawned, stroking Columbo's head. "Pretty much. She turn up yet?"

"I was about to go speak to a friend of hers who may know something. Like to come along, Charlie Blue Horse?" Beck got her a big cup of coffee first, and a minute later, they were in his truck and heading south. It was going to be another hot one, so he cranked the AC and gave her the background on the case so far.

"I saw Mercy's file," Charlie said, doing her best to fend off Columbo's advances. "She's had it rough."

"Maybe."

"You don't think so?"

The dog simply would not stop sniffing her. "Something doesn't quite add up about her." Beck reached over and pushed Bo into the back seat. "Will you leave her alone, please?" He smiled apologetically at Charlie. "Sorry, must be your perfume. Does it have gunpowder in it?"

Charlie laughed and shook her head. "Ambrette seed, sapodilla fruit, with some violet, sandalwood, and magnolia, I think. My mother makes it. But no gunpowder."

"Smells good," Beck said, trying to keep his eyes on the road.

"Hmm," she said, taking the compliment. "So, you think Jesse Roy's daughter is helping her?"

"Not sure. I guess we'll know shortly."

She shook her head. "Everything about this girl says she's a loner. Everything that's in the file.

"Could she have actually hacked into this UAV or RPA, or whatever the Air Force is calling their model airplanes this week?"

He laughed. "It is tough keeping up with the military jargon, but yeah, she did it." He explained the missing camera footage from the center. "I was sure she was the hacker thirty seconds after I sat down with her. I can't explain it. Pure instinct more than anything else."

Charlie considered the information. "Well, she did bolt right after you spoke to her. Nothing says 'I'm guilty' more than walking away from your road cleanup duty. I once tracked a guy who vanished from a work detail. Took me two years to find him."

Beck looked over at her. "Where was he?"

"In Colorado. Running for mayor, oddly enough, in Durango. Under a new name."

"A logical career move, I guess," Beck said with a laugh. "Anyway, we can't be sure she bolted." He explained the possible scenarios and why he hadn't settled on one. "The thing that strikes me, though, is her intelligence. I don't see her getting snatched from the work detail. She's just too . . . *aware*. But I guess we shouldn't dismiss the possibility that Maddox or someone else took her."

They had the time, and the highway was practically empty at this hour, so he continued south, passing the turn that led to the Double J, deciding to show Charlie where Mercy disappeared. It took a few minutes, and then he made a U-turn and slowed next to the hot springs, pointing out the dense vegetation that grew along the highway. "Lots of places for someone to hide in there."

"You could definitely conceal a vehicle," she said. "Who was aware that she was going to be on the cleanup crew?"

"It wasn't public knowledge. I'm guessing Mercy somehow got word to Shiloah." He depressed the gas pedal again. "Do you know about the Federal Reserve heist?"

"I only got the CliffsNotes. There's no real details, and you know what that means."

"It means the whole thing is classified, and that there's a lot more to the story."

"Well," Charlie said, "regardless of the real story, I can tell you that everyone from the governor on down wants this girl found *now*. I could hear the panic in my boss's voice when he called me last night, and he's not a man that scares easily."

"Mercy's not taking a thrill ride here, Charlie. She's not out to destroy. This is personal for her. If she does anything more, it's going to involve Jesse Roy."

Charlie's eyebrows came together in the middle. "I can tell you no one else I've spoken with agrees with that assessment, Sheriff. But I hope you're right. And Indian puns aside, it would be a real feather in my cap if I could get my hands on her before this Maddox guy does."

He wanted her to have that feather. "It's Beck, okay? Something else you should know. Mercy took a call from her attorney just before she went on the work detail yesterday, a guy named Sandy Barnes-Nobler."

"Is that odd?"

"It wouldn't have been, if he had actually called her. I spoke to him last night. He did talk with her the week before but not yesterday."

Charlie's head turned sharply toward Beck. "So, if it wasn't this Barnes and Noble guy, who made the call?"

Beck shook his head. "Don't know. The number recorded by

the center was the same as the attorney's. But he swears it wasn't him, and I believe him. The guy's a public defender. He's got no reason to lie."

Charlie raised her fingers to her temples. "Wait. You're saying what, that someone else, someone other than Shiloah Roy is helping her?"

Beck turned right off the highway, taking the truck onto the road that led into Dry Valley. "Someone who could make it appear the call was coming from the attorney."

"Well, who the holy hell is that?"

He looked over at her. "In my experience, the only people who can do that kind of thing are military or spooks."

"Or adolescent hackers," Charlie added. "Assuming it wasn't her, you're saying your buddy Maddox may already have her."

"I don't think so."

"Would he tell you if he did? If the military wanted to keep this a secret?"

Beck made another turn, and the road narrowed. "Definitely not. I think something else is happening here. But I'm not sure what it is yet."

Charlie sighed heavily. "I have to find this kid, Beck. She's high priority. I'm only the first. My boss got a call from the state AG's office, making it clear this is our responsibility, and he doesn't want someone from out of state doing our job for us."

He knew what that kind of pressure was like. Very quickly Charlie would be getting the same amount of heat that Maddox was getting. Ten minutes later, they pulled up to the ranch gate. The same young Latino that had been manning it a few days earlier was still there. Recognizing the sheriff, he made a quick call.

"That's odd," Charlie said. "Never seen that at a cattle ranch before."

The gate opened and they were waved through. "Trust me, you haven't seen anything yet."

As they pulled up to the house, Charlie whistled. "Wow, it's a mansion."

A picture of the old place flashed in Beck's mind, a single-story with a worn roof and aluminum siding that Jesse's dad was forever patching up. That was gone now. What stood in its place was a nearly completed white adobe fortress with three chimneys extending from the Spanish-tiled rooftops, balconies that could be accessed from all sides of the home with a view of the ranch and everything beyond it in all directions. From the outside, Beck figured it must be at least 8,000 square feet. Adjacent but unattached to the main house was a horse barn with at least ten covered stalls that matched the exterior of the house and two separate lighted arenas.

"Are we sure your friend is in the cattle business?" Charlie asked as they approached the front doors. "Have you ever seen the like?"

"Well," Beck answered, "when we were kids he seemed to have a good head for business."

She laughed. "What kind of business?"

Beck rang the bell. "He always knew where to score the best pot for the cheapest price." He winked at her. "I wasn't a party to any of that, mind you."

"What with being the sheriff's son and all," Charlie said with a laugh.

They were escorted inside by a housekeeper. The inside of the house was as impressive as the outside. The ceiling over the huge open-style first floor was constructed of massive logs that stretched out from the roof trusses like ribs from a spine. Beck had been around the world a few times, lived in faraway places, and dealt with people who liked nice things. These furnishings were designed to impress, the elegant Turkish rugs in the living and dining rooms easily costing more than a hundred grand. Likewise for the chandeliers. The furniture had been combed from a Spanish villa in Catalonia or somewhere nearby. The place reeked of wealth.

"What's wrong with this picture?" Charlie whispered as they were led to the back of the house.

Jesse Roy's study was more of a trophy case. Antelope, elk, and a bighorn ram gazed down on the two cops from their neck mounts on the walls. There was a billiards table covered in red felt and a gun cabinet as well, and an antique wooden desk that was larger than the one Beck once saw in the Oval Office when Obama was president.

"The mister will be coming," the housekeeper said in an accent as heavy as a dead donkey.

Beck plopped down in one of the fine leather chairs opposite the desk. "What do you think, Charlie Blue Horse?"

She was examining a crystal vase on a nearby bookshelf that probably cost more than her car. "I think I went to the wrong booth when we had Career Day at school."

"Yeah." Before he could elaborate, Jesse walked in with his associate, César.

"Whoa, two visits in three days, Beck. Maybe I should go buy me a lottery ticket."

Charlie snickered. "Looks to me like you already won the lottery."

An awkward silence hung in the air for a few seconds before Jesse broke out laughing, which got Beck going as well. "Jesse, this is Detective Charlie Blue Horse with the DPS Investigative Division."

They shook hands and Jesse took a seat behind his desk. César, in different but equally expensive threads than he had on when Beck met him three days earlier, retreated to a corner of the room.

Beck stared into the man's cold, dark eyes, feeling his own pulse quicken. "Might be better if we do this in private," he said.

Jesse dismissed the comment with a wave of his hand. "This about my bull? I thought we settled up on Saturday with the government."

"I'm not here about that, sir," Charlie said, looking to Beck.

Beck cleared his throat and asked if they could have a word with Shiloah. Jesse's head snapped quickly to his childhood friend. "About?"

"About a friend of hers at the Youth Center."

Jesse lifted a pen from the desk, tightening his fist around it. "She's done something wrong, hasn't she? What did she do?"

His tone revealed a lot. If Shiloah and her father were at odds, maybe she was trying to hurt him. "I'm not aware of her doing anything wrong, Jesse. This girl, her friend, has been incarcerated at the Youth Center and disappeared last night. It's technically the state's jurisdiction, but I thought Shiloah might have some insight into where she might be heading. It's awfully hot out there, and you and I both know what can happen to someone who doesn't know the desert."

Jesse stared at the two of them for a second or two before looking over their heads. "Isabella?"

Moments later, the housekeeper returned. "Señor?"

"Isabella, could you ask Shiloah to come down here please?"

She started to leave but then stopped. "Señor, she still sleeping."

César stepped out of his corner and spoke sternly in Spanish to Isabella, whose eyes retreated apologetically back into her head. She spun on her heels and left the room.

"My daughter is a late sleeper," Jesse told them. "My old man had my sister and me up at the crack of dawn every day. Apparently, it's insensitive to do that to your kids now."

Beck noticed there were no pictures of Willa Roy on the walls or on Jesse's desk. It wasn't a judgment. It had been eight years since she had died. People were entitled to move on. He could still see her face when Shiloah entered the study in a sleepy huff, wearing a T-shirt and cutoffs. "You summoned me?"

Jesse waved her over to the desk. "Shiloah, the sheriff and his colleague would like to ask you some questions." Charlie flashed her ID and introduced herself.

"About?" She sounded perturbed. Not the same glib equestrian Beck had met the other day.

Beck leaned forward in his seat. "About Mercy Vaughn."

Her gaze immediately fell to the floor. "What about her?"

He didn't answer, waiting until her eyes finally rose to his. At that moment, he lost his train of thought, amazed even more how much she resembled her mother.

Charlie jumped in. "How well do you know her?"

"Not well. I met her when I came back from school. See her in the library sometimes when I'm there. She likes to read."

Beck watched as her hands went in the pockets of her cutoffs, like she was hiding them. If she had been sitting at the desk instead of on top of it, she would have slid them underneath. That's what people do when they're concealing the truth. "I was given the impression you two were closer than that."

Shiloah stood up. "Who the fuck said that?"

"Hey," her father said, holding up a finger. "Watch the language."

"She walked away from a road cleanup crew yesterday," said Charlie.

Shiloah stared into space, said nothing.

"I believe they're asking if you know anything about this, Shiloah," Jesse said. "Right, Beck?"

Beck was focused now. When normal people are being dishonest, the mind is thinking of a lot of things. The story itself. Is it believable? What do I need to add? Am I behaving normally? Am I sweating? Mercy wasn't normal, so the rules didn't apply to someone like her, but Beck established his baseline on Shiloah the minute he saw the glee on her face when they first met, after her daddy's bull had been blown up. It was an honest reaction. He leaned in. "Did she say anything to you about leaving the Youth Center, Shiloah?"

She closed her eyes, frowning and shaking her head. "No. Of course not. Why would you think she would share that with me?" Then her hands came out of her pockets and into the air as if to say "What an absurd question!"

Another tell. Normal hand gesturing occurs while someone is talking. A liar tends to gesture after the statement.

"Look at me," Jesse said to her. "This is important. Is that the truth?"

She rolled her eyes. "Yes, it's the truth. I hardly know her."

"There you have it, Beck. Anything else?"

It didn't jibe with what Brinley told him about the girls. "Here's the thing, Shiloah. I'm worried about Mercy. She doesn't have any family, no one to go to in the area, no home to run back to. People like that can find bad luck in a hurry out here, and I don't want that to happen to her." He pulled a card out of his back pocket and handed it to her. "If you think of anything that might help us locate her, or if for any reason Mercy tries to contact you, would you please call me?"

Her head bobbed once in irritation.

"Sorry we couldn't be more help, buddy," Jesse said.

Charlie and Beck stood. "No worries. Thanks for your time." Shiloah retreated quickly up the stairs, and Jesse walked Beck and Charlie outside.

It was 9:30 now, and the sun was already beating down on

them. Beck looked up at the pale blue sky and smelled the smoke in the air. It would be the seventh day in a row they would break 100 degrees, and Mercy could very well be outside somewhere. "The house is amazing, Jesse. Just you and Shiloah under that big roof?"

He laughed. "It's a lot, I know. I wish they'd hurry up and finish. And I wish Willa could have seen it. It's the house she always wanted."

Beck's eyebrow rose into the furrows of his forehead. The girl he remembered came from humble beginnings and wasn't comfortable with extravagance in any form. His mind flashed on an almost thirty-year-old memory. They were on horseback, riding double in an open field of sagebrush and basin wild rye made golden by the setting sun. "I could live right here," she said, her arms firmly around his middle. "With you. I don't need anything more."

Beck shook loose from the image. From the outbuildings to the south of the house, he watched as a long cattle hauler was maneuvering alongside some cattle pens. He noted the two Latinos in the cab. Four more were behind the trailer in a white Toyota Highlander. "Shipping some steers?"

Jesse waved to the driver. "Yep. I sell to a few ranchers down in Mexico, after I get them good and fat. You think we're in a drought here? You should see it south of the border."

Beck asked Jesse if he had any more thoughts on what happened on the Fourth of July.

"Like what?"

"I don't know. But it seems crazy that out of all those cattle your bull drew the short straw."

Jesse's big boots skidded abruptly to a stop. "Wait. What are you trying to tell me?"

Beck removed his cap and ran his fingers through his hair. "I'm not trying to tell you anything. I'm asking, Jesse. Someone is coming after you. They blew your bull up to make a point, to send a message." He motioned to César. "You've got this guy hanging around who I'm pretty sure is a bad man. You're shipping stock to Mexico for some reason. Now I've known you almost my whole life, so I'm asking, as your friend, to tell me what's going on so I can help you before things get out of control. If there's something else you're shipping, or if somebody is jamming you up, I can help you get out in front of it."

Jesse's mouth puckered in anger. "Is that why you were poking your nose into my business last night up in Ely? Trying to help me get out in front of it? Is that what friends do?"

Beck stepped closer, their noses only an inch apart now. "No, that's what cops do. And speaking not as your friend now, but as the sheriff, I'm telling you that if you're moving drugs for these people, shit that some of your neighbors are choking and dying on, all of this, this big green ranch and oversized house, will dry up and blow away."

He waited, hands on his hips, but Jesse didn't respond. No denial. No admission. Nothing. Beck and Charlie walked to the truck. Once in, Beck cracked a bottle of water and poured a little in a dish for Columbo. Jesse stood on the lawn staring down at them.

"Well, you certainly got his attention," Charlie said. "You're not afraid that will spook him into stopping for a while or skipping out altogether?"

Beck started the truck. "He won't spook. And he won't run. His ego is too big for that hat. He'll make it a contest, and he'll make a mistake."

Charlie stroked Bo's head as he drank. "Well, the girl is definitely lying. That was obvious enough. But do you think she knows where Mercy is?"

Beck nodded. "Yep, hold on to your hat, Charlie Blue Horse. It's about to get interesting." He glanced over at her. "Hey, do you want to go see some aliens?"

CHAPTER 17

Ten minutes after the sheriff left, Jesse Roy watched as the same dozen heifers that had arrived three days earlier were now herded back into the chute and led one by one into the cage that would immobilize them. The marking and vaccinations were done and there was nothing more to attach to the young breeders to ensure their health and safety. There was something to remove, however. Jesse nodded to one of the ranch hands, who pulled a long disposable glove over his hand and stretched it to his shoulder. It was identical to the examination gloves veterinarians used, except that in this case after the gloved hand was inserted in the animal's rectum, it came out holding a packet the size of a beanbag. Then he reached back in and pulled out two more.

"I was afraid those bags would have blown apart in their asses by now," said Jesse. "But we can't wait any longer. My old friend has our scent now, and that dog can hunt."

"We should have done this three days ago," said César, "but it's good to know your cows can handle a little stomachache." He laughed and in Spanish directed the man holding the packets of

"Mexican Oxy" to give one to him. The cowboy rinsed the packet thoroughly in water and handed it to his boss. César slit it open with his pocketknife, dropping a few baby-blue pills into his palm. The pills, oxycodone pressed with fentanyl, were stamped on one side with the letter M and the number 30 on the other. "Bueno," he said, handing it back to the man, who set it in a wheelbarrow nearby. He turned to Jesse. "Should be a solid two hundred grand in this haul."

Jesse shook his head. "I hate this part of it."

César nodded. "It's pain relief, amigo. And it's a lucrative part."

Jesse turned his head and spat. "Yeah, well, I sure as hell hate it. A friend of mine died from this shit a few days ago."

"You don't know that," César replied. "You don't know where he got it."

Rage poured out of Jesse's bloodshot eyes. "Well, since over the last six months we pretty much put every other supplier out of business here, I guess I goddamned do know it. So get it loaded in the pickups and off to the stash house. And keep your eyes open for my daughter. She doesn't see any of this, got it?"

As he stomped off, Jesse had one thought in his head. *I'm going to get out of this dirty business if it kills me, by God.*

It took almost two hours to reach the tiny town of Rachel, where about fifty people reside permanently and where at least twenty times that number had already arrived for the upcoming Alien Independence Day set to kick off in three days. Tents, trailers, buses, and recreational vehicles lined both sides of the highway at the far western edge of the county, staking out the best real estate, nearly all of them either partially or fully decorated like floats in a parade. The people, too, were a spectacle, walking around in alien costumes or as their favorite Star Trek characters. And across from the Little A'Le'Inn, the town's sole motel, they were erecting a four-story flying saucer made of sheet metal.

"My goodness," Charlie said with a laugh. "It's like Burning Man."

"I hope the eventual turnout is a lot smaller," said Beck, eyeing the food trucks near the big ship and thinking about the yearly event in the Black Rock Desert, which reminded him he needed to nail down his itinerary for the trip at the end of August.

"These people don't really think they're going to storm Area 51, do they?"

Beck shook his head. "I don't know. But they're going to be very disappointed if they try."

Charlie popped her head out the window, scanning the crowd. "You really think she might be here?"

Beck took a left off the highway and pulled into the pump at Rachel's only gas station. "The guards at the Youth Center said that right at the time Mercy vanished, a parade of vehicles on their way down here passed right by them. Maybe she saw an opening and took it. It would make some sense. She could get lost in the crowd. Her crowd, really. Nerdy nerds."

They got out of the truck. What Charlie saw was a convention of weirdos. "Kind of a long shot, don't you think? She wouldn't have known any of these people."

"Maybe, but however brilliant Mercy may be with a computer, she has some impressive social engineering skills as well. She can manipulate people. She could have convinced any of these nut bags that she could tap into the comms the government guys are using. She's already hacked a top-secret drone. Turning off the NTTR security systems that monitor Area 51 might be child's play for her."

After filling the truck with gas, Beck said, "Let's get some chow. Then we'll take a look around."

On Highway 93, a few miles south of the Lincoln County line, INTRANS, a wholly owned subsidiary of Daimler Truck, was conducting its eleventh test in eight weeks of what it hoped would soon be the leader in autonomous vehicle freight hauling. Two years ago, Daimler had chosen Coyote Springs as the optimal location for its plant and control center where its engineers and team of teleoperators could bring the company into the future. It had the advantage of being a reasonable commute from Las Vegas for Daimler employees and offered a relatively low-volume highway through the desert, which meant roads generally with low traffic and weather ideal for testing. The state had been eager to have the automotive giant move in, offering generous tax incentives to seal the deal. The United States was moving almost twelve billion tons of freight every year by truck, and Daimler, like its competitors, had calculated the windfall that would be up for grabs in the next decade for providing driverless alternatives to companies.

The seventy-foot Futura, as it was nicknamed, with the shiny Mercedes three-pointed star emblem on the front, had just made a right turn onto the highway and was currently under the control of a human driver. Today's test would center around acceleration, braking control, and the collision avoidance system, all of which had been tweaked after last week's test run. Mike Weaver allowed the steering wheel to spin easily through his hands as he guided it to the center of the right lane.

"All set here," he said into the headset's microphone. "Northbound on the 93 and no issues. Good to go."

The first reply came from the much smaller white pickup following closely behind. "Chase vehicle copies, Futura." The next reply came a second later. "Lead vehicle copies, Futura. Ready for test."

"Control center copies Futura is good to go," added a third voice from the office in Coyote Springs. "Say the word."

Inside Futura, Weaver reached to the controls to the right of the steering wheel and toggled a switch to the up position. The light on the switch went from red to green, and the driver removed his hands from the wheel, picking up a clipboard from the console in the middle of the cab. "Control, Jesus is at the wheel," he said into the mic.

"Control copies, Futura. Have a good run."

The GNSS, or Global Navigation Satellite System, was the truck's central brain, and it was quite simply the best in the world. In addition to providing real-time traffic and weather data, its technology provided decimeter-level accuracy to ensure Futura stayed in its lane and a safe distance from other vehicles. Its sensor integration had the full complement of surround view, blind spot detection, traffic sign recognition, rear collision and lane departure warnings, among other features, all of which gave the Daimler truck a veritable sixth sense for overall positioning performance. In many ways, the vehicle was as complex as the remotely piloted aircraft flown by the military.

In a minute, the cruise control leveled out at fifty miles per hour, five below the speed limit, which was sufficient for today's test. Weaver stretched his arms above his head and yawned. "All right, chase vehicle, commence your run."

"Copy." The driver of the chase truck lowered the gas pedal, closing the distance between him and Futura. When he was fifteen feet from the back of the trailer, a beeping alarm activated in Futura and played over its speakers. Mike Weaver spoke in the composed monotone of an air traffic controller giving a plane runway instructions. "Rear collision warning light and audio check. Thank you." He paused a beat, then spoke again. "Lead vehicle, commence your speed reduction." As he was checking off a couple boxes on the test checklist, he added, "And no joking around this time, Wayne."

"Lead vehicle copies, Futura. No NASCAR auditions today."

A moment later, through Futura's windshield, Weaver saw the distance between them shrinking. What was a quarter mile quickly became an eighth, and Futura's operator turned his attention from the road to the collision display light. In a matter of seconds, when the two vehicles reached the preprogrammed distance limit, the display would light up, exactly as it had in all of the preceding tests. He waited. Nothing happened. Instead, the left blinker signal activated and Futura began moving left into the oncoming traffic lane.

"Whoa, girl, what the hell?" Weaver said with some frustration. Another glitch meant another full test to add to an already delayed schedule. "Uh, Control, Futura is making a lane change outside of parameters. Taking it out of auto-mode." He reached to the dash and toggled the mode switch back to manual, fully expecting the truck to respond to his hands and feet. Instead, Futura surged past the lead truck and took off. The sudden acceleration drove Mike Weaver back into his seat.

"Control!" he yelled. "Futura is not responding. I am *not* driving this rig!"

CHAPTER 18

Dal Cho was fuming. Instead of cruising the I-80 back to the Bay Area with a highly valued young hacker in his trunk, he was scrambling for a lead on the girl's whereabouts. He had been *so* close yesterday, about to snatch her, his hypodermic filled with a silent paralytic cupped in his fingers. His steps through the wash were as soft as a cat hunting mice, coming through a thick line of trees to the very spot she had entered only seconds earlier. But she wasn't there. The garbage sack was there. The long trash-grabber she had been using lay on the ground. But Mercy Vaughn was gone.

Cho looked everywhere. He drove up and down the highway several times. He checked the nearby Hot Springs Motel. Nothing. Then on the police scanner he had been provided, he heard the calls go out. The Youth Center guards and, later, the Sheriff's Department were looking for her. She had escaped them all. The night passed, his second in the rental car with almost no sleep, and now he had to report to his superiors how he had failed to capture the girl. Their first question would be if the federal authorities had custody of her. He had no answer to that. For now.

Cho had not come this far by being an idiot. His best option at this point was to follow one of the men trying to find her.

Beck ordered two tacos, one of which he gave to Columbo, and Charlie snapped up one of the last boxed salads the food trucks had to offer. They ate while they walked, stopping to show Mercy's photo to anyone who would look. "So, where's home for you right now, Charlie Blue Horse?"

She chuckled and put a hand in front of her mouth while she chewed. "You don't have to keep calling me by my first and last names, you know."

He wiped some taco shell from one side of his grin. "But I like the sound of it."

They stared at each other until Charlie couldn't any longer. "How's your dad? I worked a couple cases with him over the years. Good cop."

"Yeah, he was a good cop, a good sheriff. He's struggling with dementia now. Has been for a couple of years. Good days and bad, you know. Still recognizes Brinley and me, so we haven't hit the steep slide yet."

"Brinley? Is that your wife?"

"My sister, Brinley Cummings," he answered as Columbo, seeing Jabba the Hutt walking toward them, growled.

Charlie's chewing ground to a halt. "Brinley Cummings, Gun Girl?"

Before he could respond, Jabba's mask came off, revealing X-Files inside all that rubber. "Christ, I'm dying in here," the former journalist said, panting as hard as Columbo.

"I should have guessed it was you under that hood," Beck said with a laugh. He introduced Charlie. "You need to hydrate, pal. You got water?"

X-Files removed his glasses and wiped the sweat from his eyes. "I'm not sure. Does bourbon contain water?"

Beck shook his head, gave him Mercy's mugshot, and told him what they were doing.

"She your drone hacker?" X-Files asked, looking over the photo.

"She's a missing kid at this point, Greg," Beck answered. "Have you seen her?"

He hadn't but promised to keep an eye out. In half a minute, Beck and Charlie were walking again and resumed their prior conversation. "Sounds like you've heard of my sister."

Charlie nodded. "I've seen her weapons training videos. She may have taught me more about how to shoot than I ever learned at the academy. She's really your sister?"

He took another bite. "Adopted. Since she was little. I'll introduce you if we have time. What about you? You never answered my question about where home is."

"I'm based in Reno."

"Love Reno. I went to school there. You married?" There was no ring on her finger either.

She shook her head, laughing. "Didn't last. Job got in the way. I have a twelve-year-old daughter. My mom keeps an eye on her when I'm on the road."

He wondered what it would be like to have a daughter. "Good kid?"

"The best," Charlie answered, beaming.

They spent another half hour walking the road, peeking into vehicles and showing the photo to anyone who would look. Nobody had seen Mercy, and Beck believed them. He was about to suggest they head back to the main station when he noticed a silver sedan pull up and park next to his truck across the highway. An Asian male got out, thin but graceful and supple in his movements. He was dressed like an ad for REI, including a dusty black bandana around his neck, and he had a loose boot string that was dragging on the ground. As he passed on the other side of Beck's truck, he ducked down and out of sight, emerging a few seconds later with his bootlace retied. He took a brief look around, like someone from out of town might, and crossed the road toward the big flying disc. He was now only a hundred feet away, his eyes scanning the crowd before passing quickly over Beck.

"What is it?" Charlie asked.

Lincoln County wasn't a big tourist area, and there were only a couple of Asian families here. Alien Independence Day, or AID as they were calling it, was shaping up to be a much more cosmopolitan gathering, but something looked off about the guy. "Probably nothing."

Her phone rang. "Blue Horse," she said and listened for several seconds.

Beck held Mercy's photo up and gestured to his left, indicating he was going to show a grandmotherly blonde in a Wonder Woman outfit if she had seen Mercy Vaughn. When he was done with Wonder Woman, he did a quick about-face and found the Asian male twenty feet away now, his eyes momentarily locked on Beck's. The man turned and fell in a long line at the food truck selling shaved ice.

"Haven't seen you around before," Beck said, approaching. "I'm Porter Beck, the sheriff here. What's your name?"

It seemed abrupt, which was what Beck was hoping for. But the Asian man spun around enthusiastically. "I'm Dal Cho. Nice to meet you, Sheriff."

Beck craned his head to one side. "Dal. That's Korean, isn't it?" For the briefest of moments, the question seemed to rattle the tourist.

"Yes, it's Korean. But I'm actually from the Bay Area."

"Passing through on your way home, or do you fancy scaling the fence into Area 51 to see some little green men?"

Cho's brows knitted together. "My goodness, Sheriff, do you always take such an interest in people you don't know?"

Beck laughed. "Oh, no. Sorry. I was only wondering if you needed any directions or wanted to know about any of the historical sites. In addition to being sheriff, I'm also a member of the Chamber of Commerce, so I'm learning how to be a better ambassador for the county." He paused a second and looked Cho squarely in the eyes. "How am I doing so far?"

As he advanced in line, Cho glanced down at the gun strapped to Beck's thigh. "Well, I'm not sure the gun says 'Welcome to Lincoln County,' but I appreciate the gesture. Really, I heard this was happening, and wanted to see it for myself, though I guess we're still a few days out before these idiots try anything. Since I have you, Sheriff, I'm actually taking a few days off work, haven't been in this part of Nevada before, and was hoping to do some camping up at Great Basin. Any recommendations?"

Beck had spent a year in Korea and had observed that, generally, Koreans had light skin. Their eyes tended to be small, and they had longer noses than their Chinese cousins. Dal Cho's face was round, his nose shorter and wider, his skin a shade or two darker. In and of themselves, these things meant nothing. People came in all kinds of wrappers.

Charlie touched him on the sleeve, pulling him a few steps away. "One of those driverless big rigs from that Daimler plant down south seems to have developed a mind of its own. Driver can't take control, and the truck is headed up the 93."

While his eyes remained on the man wearing the Giants cap, Beck recalled what X-Files had said about hackers taking over automobiles. "Was the truck hacked? And how far up the 93 is it?" He was sure he saw Cho, who had turned away, slightly stiffen, his left ear tuning in on Beck's voice.

"They think so. It's fifteen minutes south of Alamo. NHP has units coming from both directions, but they'll be a while getting there. Do you think this is her? Is it Mercy?"

"Has to be," he said, watching as the girl inside the food truck handed Cho his cold treat. Beck stepped up next to him. "You definitely want to hit Lehman Caves and the Bristlecone Trail, if you can." He paused a moment, lowering his upper body about fifteen degrees, a polite bow. "*Joeun yeohaeng doiseyo.*" *Have a good trip.*

The Chinese agent bowed in return, offering an admiring smile. "Your pronunciation is perfect, Sheriff. I'm impressed. Where did you study Korean?"

"Rosetta Stone," Beck lied. His pronunciation *was* perfect, for much like his ability to recall song lyrics and movie lines, he could parrot back any piece of language he heard, regardless of origin. He added, "*Rén bù kě mào xiàng.*" *Never judge a person by his appearance.*

Cho laughed. "I think you're mixing up your languages now. That sounded like Mandarin."

Beck lifted an eyebrow. "Was it? I get confused. Hey, have you heard the joke about the guy who opposed the Chinese government?"

Cho said nothing, waiting impassively.

Beck grinned. "No one has."

Moving at sixty-eight miles per hour, Daimler's Futura was well past the county line and had, over the last thirty minutes, passed about that same number of vehicles coming the other way. Highway

Patrol was scrambling to close the highway in both directions but was still a long way out from the stretch of road that the runaway truck was on. The teleoperators in Coyote Springs had done everything in their power to sever the connection to Futura but had failed to wrest control from whoever was now operating it. Mike Weaver, the man in the cab, had pressed every button and completed every troubleshooting checklist he could. As the beads of sweat trickled from his brow, he thought about calling his wife, currently an ER nurse at the trauma center at University Medical Center in Las Vegas. If this ended badly, UMC would be the place they airlifted him to. If he wasn't pronounced dead at the scene. Better not to call, he thought. Better to pray.

While he and Charlie sped south toward the junction at Crystal Springs, Beck was speed-talking on the radio, trying to get someone close enough to the Daimler truck to take some action that wouldn't result in absolute mayhem. Unfortunately, most of his troop were helping with wildfire control far to the north. Arshal was the closest, estimated to be about twenty miles east of the autonomous big rig and traveling much faster. Charlie was on her phone trying to determine the location of the nearest NHP unit.

"How far?" Beck asked when she hung up.

"Too far," she answered. "Maybe thirty minutes before someone could intercept him."

"Damn." He keyed the radio mic again and directed Arshal to close westbound traffic on the highway and to lay down some spike strips.

"Will they even work on those big tires?" the venerable deputy asked.

Beck looked to Charlie for some help. "Might," she said, "but if we can't block the traffic ahead of and behind it first, it's really high risk. A rig like that might end up taking out other cars. And you probably don't want to be on the hook for wrecking something that expensive. It's not like it was made in China."

Beck stared at Charlie for a long moment. Then he keyed the radio again and told Arshal to scratch the spike strips and catch up to the Daimler truck. *Made in China.* Charlie's words echoed in his brain, clearing the clutter. The realization almost gave him whiplash.

"What is it?" Charlie asked.

"The Asian man I was talking to right before we left Rachel? He said he was Korean, but I'm pretty good at ethnicities, and he's Chinese. I'd bet on it."

Charlie shook her head. "So?"

"So is Mercy Vaughn, I think." Charlie wasn't following, and Beck could see it. "Not ethnically, but from one of the regions in China."

Charlie still had Mercy's file on her lap and opened it. She pulled the color photo and showed it to Beck. "This girl? You're telling me this girl is from someplace in China? The dirty blonde with green eyes."

Beck nodded. "It's her eyes. She has an epicanthic fold. Very rare in non-Asians. There's a village in northwest China. I forget the name. Almost two-thirds of their population have green eyes and blond hair. The story is that about the time of Christ, a Roman legion, mostly decimated by the Parthians, found their way into China. Their descendants, their DNA, is still there. A lot of Uyghurs are also blond. In other words, she doesn't have to look Chinese to be from China."

Charlie stared at him blankly then rifled through Mercy's file. "Says here her parents were white, both born in the U.S. The kid didn't come from China, Beck."

"I'm beginning to think everything in that file is a lie. A cover."

He quickly dialed Agent Maddox on his cell and put the call on speaker. "Maddox, Beck here. Listen, we may have another hack in progress. A driverless—"

Maddox cut in. "Yeah, I'm aware. We lost another RPA. This one is out of Creech."

Beck wasn't sure he had heard the man correctly. "What? I'm talking about a semi-truck coming out of Coyote Springs and heading north. Are you telling me she's got another drone as well?" He could hear the sounds of helicopter rotors turning.

"You tell me, Sheriff," Maddox yelled. "You're the one who lost her."

"Shit. Is it armed?"

There was too much noise from the helo. "What?"

"Is it armed?" Beck screamed. "Your RPA."

"I'm told no armament. Surveillance only."

Beck and Charlie let out a sigh of relief at the same time. "Where is it now, Maddox?"

"If I knew that we could shoot it down."

"Is it tracking the Daimler truck?" Charlie asked Beck.

Beck hung up, leaned close to the windshield, and peered up into the sky. "No, no. She already has the Daimler truck. So why does she need another drone?" He said the words as they were passing a cattle hauler coming the other way, his head turning fully as it passed them. "Jesse's cattle are headed to Mexico," he said.

Charlie nodded. "Only one road from his place leading in that direction, and we're on it."

"She's using the drone to spot his trailer," Beck said.

Charlie looked at him in disbelief. "How the hell is she doing this?"

CHAPTER 19

Though he had no crucifix or beads to hold, Mike Weaver was already deep into the Rosary when the miracle occurred. A short distance west of the turnoff for the ghost town called Gold Point, Futura started to decelerate, dropping below eighty. He felt the shift in speed and opened his eyes. "Oh my God," he said into his headset. "We're slowing. Guys, I'm slowing down."

"Copy you are slowing, Futura. Do you have control, Mike?"

Weaver moved his hands back to the steering wheel, but the rig remained unresponsive. "Negative, Control. Still decelerating though. Fifty. Forty-five. Forty." He checked his map. "Uh, approaching Pole Line Road. Could be we're going to turn. Hang on."

The supervisor in the control center was quick to respond. "Copy you're coming to a turn, Mike. That's the road to Gold Point. We have you on GPS. If you have the chance to jump, well . . ."

"Copy, Control. Are you sure? If I jump, Futura is on her own."

"You get the hell out of that cab if you can, Mike."

Weaver felt the sweat running down his brow, and he felt the tug of the heavy electronic brakes. "That's it, you big angry bitch, slow down. Slow down." Futura approached the junction at a crawl and made a right turn, just behind the lead test vehicle. As soon as it straightened out, Mike had the door open and was ready to jump to the ground below. He might get skinned up a little, but he would survive. Suddenly, the tractor-trailer came to an abrupt stop. "Control, Futura. We have stopped and are idling." Mike could see in his side mirror the driver from the chase vehicle climbing out of his truck.

"Futura, Control. We copy and see you stopped. Can you shut her off?"

Before he could answer, another voice streamed into his ears. It was female. "You have ten seconds to get out of the truck, Mike."

"What? Who is this?" he yelled.

"Seven seconds."

Mike Weaver ripped off his headset, unclipped his seat belt, and jumped to the ground. Futura didn't move. Mike motioned the driver of the lead vehicle to swing directly in front of the autonomous semi. With a truck in front and in the rear, maybe she would stay put. A Lincoln County Sheriff's unit pulled up, siren wailing, and a lanky old cowboy with a silver handlebar mustache got out. While the Daimler engineers and Arshal Jessup discussed what had transpired over the last hour, Futura sat idling.

Five miles northeast of them and crawling south on the Great Basin Highway, a long cattle truck was dropping out of the mountain pass it had been winding through for twenty minutes. At the first sign of a good stretch of open road, the cars stacked up behind the slow-moving trailer accelerated and began moving into the oncoming traffic lane, grateful to finally get around it and the animals whose stink drifted backward and into their AC systems.

The Mexican driver hauling Jesse Roy's cattle was paying close attention to the speed limit, as he always did. The last thing his boss in Caborca would tolerate was a moving violation or any police stop that might result in an examination of the trailer's contents. He spoke no English, so he used the universal middle finger as the cars now gunned their engines and passed him, not seeing the small shadow on the ground in the shape of an aircraft that seemed to parallel him. The MQ-9 Reaper was soaring a thousand feet above him and had been in the air for forty-seven minutes, on a mission to test its new Miniature Air-Launched Decoy, or MALD, designed to deceive enemy air defense systems. Neither was the driver aware that at that very moment, not far ahead on a small turnout road, an autonomous vehicle began moving.

As soon as Futura started forward, the Daimler engineers all jumped back, watching in horror as the seventy-foot truck left them standing there on the cutout. It struck the much smaller Mercedes lead vehicle almost gently, increasing its speed barely enough to nudge it out of the way. Arshal jumped back in his vehicle and began steering it into harm's way, but quickly realized his pickup was no match for the much larger semi and backed up in the nick of time. The Futura swung wide, barely missing the Ford's front end. Arshal opened his door, stood on the running board, and drew his .44. He began firing at the big rig's front tires. But the seventy-footer turned fully around and faced the highway once more. Seconds later, it accelerated toward the junction. The driver of the cattle hauler saw the tractor-trailer picking up speed as it moved toward the intersection but was sure it was going to come to a full stop before turning right or left. Instead, in horror, he and his passenger watched as the semi increased speed, crossing the highway at the exact moment the cattle truck reached the same intersection. The collision pierced the otherwise-still July air, slamming into the target's left side.

With its current load of steers, the trailer's weight was roughly equivalent to Futura's, but the collision tore a wide gash in the

lightweight polished slats that ran the length of the trailer and provided much needed air for its bovine occupants. In the few horrible
seconds it took before it flipped fully over, cattle were ejected from
the trailer and onto the road in twisted and bloody carnage.

Flying cows, Mike Weaver thought, watching in amazement.

They saw the flashing lights and flares before anything else. Both
Beck and Charlie had seen their share of gruesome vehicle accidents, especially on the open roads of the state where speeds
could get excessive in a hurry and boozy drivers could wreck lives.
Seldom, however, did one see so many dead and dying animals on
a highway.

Arshal had control of the scene and met them as they pulled off
into the dirt. Charlie's people were working to seal the road a few
miles east of the crash. For now, both lanes were impassable, but
drivers were being diverted onto Pole Line Road and then back
onto the highway. The cars and trucks going both directions were
already stacking up.

"Casualties?" Beck asked, getting out of the truck, leaving
Columbo snoozing on the back seat.

Arshal shook his head. "Other than about fifty steers, not really. The driver of the cattle hauler and his buddy are a little shook
up but otherwise okay. The cab wasn't touched. The rest of it is
a bloody goddamn mess." Beck introduced him to Charlie Blue
Horse. Arshal beamed. "It's been a while. How are you, Charlie
girl?"

Charlie hugged him. "I'm good, you sexy man."

"Charlie and I worked the Flees with Bees case a few years
back," Arshal told Beck. "Before your time."

"Flees with Bees?" asked Beck.

Charlie nodded. "Some of the farms up north were losing their bees. Lots of them. Turns out the hives were being stolen. Arshal and I actually spent three days together holed up in a shack on a beehive stakeout."

"Anybody get stung?"

"Me." Arshal laughed. "Every time I made a pass at Detective Blue Horse."

The wind was up, as it was most days, and the smell of the blood and other bovine bodily fluids was already hitting Beck's hypersensitive nostrils. Cattle were strewn everywhere, their hides starting to cook on the hot asphalt, some futilely trying to right themselves on broken legs, most of them crying plaintively. The sight and sound of it sickened Beck.

"How many dead, Arshal?"

He stroked his big silver mustache. "Maybe thirty. Three of them walked away clean. They're over there." Beck's most senior deputy pointed to the north side of the highway. "The rest won't make it."

Beck's ears caught another horrible cry. A dying steer. It wasn't a mooing like you would hear from healthy stock. It was more a strangled scream, and it was the sound those left paralyzed and bleeding out were making now. Beck asked Arshal if he had notified the folks at NDOT to get some heavy equipment out here to clear the road and remove the dead.

"Ayup, but the closest crew is in Vegas, so we're looking at ninety minutes or more."

"Long time for these animals to suffer."

Arshal adjusted his big hat. "Ayup."

Beck pulled the Glock from his drop-leg holster. "Teach me to feel another's woe, to hide the fault I see, that mercy I to others show, that mercy show to me."

They had all done it before. "I hate this part," Charlie said. She unsnapped her Colt and drew it.

Beck reached out and set his hand gently on hers. "We can do it, Charlie, if you'd rather not."

She shook her head. "Hey, part of the job. But thanks."

They separated, each taking a quadrant on the road, splitting up those to be killed, their boots making squishing noises in the quickly drying blood on the hot pavement. Even in the open air, the sound of gunshots was deafening, all twenty-nine of them.

When they were done and it was quiet again, Charlie headed down the road on foot to confer with the senior trooper that had arrived on scene. Beck regrouped with Arshal. "What are the witnesses saying?" he asked.

"The Daimler guys are saying it's a science fiction movie. That truck of theirs got hijacked by the Invisible Man. Or woman, maybe. The operator in the cab said a woman's voice came over his radio and told him to get out."

A woman. Beck wondered where Mercy Vaughn was at that moment. He scanned the sky for the missing drone. *Is she watching us right now?*

Arshal led him around the back of the overturned Daimler rig and into the center of the road.

"You were right," Arshal said. "They're Jesse Roy's steers. Same trailer you saw leaving his place this morning?"

Beck looked across the road on the other side of the southbound lane where the cattle hauler had come to rest. He almost didn't recognize it. "Yep, that's it." Normally, when there was an accident involving livestock, they would call out the State Brand Inspector, but there was no need in this case. The Double J brand could be seen clearly on some of the broken animals. "Jesse's cattle, for sure, but he sold them to somebody in Mexico."

Arshal snickered. "I imagine he won't get paid then until he delivers a load that are still alive. This is bound to piss him off."

Beck looked up at him. "Does he know yet?"

"Driver called him right after it happened. My Spanish isn't the best, but from what I gathered, Jesse was not a happy man." Arshal pointed toward the four men huddled around the Toyota Highlander that had followed Jesse Roy's trailer from the ranch. "I guess they're all together. Don't look like any ranch hands I've ever seen. Look more like banditos to me, riding shotgun, it appears."

"How so?"

Arshal raised his thumb and pointed backward. "Oh yeah, that's the interesting part. Let me show you."

Beck put two fingers in the corners of his mouth and released a whistle that could wake even a poorly trained canine cadet from a sound sleep. After several seconds, Beck saw Columbo's air-conditioned head rise behind the tinted windshield of his truck. Columbo scrambled out of the passenger side window and ran over to them. Charlie had returned, and together they walked to Jesse Roy's overturned and pulverized cattle hauler, the tractor of the Daimler driverless rig piercing its center. Columbo found an opening between the two vehicles and jumped inside the tangled mass of jagged metal, dead steers, and blood. Beck followed and then pulled Charlie up. "Careful, slippery in here."

The scene inside the trailer was much worse. The few animals that weren't ejected were piled up, crushed and cleaved and eviscerated. Between the carcasses, Beck and Charlie could see the real transport.

Beck surveyed the semiautomatic rifles and handguns pushing up through what was left of the metal floorboards. Columbo circled a few times and sat down next to the arsenal. Beck frowned at him. "Yes, thank you. We can see them. Solid police work."

Charlie reached down and picked up a black AR-15 rifle, easily converted to a fully automatic weapon. "So, where do you suppose these are going?"

Arshal, peering up into the truck from the ground, fiddled with the furry handlebar under his nose. "No place I want to vacation."

"Sonora," Beck answered, thinking of Jesse's guy César and the information Sev turned up. "I was hoping for drugs."

"Why?" asked Arshal.

Charlie ejected the magazine from the rifle. "Because we can't arrest Jesse Roy for this."

Beck shook his head. "Assuming they're legally purchased, which I'm sure they are. Jesse's a lot of things. Stupid isn't one of them." He reached over one of the dead steers and pulled an STF-12 tactical shotgun out, then tossed it to Charlie. "Ideal for home defense or for killing the local *federales*. We might not be able to arrest Jesse, but we can slow him down. Impound it all, Arshal."

"Ayup. What about the two guys who were transporting all this hardware? Do we bust them?"

Beck shook his head. "Couldn't hold them. They haven't broken any law." He looked down again. "There's ammo in here as well."

"Enough to start a war," Charlie added.

Beck braced himself between two of the shattered floorboards, picking up a box of .223 Remingtons. "Or to keep one going." He looked up at Charlie. "Smart. Phony floor. Border guys aren't going to unload a bunch of cattle to look for these."

Charlie slid up alongside him. "Especially for something going south. I'm sure they just wave a cattle truck right through. The smell alone might mask any scent of gunpowder."

Suddenly, the air filled with the noise of helicopter rotors, and the three of them peered out of the mangled wreck. A sand-colored eggbeater was landing off the Pole Line Road exit. There was nothing nondescript about this chopper. It was an Armed Black Hawk, big and menacing, with everything from electro-optical IR sensors to two large machine guns and Hellfire missiles. Maddox hopped out and jogged over, surveying the scene along the way, with the ashen face of a man whose career had slipped over the cliff. The four men from the Army of Northern Virginia followed, all fully outfitted now in military tactical gear, all strapped for a war and looking like they had recently returned from killing Osama bin Laden.

Maddox's foot caught some of the slick cow blood, sending his feet out from under him. Beck hopscotched over to help him up, but before he could, the OSI cop pitched over and vomited. It was clear the man had never been close to a war zone or a livestock accident. He had blood on his slacks and shirt now, and the sight of that made him retch again. Finally, Beck reached down, grabbed him under the elbow, and hauled him to his feet.

Maddox wiped his mouth with a sleeve. "Thanks." After a few deep breaths, he was able to ask, "Do I need to guess whose cattle they are?" Beck walked him through what had happened, showed him the guns. "If I have this right, then," Maddox said, "this Mercy kid wants to bring down Jesse Roy and screw with some Mexican drug cartel? That's what this is all about? Why didn't she send you an email and tell you where to look?"

Beck thought about the email he had received on the night of the Fourth. She hadn't told him where to look, only that she might need his help. "I guess she prefers to handle things more directly."

Maddox brought a hand to his mouth, stifling the urge to toss what was left of his lunch. "Do you . . . have any idea where she is?"

Beck shook his head, his eyes and ears suddenly drawn to the west. Through the heat haze that rose above the highway, a large gray bird came into focus. It was so close to the ground the untrained eye might have taken it for a vulture of some kind, flying low and looking for roadkill, but Maddox and Beck both recognized it instantly. "Get down!" Beck yelled.

Everyone but the kill squad dropped to their bellies. Gunsights trained on the target, they fired in concert, watching as the MQ-9 Reaper shredded the sky twenty feet above the highway, its 900 HP turbo prop engine powering it close to its 300 mph maximum speed. The carbon fiber bird screamed north, rising higher at a steep and fast climb.

"Idiots!" Maddox screamed at the special operators. "You're not taking that thing down with a rifle."

Beck and the others rose slowly to their feet, watching as the Reaper suddenly banked left, heading north and quickly out of sight. All eyes were glued to the sky now, watching and waiting for the drone to reappear. It didn't.

"We'll try to find it," Maddox said. "The Reaper doesn't put out much of a heat signature, so that might be tough. Maybe the girl will turn control back over to us, like she did after blowing up that stupid cow. Maybe it will run out of fuel, I don't know." He pulled his eyes from the sky and turned to Beck. "I have to tell you, Sheriff, my ass is already in a sling over this. I need this girl in custody."

The military, Beck knew, was a very unforgiving institution. "We're looking. Maybe she's done now. Maybe she's caused Jesse enough pain. At least she's not taking out a nuclear power plant or the White House."

Maddox raised an eyebrow. "I honestly don't care how personal this might be for her, Sheriff. I'm agnostic when it comes to crimes outside my purview." He pointed to the special operators twenty yards away. "The only reason your county hasn't been invaded by a battalion of those guys is because we want to keep a lid on this. But if that team over there gets to her before you do, well . . ."

The rest of Maddox's sentence was drowned out by the arrival of two more NHP units, sirens blaring. Beck didn't need to hear those final words. He knew what they were. The last thing the military would tolerate would be word getting out about how some teenager hacked into and took over not one but two of the most sophisticated aircraft in its arsenal and used them to fuck with a gun-running rancher in Bumfuck, Nevada. They would take her out. It was a national security issue now, and along with Mercy Vaughn, it would be buried under six feet of desert.

CHAPTER 20

The dead steers would not be buried six feet under. Not immediately anyway. They would be transported to a nearby landfill and discarded on a mountain of trash where the crows, turkey buzzards, and coyotes would feast for a few days until the next load of trash covered them. The image got Beck thinking about other mountains, and after pouring Columbo some cold water from a cooler in his truck, he turned slowly in a circle, looking at the peaks in every direction.

"What is it?" Charlie asked, taking the bottle from Beck and stealing a sip.

"Charlie, where would you go if you needed to tap into a satellite and be confident no one was watching you?"

She looked to the horizon to the east, where the earth rose sharply into the sky. "The mountains. High enough to get a strong signal. Maybe one of those old mining towns you have here."

His satellite phone buzzed, and Beck could see it was Brinley, who had been out all night looking for Mercy. He put her on speaker and introduced her to Charlie.

"Any luck?" he asked.

"I've been to every barn and abandoned building within twenty miles. Talked to every person. Nobody has seen her. She could be anywhere by now. She could be hiding in Shiloah Roy's bedroom for all I know." Beck filled her in on their visit to the Double J earlier in the day and their discussion with Shiloah. Then he told her about the Daimler truck hack and Jesse Roy's dead steers, as well as their trip out to Rachel. "That was going to be my next stop," she told him.

He ran the idea of Mercy hiding in the mountains by her. "Oh, shit!" she yelled. He heard the high-pitched scream of her tires braking and spinning.

"Brin? What is it? You okay?"

"I'm such an idiot," she said, followed by a few expletives. "I was filling up in Caliente earlier, and a Land Rover whizzed by heading west."

"So?"

"I've seen it in the parking lot at the Youth Center a few times. Black over orange. Maybe it's Shiloah's. Don't know who else it could belong to. Big cargo rack on top, floodlights, all the bells and whistles. And if you guys haven't seen one of those come past you . . ."

"We haven't," Beck said. With a shake of her head, Charlie agreed. Beck looked southeast toward the closest mountains. "You're heading to Gold Point, then?"

"You might want to meet me there," Brinley said. "You're close enough."

Beck looked at Charlie. "It's about fifteen miles south of here. Worth a shot." He heard gravel spitting under tires and turned to see a cloud of dust emerging from the north side of the highway, behind the line of stopped traffic. An expensive black Escalade skidded to a stop on the side of the road. Beck didn't have to see the driver to know who it must be. "Okay, Brin," he said into the phone. "I've got a little cleanup still out here, and then we'll take the other road to Gold Point and meet you there. We should be ten or fifteen minutes behind you, tops. Careful on that road. It pops a lot of tires."

"I remember," she said and hung up.

He was sure she did remember. It wasn't far from Gold Point, up on Slidy Mountain, that Pop had found Brinley and her dad living like animals. Thinking of animals, Beck could see Jesse's wolfish face as he climbed out of the expensive SUV and ran over to the driver of the cattle hauler. After a lot of shouting, one of the men who had been following the trailer walked over and inserted himself between Jesse and the driver. He was taller than Jesse, younger by a decade, and when Jesse got in his face, he shoved the rancher backward.

"Well, that's interesting," Charlie said. "Should we intervene?"

Beck shook his head. "Never interrupt a good unraveling."

The interruption came from a Mariachi ringtone Beck didn't recognize. The man who had shoved Jesse answered the call, listened for a few seconds, then directed his compatriots back to their vehicle. They made a U-turn from the shoulder of the highway and headed east again. Jesse watched them go, then crossed the highway slowly, surveying his dead animals.

"Where's the driver, Beck?" he yelled. "Where's the guy who killed my stock? I want the son of a bitch."

Beck grabbed another water bottle out of the cooler and handed it to him. "Looks like you're in some hot water, Jesse. Would you like something cold?"

The rancher swatted it away. "I don't need your goddamned water!" he screamed, storming back out onto the highway. "Is he dead? He better be dead."

Beck and Charlie followed as Jesse ran toward the Daimler

truck. "There is no driver, Jesse," Beck yelled after him. "The truck that hit yours was autonomous. Didn't your driver tell you that?"

The rancher spun on his heels, his eyes reduced to tiny slits. "What? No. He said he got T-boned by a semi. What the hell does that mean, autonomous?"

Beck really wanted to slap the man, but he was out of time and a better alternative at this juncture was to come clean with what he knew. He had promised Maddox those details would remain confidential, but Jesse needed to understand what was happening to him. "I told you. You're being targeted. Your bull the other night wasn't hit by a fuel tank. It was a missile fired by a military drone. That drone was hacked. Hacked by the same person who rammed your cattle truck an hour ago. The same person we were asking your daughter about this morning. A teenage girl, Jesse. A teenage girl who has an axe to grind and the ability to kill you. So maybe you want to tell me what's going on before she turns her focus away from your animals and decides to come after you."

"That's impossible," Jesse said with a shake of his head. "People can't do what you're describing."

Beck raised his arms to the sides, gesturing at the dead animals, strewn over fifty yards of road. "Well, clearly they can." He paused to take a breath and collect himself. "Tell me about the guns."

Jesse walked between several dead steers, gazing down at the broken backs and torn limbs. He crossed his arms over his chest. "The guns are legal. All purchased through private individuals. I have the paperwork."

"Uh-huh. You're trafficking them in bulk to Mexico under a load of cattle."

Jesse kept walking, shaking his head, calculating his losses. "Like I said, legal."

Beck kept up with him. "There were about twenty thousand

gun murders in Mexico last year, Jesse. And you're making money off them. Lots of it, I'm guessing. How do you feel about that?"

Jesse removed the straw hat from his head, fiddled with it a second. "I feel really good about the profit I'm getting. It's normally about ten times what I pay for them." He smiled. "Look, buddy, I have no idea what happens with those guns when they get there. It's a financial—"

Beck's right hand moved so fast, Jesse had no time to pull back, the major knuckles contacting the rancher's nose. The blood flooded on to his face before he even hit the asphalt.

Fifteen feet back, Charlie raced toward the two men and yelled at Arshal, who was across the highway cataloging the guns in Jesse's cattle hauler.

Jesse had been in more fights than he could remember, and the fact that this one was with the county sheriff didn't matter at all. He knew better than to lie on the ground and grab in dismay at his broken nose, knew you couldn't win a fight on your back. He was scrambling to get to his feet when Beck's boot caught him in the left shoulder, launching him backward again.

Beck saw Jesse's head collide with the road, saw the whites of his eyes momentarily flood those compartments, then saw his mouth screw into a bloody knot. Beck reached down and seized him by the collar, curling the cloth into his fist, and rolling it into Jesse's neck. Charlie, and now Arshal, tried to separate the two.

"My lawyer will have your shitty little job for this, Beck," Jesse said through gritted teeth. "After I kick your ass."

Though they had his arms, Beck's legs were still free, and he managed to kick Jesse's out from under him as he tried to rise again. "You running drugs for the cartel now, Jesse?" Beck shouted at him.

Suddenly, Columbo was at Jesse's neck, snarling at him. Jesse covered his face, his eyes narrowing. "This is about Willa, isn't it, Beck? You never got over her, did you?"

Arshal ordered Columbo back and hauled Jesse to his feet. Beck held up his hands, letting Charlie know he was done fighting. He spoke calmly this time. "You're killing people. Killing them with guns and with dope. And all for what? So you can have a ranch bigger than your daddy's?"

Jesse spat in Beck's face. "Fuck you. You have no idea what you're talking about."

Beck ran his white sleeve over his cheek, catching most of Jesse's tobacco. "What's going to happen when your guns don't show up in Mexico? What are your buddies in the cartel going to do? Talk to me now. Before this goes any further. Before you end up on a slab in the mortuary, or worse, with an *aneurysm* like the one that killed your wife."

The arrow found its mark. Jesse's eyes were glistening now, bloodshot and strained. "What the hell is that supposed to mean?"

Beck's laugh dripped with derision. "What really happened to Willa, Jesse? She would never have been okay with you making money on illegal drugs. Did she tell you she was going to leave you? Expose you? Turn you in? Did you kill her, Jesse? Did the cartel? Did they kill your wife, you selfish prick?"

Jesse stared back at him, said nothing. He looked at the three officers surrounding him. He looked at the dog. "If you want to ask me questions, do it through my attorney."

Beck took a step forward. "I'll tell you what I'm going to do. I'm going to get a warrant to exhume Willa's body. I'm going to dig her up and have her autopsied. See what really killed her."

Jesse's eyes rose slowly and met Beck's. "I'll kill you first. How about that?"

"Get him out of here," he told Arshal, his breath fast and angry. He turned back to Jesse. "You come for me. You do that. Let's see what happens."

As soon as Jesse was back in the Escalade and heading home,

everyone huddled at Beck's truck to discuss next steps. Charlie pulled out a handkerchief and wiped the remainder of Jesse's spit from Beck's face. "You're not really going to dig up his wife, are you?"

"Haven't decided," he answered. "Shook him up, though, didn't it?" He told Arshal that he and Charlie were heading out to Gold Point and that Brinley was already on her way there. His sat phone rang again, a number he didn't know. "Hold on," he told them, hitting the speaker button. "Beck here."

He recognized the incredulous voice instantly. "You are letting him go? You caught him with all those guns, and you are letting him go?"

Beck looked up into the sky for the Reaper but gave up quickly. It could be circling at 25,000 feet and filming them. "Mercy, I'm afraid you are now officially in a world of shit. Let me introduce you to Detective Charlie Blue Horse of the Nevada Department of Public Safety. She's in charge of finding and arresting you."

"Forget about that," Mercy snapped. "That was never going to happen. Please answer my question. Why are you letting this criminal go free?"

Her tone was full of irritation, not like when they met at the Youth Center. Beck mulled quickly over how best to use that. "You should have done your homework, Mercy. I'm disappointed in you."

She shouted into the phone, as angry as Jesse had been only a few minutes earlier. "What are you talking about?"

Charlie jumped in. "Selling guns to Mexico is not illegal, Mercy."

There was a pause on the line. "That cannot be true. He is fueling a war. People are dying. If it was not illegal, he would not be hiding them in those cattle trucks."

"Hate to spoil your fun," Charlie added, "but that doesn't

make it illegal. It's a horrible law, and you can take it up with Congress, if you ever get out of jail."

Mercy didn't respond, so Beck did. "What did happen, though, is you maimed and killed a bunch of animals. For nothing. Congratulations."

The silence on the other end persisted. Finally, in a much softer, contemplative voice, Mercy said, "We butcher animals every day for food."

The remark got Beck's blood up in a hurry. "Well, there are no hamburgers being grilled out here today, Mercy. Is that your excuse for what you did to them? Because I didn't see you putting bullets in their heads. We had to do that."

"I am sorry." Her voice had dropped an octave. It was sincere, not an ounce of acting.

Beck heard someone whispering in the background and decided to take a different tack. "Mercy, is that Shiloah with you? You're getting her into a bad situation. Is that what you really want to do?" Charlie and Arshal nodded in unison, approving of the plea to the girl's conscience.

"What I really wanted to do, Sheriff, was have you arrest her father. I still cannot believe you are not going to do that. How can supplying guns to murderers not be a crime?"

Beck was still hot. "Stop lying to me. You're smart enough to hack the military's best technology. You're so clever you stole almost a billion dollars from the Federal Reserve. But you didn't take the time to research the law surrounding transporting guns to Mexico? I don't buy it. Not for a minute. Tell me what's really going on here, Mercy. What is this really all about? Because it isn't about guns. There are people out there looking for you, and they're much more of a threat to you than I am. So tell me. Let me help."

There was silence on the other end of the line, leaving the three cops wondering if she had hung up. "You are kind," she finally said. "But there is nothing you can do. Whatever will be will be. But I can help you a little more. When I get a minute, I will send you additional information. I have to go now."

Beck snatched up the phone, bringing it directly to his mouth. "Give it to me now, Mercy. Don't do this by yourself."

"Patience is power, Sheriff. With time and patience the mulberry leaf becomes a silk gown."

Beck nodded appreciatively. "I love Chinese proverbs. Are you from Liqian or one of the Uyghur regions?"

"You have quite the discerning eye, Sheriff," Mercy said. "Your military records do not do you justice. I am even more impressed with you now."

"That's good," said Beck. "Because proverbs aside, we're coming for you. We're coming for you both."

"I suppose I would be disappointed if you did not try, but I do not advise it. It is dangerous. Please do not put yourself at risk." Her tone had returned to its normal "I'm the most confident person in the world" inflections.

The line went dead. "She likes you," Charlie said.

Beck gazed into the sky one more time. "I hope you're right. I don't want this girl getting pissed at me."

CHAPTER 21

Just as he and Charlie were leaving the scene, Beck took another call, a quick update from Esther Ellingboe on the wildfire situation. A new one had started in Patterson Pass, in the northwest corner of the county, the result of a campfire not properly extinguished. He promised to divert the Jolly Greens to help with resident notifications and traffic control and asked Esther to do a rain dance.

"Hell, I'd dance naked in front of the president if I thought it would help," she said.

Instead of getting back on the highway, Beck and Charlie drove south on Pole Line Road. The pavement ran out quickly. It was probably no more than a dozen miles to Gold Point, but the road was seldom traveled, and the climb over the rocks and pits to 8,000 feet could easily take forty-five minutes or more. Long since abandoned, the old mining town sat at the base of Slidy Mountain, a peak that had a number of radio repeater towers and radar equipment on it, the perfect place for someone who might need to hack into a satellite and control an RPA.

As Beck maneuvered his F-150 up the narrow trail through

mostly desert scrub and choking dust, Charlie held tightly to the bar above her head. "This road is like bull riding. You really think they could have made it out this far?"

Beck was about to answer when they were treated to a small herd of elk crossing in front of them. He slowed to a stop.

"Good omen," Charlie said, as the dozen or so animals took their sweet time moving to the other side. "The wapiti are protectors who bring strength and patience."

There was no use honking at them. Elk are predisposed to loitering. It gave Beck time to reflect. "I'm about out of both." He looked over at her. "Don't you think it's strange that Mercy and Shiloah happened to fall in together? I mean, Mercy is the brains of the operation, right? She's the one with the technical skills to pull this off. But we have to assume Shiloah is the instigator or is at least an equal partner in all this. It's her father who's being targeted."

The majestic bull bringing up the rear was in his prime, between six and nine years of age, easily 1,200 pounds, his neck and shoulder hump prominent with long dark hair, and a rack with seven points on each side that wouldn't be full grown for another month. He stood in the middle of the road, about five feet tall at the shoulders and guarding it as the cows and calves and juveniles took their sweet time moving up the other bank. After much consideration, he decided to give the humans the road.

Charlie drummed two fingers against her lips. "Okay, but Mercy has been in the Center since January. Shiloah started working there less than two months ago."

Beck nudged the truck forward, skirting some larger rocks. "And that's not a lot of time to develop a relationship, let alone join in a conspiracy that involves the theft of military aircraft and state-of-the-art driverless trucks."

"Which means they've probably known each other longer than

a couple months, maybe before Shiloah came home. Something brought them together."

That struck a chord, and Beck's eyes found hers. "Or someone. Maybe there's a string puller behind the curtain. Someone we're not seeing."

Charlie cackled.

"What's funny?"

"This case. Drones, guns, self-driving trucks, a teenage hacker, and the murder of ruminants. You guys get all the good ones down here."

He liked her laugh. It tugged at him. She was an attractive woman, with kind eyes and a husky voice he found alluring. She was confident and funny. He had the feeling that she would get his jokes. Somehow they got on the subject of Burning Man again and realized they had the yearly event in the Black Rock Desert in common. Both volunteered to provide security and emergency medical care at the festival. Maybe they would see each other there next year.

"We could go together," Charlie suggested with a perfectly raised eyebrow.

Before he could respond, the truck's radio crackled to life. "Beck, you there?" It was Arshal, his voice so hoarse it sounded as if it had to pass through a scraping tool before leaving his mouth.

"Copy," Beck answered. "How's the cleanup coming?"

"NDOT is here, and they're getting the highway cleared. Should be back up to speed in the next thirty minutes. I'm already headed back to Pioche with Jesse Roy's guns. Charlie's guys have the scene now."

Beck's mind turned to those guns, which made him think about the four Mexicans that had left the crash site heading east instead of southwest. "Arshal, did you happen to run the plate on that white Highlander, the guys who were riding shotgun on Jesse's load?"

"Ayup," he answered. "Rented at the Vegas airport last night."

"So why do you suppose they didn't keep going back to Vegas?" Beck asked. "Why turn around?"

"Probably heading back to Jesse's to get a refund on all this hardware they bought."

Beck looked at Charlie. "I don't think it's only guns, Arshal. Jesse collects the guns and ships them south. The cartel sends the trailer full of cattle back but with a bunch of dope. Once the cows get here, the drugs get packaged and mailed from any post office within a hundred miles, possibly using prostitutes as couriers." Though he was aware of just the one in Ely, Beck was fairly confident Jesse was using both rural and city sex workers, legal and illegal both, to mail those drugs. They were good at keeping secrets and were always looking for extra cash.

"Hmmph," growled the old deputy. "Well, if you need me to interview any call girls about their mailing habits, I guess I could make myself available."

Charlie laughed. Beck rolled his eyes and told Arshal to take the east road into Gold Point, the same road Brinley traveled. "I'm guessing we might need the extra help."

"Roger that."

As they drove, Beck mused on Shakespeare's trope about jealousy being a green-eyed monster. He envied the cops in big cities sometimes. Not because of the higher salaries or the cool gear and technology, but because they could get places quickly when they needed to.

Not like him, driving across bumpy, unmaintained roads, losing time. Losing daylight.

CHAPTER 22

At its heyday shortly before the First World War Gold Point was a decent gold producer, its mines in the eastern mountains drawing prospectors and merchants from all over the west in search of a better life. It had three saloons, a handful of stores, and a post office. By the end of the war, the mines were played out, and the town evaporated about as fast as morning dew on a cactus. Even at 8,000 feet, there was precious little moisture in the air most days, so finding a natural water source could be the difference between life and death.

The town's few dozen remaining structures, in various states of decay and worn by wind and sun and vegetation, appeared as abandoned as ever, roofs caved in or blown off, wood slowly devoured by insects and brick broken by time. Shiloah and Mercy were tucked into the woods behind a log shack, the last building in town and at the base of the old cemetery, built on uneven ground and supported by a rock foundation. It had a single entrance and probably once served as a toolshed for the shovels and picks men used to dig and cover the graves of the dead.

It had been a long time since Shiloah had been camping, since before her mother died, but somehow it all came back to her. She had quickly erected an orange backpacker's tent and a couple of folding camp chairs and table, careful not to trip over Mercy's many black computer cables that were strung everywhere.

"I still don't understand," said Shiloah as she removed a sleeping bag from its stuff sack, fluffed it, and threw it inside the tent. "How can transporting guns to the drug cartels not be illegal?"

Mercy, surrounded by electrical cords, a power strip, and a small Honda generator, shook her head, typing some commands with her left hand into the special laptop PC Shiloah had procured for her. In addition to the computer, she had two larger monitors relaying critical instrument data, chief among them fuel state and altitude. Her right hand was on the control stick piloting the Reaper, its camera relaying video of the sheriff's truck as it moved through the desert. There was no hurry in returning the military's principal unmanned killer. It had been airborne for almost four hours now, and it would fly for another twenty or so if needed. It would take even longer than that for the Air Force to crack the code she used to get it. Even then, the multiple VPNs she was using were bouncing her signal all over the world, concealing her location.

Shiloah stood up. "Did you hear me? How can transporting guns to the drug cartels not be illegal?"

"Well," Mercy responded, clicking her mouse a few times. "I have done some quick checking on that. I admit I should have done that at the beginning. Your father is breaking no state or federal laws in transporting the guns. They can be seized at the border, but it says here it is very infrequent that this happens. Most of the time, you can cross with no questions asked. And if it looks like he is merely moving cattle, I doubt he would ever be stopped."

Shiloah checked her watch, a sparkling Apple Series 7, another gift from her father. She tore it off her wrist and threw it into the nearby grass. "I hate him."

"We could have used that," Mercy said, without taking her eyes from the screens. "Pawned it perhaps."

Shiloah dropped to the blanket on the ground and onto her back, flustered. "Before or after the sheriff arrests us?" She rolled back onto her stomach. "Can you see where he is now?"

"Oh yes, I have him right here. He is one smart potato, this Sheriff Beck. I will give him a few minutes to see if he turns off somewhere, but he obviously suspects where we are."

Shiloah covered her face with both hands and screamed. "Fuck!"

Comfortable with the drone now tracking the vehicle on the ground on its own, Mercy lowered herself next to her friend. "It will be okay, Shy. We should give the sheriff a little credit and some time. I do not believe he is done with your father yet."

Shiloah propped herself on an elbow. "You're forgetting they're old friends. Don't you see? That's why he let him go. He's never going to arrest my father. Not for guns or drugs or anything else. And my father will know it was me who helped you. He probably already knows."

Mercy carefully pulled Shiloah's blond curls from her face and kissed her. It was only their second kiss, and Mercy desperately wanted to be better at it. "Not if you head back now. You tell him you were taking a drive somewhere."

Shiloah pulled away. "Won't work. He always knows when I'm lying."

"Be more convincing. The best way to tell a lie is to tell as much truth as possible. Tell him you drove to Gold Point to check out the old buildings. You had to get out, find something to do. Show him the pictures you took with your phone. Be forthcoming.

Admit that you and I have become friends and that I had asked questions about him, questions that seemed harmless. When he pushes you, admit that you gave me the password into your computer, but say that I was cleaning up some viruses for you. Let him reach the conclusion on his own that I must have used that to gain access to his system." Mercy drew her knees to her chest. "It is a perfectly plausible explanation, one that will make it clear that I used you to get information. And then tell him you are sorry for being stupid. That should win him over." Before Shiloah could argue, Mercy asked her for her cell phone.

"Why?"

"I want to take off the programs I installed so if your father looks, he will not find anything."

Shiloah laughed and handed it to her. "He wouldn't know what to look for."

Mercy got up and plugged the phone into the laptop, navigating around the phone's apps and installed software, deleting the photos of people and things around the ranch Shiloah had sent her over the last several months, critical information she used to piece together what Jesse Roy was up to, information she kept carefully concealed in Dan Whiteside's desktop computer. She liked the Youth Center's superintendent and felt bad about the abuse of trust, but his office had been the easiest to access, his passwords the easiest to break in the dead of night.

Mercy wiped everything from Shy's iPhone that might incriminate her but noticed something strange. Suddenly, her jaw dropped. "What is this?"

Shiloah sat up. "What?"

"You use the Find My app? When did you activate this?"

She shook her head. "Are you kidding? I don't want anyone knowing where I am."

Mercy glared at her and tapped a number of keys on the laptop. "It was activated . . . this morning."

Shiloah stood up, grabbing the phone. "What? No way. I've had my phone with me the whole time."

Mercy inhaled deeply. "You smell nice. Did you shower before coming out here?" Shiloah didn't answer, which told Mercy everything she needed to know. She shook her head. "Probably your father's friend from Mexico, which means they are tracking you."

"There's no internet out here, so he couldn't know where we are."

Mercy disconnected the phone from the computer. "You need to leave now, Shy. You would have had a signal for most of the way here. Trust me on this. It would not take an abundance of brain cells for them to figure out where you were going. I have studied the maps. There is nothing else out here." She put her hand in Shiloah's. "I will be okay tonight. Come back tomorrow if you can sneak away, and only if your father believes I must have been using you. But leave your phone at home. Do not worry about it if you cannot get away. Send an email to the address I gave you and use the code I showed you. That way, if he looks, he will think you were talking to a friend from your school."

Shiloah threw her hands into the air. "Why not just leave? Both of us, I mean. We can cut east through Utah and be in Salt Lake or even Phoenix before tomorrow."

Mercy placed a hand under Shiloah's chin. "Because it is too soon. They will be using all their technology to find me right now, facial recognition chief among them. You would be surprised how many cameras there are that can capture your pretty face in a major city. We need to stay off the grid, so to speak, let the search spread out and die from lack of nourishment." She motioned to the grocery sacks on the ground. "And speaking of nourishment, you brought me enough to last a couple of weeks. I will be fine. So go, my love."

Mercy's eyes moved back to the laptop screen. "Amazing, this sheriff of ours. He is coming this way for sure." She typed a command and the image of Beck's truck enlarged on the screen. "Hang on, let me do this one little thing."

CHAPTER 23

Dal Cho was having a difficult time of it. The rental car was two-wheel drive and had very little ground clearance. Cho cursed every time a tire collided with one of the sharp rocks that lay like land mines half-buried in the dirt, sure that he would have a flat and be out of business very soon. He had been trained in all manner of surveillance in his time with the Ministry of State Security, but all of that had been done on busy city streets with dozens of cars and buildings helping to conceal him. In this place, there was miles and miles of open road. After meeting the county sheriff, Cho suspected the man was far more intelligent and seasoned than his bio suggested. His use of Korean, expertly spoken, and then the jump to Mandarin. Though he was careful not to show it, the words so unnerved the MSS agent that he immediately fired off an encrypted email demanding more information on Porter Beck.

For now, all he could do was follow the lawman at a great distance, which was easy considering there was only the single road. But Cho's rental car was churning up so much dust, he was sure the sheriff would wonder who was behind him. While he had managed to affix a tracker inside the wheel well of the sheriff's truck in Rachel, the signal his receiver was getting had been intermittent shortly after he turned off the highway. Cho's only advantage was that the farther he went, the more the road rose into the higher elevations, and the rockier and less dusty it got. The disadvantage was the car itself. It was two-wheel drive, and he needed four. He was moving at a snail's pace to avoid getting a flat tire. The sheriff, in his rugged pickup truck, was no doubt moving much faster.

After thirty minutes of bucking and bouncing, Cho pulled the Hyundai to a stop at a fork in the road. He had a choice to make: turn east and follow the sign to someplace called Gold Point or continue on the road south. He pulled one of the topographic maps out of his duffel bag and studied the options. There was nothing to the south, no reason for the sheriff to look for Mercy Vaughn in that direction. To the east lay the mountains and a tiny dot on the map called Gold Point. There were ghost towns all over the west, mostly old mining operations. Gold Point surely had to be one of those.

"Places to hide," he said, turning the wheel to the left.

With no further word from Brinley, Beck feared she must be out of cell range. Signal strength off the county's main highway plummeted as fast as the mercury on a winter night. He'd considered getting her a satellite phone like the ones he and his deputies carried, but it was only recently that she was spending time close to home. He thought for sure she would have passed them by now, coming the other way from Gold Point with Mercy and Shiloah in tow. Now he was starting to worry.

Beck admired the sat phone Charlie had brought along, smaller but with a longer antenna than his. *Her budget's bigger than mine,* he reminded himself. She was on with her boss in Carson City, updating him on the search for Mercy. From where Beck was sitting, it didn't sound pleasant. He waited until she hung up. "I take it he's not pleased with our progress so far?"

"The governor is all over him about Mercy Vaughn," she replied. "Word's already spread about the Daimler truck hacking."

The road was smoother here, with fewer rocks and without all the deep divots, so the truck was bouncing around less, but the dust made it harder to see the dark shape in the smoky midafternoon sky through the windshield. "Hardly seems fair. You've been here less than eight hours. And it's not like she's killed anyone. Humans anyway."

Charlie had half of Columbo in her lap now and was giving him a good ear massage. "I guess those points are lost on him."

They were climbing steadily now, the road spanning a deep arroyo on either side. Beck slowed the truck, leaning forward and straining to see something moving in the haze. He activated the windshield washer and wipers to clear off the dust. What he saw then was a long cigar-shaped aircraft with a propeller on the back moving through the wildfire smoke to their right. Even before it banked toward them, he recognized it. It was an MQ-9 Reaper.

Charlie leaned forward too, tracking it with her eyes. "Uh, is that—"

"Yep." In seconds the Reaper closed the distance between them, maybe only a mile out and directly south now. In no time, it swooped down, crossing directly over the top of them, its engine buzzing like a huge lawn mower. Beck brought the truck to a stop. "It's her. But what is she doing?"

The drone was north of them now and turning back. Charlie dropped her window and leaned out. "Well, Maddox said it wasn't armed."

"It doesn't have to be." He did the math in his head. The trees were several hundred yards away, but on this road, strewn with sharp rocks and huge divots, there wasn't enough time to reach that cover. The Reaper was headed right at them. "Get out, Charlie." Suddenly, the two of them, plus Bo, were out of the truck and running back down the hill.

But they were too close. In that final second, Beck looked back, his brain taking a snapshot. The Reaper was just above the ground. He grabbed Charlie by the arm. "Jump!" They were in midair when the nose speared the engine block, tearing through two yards of metal, the impact launching the truck high into the air, catapulting it end over end, the explosion sending a shock wave of highly compressed air outward in all directions at supersonic speed. It caught Beck, Charlie, and Columbo before they hit the ground.

Dal Cho glimpsed what was left of the sheriff's truck through binoculars from a half mile away. It was shredded and burning well off the road in the bottom of a gully. Fire was chewing through the surrounding vegetation in a radius of more than two hundred feet, charring the ground and, no doubt, the bodies. He had heard the boom clearly and now watched for a full minute until he was satisfied the county sheriff and the detective had not escaped. He saw small pieces of what appeared to be an aircraft of some kind.

"Ó cao," he whispered in awe. *Oh fuck.* Seeing what he believed was one of the military's unmanned aircraft pass over him minutes earlier, he wondered now if this was the work of Mercy Vaughn. Was she so good she could take control of these weapons at will?

Cho's plan had been to follow until the sheriff led him to the girl. Now he would have to improvise and hope to locate her on his own. And he would have to be at his best because she was

pants pocket and dabbed at the blood that was trickling through Beck's hair. "Hold this there. Now let me see your back." She lifted up the tail of his shirt. His skin was red but thankfully not blistered. "It was those elk we saw earlier that saved us. Told you, good omen."

Beck started to laugh but even the slightest movement of his head made him dizzy. "What I'm saying is she flew that bird right over the top of us first. It was a warning. She gave us time to get out. If she wanted us dead, they would be picking pieces of us up with tweezers for the next two weeks."

Charlie groaned. "Time to get out? Is that what you would call that, because I would have preferred about five minutes."

Beck fought the almost irresistible urge to close his eyes. If he had a concussion, he needed to stay awake. "Help me up, Charlie. We need to kick some dirt over the rest of what's still burning and then get moving. We're going to have to hoof it from here. About two miles. Maybe less."

Charlie grabbed onto Bo's harness for support and reached down for Beck. The dog seemed to understand the intent and pulled forward. When Beck was on his feet and steady enough to walk on his own, he turned to both of them. "Everybody having fun?"

CHAPTER 24

Mercy shot up from her chair at the camping table, gazing down in disbelief at the now black computer screens in front of her. "What happened?"

"What?" Shiloah responded, getting to her feet quickly.

Moments later they heard it, the low roll of thunder that climbed up through the trees from the west. Both girls' heads moved on a swivel. They saw nothing at first, then a spiral of smoke rising into the distant sky.

"Change of plans," Mercy said. "We both have to get out of here. Now." But there was another noise, and her ears caught that too. She held up a hand. "Someone is coming." She turned back to the northeast, to the high side of the cemetery. The sound was unmistakable, a vehicle and the crunch of tires on dirt and rock, riding the heat waves in the otherwise still air. It was a midsized engine, probably a V-6, its low hum straining against the climb to the old mining town.

"That is the road you came in on, Shy," she said. "Who would be on that road?"

Shiloah stepped up next to Mercy. "My dad might."

Seconds later, the vehicle, a white SUV, appeared through a break in the trees on the road two hundred yards away, skirting the western edge of the cemetery. Mercy snatched up the laptop, crammed it into a backpack, and grabbed Shiloah's hand. "Quick," she said.

They ran in the opposite direction, finally ducking into the ramshackle post office that had closed a century ago. They took cover behind what was left of the old service counter. Mercy held a finger to her lips. They waited, listening. Half a minute later, they heard footsteps outside, then inside the small structure ten feet away. Shiloah was ready to scream, so Mercy put her hand over her mouth.

Brinley, glistening in sweat and looking like she had popped off the cover of *Outside* magazine, looked over the counter. She was holding a small gray pistol in her hand. "Hey, girls," she whispered.

"Oh, thank God," Shiloah said, rising up. "It's you."

Brinley held up her hand. "Get back down. It's not me. It's somebody else. And stay quiet. I'll be right back. Don't move until I come get you. Clear?"

Exiting the post office, Brinley ducked low, moving across the road and into the thick grove of pines. She looked for movement. Through the trees she saw the vehicle stop and two bearded dark-skinned men get out, both carrying rifles. These were not the special forces guys her brother had mentioned. They were young, mid-twenties, not fit, not clean-cut. If Jesse Roy was moving drugs, then there was a good chance these soldiers were from a different army. The two men followed on foot as the Toyota Highlander continued slowly down the winding road in Brinley's direction. Her view partially obstructed, she dropped into a crouch and moved closer. One of the cartel men walked over to Shiloah's

Land Rover, and finding it empty, returned to his partner. She watched and listened as they conferred with the driver in Spanish. There were a total of four voices now. Four men.

Brinley retreated slowly, avoiding sudden movements and sliding her boots silently backward through the mountain grass. She heard the Highlander's engine rev higher and saw it quickly round the corner only a hundred yards in the distance. There was no way to make it across the road and back to the old post office without being seen. Immobile, she watched as the SUV navigated the rocks and divots, its two occupants peering out the open windows for their quarry. Brinley calmed her breathing now, wondering who that quarry was. Shiloah? Mercy? It didn't really matter. They were hunting someone, and the two guys on foot were moving south now. It made sense. They would cover both ends of the old town and work their way in to the center.

Once the car took the next bend, Brinley slipped back across the road and into the post office. Shiloah and Mercy were where she had left them, crouched behind the counter, a twelve-foot-long piece of splintered mahogany, probably cut from these very mountains. Mercy's laptop was open and she was typing.

"Are they gone?" Shiloah asked.

Brinley put a finger over her lips and shook her head. She whispered, "Four men. Latinos. Armed and looking for someone." Mercy continued to type frantically, and Brinley could see the screens changing every few seconds.

"They're from Sonora," Shiloah said, the fear spreading across her young face. "Friends of my father. They came this morning."

"Cartel," Mercy responded without looking up. "Bad guys." Brinley asked what she was doing. "Sending your brother some information he is going to need."

Brinley waited a moment. "Listen, girls, we have to move. They're on both ends of the town now and will be searching every building." She rose slowly, motioning for them to follow. Mercy closed the laptop, stuffed it in the backpack, and carefully climbed into a crouch. But Shiloah couldn't move. She started to sob. Brinley seized her by the arm and hauled her to her feet. "Listen to me, Shiloah," she said into the girl's ear. "We are leaving this place right now. You will follow me and do whatever I tell you, and if you do, I will get you out of here. Do you understand?"

Shiloah nodded, and together the three of them worked their way to the front of the decrepit building. Brinley peeked around the open entrance and then turned back to the girls. "Stay low and move quickly. Follow me." Pistol in hand, she led them around the back of the structure, away from the road and where there was taller grass in which to hide. Behind the post office on either side were a number of other partial buildings, and Brinley pointed to one where all that remained were two sun-bleached brick walls that came together at a ninety degree angle. The rear wall had the opening for a window and a long, rotted wooden beam standing against it. It was a fifty-foot run up a gentle slope through some rough brush. They were quiet but kicked up dust the whole way. Brinley cursed quietly, watching as the dust floated through the blue sky, easily seen for a hundred yards or more. She looked north to the cemetery and wondered what was taking Beck so long to get here.

Behind them was the mountain, filled with Joshua trees, yuccas, and jacarandas well past their pretty purple spring bloom. Plenty of stuff to hide behind, if they could get up there without being seen. Still, there were only so many disintegrating buildings left in the town, and it wouldn't take long for the cartel men to check them. The girls moved slower now, one at a time, from bush to bush and tree to tree. In a few minutes they had reached the high side of the cemetery and a long, crumbling wall that had once set the eastern edge.

The grass was tall in the cemetery, towering over the uneven headstones and grave markers by two feet in most places. Brinley peered over the wall, looking west into the late-afternoon sun. Not an optimal position for a firefight. From her vantage, she could see the Highlander was returning now, only the driver inside, which meant the third man was also on foot. They would have found Brinley's car as well and would know now that Shiloah was here and not alone. She saw the SUV come to a stop south of the post office and watched as the driver exited the vehicle. He was older than the first two, tall and lean and dark. Seconds later, she saw the other three converge in the center of the road. They talked and then fanned out. One of them entered the post office, exited a moment later, shaking his head. There was only one place left to check, and that was up the hill.

The wall Brinley and the girls hid behind curved north and then west. Since the men from Sonora were now walking east, it was time they moved as well. Staying low, they scrambled on all fours behind the mortar and brick, disintegrating in places, fully collapsed in others. When they were well on the north side of the cemetery, Brinley told the girls to stay put. "I'm going to the west side. If they come at me, you stay low to the ground and go straight up into the trees. Hide and do not come out. If I don't come back for you, stay hidden. My brother will get here soon. He'll look around and fire three shots in the air. That's when you'll know it's okay to come out. Clear?"

They stared at her, their breath hurried and shallow, Mercy unable to summon the courage to tell her that the sheriff wasn't going to make it. Brinley peered over the wall one last time and bolted for the west side of the graveyard. She was now back on the far side of the road and could see the men walking north through the cemetery, moving through the high grass straight toward the girls. She noted two rifles and two handguns. The younger men were inexperienced with weapons, both rifles pointed to the ground. It was a potentially deadly mistake. She repeated Pop's mantra in her head. "Always point the gun in front of you. The extra second it takes to raise it may be your last." Her eyes wandered to the other two men. Their pistols were pointed straight ahead. They were hunters.

As the group reached the center of the field, Brinley did the math. Judging by their guns, the bad guys were packing a lot more rounds than she was, probably a hundred or more between them. Even if they didn't have extra magazines, the total far exceeded hers. Brinley had eight in the magazine and one in the chamber, and a spare mag in her side pocket. But she also had the high ground and the best friend outside of another shooter you could have: the sun at her back. She took a quick peek behind her. They would be staring directly into it, and the shadows cast by the towering ponderosa pines wouldn't help.

She had to keep them away from the girls. Sliding behind one of the massive trunks, she called down. "Sheriff's Department. What's your business?"

The four men froze but only momentarily. Straining to see up the grade, each held a hand in front of his eyes to block the sun. They could not see her. They conferred quietly in Spanish but not loudly enough for Brinley to make out what they were saying. She didn't need to hear the words. She knew what was coming.

The tallest man, the one who had been driving, spoke in broken English. "We are looking for Shiloah Roy. Her father sent us to find her."

"I see," said Brinley. "And you need all those guns to convince her to come with you?"

The men conferred again, more quickly this time. They fanned out, advancing slowly, guns coming up. "Give us Shiloah and the other one," the man said. "You can go home and live your life."

Brinley watched as the men dispersed. She called out, "I'm a really good shot, fellas. You should really think this through."

They didn't. They moved in her direction, exactly what she needed them to do. When the man closest to her was forty yards out, she popped out from behind the tree and fired a single round into his chest. He crumpled to the ground. The remaining three fired wildly, dozens of rounds smashing into the dirt and tree trunks, dramatically reducing their ammunition advantage. Looking for a target, one of the men, older and heavier than the rest, ran to what he hoped was Brinley's right to flank her, but he tripped over an old grave marker and went down. When he popped back to his knees, Brinley braced her extended arm against the side of the tree and shot him in his left shoulder, spinning him. Her next round caught the man in the back just below the neck.

The adrenaline surged through her veins, and she called out again. "I gotta say, I'm really liking my odds now." She sprinted south, weaving through the trees, drawing fire once more. But this time, the two remaining killers advanced methodically, one firing while the other was moving, and keeping her pinned. Though the sun was behind her, she was down to a total of fifteen rounds. *More than enough,* she told herself. She drew in a deep breath and began releasing it slowly, her right arm swinging around the tree trunk. The man to the right, the leader, was only twenty yards away and out in the open. "Night, night," she murmured on her exhaling air.

She did not see the man behind her, the man whose passport bore the name Dal Cho. She was vaguely aware that her shot had missed badly and of the slight pinch in her neck. Then there was darkness.

CHAPTER 25

Arshal saw the twisted, smoking wreckage of Beck's over-turned pickup from the road and was certain he and Charlie must be dead. He ran down into the arroyo anyway, and not finding them, returned to his truck and gunned it up the trail. He found them high on a bluff overlooking the old town, scraped up and somehow ambulatory. As they climbed into the vehicle, Beck waved off Arshal's offer of the first aid kit, saying there was no time and that they had heard what sounded like gunshots about fifteen minutes earlier. Beck drew his Glock as they rolled into Gold Point and saw Brinley's Subaru.

When they reached the cemetery, he pointed toward some trees. "That's the Land Rover Brin described. They must be here." Acutely aware of how many rounds they had used euthanizing twenty-nine of Jesse Roy's cows, Beck popped the twelve-gauge out of the rack between the seats and looked back to Charlie.

Charlie ejected the magazine from her Colt. "I've still got seven or eight and one more in the pipe. You guys take those."

"Don't forget," Arshal said, "we've got the arsenal Jesse was shipping to Mexico in the back." He pulled the AR-15 out of its holder, and the three of them exited the truck in a hurry, spreading out. Behind the small log building, they found the camp but no campers. Charlie ducked inside the tent and backed out. "It appears they were planning on staying a while. Tons of gear and supplies."

Beck gazed down at the electrical cables and computer monitors. He felt one of them. "Still warm." Columbo, nose in the air, sprinted away. Seeing no one, Beck called out to his other deputy in the middle of the graveyard. "Arshal, anything?"

The man who had tracked man and animal alike since before Beck was even born had his eyes squarely on the ground. "Blood here."

Beck and Charlie moved quickly into the tall grass, flanking Arshal on both sides. Moments later, Charlie crouched to the ground. "Blood here as well. Shell casings too. Lots of them." She held one up. "All .223s, shiny and new. Somebody was using a rifle."

Beck surveyed the scene. Blood in two places. Spent rifle shells. A gunfight. He bent over and reached into the grass, feeling the blood on his fingertips, still warm and sticky. The blood trail led back through flattened grass to the camp and the wide tire tracks of another vehicle. "They dragged the bodies here. Took them away."

Beck pointed to the higher edge of the cemetery grounds to the north and west, saw Columbo's head moving around in circles. "Assuming Brinley was with them and somebody else came along, somebody with guns, she would have moved up there somewhere. Sun at her back, higher ground, better cover. Even the odds."

Columbo barked once. Beck and Charlie trudged to the western edge, across the road and into the trees. "Whatcha got, Bo?"

Columbo circled something on the ground and sat. Beck noted the footprints in the dirt and then saw what the dog had found. "More shells." He scooped one up, giving the dog a nice pat on the head. "These are .380s. These are Brin's." He turned and looked down over the cemetery, pointing with one arm. "She had a good line of sight to the two spots in the grass where we found blood."

Charlie was stunned. "That has to be more than a hundred feet from here."

He nodded. For Brin, a hundred feet was the same as if they were standing right in front of her.

Charlie watched as Beck's face tightened. "We'll find her," she said.

Arshal called out from the wall to the north. "Up here."

When they got there, the deputy pointed to what he had found. On the other side of the wall, tucked up against the base, was a black computer backpack. Beck bent down. There was no reason in the world for a computer bag to be all the way out here. He picked it up and looked inside. Nothing. No computer. No power supply. No papers. He turned it upside down and shook it. A twenty-sided blue die fell out and onto the rocks at his feet. "This is Mercy's. They were right here. All of them."

Charlie holstered her Colt. "I can see Maddox taking Mercy, but a gun battle doesn't make sense."

Beck started walking down the hill. "I don't think it was Maddox. Brinley isn't stupid. She's not going to get between the feds and a teenage hacker. So that leaves whoever Jesse is working for."

"Those boys we saw down at the crash site earlier," Arshal said.

"More than likely. But how did they know to come here?"

"Tracked Shiloah's phone," Charlie offered. "Or maybe Jesse has something on her vehicle."

The three cops walked down to the sporty SUV, caked with dust from the ride in, and took a quick look inside. "Whoever grabbed the girls doesn't need Brinley," Beck said, swallowing hard. "Check every bush and building. If they killed her . . ." He didn't finish the thought. Didn't need to. They knew what he meant.

Ten minutes later, they reconvened at Arshal's Police Responder. "Anything?" Beck asked.

Charlie shook her head. "Nothing."

Beck pulled his Glock again and fired three shots into the air, knowing the sound would carry a mile or two. It was a signal that it was safe to come back. When the echo of the last shot died away and no one responded, Beck said, "We need to get to Jesse Roy's in a hurry."

They climbed into Arshal's truck. "Why there?" Charlie asked. "They'd have to know it would be the first place for us to look. Maybe they're heading south to Mexico."

"I think Mexico is right," Beck said, looking in the opposite direction. "But Jesse Roy has a plane."

"No, I don't have her," Maddox yelled into the phone. "I would have told you. We've been looking for her since we left you. I thought you were calling to tell me *you* had her."

Beck was steamed, and the bumpy road driving nails into his already injured brain wasn't helping his mood. He debated for a moment over whether to tell Maddox about the Reaper attack and decided against it. "Where are you now, Ed?"

The voice crackled in Beck's ear. "Landing back at Nellis. We need to refuel."

Beck could hear the rotors in the background and the helo's

engine shutting down. "I think Jesse Roy found her first. I'm heading to his place now. He's got that Beechcraft we saw when we were there. If he gets her on that plane, she's gone. Can you get something in the air?" The last thing he wanted to do was put Mercy together with a guy that would make her disappear, but he was more worried about Brin at the moment.

"Shit, hang on a sec," Maddox said loudly. Over the next several seconds, the noise abated, Maddox walking to a quieter spot. "You there?" Beck said he was. "Best I can do on short notice is get this bird back up as soon as we refuel. But it'll be forty-five minutes at the earliest. And if he does try to fly her out and stays below radar, we'll never see him."

Beck kicked the floorboard in Arshal's truck, knowing Maddox was telling the truth. "All right, we're about thirty minutes out. I'll keep you posted." He hung up.

Charlie sensed it wasn't good news. "No good?"

Beck shook his head. He tore open a packet of extra-strength Tylenol and popped the caplets in his mouth, handing another packet back to Charlie. "We're on our own."

Charlie downed the pills, asked how they were going to get into the Double J. "We don't have a search warrant and no evidence that will get us one. Probable cause is a stretch at this point."

She was right. Beck dialed Tuffy at the main station and filled her in. She didn't hesitate. "Sev and I can be there in twenty minutes. We'll knock down the gate if we have to. Call it a livestock inspection. Worry about a judge later on."

Steering as fast as he could over the uneven road, Arshal flashed a grin Beck's way. "My kinda girl."

Charlie pulled another shotgun from a rack behind the driver's seat. "My just-in-case is on my phone," she told Beck. "My thumbprint will open it for you."

Beck reached back and took her hand. Twenty-plus years in the Army had taught him what the just-in-case was. It was the letter soldiers wrote to their loved ones, to be delivered by a trusted friend or colleague in the event of their death. "Okay, Charlie Blue Horse. Okay."

CHAPTER 26

In the fog of her brain, Brinley saw him behind her, reaching out with those long, tattooed arms and grabbing her by her hair, yanking it so fast and hard she thought her head was detaching from her neck. She threw her arms upward, allowing her head to bend back over her spine, straining to reach his arms and chest with her fingernails, to at least draw some blood before he finished her. In an instant, he ripped the T-shirt from her small back and was reaching for her bottoms. She screamed, the last cry for help she was sure she would ever make.

"Wake up," he said. "You're having a nightmare."

Her eyes came awake but couldn't see. Something was covering them, a rag maybe. Was she still dreaming? She wriggled her body and felt the restraints pull at her hands and feet, bound to a chair she couldn't see in a building she couldn't see, the air dank and chilly, smelling of wet stone and maybe a day-old roast. Her head hurt like someone had used it as a soccer ball.

"What were you dreaming?" the man with the accent asked, his voice reverberating off the walls of the cave.

Still woozy, she couldn't place it, maybe Mexican? Italian? Her ears seemed stuffed with cotton, and the images of her father were still ebbing from her mind. "Uh, nothing," she managed to say, her mouth dry, her lips swollen and achy. "I don't remember."

"Well," said the man, "it really sounded like—"

She cut him off, her words slurred and slowed from the drug. "Hey, champ . . . here's an idea. Why don't . . . you . . . take this blindfold off. Cut me loose . . . you and I can square off. How 'bout that?"

She heard them laugh, noted three distinct voices, cataloged them. Then someone lifted the rag from her eyes. Right eye only. Left swollen shut. She remembered the pinch in her neck, someone grabbing her from behind. They had beaten her first, probably payback for the two shit bags she had dropped among the gravestones. It took her a minute to focus. She was surrounded by walls of big block stone and wooden racks from floor to ceiling. Wine bottles. Hundreds of them. She was in an immense wine cellar. It was similar to many she had seen in Hollywood but most resembled the one in George Clooney's house, the one in Studio City, and it had a long wooden table in the center with six chairs around it.

A pair of long fingers snapped in front of her good eye. They belonged to a tall, slender man in his late thirties, the man in charge at the cemetery. To his left was the other still-living cartel man, shorter, square-shouldered and muscled, and much younger. He was twirling what appeared to be a branding iron in a propane heater that sat atop the table. She could see the iron glowing hot and red. Brinley craned her head to her left, the pain searing through the trapezius and deep cervical flexor muscles of her neck, confirming they had hit her many times. Her right eye locked on an Asian man, six foot and with the lithe physique of a swimmer. Next to him was Jesse Roy, a man she hadn't seen in many years, his nose red and slightly askew, maybe broken. Alongside him was another Hispanic heavyweight.

"I see you're hanging with all the right people these days, Jesse," Brinley said.

The cattle rancher stepped closer, his features captured more prominently now under the recessed lighting. Even with one eye shut, she could see the time on his silver Omega watch. It was almost five o'clock. She had been out for close to ninety minutes. "Who are you?" Jesse asked. "How do you know me?"

She had been off her cyclothymia meds for two days already—not by choice, she simply hadn't been home—and these guys keeping her would not help. With the drugs and the meditation techniques Dr. Bishara had shown her, she had managed that precarious balance between depressive and manic symptoms for almost a year now. In a short time, if she were still alive, she would be bouncing off the walls.

Jesse grabbed her roughly by the chin. "I asked you how you know me."

She shook loose of his hand. "My brother used to be a friend of yours." Jesse's expression told her he had no idea what she was talking about. She laughed. "Yeah, Porter Beck. He's not going to be too happy about this, Jesse. You should start running now, maybe south of the border with your buddies here. You might squeeze in a few more days of life. I can't promise that of course, but anything is possible."

Jesse reached for her again but was caught on the arm by the guy next to him. Brinley could see the irritation and the fear in the cowboy's face. "You're that girl Beck's old man rescued up in the mountains. The one they adopted. God, you turned out good." He looked at the others. "We need to know what she knows," he told César. "What her brother knows."

"Nando," César said.

The taller man walked to the propane heater, donned a thick silver oven mitt over one hand, and removed the glowing branding iron from the red and orange flames. Slowly, he approached Brinley. He held the iron in front of her nose so that she could smell and feel its searing heat. César walked behind her and seized her hair in his hands, yanking it backward. "You killed two of my men. Tell me what the authorities know about our operations, and I promise to kill you quickly."

Her eyes rolled upward to see him. "I've been burned before, asshole." The images flooded back, the cigarettes he liked to stub out on her chest and back. The smell. She was only ten when the man named Joe Beck arrived at their trailer in the mountains. He had probably smelled their fire. But Tom Cummings had clubbed the lawman with a two-by-four and was getting ready to hit him again when Brinley separated her father's head from the rest of his body with a shotgun blast. It was the first time in her life she had fired a gun. Joe Beck had lied for her, said it was he who killed the child abuser, protected her from the state taking custody of her. It had been their secret, one she hadn't shared with anyone, not even Porter. And now she would take that secret to her grave.

Nando moved even closer with the hot, smoking iron, the J^J brand merely an inch from her cheek. She thrashed under César's grip. "Hold her tight," Nando said.

Jesse's cell phone rang. He could see the number. "It's the sheriff," he said. It rang three more times before falling silent. Ten seconds later a text appeared and Jesse read it aloud. "Hurt any of them and you're dead."

César ordered his last man out of Jesse's wine cellar to keep watch. Another text pinged on Jesse's phone. "What does it say?"

"It says the military is closing the airspace, and if we try to leave they will force us down."

César relaxed his hold on Brinley. "Is it a bluff?"

Jesse shook his head. "Maybe. I don't know. We need to get

out of here. Now." César seemed uncertain. "Put this one on the plane," Jesse instructed Nando. "Her and that Mercy girl."

César turned to Nando. "All three females on the plane. Please."

The blood drained from Jesse's face. "César, not Shiloah."

The cartel enforcer put a hand on Jesse's shoulder. "It will be okay. Señor Cordero will decide."

His phone ringing again, Jesse took a quick step toward Nando, raising his fist. "No, I decide. My daughter stays here."

César held up a hand. "Please, old friend. Don't push."

Jesse folded his hands in front of him, and prayed to Marco Cordero's chief enforcer. "I'll talk to her. She won't say a word."

César stood expressionless. Enraged, Jesse punched him in the face. It was a vicious blow that sent César's jaw sideways but not enough to knock him down. Nando raised his nine millimeter and pressed it against Jesse's right temple. Bringing his fingers to his mouth, César felt the blood. "Control yourself, Jesse. Shiloah will not be hurt. It's insurance only, and we may need her to get the other one to talk."

Dal Cho, who was sampling a 2001 Colgin Cellars cabernet and observing from a distance, finally moved toward the group. "And once she does, gentlemen, the hacker is mine, per our agreement." Cho had been forced to improvise at the cemetery. Though he was confident he could have killed the remaining gunmen, the situation had become much more complicated than he initially believed. And he needed to understand the complete picture.

Jesse spun toward the stranger. "Who the fuck is this guy, and why is he drinking my wine?"

"You get her when we've finished with her," Nando told Cho, before turning his attention to Jesse. "Mr. Roy, your daughter will not be harmed. You have César's word. You have mine. But she cannot be here when the police arrive. And César is correct. The hacker is more likely to talk if she thinks some harm could come to Shiloah. Once we have what we need, we will get her back to you."

Jesse reached out and grabbed Nando by the collar. "You do what you have to with this one and the other girl. My daughter is—"

"Dead," Nando said, with a sadistic grin. "Or worse, if you don't take your hand off me and do as I say."

It was the words *or worse* that Brinley could see did the trick. Jesse withdrew his hand and backed up, defeated. "You ball-less piece of shit," she said to him. "You're going to let them take your own daughter?"

Nando moved toward her. She saw his fist coming, and that was all.

Jesse looked down on Beck's unconscious sister. There was no going back now. He could not undo this. Hadn't been able to undo any of it since that day in Mexico fifteen years ago, that day a man climbed into the passenger seat of his pickup and told him that after bringing guns across the border and selling them for a tremendous profit, he was going to be taking narcotics back to the United States. The man, who would later become the head of the Caborca cartel, showed Jesse a photo of Willa and their baby daughter, a photo taken a month earlier at Shiloah's baptism. The message was clear. He'd felt a tremor of panic then, the same tremor that raced through his body now.

But there was one final straw to grab, and Jesse reached for it. He turned to César. "The plane only holds six. I count seven, and I have to fly it. Leave Shiloah here."

César checked his watch. "No." He pointed at Brinley. "We don't need this one." Powerless, Jesse turned to leave. "No, amigo," César said, handing him his revolver. "This is your mess. You clean it up."

César, Nando, and Cho ascended the stairs. Jesse stared down at Brinley, who was coming around now and wishing she hadn't. He raised the Ruger .357, pointed it at her face, cocked the hammer. Brinley's eyes stared into the barrel and watched as Jesse's hand trembled. She held her breath. Finally, he lowered the gun, walked behind her. The air escaped her chest as she heard his footsteps trail away, stop, then return toward her. Coming around her right shoulder, he dropped a small, soft blanket over her head, covering her face. Brinley thrashed, struggling against the zip ties that bound her wrists and ankles to the chair.

"I'm sorry," Jesse said. In the rock cave he had spent months designing, the noise of the gun was deafening.

CHAPTER 27

There had been no response to Beck's call or texts, and he could feel the panic rising within him. Arshal drove through the Double J gate at speed, accelerating toward the main house where Sev Velasco's patrol truck was parked. Beck and Charlie, guns drawn, were out even before Arshal pulled alongside it. They were sprinting up the massive lawn when Tuffy ran out the elaborate front doors shaking her head.

"Empty," she yelled. "Just the housekeeper."

Beck scanned the grounds. There were almost a dozen total structures on the property. "Spread out. Search every building," he shouted, climbing into Sev's Interceptor. He punched the gas pedal to the floor, the tires rotating so fast they spat rocks and dirt as the pickup shot forward. His eye caught Sev coming out of one of the outbuildings and sprinting south, waving for Beck to follow.

The engine in the Ford was a big one, and in a second he was flying between the equipment buildings and barns and onto the road that led to Jesse Roy's private airstrip. Through the windshield, he saw Sev cresting a hill a quarter mile ahead, and all he could think about was Brinley, the jumpy, frightened little girl Pop rescued, the girl who idolized him as a brother and grew into a ferocious woman who could shoot the eyes off a fly. When he crested that same hill, he saw that the propellers on Jesse's Beechcraft Baron G58 were turning, and the plane was slowly turning at the east end of the dirt runway.

He slowed enough to let Sev jump onto the running board, where he clung to the doorframe and side mirror, gulping air.

"Hang on!" Beck yelled. In three seconds, they were going much faster than the plane as it started its run toward takeoff. There was only one way to do this, and that was to put the truck squarely in front of the aircraft. When he swung onto the runway, the plane was accelerating toward the Interceptor at full throttle. Beck was certain Jesse Roy must be estimating the distance between them.

Sev had somehow not only managed to hold on but had executed a spectacular gymnastic feat, vaulting himself and his rifle through the open passenger window and into the seat. Beck looked at him in amazement. "Well, if this doesn't work, you can always join the circus."

Sev Velasco already had his AR-15 off his back. Without hesitation, he repositioned his upper body outside the window, the rifle pressed tightly to his right shoulder, the barrel resting on top of the side mirror. His right eye was already looking down the front gunsight, but the Beechcraft was still six hundred yards ahead and jumping in and out of view as the Ford's shock absorbers adjusted to the road and speed. "Bring it down a notch," he said calmly, never taking his eye off the target.

Beck eased off the gas. Sev let out a long, slow breath and fired three quick rounds. Beck saw the belly of the plane spark and understood what his deputy was trying to do. The Beechcraft swerved on the dirt runway but didn't slow. Beck reached over and pulled Sev back into the seat. "He won't stop, and you could hit Brinley or one of the girls. Let's put something a little bigger than a bullet on it."

His eyes squarely on the plane's nose wheel, Beck kicked the truck up to eighty. They were a football field away now. Even above the roar of the truck's motor, he could hear the twin propellers winding up to full throttle. "Seat belt," he said to Sev without looking away. Sixty feet from the nose wheel, Beck turned five degrees right, aiming for the left wing. He caught the briefest glimpse of Jesse Roy in the pilot's seat. The collision never happened. The Beechcraft cleared the pickup by inches, but it might as well have been miles.

The airplane climbed into the sky. They were gone.

Beck drove back toward the main house, processing the possibility he might never see Brinley again and that he had also managed to lose Mercy Vaughn. There was no doubt in his mind that they were both on the plane.

As they passed the large central barn, cattle-ranch-red and reflecting the last hours of scorching sunlight off its siding, Tuffy and Charlie waved them over. Beck skidded to a stop in the gravel and jammed the gearshift into park.

"Inside," Tuffy said as Beck climbed out. "Arshal found something."

Jesse's ranch hands, six of them, were out front and herded tightly together by Columbo. Beck studied them as he walked toward the barn. They were all Latino, possibly undocumented, and looked to be legitimate cowboys.

Beck turned to Sev. "Question them. Find out who was on that plane and where it's going. Anybody whose immigration status is in question might be willing to play ball. Talk to the housekeeper, too."

"Boss, if they're linked to the cartel in any way . . ."

"Yeah, I know. Try anyway."

Sev broke off and was already interrogating the men in Spanish before Beck entered the main barn. The inside was huge, much larger than it appeared from the outside, and it contained a good amount of equipment and vehicles and the tools to service them. Across the expansive dirt floor, Arshal was bent over and looking into the front seat of a car. A silver sedan covered in dust. As Beck got closer, he recognized the Hyundai driven by the man he had encountered in Rachel earlier in the day. The man named Dal Cho.

"Two bodies in the trunk," Arshal said. "Two of the steer haulers we saw at the crash site. Must have been their blood at the cemetery."

Charlie stepped around back and examined the wounds to both men. "Wow. That girl can shoot."

Beck noticed multiple sets of boot prints in the dirt. None of them were Brinley's. "Small amounts of blood here and there," Tuffy said, also scanning the ground. "They probably carried those two fellas in and set them in the car."

Arshal said, "You can see they kicked around the sand here, trying to cover the blood." His eyes moved to the man who had once sat on his lap as a small child. "Brinley and those girls are still alive."

"Maybe . . . but they're gone."

Arshal put a hand on his shoulder. "Then we'll get 'em back."

Beck looked around the barn. "Nothing else?"

The deputy pulled on the handlebars under his nose. "As far as forensics goes, doubtful."

Tuffy appeared at his side with her crime scene kit, lowering herself onto the compacted sand. "I'll process the car and try to get some of the blood here in the dirt to rule out it belonging to the girls. Sev can process the SUV out there on Jesse's airstrip."

Beck shook his head. "Waste of time. Time we don't have."
He addressed his crew. "The girls are still alive. For now. Ideas?
Anybody?"

Nobody had anything to say. Finally, Charlie touched him on
the arm. "Jurisdictionally, this is the point we should hand things
off to the feds. At a minimum, it's a kidnapping case now." He
looked at her, and she could see the hope draining from his face.
"But I have some connections with DEA. I'll see if I can get us a
plane."

Beck dipped his head. "Thanks, Charlie." He wasn't handing off anything to the feds. Not while Brinley was a hostage, or
worse. Right now, he wanted to kill someone: Jesse Roy, César, the
head of the Sonoran cartel, all of the above. To get that opportunity, he needed a plan. "Okay," he said. "Jesse's plane is in the air.
Destination unknown, but probably Mexico. Let's see if Sev has
got anybody talking. If not, we head back to the office and start
calling everybody who might be able to help."

Moving out of the barn, Beck headed toward Arshal's truck.
He yelled to Sev. "Where's Columbo?"

Still interviewing Jesse's ranch hands, Sev turned and shook
his head.

Beck checked Arshal's truck, but he wasn't inside. "Damn it,
dog, where are you?" He climbed onto the running board and
moved his eyes slowly over the entire property, but Columbo was
gone.

Tuffy headed back toward the barn with her crime scene kit.
She called out to Beck. "I'll look for him when I'm done and bring
him back with me."

As Beck and Charlie climbed into the cab, they heard a bark.
Then another. Beck got out and stood on the running board again,
looking up the hill toward the main house. The dog barked again

and kept barking. Beck took off at a run, Charlie, Tuffy, and Ar-shal behind him.

They found him inside, circling the large rectangular island in the kitchen. "What is it, pal?" Beck asked.

Beck watched Columbo do another loop around the island and then sit. He extended his long tongue and licked his chops. The communication was clear. It was how he had been trained. And it was exactly what he had done at the Daimler crash site earlier in the day. But this was a kitchen island, larger than most and with a granite top that had probably been quarried in Italy or Brazil.

"I don't understand. It's an island, Bo," Beck said with some irritation. He reached down to open the cabinet doors on the long side, certain he would fine pots and pans, but when he pulled on the ornate handles, the doors held fast. The hardware was purely decoration. Bo barked once more.

Tuffy walked to the other side of the granite top, dropped into a squat, and felt underneath the lip. As she ran her fingers along the edge, the top moved to her right, rolling an inch away from the shorter end of the cabinet. She looked up at her boss. "My hell, will you look at that?"

Beck stepped around to the short side, put his hands on both sides of the top, and pushed. The granite moved easily on its metal gliders, revealing inlaid tile steps leading downward with wooden hand railings on both sides. As he slid the island's top farther, a light came on below.

Charlie drew her Colt, followed in quick succession by Beck and Tuffy. The front of the island's short side opened easily, and they took the stairs in single file, descending slowly. At the bottom of the stairs, Beck could see a rock wall that curved to the left and turned into rows of wooden wine racks, most of them filled with bottles.

He popped around the corner, Glock aimed straight ahead, and immediately saw the far end of the long room. "Oh God," he said, seeing the figure in the chair, the body's top half covered by a blanket and a deep red stain starting where the head was. Beck's eyes moved down the corpse to the Spanish-tiled floor and a pair of boots. He recognized them. In agonizing increments, he moved closer, knelt to the stone floor, hesitantly reached for the blanket, and slowly peeled it from her head. Brinley's face was turned to the side, her hair matted and sticky red. Slowly, he rolled her chin toward him, pulling the hair from her swollen, blood-smeared face.

Her head shot forward, one eye opened and filled with rage, her teeth bared and reaching for his throat, a blood-curdling scream escaping her own. Beck flew back onto his tailbone, Charlie and Tuffy jumping too, as Brinley continued to scream.

Tuffy shrieked back, her body smashing into the wine racks.

"Brin!" Beck yelled, grabbing her head with both hands. "It's me, Brin. It's me."

But Brinley couldn't hear him and couldn't see him. She screamed once more and suddenly went silent. In the next instant, Beck saw the blood drain from her face and her head fall to her chest. "Brin!"

Charlie moved behind Brinley, cut the electrical ties binding her to the chair with a pocketknife. Brinley's arms, free now, swung limply to the sides of her body. Beck caught her and laid her gently on the floor, feeling for a carotid pulse. He looked back at Tuffy and shook his head. "Get your kit." She sprang up the stairs.

"No pulse," he said to Charlie as he started to straddle her hips, positioning his body above hers, his fingers interlocking, arms rigid above her chest.

"Wait," Charlie told him. She reached down and sliced Brinley's

T-shirt vertically, tearing it off her chest. "Let's try this." She raised a fist into the air and brought it down hard on the lower third of Brinley's sternum. "You can do a precordial thump when—"

Brinley's right eye opened again, and she sucked in a loud lungful of air. Seeing Beck above her, she looped her hands over his neck and pulled him to her. She started to cry, great convulsive sobs heaving out of her.

"I thought you were dead, Brin. Jesus, I thought you were dead." His fingers moved into her hair, looking for the wound.

"Thought so, too," she gasped. "The last thing I remember was Jesse Roy pointing a revolver at my head."

Beck looked shocked. There was no bullet wound. "But he didn't—"

He felt the red blood on her face, bent closer, smelled it. "I don't believe it."

"What?" Charlie asked, bending closer.

"Wine," Beck said. "It's not blood. It's red wine." He pulled her to a sitting position, braced her against Charlie, looked over the chair she had been fastened to and beyond it to the wooden wall twelve feet away. There was a nice, round hole in it.

Charlie saw it, too, grabbed the soaked blanket from the floor and smelled it. "Oh my God."

Beck pulled Brinley back into his arms. "He faked it. With a nice cabernet, I think."

"I'm sorry, Porter," Brinley cried. "They have the girls. I got two of them but—"

He squeezed her. "You did fine. We'll get them back, sis."

Tuffy shot back down the stairs, med kit in hand, saw her best friend alive and sitting up. "Oh, thank God." She dropped to the floor and joined in the hug.

Beck pushed himself up from the floor. The adrenaline he had been running on for two hours drained from his body all at once, and he staggered backward into the long tasting table. Charlie caught him before he fell. "Easy, Beck."

Tuffy wrapped Brinley in an emergency blanket and helped her to her feet. She looked up at Beck through her one good eye, seeing the cuts on his face. "What happened to you?"

"We ran into one of Mercy's drones," Charlie said, her eyes gleaming. "Your brother saved my life."

Beck regained his footing. "That's why we were late getting to Gold Point. Sorry."

Brin squeezed her eyes shut, remembering. "After I put the first two down, I got jumped from behind. I think it was this Asian guy. Drugged me. He wants Mercy. They talked about it before they left. He made some kind of deal for her."

Beck recalled the face of the man he suspected could be Chinese. Dal Cho. "About my height, lean, moves well?"

"That's him."

He examined her more closely. She had a small laceration below the right eye. The left one was a deep black and blue under the eyelid, and it was badly swollen. "Can you see out of this one?"

"Not so much."

She had a serious bump on her forehead as well. "Who hit you?"

She knew why he was asking. There would be payback. "One of the Mexicans, but I woke up in the barn already feeling like they'd gone at me, so maybe all of them."

He carried her out of the wine cellar, back up through the kitchen island, and out to Arshal's truck where Columbo licked her up and down. "First stop, hospital."

"I'm okay," she said, grabbing his hand as he buckled her in. "Let me help."

He leaned in and kissed her forehead. He had her back and now he had Jesse—if he ever found him—on numerous counts of kidnapping that would put him away for the rest of his life, which would not be long if he had anything to say about it. There were still two young girls on a plane to Mexico, one of whom the government badly wanted. Maybe it would lend its mighty hand to getting them back. If not, he was going anyway.

CHAPTER 28

On the way back to Pioche, they dropped Brinley at the twenty-bed county medical center in Caliente. Hadji Bishara met them in the parking lot and quickly assessed Brinley's balance and dazed look. A Sunni like most Turks, Bishara wore an off-white jubbah with his name on it in lieu of gray hospital scrubs, and a navy blue sandal turban hat. "Possible concussion," the doctor mumbled in his heavy Turkish-accented English. "I will call you with an update when I have it."

Brinley raised her head, wincing at the pain. "I told you I'm good."

"What day is it?" Bishara asked her.

"Uh . . ."

"Stick around," he said.

They helped her into a wheelchair and a young nurse rolled her inside. "Thanks, Hadji," Beck said. "I'm in the middle of something that can't wait, so I'll have Pearl drive Pop over so he can sit with her. Brin's tough, as you know. Her heart stopped for a few seconds, and they drugged her, so run a tox screen, and check her cyclothymia meds for me. She hasn't been home in the last two days."

Bishara slapped Beck's forehead. "You fucking guy! Tell me again where you graduated medical school." A tiny reed of a man but with the bearing of someone much larger, he knew Brinley as well as a mechanic knows his best car. He grabbed Beck's arm as he was turning to leave, beaming his bright flashlight into his friend's eyes, noting the scrapes and bruises on his face. "What happened to you?"

Beck squinted at the light beam. "My truck collided with the military's most deadly attack drone."

Bishara held up a finger and moved it back and forth, directing Beck's vision to track it. "Fine, don't tell me. How is your RP?"

The question about his night blindness was becoming as both-ersome as the actual disease. "No worse than when you asked me last week. I have to go, Hadji."

"You're taking the vitamin A?"

It was always the same. "All 15,000 units. Gotta go, buddy. If I'm still alive on Friday, I'll see you for our weekly chess game." It wasn't really chess. The two men just called it that. It was a ju-jitsu match, requiring the same ability to think ahead five moves that the ancient board game did. Beck climbed back into Tuffy's Bronco and signaled her to go.

Tuffy backed out of the parking space, Bishara rapping on Beck's window and calling after him. "I want to talk to you about some clinical trials."

From behind the glass, Beck pointed to his ear, feigning deaf-ness. The pain in his back was becoming extreme and his head now felt like it was loosely wired onto his neck. By the time Tuffy got him back to the office twenty minutes later, the sun had dropped beneath the western peaks, and with it so had the light from his eyes. She guided him inside.

He sat down at his desk and checked the time. It was 8:30. He popped four Advil and swilled them with the cold coffee still in his mug from twelve hours earlier. While physically depleted and badly in need of some rack time, Beck felt strangely elated. It was because he had Brinley back, that he hadn't lost her. He needed that boost right now because there were still two missing girls out there somewhere. And there was an old friend that needed to be put down. As he was envisioning how he was going to make that happen, Columbo sauntered into his office, carrying himself with great pride, putting his front paws up on Beck's lap.

"Yeah, that was nice work, bud," said Beck, stroking his head. "We might never have found her. You saved her life. And I almost walked away." He pulled one of Pearl's homemade dog biscuits out of his top drawer and let the dog gently take it out of his hand. "Good thing one of us was paying attention."

Tuffy brought in some fresh coffee and a hot sandwich, setting both on his desk. "Maddox called. He said that at any given time, there are close to ten thousand planes over the U.S."

Beck shook his head in dismay, and that hurt even more. "I'm sure he's great on trivia night. Did you tell him that wasn't particularly helpful information?"

She took a seat across from him. "They haven't seen Jesse Roy's plane, but they're looking. If they're heading for Mexico, he isn't hopeful."

Beck took a sip. As hot as it was outside, the hot coffee seemed like the best thing he had ever tasted. "He sound pissed?"

"Very. Said we totally blew this, and that he'll be calling the governor."

"Well, I don't report to the governor."

Tuffy shrugged. "Charlie does, I guess, indirectly."

Beck picked up the receiver on his desk phone. "Yeah. What's she doing?"

"She's at my desk. Sounds like she was getting an earful from her boss."

Tuffy got up to leave, and Beck asked her to close the door behind her. Then he dialed a number from memory. He heard a series of clicks and clacks and digital noises, which told him it was bouncing around the world. Finally, she came on the line.

"Well, this is a nice surprise," said Sana Locke of the CIA. "To what do I owe the pleasure?"

"I need a favor, Sana, and I need it now."

Sana immediately barked some instructions in Arabic to whoever was in the room with her. "I owe you. We both know that. I'm not really in the office right now, but tell me what it is."

He gave her the rundown on Mercy Vaughn. The drone hacking. The hack into the Federal Reserve last year. The Sonoran cartel. Jesse Roy's plane. The Asian guy named Dal Cho.

"This is all the same girl?" she asked incredulously. Sana was Jordanian and Egyptian on her mother's side and English on her father's. Her voice was the perfect blend of all three, and in Beck's sensitive ears, it was a mating call. They had been through the thick of it together, and they had coalesced under the sheets. He missed that, missed her, knew that she would have permanent residence in his dreams. But he also knew this wasn't the lifetime they could spend together.

"I'm going to have to wake some people up," she added. "It's late in D.C. Give me an hour."

"Now I owe you."

She laughed. "Let's hope we can settle any outstanding balances sometime soon."

He hung up and tapped his keyboard, lighting up the large monitor, and did a Google search for a map of the Mexican state of Sonora. Sev had done a lot of digging on Jesse Roy in the last few days, and the most likely connection to drugs and weapons south of the border was in Sonora and the Caborca cartel, run by a man named Marco Cordero. Unfortunately, the drug boss almost certainly had numerous residences and kept his movements unpredictable. Beck would need Sana to help him find the man.

But he had to get there first. There was an airport, Mar de Córtes outside Puerto Peñasco, a city American tourists called Rocky Point. They would have landed there by now, he thought, if that's where they were going.

And that's what nagged at him. One of the reasons for his success in the Army was his ability to think critically and analyze data. Right now, every synapse in his brain was telling him that something was off. Maddox, Mercy, the whole enchilada, so to speak.

A half hour elapsed before Charlie interrupted his contemplations. "I got us a plane."

"Us?"

"Hey, Mercy Vaughn is still my responsibility."

Beck gave a slight shake to his head. "We don't have any legal authority in Mexico. And you have a daughter. Nice try, Charlie Blue Horse, but I'm not taking you down there."

She closed the door. "Then you're not going either. It's my contact." She told him the pilot was a guy she met while working a DEA task force a few years ago. He lived up north in Elko. "The cartel thinks he's working for them, but he works for us. Flies a little cactus dodger. If he agrees, it has to be off book, so we'll have to come up with some money. He wants ten grand. Say the word and he's on his way."

Beck stared at her. "You could lose your job. Your pension. Your life."

"Nah, I have some days saved. I'll take a few. And from what I understand, you could use someone who can see in the dark."

"Reports of my vision's demise have been greatly exaggerated. Besides, you only met me this morning. I don't normally take a girl to Mexico on a first date."

She flashed a wide smile. "Hey, if tamales are on the table, I'm in."

Beck had some money in his savings account, a little more than ten grand the last time he bothered to look, and he could live well enough off his salary and his military pension. "I'll cover the pilot," he said to Charlie.

Charlie checked her wristwatch. "It'll take him ninety minutes to get here."

"Okay." He toggled to his email and a quick glance for anything important. If he was heading to Mexico, a trip that might well result in Lincoln County needing a new sheriff, it made sense to take care of anything that required his immediate attention. There wasn't. A dozen or so emails containing purchasing orders, time-off requests, notes from business owners, a bunch of spam. He made a mental note to talk to Tuffy about a better crap filter and was about to close out the program when he saw it, sandwiched between the others. "Charlie." She was already halfway out the door. "I might have something."

Charlie moved around his desk and peered down at the screen. "What?"

It was the sender's name that caught his eye, and Beck pointed to it. "Remember that email I told you I got the day Jesse's bull got barbecued?"

"The one you think was from Mercy?"

"Same sender. 0DayMei@proton.me." The subject line was brief: *HELP!* He noted the time stamp, saw the message had been sent shortly after he and Charlie had nearly been killed and about the time of the gun battle in Gold Point. He opened it.

Sheriff, if you're still alive, now is the time I could use your help. I know you have no reason to trust me, but I trust YOU. First, I've encrypted your email. The NSA has been snooping around your computer, but now it's overloading their own servers with spam bombs. Contained herein is everything you need, and everything I need. Counting on you, my good sheriff. You have the key now.

"She's attached some files," Charlie said. "The first one is a video." Beck opened it. They could see Mercy's face, sitting in what appeared to be her room at the Youth Center. He hit the play button.

The room was dark except for a lamp next to her bed. She smiled for the camera and spoke quietly. "Hello, Sheriff Beck. My name is Mercy Vaughn. You do not know me. At least not yet. But if you are seeing this, it is because everything has gone to shit, and I am going to need your help."

She kept her voice low, probably to keep the girls on either side of her from hearing. Beck could see she was twirling her twenty-sided die. The video had been made before the interview at the Youth Center. "I am going to deal you into the game, so to speak."

They saw her reach down and touch her keypad. Suddenly, the screen filled with columns and columns of data against a black background. "What you are seeing here are transactions initiated over the dark web. I am going to assume you already know what that is, given what I know about you and your history. And what you will learn about me very quickly, I think, is that I know what I am doing when it comes to these things." She chuckled. "Anyway, these are transactions—initiated by various parties in Mexico to obtain weapons from a Lincoln County resident by the name of Jesse Roy. Mr. Roy is a bit sloppy with his email accounts—and yes, I know it is illegal for me to have read those—but he is getting these guns from straw buyers from all over the southwest, and then he is moving them to Mexico in his cattle trucks."

Mercy paused, a sound coming from the cell on her left. She held a finger up to her lips. Beck and Charlie looked at each other.

"She made this before she even met you?"

Beck nodded and watched as Mercy rose to her knees, put her

ear against the wall, listened a moment, then sat down on her bed again. "You may already know most or all of what I have just told you, Sheriff. I would not be surprised if you do. When I started this, I researched you, your background. Really quite impressive." She grinned.

"That's all classified stuff," said Beck.

Charlie laughed. "I think we can safely assume she's probably reading the president's emails at this point."

Mercy continued. "I am sorry for the intrusion into your personal life. But I needed a fail-safe in case things went upside down, and I was greatly encouraged when I discovered that you were a person who could be trusted to do the right thing."

Beck looked at Charlie. "What's the right thing?"

Mercy giggled. "What is the right thing? Glad you asked. Open the next attachment. It details all the transactions. This includes banking records of Roy's dealings with the Caborca cartel in Mexico, run by a man by the name of Marco Cordero." She paused a second for effect. "It is not just guns, Sheriff. It is probably drugs. Lots and lots of drugs. I have not had time to look into that end of it, but I am sure you know people who can."

"This girl is smart," Charlie said. "This is all dark web stuff. Look at those codes. Those transactions will help the DEA guys build their case."

"If you are aware of that aspect already," Mercy continued, "kudos. Pass Go and collect two hundred dollars, as they say. Regardless, I have sent you these because something has gone horribly wrong. Open my last attachment. That is the one you are really going to need. To help Shiloah. Do not let anything happen to her." She looked directly into the camera, moving even closer. "Oh, one more thing, my dear sheriff. My name is not Mercy Vaughn. It is Mei Wu." She reached for the camera again and the video ended.

Beck and Charlie stared at each other. "Then who the hell is Mercy Vaughn?" asked Charlie.

A legend, Beck thought. *Like Dal Cho.* He opened the final attachment. "Let's see what's behind door number three."

Beck clicked on the file and read quickly. It was a lot of text and a lot of numbers. When he was done, he rose abruptly out of his chair. "My God. She's playing with fire."

CHAPTER 29

Mercy knew the food was an offering. A transaction, really. She also remembered that in a dangerous situation it was important to eat whenever the opportunity presented itself. Her mother had taught her that. She would need the energy, and the next meal might be a long time coming. It was dark outside, probably the middle of the night, which meant that they had not traveled more than several hundred miles. Teeth chattering and heart pounding, she forced down every bite of the beans and tortilla. It wouldn't be long now. The doors to the small, dimly lit room would open, they would drag her out, and then they would all get down to business. They would want to know the extent to which the American authorities were aware of Jesse Roy's operations, and by extension, the Caborca cartel's, and once she was done spilling those frijoles, they would give her to the Chinese man.

Yes, the Chinese man. She wondered how much he knew. Was he here for Mei Wu, the girl who watched as two MSS agents first beat and then killed her mother four years earlier? Or was he here for Mercy Vaughn, the teenage hacker who had discovered and thwarted the CCP's intrusion and manipulation of the Federal Reserve?

She considered all the facts, then weighed the probabilities in her mind, something her mother would have done. God, how she missed her! She might have died as well that night had she been in that same filthy Philadelphia hotel room, but she was two miles away in a plush apartment watching on the cell phone her mother provided. The attack had come after a year on the run, time her mother used to explain that she was an agent of the Chinese government. She had been in the United States since she was a teenager herself, trained and educated in the best American schools and meticulously positioned in society to marry Michael Wu, a Chinese American and rising star in Silicon Valley. Their adoption of a toddler with strange blond hair and green eyes from China during the final years of that country's "one-child policy" had been an orchestrated intelligence operation, one the compromised Michael had no choice but to acquiesce to.

Mei's adopted parents taught her everything. She was a DNA dream with a genius IQ, a tech prodigy who would one day work for the CIA or NSA, all the while feeding vital intelligence back to her handlers in the MSS.

What went wrong was simple enough. It was democracy. Freedom. Mei's mother, Lucy, had come to see her country's views toward the West as not only false but tremendously naive. When her case officer informed her that Mei was old enough for her real training to begin, Lucy decided to run. Not to the American authorities. She had no desire to go to prison. She created new identities, one for her and one for her daughter. She taught Mei how to become someone else, how to con and steal using the internet. Together, they would disappear into the vibrant digital economy. Whatever happened to Michael, Mei's pretend father, was his problem. They would never find Lucy and her daughter, two orphans from different times, sent to do unspeakable things.

But they did find them. Since the day of her mother's murder, Mei had been on her own, moving every few weeks, pulling all the right levers in e-commerce and the dark web to stay afloat, using bribes, tech favors, and sometimes extortion to convince landlords to provide an empty apartment so she could stay hidden and out of the arms of law enforcement. She took her mother's knowledge of hacking and grew it exponentially. By fourteen, she was selling software exploits on the open market. A year later, she brilliantly detected a plot by the Chinese government to steal a billion dollars from the central bank of the United States and took great pleasure in stealing it from them. And nine months ago, trying to score a windfall at a hacker conference in Las Vegas, she was arrested. Or, more accurately, Mercy Vaughn was arrested.

Now she was back in the arms of her Chinese masters. But did they know who they had? While she gobbled down the tortillas and beans, she wondered. And she worried about Shiloah. Mercy had been drugged and unconscious during the flight, so she wasn't sure if Shiloah was even on the plane. If she wasn't, then there was a good chance Mei would never see her again. But she would be alive.

What little light was in the room was coming from underneath the door, so Mercy set the tin plate down on the wooden floor and walked to it. She tried the knob. It would not turn. That settled a lot in her mind. She would have to wait. Reflexively, she felt for the twenty-sided die in her fingers. It wasn't there. She had left it in the backpack for the sheriff to find. Before Brinley went down and the Chinese man appeared. Everything was a blur after that, the three of them blindfolded, gagged, and bound with electrical ties, the very brief stopover at what she was sure must have been the Double J Ranch, and then the flight here—wherever here was. The thought of that entire ordeal made her shake even more.

She thought about Brinley, the counselor from the Center who connected so well with all the kids, a signal to Mercy that she had a troubled past of her own. Was she dead? Did they kill her? They had beaten her terribly after she shot the two cartel men. Mercy had heard the men yelling, taking out their rage on her, kicking and punching. She hadn't planned on Brinley becoming involved. And now she was probably dead.

And the sheriff, what about him? When she dashed off the email at the cemetery, she had considered him a potential ally. But would he be now, especially if his sister was dead? He would know it had been her fault. All of it. And never come after her.

"I am sorry, Mother," Mercy whispered in Mandarin. "I have failed." As she was wondering if she would ever step foot on American soil again, the door to her room opened.

CHAPTER 30

S ana was late. It had been well over an hour since they had spoken. The office smelled of strong coffee, as Tuffy did everything she could to help them all stay awake. The email from Mercy had also given Beck a new email address she wanted him to monitor round the clock, but he couldn't do anything with that until she contacted him. If he didn't hear from her within the next day, he was free to use it however he saw fit and assume that she was dead. He had been checking the new email account every five minutes for the last hour.

While waiting, and without knowing where precisely in Mexico to go, Beck had little to do but catch up on the latest wildfire situation reports coming from the Forest Service. His deputies were already stretched the length of the county helping deal with the residents of some of the mountain communities, and the Jolly Greens had been sent to the new and growing Patterson Pass fire earlier in the day. There were now only four separate wildfires burning in Lincoln County, but they were big and growing. That left Beck with Tuffy, Arshal, and Sev at the main station, Sally

Goodnight at the southernmost station in Alamo, and the semiretired Sam Hitchens in Caliente, now covering for the Jolly Greens.

As he was plotting those fires on the big map in the main office, that nagging feeling that he was missing something returned.

"Boss?" Tuffy called out from her desk.

Beck turned from the map on the wall. "Yeah?"

"Sana Locke on line two."

Beck motioned for Charlie to follow, and together they went into his office, where he depressed the speaker button before sitting down. "Go ahead, Sana. I've got Charlie here with me."

"Sorry, this took longer than I expected," she said. "I have some news. I'm not sure how much it will help."

A dozen possibilities flashed in Beck's mind, a dozen landing strips in the Sonoran desert. "Fire away."

"The plane you described to me has not entered Mexican airspace in the last six hours."

That was not what he expected to hear. Beck and Charlie stared at each other, dumbfounded. "How can you be sure?"

"Do you trust me, Beck?"

He thought back to what had happened five months earlier. Theirs was a professional relationship that had begun as competitively as two Thoroughbreds at the Kentucky Derby but which had evolved in different, personal ways. "Yes."

"I can be sure because—and this is not for public consumption—our satellites see every aircraft going across our southern border every second of every day. That plane is not in Mexico."

He believed her. The United States of America had the best technology in the world, a good deal of it not publicly acknowledged. "Okay, Sana. I think that's good news. Jesse Roy has some property down near Tucson. We'll see if someone can get eyes on it for us."

"Way ahead of you, sport," said Sana. "Jesse Roy's plane is

nowhere near Tucson, I'm afraid. Unless it's parked inside a hangar, which I suppose is possible. But I don't think it is."

"Why would you say that?" Charlie chimed in.

"Because Marco Cordero has a plane. And his plane took off from Caborca, Mexico, approximately three hours ago, and when it crossed the border into Arizona it was on a northwest heading."

Charlie sat down on the corner of Beck's desk and swallowed some coffee. "Marco Cordero is in the U.S."

Beck asked, "Sana, I don't suppose whatever satellite caught him crossing the border can track him to wherever he lands?"

"I'm afraid not. They're geosynchronous, and we typically only track planes going south. But DEA automatically gets a heads-up whenever the sats pick up a cartel bird coming our way. They'll be out looking for him, and if they know he's connected to Mr. Roy, you'll probably be hearing from them."

Beck rubbed his jaw. "On the one hand, it would be nice if they could find him fast. It's too much of a coincidence for him to be crossing the border and not be coming to see Jesse."

Sana sensed what he was thinking. "On the other hand, if DEA finds him before you do, it might put the girls at risk."

"Exactly," Beck said. "Anything else?"

"Lots more." She let out a long, deep breath, the kind you release when you're going to say something you shouldn't. "You were right about Mercy Vaughn. She's not real, at least in the documentation sense. Everything about her is a smoke screen. It's an extremely well-crafted legend, but it is a legend. The question is, why? Why does a sixteen-year-old need a legend?"

Beck pondered the information for a moment. "I don't know, but her real name may be Mei Wu. That first name is M-E-I."

"What makes you think that?"

"She emailed it to me." He decided not to share the contents of the rest of Mercy's emails, but not because he didn't trust Sana. He did. Mostly. But she was going way out on a limb for him, and he didn't want her falling off.

"Hmm," Sana said. "Okay, I'll check on that. Doesn't ring any bells."

Beck switched gears. "What about the Federal Reserve hack?"

"That part is true. She did it. It was absolute genius. But it's not why she landed in your backyard."

"Huh? What do you mean?"

"We actually didn't know who the hacker was. Didn't have a clue apparently. That's how well she covered her tracks. But she tried to sell a zero day for a Defense Department networking system while she was at a hacker conference in Vegas last year, and she confessed to the fed hack in exchange for leading them to the money and what has amounted to juvenile detention until she turns eighteen."

Beck shifted in his chair. "And where was the money?"

Sana laughed. "This is the kicker. She actually only stole about eighty million. The Federal Reserve shut down the money transfers at that point. And that eighty million she was anonymously parceling out to eleven separate charitable organizations that support the Uyghurs in China through advocacy projects and grassroots initiatives. She didn't keep a dime of it." Beck didn't respond. "I can hear your thoughts," Sana said. "And you're thinking what I'm thinking."

"Yeah. Why would a girl who was so careful to not get busted for stealing that much money be so careless as to get arrested, let alone show up, at a hacker conference?"

"Agreed," Sana said. "It makes no sense. And when things like this make no sense, there's usually a good, really dark reason for it, if you take my meaning."

He did. He had seen it a dozen times in his years in the Army. "What about this Dal Cho guy?"

"Just sent you a photo. Should be in your inbox. Let me know if this is the same person."

Beck opened the email and looked at the passport belonging to Dal Cho of South Korea. "That's him."

"Not good," Sana said. "And by that I mean we have nothing on him. As far as we're concerned, this guy is from South Korea and has been working as a political consultant for several years. UC Berkeley, degree in economics, goes home to visit family a couple times a year. Unmarried. Has worked on several political campaigns, all very left-leaning. But that could be almost anyone in California. If he's Chinese, he's been very careful."

"He's Chinese, Sana. I'm sure of it. Our girl Mercy—or Mei—is a Chinese Uyghur. Can't be a coincidence."

"I'm not doubting you, Beck. A few years ago, I attended a briefing on China's approach to intelligence gathering. The guy who gave it said if a beach was an espionage target, the Russians would send in a sub, frogmen would steal ashore in the dark of night and with great secrecy collect several buckets of sand and take them back to Moscow. The Americans would target the beach with satellites and produce reams of data. But the Chinese would send in a thousand tourists, each assigned to collect a single grain of sand. When they returned, they would be asked to shake out their towels. And they would end up knowing more about that beach than anyone else." She took a breath. "The question is, what sand is Cho collecting?"

"Mei Wu," Beck replied. "She's the sand. They need her to break into something. They need a zero day."

"Okay, we'll do a deeper dive. I'll alert our FBI partners." Sana paused a moment before adding, "Be careful, Beck. Everything you've described scares the hell out of me. Brinley is safe. Maybe it's time to take a step back."

Beck sat them all down in the main office—Charlie, Tuffy, Sev, and Arshal—while he stood in front of the big fire map. "A little good news, a lot of bad," he said. "Jesse Roy's plane is not in Mexico. That's the good news. The bad news starts with we don't know where else it could have gone. We have some intel from our old friend Sana Locke that Jesse's business partner in Mexico, Marco Cordero, is now in the U.S. We don't know where." He winced as hot pain shot into his side, his discomfort visible to everyone. Sev shoved a rolling chair at him with his foot, and Beck leaned on the backrest with both hands. "More bad news, potentially at least. You guys were right about Mercy Vaughn. It's a fake identity. She claims her real name is Mei Wu, but that's all we have. She's from China, and I'm equally certain that the guy Charlie and I saw out at Rachel today, the guy Brinley saw in Jesse Roy's wine cellar, is also Chinese. So . . . what's the link there? There has to be one." He pointed to Sev. "I forwarded you some info on him. Call every source we have from the old days. Maybe Army intelligence knows who Dal Cho really is. The rest of us need to determine where Jesse's plane might have flown and where this meeting between him and Cordero is going to take place."

Tuffy took the lead, holding up a manila folder. "We know Jesse owns property outside of Tucson and in Newport Beach and Vail."

"Tucson is out," said Charlie. "His plane is not on the ground there."

"Right," Beck said. "But it is on the ground somewhere. Has to be by now. Sev, what's the max fuel range of his plane?"

Sev answered almost immediately. "About 1,400 miles. At typical cruising speed, he's now out of gas. Or he's refueled somewhere."

Tuffy threw a plastic cup at him. "Is there anything you *don't* know?"

That's when Beck realized what he had been missing. "Hold on. Jesse knew we were coming. I texted him, warning him about hurting the girls, and that the military was closing the airspace. That was a lie but he didn't know it. He had every reason to believe that the feds would be looking for Mercy and his plane."

Tuffy shook her head. "So?"

Beck turned and looked at the big map of the county on the wall, the one with wildfire pins in it. "Well, if you were sure everybody and their brother was looking for this girl, especially from the air, you'd know that your plane might be spotted. Might even be forced down by the military. Would you risk a long flight somewhere?"

Charlie got out of her chair and walked toward the map. "Not unless I was sure you were bluffing, and he couldn't have been sure. I wouldn't go to Newport or Vail either. Too much chance of being seen moving my hostages at my landing site. I'd go somewhere remote."

Arshal removed his big straw hat and set it on the desk. "Logic isn't always my strong suit, folks, but if you were Jesse Roy and you took this girl up in a plane, the girl who had just turned your world upside down, why wouldn't you boot her out over some wilderness area or a lake somewhere? You drop a body from ten thousand feet, there isn't going to be much left to pick up, if it's ever found."

Beck turned to face the group. "Because she's not just any girl." He looked at Charlie. "That's why Marco Cordero is coming. It's also why Dal Cho wants her." He thought about Mercy's final email, the key she had left him. He turned around, gazing at the map again. "Jesse's got a hideout here in Lincoln County. And we have to find it. Sev, forget Dal Cho for a minute. Get me every satellite map you can find. We're looking for anything that can be used as an airfield."

Charlie sidled up next to him, lowering her voice. "Sana said Cordero was on a northwest heading. What makes you think it's in Lincoln County?"

He turned so that everyone could hear. "I was looking at some maps of Mexico earlier, thinking that's where we were going. Cordero is from Caborca in Sonora. A heading northwest of Caborca takes you right to Nevada." Beck looked back at the map, seeing the topography in his mind. "He's coming here."

CHAPTER 31

The door opened. Two men Mercy had not seen before entered. They made no effort to drag her through the hacienda. They both had guns, and that was enough. She was led down a tiled hallway, somewhat surprised at the numerous cracks in the flooring, past a spiral staircase and through a large, ranch-style kitchen where she noted food scraps on plates on the counter by the immense copper sink and a number of used coffee mugs. The appliances looked old, not what she expected to see in the kitchen of the head of the Caborca cartel. They kept moving through a dining room, dimly lit and questionably decorated, leaving Mercy unimpressed. Large picture windows spanned the home's great room, accenting the high ceilings and allowing for maximum light but again the furniture was far from magnificent, with uncomfortable-looking chairs and a rust-colored leather couch that had seen better days, all placed over a rectangular area rug in the center of the dark wood flooring. The fireplace was blackened and much used, its tired bricks shaped like a ceramic kiln.

The Chinese man sat on the couch, tall and slender, and smiling politely. To his left was the man Shiloah had described as her father's friend from Mexico, the man named César. Across from both, in one of the two leather chairs, sat a third man. Physically, he resembled the old house, unassuming and badly in need of repair. He was fifty-three, diabetic due to heavy drinking and a diet rich in fat, and had survived three separate gunshots which left him with a limp and a shoulder that ached whenever he turned on that side in his sleep or became agitated. He was rubbing that shoulder now.

Mercy could see the amazement on Marco Cordero's face. He had been expecting someone older, someone who had developed her technical chops at college with work experience at Google or Apple. Not some girl who looked like she was in high school.

Cordero watched as Mercy was directed to a chair opposite him and then turned to the man called Cho. "I don't understand. I thought we were dealing with—"

"Don't be fooled," Cho said. "She's very good. Her skills are remarkable."

That confirmed a lot for Mercy. If Cho was aware of her skills, he had knowledge of her past. Once she was seated, Cordero directed one of his men to pour her some water. "Do you know who I am?" he asked her.

She raised the glass to her mouth. "I recognize your face. You are Marco Antonio Cordero."

Cordero's eyebrows rose, the skinfolds in his forehead more pronounced now. There weren't many photos of him in existence. He had made sure of that. "I wish I could say it is a pleasure to meet you, Miss Vaughn, but that is hardly the case. May I call you Mercy?"

Mercy drank and nodded all in the same motion.

"Such an interesting name, Mercy. I hope it speaks to your nature and that we can dispense with this unpleasant business quickly."

Mercy set the glass of water down on the side table. "Well, that depends on what you are offering, I guess."

She was dirty and exhausted, the best time to get information from a prisoner, when the fight was low and the fear was high, but this had not been the response Cordero had expected. "I'm sorry?"

"You want to know what I know, and how I know it. You want to know what the U.S. authorities know about Shiloah's father and, by extension, you. But what you are really curious about is if I am the one who has your money. As for me, I have most of the federal government trying to track me down and could use a place to lay low, at least for a while. Could I possibly get a glass of orange juice, please? Apple will do if you do not have orange."

Cho, his face impatiently red, began to rise from the couch. César put an arm on his, urging him to take his seat again. Cordero motioned to one of his men to get the insolent girl a juice. "I have to tell you, I am not used to having someone in my presence, someone I could kill without a second thought, attempt to negotiate with me from such a point of weakness."

Mercy laughed, the effort requiring every ounce of courage she had left. "Why would you assume I am at a disadvantage, sir, considering what I know and what I have? Has it not dawned on you that I have, through Jesse Roy's stupidity and abhorrent lack of cybersecurity, snaked my way into every corner of your organization? Your security is not much better than his, by the way. Your firewall is poorly configured and the lack of intrusion prevention systems made it a snap to get in. I have records of transactions, shipments, bank accounts. I have everything. I have access to your offshore money, which, as you know, has disappeared." Cordero's servant walked back in the room with a glass of orange juice, and Mercy took a long drink. "Now you can kill me and Shiloah, I suppose, but that will not get you your money back. So, no, I do not consider myself to be negotiating from a point of weakness. That is really good juice, by the way. Fresh-squeezed. We do not get fresh-squeezed in the Youth Center, as you can imagine. Thank you."

Cordero's pupils constricted to pinpoints. He turned to Cho. "Could this be true? Could she do all of this?"

Cho looked at Mercy in admiration. "It could be. She is capable of doing these things. You should have your people delete any incriminating information at once. As for the part about the Americans trying to find her, I can vouch for that. My government has been monitoring their communications, and the authorities have been directed to stop her at all costs."

Cordero slowly rose from his chair. He was not a man who made rash decisions. He had not risen to the top of the Caborca cartel by acting irrationally. But at this moment, he wanted to strike this little bitch, to stomp her face with his $12,000 Lucchese alligator boots, to watch her bleed. But if she had his money, she was in control. For the first time in his adult life, Marco Antonio Cordero felt paralyzed.

Mercy shifted in her chair. "I know what you are thinking. You are angry, and that is understandable. But this is a simple business transaction, really. You will release and transport my friend and me to the United States. California would be nice, Arizona will do in a pinch. Once on American soil, I will transfer your funds back to you. And I will not share any of the information I have with the authorities or with your liege lord, Mr. Salazar."

Cordero's fingers curled tightly around the armrests of his chair as he listened in fascination and horror. She thought she was in Mexico, which might work to his advantage. But could she actually know how much money he had been skimming from Salazar? Without a word, he stomped out of the big room, César behind him.

Mercy watched them go and then turned to Cho. "What do you think? Too much?"

Cho rose and walked slowly across the room to a large bay window where he drew the shades to the side and looked out over the magnificent sun-drenched valley. "You're very impressed with yourself, Mercy." He paused. "Or should I call you Mei?"

She didn't respond. She was too busy shaking and she needed to get that under control before the Chinese MSS agent turned around. She had just blackmailed one of the most dangerous men in Mexico, and the man across the room knew who she really was.

Cho loved the light filtering through the trees. He hadn't anticipated finding this level of beauty in the Nevada desert. "My compliments. You anticipated this. You found the leverage you believed you might need. I'm guessing you inherited your impudence from that whore we placed you with."

Mercy didn't take the bait, focusing on her breathing. "I do not think we have been properly introduced. You are?"

Cho turned. "I'm the person who's been looking for you for four years. I made a deal for you. You're coming with me. You're coming home. But first you'll do something for me."

Mercy reached down and pinched the tender flesh under her arm until the pain made her want to scream but forced her to focus. "Well, I suppose we will see about that."

They began a staring contest that lasted a full minute before Cordero and César reentered the room. Behind them, two men were dragging Shiloah Roy.

Brinley wandered into the main station a little after 9 P.M., insisting she was fine and that Hadji Bishara had released her. Her face was still swollen and she was walking with a bend to her right side, so Beck knew she was still hurting. As he was reaching for his phone to call Hadji, it rang.

"She is gone!" Hadji yelled into the phone. He began rambling in Turkish, and Beck held the phone away from his ear so Brin could hear.

"She's here, Hadji," he said, when the doctor finally took a breath. He listened for another minute while Brin took her brother's winter Duluth jacket off the hook next to the door and pulled it on. It swallowed her tiny frame. She sat down in a chair opposite the desk, put her feet up, and was asleep before Bishara finished his rant.

Beck let her sleep and spent the next few hours poring over Google Earth and other satellite maps of the county. Sometime after midnight, he popped four more Advil to help with the pain in his head and back. He and Sev had studied every inch of terrain on every map and were certain that Jesse Roy did not have another airfield in Lincoln County. Strike one.

The email account Mercy had directed him to monitor still showed nothing in the inbox, which either meant that she was dead or that she had not yet achieved the upper hand over Cordero. Emptying the man's bank account was the riskiest of moves, and as he twirled her Dungeons and Dragons die between his fingers, he feared it had been too big a gamble. A man like Cordero might simply strip the skin from her body or stick her hand in a vat of acid to get her to return his drug loot. Strike two.

Beck was dead on his feet, having had about two hours' sleep in the last forty-eight, and out of pure survival instinct, his eyes finally closed around 6 A.M. He was out for all of five minutes before the phone rang.

"Beck," he said, lifting the receiver without opening his eyes.

"Beck, it's Esther Ellingboe." Her voice streamed into his ear on a soundwave of airplane propellers. "Didn't expect you in so early. Was going to leave you a voicemail."

Here we go, Beck thought, another wildfire somewhere. It was the last thing he wanted to hear from the BLM's northern district manager. He opened his eyes and saw that Brinley was lying on the floor now, sleeping like a baby. "How's it going up there, Esther?"

"Well, don't you know, that's what I'm calling about." Esther was originally from West Texas and still had the idiom and accent to prove it. "The Patterson Pass fire is spreading north faster than syphilis through a squad of Catholic high school cheerleaders. The wind kicked up during the night, and it's licked its way along into those mountains. Given all the other fires we've got, I expect it'll be six thousand acres before I even have the planes and hotshots to send in. Gonna be a long day."

Beck sat up and rubbed his eyes with his thumb and forefinger. "Okay, Esther. How can we help?"

"Oh, I guess the Green brothers are up there already assisting with road closures, and I don't know of anybody we'd have to evacuate, given how remote it is. But you might get someone out to that ranch in Grass Valley and put them on alert. If that fire comes down those hills, it could be on them in a hurry."

Beck took a sip of air from his now empty coffee mug and shook his head. "Not necessary. The couple that own it have been trying to sell it for a couple of years. They live in Arizona now, so there's nobody there."

There was a pause on the line. "Hmm," Esther said. "Well, if you're sure, okay, but they left two airplanes behind. When did they put in that airstrip anyhow?"

Beck shot up straight in his chair. "What did you say?"

"I flew over the place a half hour ago, and I'm telling you

there's two planes on the ground west of the main house. I don't remember those people even being pilots."

Stan and Sue Morrow were not pilots. They had operated the ranch for twenty years until age and a shortage of heirs forced them to retreat to Prescott, Arizona. And there had never been any semblance of an airstrip on the 41,000-acre ranch. "Esther, you didn't happen to take any pictures?"

"Texting you now," she answered.

Beck's cell pinged. He picked it up off his desk and expanded the photo with two fingers. Esther had probably taken the shot from a mile up at least, but what Beck saw was unmistakable. There were two planes on the ground at the end of a dirt airstrip that had never been there, and one of them looked like it could be Jesse Roy's.

"Esther," he said. "I need you to listen to me very carefully because I'm going to need your help."

CHAPTER 32

Shiloah was blindfolded when they brought her in, kicking and screaming the whole way. Finally, one of the men had had enough and slapped her so hard she fell to the ground and didn't move for several moments. She began crying and shaking uncontrollably. Though the fear Mercy felt was as palpable as a hand reaching into her chest and grabbing her heart, she knew without looking that Cordero was watching her closely, looking for any sign of weakness, any indication of submission.

Cordero didn't speak. He waited as the prospect of what would happen to Shiloah sank into Mercy's brain. He had done this many times to many different people. An avid student of human psychology, the cartel boss understood the lizard brain in people was where instinct overrode logic. Fight, flight, fear, all of it more powerful than a person's ability to think critically in a time of crisis. When a loved one is threatened, people break quickly. That threat was much more effective than torture. He waited and watched the young hacker's face as Jesse Roy's daughter wept and cried out, "Mercy!"

Nothing. Mercy's eyes turned to him. No hint of emotion.

Only calm. "I wonder," he said, "is she begging for mercy or calling your name?"

"I warn you, sir. I will—"

"Rape the girl," he commanded.

Both men reached for Shiloah's clothes. And that was all it took. Mercy's eyes narrowed to slits, her words as calm as a person reciting a grocery list. "You have ten seconds, Mr. Cordero."

Purely in admiration of Mercy's self-control, Cordero signaled his men to wait. He glanced at Cho standing by the window and looking out into the desert, refusing to see what must be done. "And what do you think happens then, my dear?"

Mercy curled the bottom of the beautiful white top Shiloah had given her, now dirty and sweat-stained, around her fingers. "My deal will be off the table. You will never see a penny of the twenty-three point seven million dollars I have taken from you. Your boss, Mr. Salazar, will receive an email already queued in my outbox by noon Pacific time today. That email will contain details of how you have skimmed more than four million dollars from him over the last three years alone." She paused a moment, taking a breath. "You can torture us, rape us, and kill us, but you will be on the run for the rest of your sad, all too short, literally bankrupt life."

Cordero stood frozen. He knew to the penny how much he had managed to conceal from Salazar, and Mercy's figure was accurate.

Mercy continued. "I am under no illusions, Mr. Cordero. I understand how awful the next minutes or hours might be for us. But you can only kill us once. It will eventually be over. We will be dead, and so will you." She leaned forward. "Man has a thousand plans, Heaven but one. I imagine the afterlife will be much nicer for us than it will be for you."

Cho stood by helplessly. He had no feelings one way or the other about the rancher's daughter, but he could not allow Cordero to kill Mei Wu. She was an asset of the People's Republic of China, and Cho's own future hinged on getting her home.

Mercy's eyes moved to Shiloah, writhing on the ground against her captors. "Decide, Mr. Cordero. Your time is up."

"Where is my money?" Cordero demanded, his voice thundering off the walls.

"Safe," Mercy answered. "Simply in another account with new credentials, transferred, I might add, over a three-day period which you and your people obviously slept through." Mercy ran her fingers through her dirty hair, thought about demanding a shower. "I guess nobody was minding the store."

Cordero paced while his men stood over Shiloah ready to violate her on his command. "If I agree, you will transfer the money back."

"No, silly," Mercy said, shaking her head. "International wire transfers, especially of this size, take a number of days, and I do not think you want to wait that long. Do you? No, I will simply give you the credentials to the new account so that you can access it. The bank will be new, but the security is much better."

Cordero pulled at his thick mustache. "Release her," he told his men. "Take her out, get her some food and water."

As Shiloah was lifted to her feet, Mercy fought back her emotions one last time. "It will be okay, Shy. I will be with you shortly."

When she was gone and the doors closed again, Cordero approached Mercy, pulling up a chair directly in front of her. "You are a good negotiator. I know because I am a good negotiator. I will allow your friend to leave. I cannot offer you the same deal, I'm afraid. You will have to do something for Mr. Cho here. I am not part of that. When that is done, you will work for me until my cybersecurity is what it should be. That keeps you away from the American authorities. If that isn't acceptable, then I guess you and the other girl will die, and I will die sometime later, as you say."

She could see he was telling the truth. His body language confirmed it. "You would kill the daughter of your business partner?"

Cordero shrugged. "Why not? I killed his wife. Does that surprise you?"

Mercy offered a slight shake of her head. "Not in the slightest. Where is Shiloah's father, by the way?"

"Who cares? Are my terms acceptable?"

Shiloah would live. She would have some bad dreams, need some counseling perhaps, but she would live. That was the only thing that mattered. Mercy focused on her breathing again, commanded her pulse to slow in the way her mother had taught her. She stood, stretched her arms high into the air, arched her back and yawned. "So, how shall we do this?"

CHAPTER 33

Dal Cho walked out of the sprawling ranch house into the late-morning sun. The high desert air already felt as warm as a hot July in his own Gobi. Even the terrain here, with its rocky hillsides, reminded him of the survival training he had endured in the People's Liberation Army. He liked places where a man had to depend on his instincts and fitness to survive.

As he went about his series of morning stretches, he took note of Cordero's men. The pilot tinkered with his plane, and the one they called Rico, who survived the gunfight with the sheriff's sister, walked a continuous circle around the house. Two other men Cordero had brought along were stationed at the big barn with the blue roof, which Cho surmised was where they were holding Jesse Roy. He had no illusions about what would eventually happen to the man. It was clear that his only remaining value had been flying them here, and his attempt to take off with his daughter immediately after landing was dealt with quickly and harshly.

That left Nando and César inside with Cordero, each with his own handgun. Rico and the two men at the barn all carried automatic rifles. Cho casually picked up a pair of field glasses from the railing of the wooden deck behind him and scanned the horizon in all directions, pausing only long enough over each man to assess his ability to kill.

As he looked out into the cactus and other desert shrubs that dotted the landscape, Cho saw some dust rising above the dirt road to the southwest, one of the two points of access to the valley from the south. Beneath all the dust was a green SUV. Cho brightened. His team. They had driven all night from San Francisco. Beijing had been thrilled by the news that Mercy Vaughn was actually Mei Wu and had updated Cho's marching orders. He watched his team through the binoculars for a minute, slowing and bouncing over the rocks in the road. At their current speed, it would be another half hour before they arrived. High noon, as they said in the movies.

Cho panned to the southeast and the plume of smoke coming from the hills. When he adjusted the focus, he could see the flames from the fire that had begun the previous afternoon, what the government was calling the Patterson Pass fire. It was expected to grow over the next several days, and while he gauged its current distance from the ranch to be about five miles, Cho was sure it could pick up speed in a hurry. An approaching fire would mean people and prying eyes. Thankfully, he expected to have completed his mission long before it had a chance of coming down into the valley.

He walked back into the main house, where Marco Cordero and Mei were discussing what the local police knew about Jesse Roy's gunrunning operation, as well as how Cordero's drugs moved into and out of the county. She appeared to hold nothing back, and Cordero was equal parts impressed and infuriated. With that done, they began negotiating the details of their bargain. The smug hacker, showered and fed now, sat at one end of the long dining table with her unopened laptop computer in front of her. Cordero, at the other end of the table, was eating a plate of eggs and talking with his mouth full.

"I'm afraid that is not possible," he told her.

"But you have a pilot. He can fly her back across the border. Or her father can fly her."

Cordero shook his head and dabbed at the corners of his mouth with a beautiful, multicolored napkin. "There's no need. We're still in the U.S."

Cordero turned his attention to Cho, who had taken a seat on a bar stool nearby. "Your people?"

Cho nodded. "On their way in. Twenty minutes or so now."

Mercy pushed back from the table. "Remember, I am not doing anything for him or you until Shiloah is free." She motioned to her laptop. "May I verify our location?"

Cordero took another bite. "Please."

Mercy connected to the home's network, brought up Google Maps, and instantly saw where they were. She was elated. "We are still in Nevada?"

"Evidently," Cordero said, holding up a finger. "I was here a few days ago for Shiloah's birthday. Thank you for the fireworks, by the way."

Mercy laughed. "My pleasure. Is there a horse on the property?"

"Several, in the barn."

"Then I propose the following: You will give my friend some water and food, enough for two days, and put her on a horse." She looked down at her screen. "We appear to be about . . . thirty miles from the nearest town. Shiloah will head into the desert away from any road so that your people cannot follow, and you will know she will not get anywhere fast enough to contact any- one. After she has been gone for one hour, I will provide you access to the new account."

Cordero set his fork down and folded his hands in front of him. "And how will you do that?"

"I have an associate in Europe. I send her an email and she sends the new account information and new credentials."

"Why can't you do it?"

Mercy frowned. "Because I am not stupid. I do not have it. Only my associate can access the account where your money currently resides."

Cordero checked his wristwatch. "My time here must be short, you understand? Shiloah Roy gets a thirty-minute head start." The head of the Caborcan cartel turned to Cho. "How long for her to do what you need?"

Cho got off his bar stool. "Difficult to say. A few hours perhaps."

"I don't like being blackmailed," Cordero said, rising from his chair.

The teenager leaned back and stretched into a big yawn. "Please, Marco, we have been through this. You are losing time."

"Thirty minutes," he said, after staring into her green eyes for several seconds. "That's all she gets."

"That will have to do, I suppose," answered Mercy.

He walked over to Cho and spoke softly. "You helped us get the girl, and for that I owe you. But I am pressed for time. The minute your people get here, you start work."

Beck hadn't been to the Lincoln County airport since a cold snowy night in February, and pulling through the single wire-mesh gate, his mind wandered back. Brinley and Pop had almost lost their lives, and Beck's own life had been turned on its head. On the sleek government Gulfstream jet, he'd once again learned the hard way that things are often not what they seem. The airfield itself was tiny, with a single runway, a few outbuildings, and a pilot's lounge, more than enough for the occasional civilian pilot who liked to fly on the weekend. But being this close to the top-secret Nevada Test and Training Range, the most frequent customer was actually the United States government, and those stopovers were all classified.

Esther Ellingboe, a short, wiry fifty-year-old with dirty blond hair, was waiting outside the DHC-6 Twin Otter aircraft operated by the Bureau of Land Management. The Otter looked like a flying school bus with its mostly yellow body and three black stripes running from nose to tail. Parking behind the plane, Beck saw Sev Velasco and Brinley already loading their gear.

"You know, I could get in a crapload of trouble for this," Esther said, when Beck got out of the truck. "But that's not anything new. This little scheme of yours have any chance?"

They shook hands, and Beck felt the calluses on her fingers. "I'm out of time, and this is what I came up with."

The district chief let out a laugh. "Well, it's original, I'll give you that. See you onboard."

He wandered over to Brinley. The swelling on her face had receded some, but her bruises were still as red as the gooseberries that grew in the higher elevations. "You good?"

She hauled a big pack over her small shoulder. "Pretty sore, but I expect I'll manage." She looked at him, scraped up, in obvious discomfort, feeling as bad or worse than she did. "I aim to misbehave."

Beck laughed. It was their favorite line from their favorite movie, *Serenity*. He recited his personal favorite: "My grandma always told me: if you can't do something smart, do something right." Their hands came together in a time-honored tradition: "Slap, slap, slap, pound, up, down, snap."

The Otter could normally carry eight to ten smoke jumpers

and their gear. In this case, there would be only three. Beck and
Sev each had more than fifty jumps from their days in the Army,
and Beck had taken Brinley a number of times since he retired. She
was a daredevil anyway, jumped every chance she got, and already
exhibited great technique. Inside the plane, they transferred their
gear to two of the fireboxes that normally follow the smoke jumpers after they dropped. What usually contained saws, axes, water,
and food now held a number of munitions, including flashbang
grenades, and a Barrett M82 .50 caliber rifle designed to destroy
sensitive enemy equipment.

"You bring the Axe?" Beck asked Sev. It wasn't a fire axe he
wanted. The Henry .410 Axe was a short-barreled lever-action
firearm that resembled something from a western movie. It had a
lot less firepower than a twelve or twenty gauge, but it was small
and concealable and good in tight corners, and it was Beck's personal favorite.

Sev rolled his eyes. "Yes, but I wish you would use a proper
shotgun."

"I keep telling him," Brinley said with a laugh, "but you know
what they say about a boy and his toys."

Beck looked into the last firebox. It contained a Winchester
.308, the standard sniper rifle for police, and a bunch of spare
magazines. Lastly, there were three sets of NVGs, the night vision
goggles that might even the odds a tad should this thing extend
beyond sunset.

Esther looked down into the boxes. "Must be some pretty bad
dudes over at that ranch."

Beck smiled. "Can you suit us up?"

"Sure." Esther introduced them to Dirk, a thirtyish man almost
six and a half feet tall with thick red hair that extended his height
by at least another four inches. He looked like he could carry a

one-hundred-and-twenty-pound pack on his back all day, and he explained each piece of the tool kit in detail. The jumpsuit itself was made out of Kevlar to be puncture resistant but also fairly lightweight, with a high collar to protect the neck if the jumper was unlucky enough to fall through the trees. It had an internal hard shell and a number of large pockets to hold radios and other gear. "You're on channel seven," Dirk said, handing them each a radio. "If you tune it to anything else, you're going to be interfering with people fighting actual fires, so please don't do that. We've got people moving into the pass now, so depending on where you drop, you might run into them."

Beck looked at Esther with some concern. She shook her head. "We haven't advertised this yet, per your request. But once you're on the ground, you're my problem, so get to where you're going as fast as you can and away from that fire."

"We'll stay out of your way."

They each got a ski helmet with a metal face mask. Dirk grabbed the one over Beck's face. "This grille will keep tree branches out of your face while you're trying to land. Once you're on the ground, you can strip it off like this."

Esther had requested their shoe sizes up front, and Dirk handed them each a pair of boots. They were heavy-duty and not as light as Beck would have preferred, but they needed to look the part. Dirk helped them on with their backpacks. "You've got some additional tools in these like first aid, gloves, water, and we're sending down an actual firebox with you along with those guns. If you get anywhere close to that fire, they'll come in handy, so keep them close."

They strapped on some knee pads and gloves, and then it was time for the parachutes, two of them, a main and an emergency. "We'll probably drop you about twenty-five-hundred feet above the ground," Dirk said. "The main chute opens immediately. If there's a problem, the reserve will open automatically when your AAD indicates the time is right."

"Got it," Beck said. The AAD was the Automatic Activation Device mounted on the reserve chute that determined vertical speed and altitude by measuring barometric pressure. It was configured to activate if vertical speed and altitude criteria were met.

"I hope so," said the big smoke jumper. "Because if you fuck up, you die."

Esther patted her man on the back. "Thanks, Dirk." She looked at Beck and his team. "Listen, I've finally got some hotshots and tankers in the area, so we'll do our best to keep that fire from coming your way. If you need us, you switch to channel three on the radio. You guys ready?" They all gave the thumbs-up and took seats on the green bench seats that lined both sides of the plane. "Then let's go drop you into a fire."

A minute later, Beck felt the propellers rotate to full speed and the plane turn onto the runway, but then it stopped and sat motionless. Beck turned toward Ellingboe, who was in the front seat next to the pilot. "What's the problem?" he yelled. "We need to get moving." He watched her peel off the large, noise-canceling headset, unbuckle her lift-cover seat belt, and swivel out of her chair.

She motioned with her thumb toward the front window. "Any idea who this might be?"

Beck leaned forward and peeked around her. In front of the plane a Black Hawk helicopter had set down. *Damn.* "Yep, I think I do."

A minute later, Special Agent Maddox boarded the Twin Otter and showed Esther Ellingboe his credentials. "We're on our way to a fire, Maddox," Beck said. "Aren't you supposed to be out looking for Mercy Vaughn?"

Maddox gave Beck and the others a hard look, paying special attention to their jumpsuits and to Brinley's facial bruises. "Since when do you fight wildfires, Sheriff?"

"Since global warming started turning fire seasons into year-long events. And since in my county, we help where we can. My deputies and I are also volunteer firefighters. Now what the hell can we do for you? And make it fast because we're leaving in one minute."

Maddox eyed the contents of the plane suspiciously. The fire-boxes were sealed now, so he couldn't see what was inside them, and Beck wondered how far the OSI man was going to push. "Mercy Vaughn communicated with you the night Jesse Roy's bull was killed."

Beck did his best to appear skeptical.

"Zero Day Mei?"

"Have you been reading my emails, Agent Maddox? 'Cause without a warrant, that's a felony."

"So is harboring a fugitive and impeding a federal investigation."

Beck unbuckled his seat belt and stood up. "You think I'm harboring her? Are you telling me she's not in Mexico now?"

Maddox stared into Beck's eyes, trying to get a read. "We don't think she's in Mexico," he said above the prop noise. "We think she's here somewhere."

Beck looked around. "You mean like here on the plane? Like we're hiding her?"

Maddox cocked an eyebrow. "Where is your state trooper friend, Sheriff? Detective Blue Horse, is it?"

"On her way home, I imagine," Beck said with a shrug.

Ellingboe stepped up to Maddox's ear. "Hey, jackhole. If you want to pitch in, I've got a spare suit for you. Otherwise, get the fuck off my plane."

Maddox kept his gaze on Beck. Then Dirk got out of his seat, and that was all it took. Maddox exited the plane and the helicopter lifted off seconds later. The Twin Otter sped down the runway and climbed.

"What do you think?" Brinley asked.

Beck sat down and gazed out the window, watching the helicopter in the distance. "I think the guy is like a bad penny and that he's going to keep turning up."

CHAPTER 34

Cho's team constructed the data network like two spiders joining their intricate webs. Mercy watched with concern as the Chinese agents unpacked boxes, especially noting the satellite receivers, a number of large monitors, routers and switches, extension cords, laptops hooked to boards with LAN Turtles, a number of USB drives that Mercy recognized as keyloggers, and a suitcase that when opened revealed a large screen and keyboard with wires hooked to a number of drives. She guessed it was a mobile duplicator of some sort, which made her wonder what the intelligence operatives would require her to do and how soon that was going to happen. As she listened to Cordero bark orders to his men to saddle a horse for Shiloah, Mercy knew she needed to play for time.

As they hooked everything up and powered it on, she studied the new arrivals. The woman was a beanstalk, tall, thin, and fit. The male was considerably shorter than Cho and thicker too, with the intense eyes of a rat looking for meat. Cho spoke briefly to the female and walked her over to Mercy, where they sat down facing her.

"Mei," he said, "like it or not, you are one of us. You were brought to America for one purpose, to serve the People's Republic. You were to be taught about America and its systems so that you would eventually be in a position of great responsibility within its government. You were to be trained as we all were, to gather and pass along intelligence to the Party. By all accounts, your skills have exceeded our wildest expectations. We have seen what you have done with the military drones. We searched unsuccessfully for you for years, a testament to how capable and fearless you are, and we have only the highest respect for you. Your mother's crimes are not yours. But it is time now for you to assume your rightful responsibilities. My associate here is going to explain what we need from you. You may call her Daiyu."

Daiyu's voice was smaller than she was, soft and unthreatening, and her English was flawless, having been perfected at San Jose State. "We need you to get us into Watcher."

Mercy stared back blankly. Watcher was the ultrasecure encrypted network the American government had recently adopted and mandated for all intelligence-gathering and military agencies. "I am sorry. What is Watcher?"

Daiyu's eyes shifted to Cho, who blinked his approval. She raised her left hand and adjusted the large ring on her middle finger so that the bulk of the setting was facing outward. Her response was a backhand perfected over countless hours of table tennis. It connected with Mercy's face, the force of the blow propelling her out of her chair and onto the floor, Daiyu's ring tearing a diagonal gash across her cheek. "We are not fools," she said with great calm. "You tried to sell an exploit into the program last year. But you were careless and the FBI arrested you."

Mercy put a hand to her face and felt the blood. She stared up at the young Chinese agent with fear and anger. "It was a scam. I needed the money. I heard there were buyers, but I did not actually have the exploit."

Daiyu's long leg shot out, her foot catching Mercy square in the solar plexus and causing the air to explode from her chest. "You already had eighty-one million in U.S. currency that we had managed to have transferred to the Philippines. I don't think you needed the money. The Americans made you show them how the exploit worked, so that they could close that hole in Watcher, correct?"

She thought about lying again but then envisioned what else Daiyu might do to her. Instead, coughing and gasping for air, she said, "Correct."

"But you didn't show them everything, did you, Mei?"

They wanted her to create a backdoor. Mercy wasn't surprised the Chinese hadn't figured out how to crack Watcher. Their thinking was one-dimensional and lacked creativity. "You were careless," she told Daiyu. "With the Federal Reserve exploit, I mean."

Daiyu coiled her foot for another cobralike strike, but Mercy held up a hand, a white flag. "Do not worry, the Americans have no idea it was you behind the theft. They believe it was North Korea, and I did not disabuse them of that notion."

Cho reached down and clamped on to her bicep, lifting her to her seat in the rolling chair. "And we'll talk about where that money is later." He handed her a handkerchief from his pocket. "Your face is bleeding."

She pressed the cloth into the gash on her cheek, and it stung. "And after I am done helping you get into Watcher?"

Cho rose from his chair. The impudent teenager had caused him many sleepless nights and raised concerns within the MSS over his inability to locate her after terminating her traitorous adopted mother. He smiled. "Then you come home. Meet your real family. Do some real good in this world."

Mercy scoffed. "My family are Uyghurs. You expect me to believe you are going to throw me a party?"

Cho squatted down near her. It would have been perfect, he thought. This little blond, American-looking girl could have done so much good here. But there was a reason so many in China referred to her kind as the "two-faced people." Uyghurs could not be trusted, could not be loyal. The sooner his country cleansed itself of this dirty ethnic minority, the better. "You will come. You will work."

"I think Mr. Cordero has other plans for me."

Cho shrugged. "Let me worry about that." With that, he left the room. Daiyu motioned over the male agent. "Tell us how it works," she told Mercy.

Mercy had lived the last four years fending for herself. She felt no particular allegiance to anyone or anything, certainly no country, including her own. She had been taken from her real parents at birth and given to another to raise and program like a computer, to perform as emotionlessly as software. Had she not been conscripted at birth, she had little doubt she would either be in a concentration camp or already be running the unit Daiyu was part of. So, if handing over a piece of code would eventually allow the Chinese to stage a supply chain attack or see what the bigwigs inside America's military-industrial complex were up to, then that's what she would do.

She took a deep breath. "The first thing the code does is tell me what kind of processor is running on the system."

"Thirty-two or sixty-four bit, you mean?" asked Daiyu.

"Correct. If it tells me that, I know I can get into pretty much any sealed software and modify the existing code. And I can do it without the system detecting that modification, which is how I was able to see what you were doing with the Federal Reserve. When I saw that someone on your team was going to be installing an update I created a temporary update file and swapped my version with yours at the last minute, right before the update was scheduled to go live."

Daiyu stifled a laugh. "I'm impressed. What else? How does the code work once it gets inside?"

Mercy sat back in her chair, her eyes staring into blank space, seeing the lines of code that trailed endlessly through her brain. This was what they were really after, she told herself. *Let it play. Survive. Everything else is someone else's problem.* "The code creates a profile of potential targets, looking for systems and users that are the easiest to exploit."

"Interesting," Daiyu said. Her dark eyes were suddenly cast downward, her shame pronounced. "We have tried many times to gain entry. Without success."

Mercy continued. "So, if you are inside Watcher, it should, hypothetically, tell you which dot govs or companies doing business with them are useful targets."

The male agent then asked the obvious question. "How is this not immediately detected by the software? I can see how the code could let you in, but once it starts working, how does it stay hidden?"

Mercy looked at the professional hackers. They truly did not understand. "The code reverse engineers how the software communicates with servers and builds its own coding instructions which mimic syntax and formats, so it appears, in this case, to talk like Watcher. It looks like normal message traffic to the software. There is nothing to detect."

They seemed to confer among themselves with only their eyes. Finally, Daiyu turned to Mercy. "Show us."

It wasn't what she had expected to hear. "I have a great many federal agencies and the U.S. military trying to find me right now. It would be much safer to do this when we get to China."

Daiyu smiled. "We didn't bring all this gear so that you could show us at home. You will need to prove your worth to us before we take you back."

Mercy pointed to a black box on the table next to her, the one that resembled the DIRECTV box they had in the common room at the Youth Center. "I will need that satellite link."

The male agent completed the hookups as Daiyu and Mercy watched. When it was done, Daiyu seemed satisfied. "If you had to guess, how long will it take?"

Mercy was already typing a series of commands on her keyboard. "To load the code so that you can study it, not long. Depends on how good your link is. For you to use it on Watcher, that's up to you."

"We would like you to use it on Watcher, Mei," she said.

"Why me? You need my code. You don't need—"

Then it hit her. She was the girl who stole almost a billion dollars, the girl the American government had incarcerated, the girl who had escaped her captors and hacked two military drones. And if necessary, she was the girl who could be blamed.

Twenty minutes after taking off, Beck stood in the open door gripping the vertical metal tubes on each side of the cabin for support. The hot air currents and smoke plumes were making for a rocky ride, and he was sure that if he stayed on the plane even one more minute, he would vomit right into his face mask. Beneath him was a mountain on fire, the flames engulfing the vegetation in some sections but licking the treetops in others. It amazed him how some trees had evolved to be fire resistant, keeping branches and leaves high off the ground with a trunk bark born to withstand tremendous heat. He felt a sense of awe not only for the forest fighting for its life below, from Mount Grafton in the north to

Mount Montezuma beneath him, but for the guys like Dirk who jumped into fire for a meager living and the thrill of matching wits with the worst nature could throw at them.

To the west at the base of the foothills was Grass Valley and the Morrow ranch. The two private airplanes were still on the ground. From the map he studied, he assumed the distance to be about two miles, though it was difficult to see from the plane. The smoke was everywhere, literally clouding his vision.

Dirk was next to him and pointed below to a small clearing in the middle of the thick forest. "We're twenty-six-hundred feet above ground level now, about ten thousand feet up overall. It's a lot higher than we would prefer to drop you, but it will keep you from being seen and it's well away from the fire for now. Collect your gear as fast as you can and get out of there. We'll radio if anything is getting close." He looked at the three of them. "Activate your AADs now." All three reached down to the reserve chute on their bellies and pulled up on the arming tab.

It didn't look like much of a landing area to Beck, from this height no bigger than a postage stamp. "Are you ready?" the big smoke jumper yelled.

"Ready for an ice-cold beer. Want to join me?" Though he had jumped dozens of times, none of them had been into a heavily wooded area where tall pines and spruce could split you open like a sack of grain. He bent at the knees, dropping into a crouch.

"Go!" Dirk commanded. Beck launched himself forward. He felt the drogue chute deploy to stabilize him and then another tug as the main chute pulled off his back. The harness jerked as the canopy inflated and the hot air grabbed it. *So far, so good.* The wind wasn't bad. A good mile from the closest flames, he could still feel the waves of heat wash over him.

He reached up and took the rear risers in both hands to aid in steering, then completed his opening check. When he looked up he saw Brin above him over his right shoulder and Sev above her and equidistant. Their chutes were open. Both gave a thumbs-up. Eyes firmly set on the ground now, he had about thirty seconds to pick his spot. Using the right rear riser, he turned slightly, aiming for the center of the opening in the trees. It was no longer a postage stamp.

Beck turned perfectly into the wind and placed his hands at half brakes, tucking his arms and elbows to his sides and bending his knees slightly, legs pressed together, all of which would spread the shock when contacting the ground. Some jumpers had an instinct to stick their arms out to break their fall. Beck had learned early on to resist that and had taught Brinley the same.

He switched his stare to the horizon and three seconds later felt the balls of his feet touch the ground. The roll was all muscle memory for him, and he was on his left side and then back on his feet well before Brinley touched down. Thirty seconds after that, Sev stuck a brilliant, almost balletic landing that left him on his feet.

They spread out a single chute in the center of the clearing, and on its next pass, the Twin Otter dropped three fireboxes, one with real firefighting gear, the others loaded with weapons. Beck removed his radio from his jumpsuit and keyed the mic just as Sev and Brinley were breaking out the guns. "Thanks for the lift, Esther. I owe you one."

"Yes, you do," came the reply along with a short laugh. "Godspeed, Beck."

The airplane roared and climbed north into the smoke.

CHAPTER 35

Marco Cordero and Dal Cho walked Mercy and Shiloah outside and onto the large dirt semicircular driveway in front of the main house. In front of that was miles and miles of unforgiving land that had been fought over, stolen, and fought over some more for a hundred-and-fifty-plus years. It was largely empty of people, which made it ideal for Cordero's new staging area for the painkillers he was moving to the Pacific Northwest and the waiting hands of the addicted. It was why he had acquired it, offering the elderly couple more than twice what the place was actually worth. Pity, he thought, that it was all ruined now. Ruined by the stupidity and laziness of Jesse Roy.

A single roan quarter horse mare was saddled at the end of the drive, her reins held by one of Cordero's men. Shiloah recognized the horse instantly, with her brown and white hairs spread evenly over the bulk of her great body and the bright white blaze running down the middle of the otherwise chestnut face. The dark mane and tail were distinct and bristled in the air as the horse, in turn, recognized the girl. Shy had ridden her mother's favorite many times but hadn't seen her in more than a year, her father telling her the mare had been sold while she was away at school, a decision that enraged her.

"Cinnamon!" Shiloah yelled, running to the horse in tears.

Cordero could see the heavy smoke from the forest fire in the mountains to the east. It had grown substantially since he had flown over it during the night. He watched as a large airplane swooped low over the burning treetops and dropped a load of pink fire retardant. For a moment, it seemed to snuff the towering flames, but they quickly reappeared, reminding him that he needed to get on with his business and get out of here, for where there were fires, there were government agencies, just like in Mexico. He looked at Mercy and pointed to the fire. "Enough food and water for two days, but I wouldn't recommend she go in that direction."

Holding Cho's handkerchief to the wound on her face, Mercy walked slowly toward her friend. "I tripped. It is nothing. You know this horse, I guess."

Shiloah didn't believe her. "She was my mother's. Are we riding double?"

Mercy took her by the shoulders. "You get on Cinnamon, Shy, and you ride out of here. Do not stop. Do not wait for me."

All the breath seemed to leave Shiloah's body at once. "You said we were going together."

Mercy shook her head and pulled Shiloah in close, speaking softly into her ear. "I could not make that happen. I am sorry."

"I'm not leaving you, Mercy," said Shiloah, sobbing quietly. She looked at Cordero fifty feet away and yelled at the man. "We're both leaving or I'm staying. Do you hear me?"

"I hear you quite well, my dear." He raised his hand in the air and motioned with two fingers. Out of the large blue barn to the west came three men. Shiloah saw instantly that the one in the middle was her father and that he was bloodied and limping. On instinct, she tried to run to him, but Mercy grabbed her into a hug. "No, Shy," she said. "There is nothing we can do about this."

It took a full minute for Jesse Roy to make his way to the main house, traipsing through the wild grass that grew between the buildings, falling once along the way. As he got closer, Mercy could see the man had taken a good beating, confirming her belief that he had lost Cordero's trust and had outlived his usefulness in their business arrangement. She felt nothing for him. He deserved whatever he had coming, and that was a lot. When he finally reached the drive, Cordero marched him over to his daughter.

Jesse reached out for Shiloah only to be restrained by César and the taller one they were calling Nando. "Did they hurt you?" he cried out. "Did they touch you, baby?" Shiloah stood in horrified silence at the sight of her broken father. "I'm sorry, Shiloah," he said, hanging his head. "Everything I did was for you. For us."

Cordero stepped between them. "I thought you might be reluctant to leave your friend, so I'm going to make you this deal, Shiloah. Unfortunately, your father's worth to me is only as a hostage now. The police here already know too much. Because of his carelessness, I will have to set up another network. But that's business. You get your life back. I get my money back. If anyone comes looking for me over any of this, your father dies. My arm is long. Remember that."

She reached out to him. "Daddy!" but Nando yanked Jesse backward and onto his back.

"You have to go now, Shy," said Mercy. "Right now." She walked her the few steps back to Cinnamon. "Up you go."

Shiloah grabbed the pommel, put her foot in the stirrup, and climbed up on the big horse. "They're not letting you go," she said, looking down at Mercy. "Are they?"

They had known each other all of seven months. Mercy had been at the Youth Center only two weeks before she first contacted

Shiloah, carefully laying out the events leading to her incarceration, her chronic insomnia prompting her to circumvent the center's security systems, and the internet snooping that led her to the story in the local paper about Jesse Roy's return to the county and the extravagant ranch he was building. There was a photo of him, his daughter, and his now deceased wife, who had also grown up in Lincoln County. Mercy explained—apologized really—that this was a tough habit to break, a game she played, using her cyber tentacles to find out about the secret lives of prominent people. She admitted to snooping around in Shiloah's social media sites and said she felt a connection with her; they had both lost a mother. And then she explained what she had uncovered about Jesse Roy. At first there was silence on the other end. Mercy waited for days for a visit from the feds or some kind of lockdown imposed by the superintendent, certain that Shiloah had reported her. But neither of those things happened, and soon thereafter, she received a reply. The response was more than she could have hoped for. It was short and to the point: *How can we stop him?* As the weeks went by, a plan was hatched and solidified. Once Shiloah's summer break started, her internship at the Youth Center became an integral part. What Mercy hadn't planned was how emotionally inseparable she and Shy would become.

"I have some things to do for them," Mercy told Shiloah. "But I will see you soon." It was a lie, but what she said next was the absolute truth. "You only get a thirty-minute head start, Shy. If you stay off this access road, they should not find you, but do not think for a minute they will not try. Ride fast." She paused a moment and then took Shiloah's hand. "I love you."

Shiloah squeezed Mercy's hand and then wiped the tears from her eyes. She glanced at her father a final time and pulled gently back on the reins. Cinnamon responded from pure memory, backing up several steps. Shiloah turned her with her right knee and clucked, cuing the mare into a trot. She headed south, away from the ranch, having no idea where to go, only where not to. In seconds, she had Cinnamon galloping over the rugged landscape and through a grove of Joshua trees.

Cordero checked his watch. "Thirty minutes," he said to Mercy. Then he turned to the man from China. "You have twenty-nine."

A little more than a half mile from the ranch, Beck, Brinley, and Sev were watching the events unfold below them. Tucked behind a rocky ridge 8,000 feet above sea level, each was using high-powered optics. Sev's Nightforce ATACR scope was the best of the three, and it was mounted to the .50 caliber rifle.

"I can take Cordero's head off right now, boss," he said calmly. "Say the word."

"No," Beck said. "Too much chance they kill Mercy before we can get down there, and Charlie and our people need a bit more time to get into position. For now, everybody's still alive. Jesse looks like he's seen better days, though."

"They're letting Shiloah go?" Brinley asked as they watched her ride south. "Why?"

Beck lowered his binoculars and removed a laptop and the small Wi-Fi hotspot that would give him an internet connection via satellite from his backpack. He gazed up at the mountainside they had descended, clouded in thicker smoke now. "Mercy's made a deal, which is my cue."

"Cue for what?" Sev asked, still surveying the ranch and counting guards.

"I should get an email shortly. We'll wait for that. Meanwhile, let Tuffy know that Shiloah will probably skirt south of Patterson

Pass. Get someone to pick her up on the other side. And Sev, if anyone tries to board one of those planes with Mercy, feel free to punch some big holes in it."

Brinley noted the time. It was already 5:25 P.M. The hike down from the landing spot had taken longer than they had hoped, mainly so they could be careful about their movements and avoid detection from below. "We should wait until dark. We have the NVGs. I doubt they do. We can locate the power and kill it."

Beck understood her point. In a firefight—the kind with guns, not hoses—you go when you have the advantage. "We can't wait that long. Cordero needs Mercy to give him back his money, and he's not going to sit around until the DEA finds him." He turned on the laptop and connected it with the hotspot. Once connected, he opened his web browser and the email account Mercy had given him.

They were still in their jump gear, and by all appearances they looked like trained smoke jumpers except for the guns. "We should at least get out of these jumpsuits," Brin remarked. "I'm burning up and they're extra weight we don't need to carry."

Beck shook his head. "Drink some more water and cool your jets. We're going to need them a while longer."

Sev kept his eyes on the compound below, assessing points of entry and cover. "Operation Trojan Horse. I like it."

Brinley took a long drink from one of her water bottles. "Costume party, huh? Sounds risky. Count me in."

"This is truly brilliant," Daiyu said, watching several monitors, all showing different data points the program was scanning. "I look forward to studying it in greater detail."

"Whatever," said Mercy, her eyes traveling across the room

where the short guy was setting up more equipment. "You have the code now. Once it finds the software updates, you will need to pick your entry point. My personal recommendation would be to let it sit idly in Watcher for a few weeks without doing anything. Allow it to be dormant for a while."

Daiyu wondered if the teenage girl could actually be that gullible. "I believe we're looking at a shorter time frame."

Why? Mercy wondered. It was foolish to not allow the exploit to penetrate to its maximum depth inside the network that allowed the entire Defense Department and all of its contractors to communicate. *What's the urgency?*

Cho paced the room. Strictly a field agent, he had no interest or affinity for any phase of an operation that was out of his immediate control. He pointed to the last of the four large monitors his team had set up. "Why is there nothing on that one? Is it working?"

"It is working fine," said Mercy.

Seconds later, lines of data began appearing on the monitor. It was a list of scheduled routine software updates, who was performing them, and what was included in the update.

Mercy walked by him. "See?"

Cho glanced over at Daiyu, who nodded. "Excellent, Mei. Now, there is one more thing we need you to do. And then we can get you safely home. If you would?" He motioned for her to follow.

They walked to the far table, where the man with the rat face sat behind a small console which contained a keypad with Chinese characters built into the left side. Above the keypad were two side-by-side small screens. They were lit up but currently showed nothing. Sitting on top of the console was a larger monitor, which was not active. But it was what was built into the right side of the unit that unnerved Mercy, the thing the MSS agent had his fingers around. It was a black flight stick, the kind used to pilot an aircraft, and it had three buttons on top of it.

Cho toggled a switch on the larger monitor. The screen showed what Mercy gathered was a view from a satellite in geosynchronous orbit. The image was at the lowest resolution and simply showed a large tract of mountainous desert. *"Fàng dà,"* he instructed in Mandarin. *Zoom in.*

The operator touched a key on the keyboard several times, and the image on the screen grew closer and closer still, until it showed a highway snaking through the desert hills with a few vehicles moving in both directions and what appeared to be a small community nestled along each side with the occasional patch of green or blue. Okay, Mercy told herself, some farms and lakes. The image expanded even more, until one section of green covered the monitor. And at the bottom of the image were a series of buildings with white roofs to reflect the sun, and above them seven separate round buildings connected by walking paths. Though she had never seen it from above, Mercy recognized the Lincoln County Youth Center immediately.

Cho placed his hand on Mercy's shoulder. "The American government now believes you have been taken to Mexico by a Mexican drug lord and that you are, most probably, dead. As a result, their military is returning to normal operations. There is an American MQ-20 Avenger which left Creech Air Force Base outside of Las Vegas an hour ago on a training mission. Our intelligence indicates it is scheduled to be in the air for many more hours. We would like you to assume control of this aircraft."

"For what purpose?" she asked, her breath uneven and shallow.

Cho leaned close to her. "So that you can fly it to the place where you have been imprisoned for the last seven months, as you did with the other two RPAs." His mouth grew wide at the corners. "As I mentioned earlier, we know about those. Now, please."

Mercy stepped back. "You are going to destroy the Youth Center?"

"No," Cho said. "*You* are going to destroy it. They will no doubt be surprised you are still alive, and what better way to solidify your role in all this than with an angry, vengeful attack on your jailers? What better way to ensure there is no trace back to our great country?"

She took another step back. This was not part of the plan. The image on the screen resolved even further, and Mercy could see dozens of people moving about the campus. Kids.

"I will not," she said.

"Oh, yes," Cho said, grabbing Mercy by the neck, "you most certainly will. Or I will leave you dead on this floor."

Her heart was pounding. She was not going to China after all. "I will be in good company, then," she said. "Because unless Mr. Cordero gets his money back, I imagine we will all be dead on this floor."

Cho's fingers tightened at the same instant Marco Cordero entered the big room.

"It is time," he said. "Your thirty minutes are up."

Through the glare of the late-afternoon sun, Beck saw the email appear on his screen. The message was brief and prearranged: *Lisa, send the credentials now. Roll a 1.*

"Damn," he muttered. From her previous instructions, Beck knew that Roll a One was one of two possible valedictions, a reference to Mercy's Dungeons and Dragons icosahedron die, her way of telling him her status. A one was the lowest roll and indicated that she had failed and all was lost. He should not respond, assume she was dead, and do with Cordero's money whatever he felt was appropriate. Had she signed off with Roll a Twenty—the highest roll of the die—it meant that her strategy had so far been successful, and that she needed him to reply with "Understood," followed by the new account number and password to access it online.

She had given him only the two options, but she didn't know that he was now only half a mile away. He set the laptop on his pack and slithered up the rock face next to Sev.

"Problem?" his deputy asked.

"What's our total count on bad guys, excluding Jesse?"

Sev counted them off as he eyed them through the rifle scope. "Outside of Jesse Roy, we have Cordero, our good friend César, and a minimum of five more cartel guys."

Sev paused the scope over each of the windows on the back of the house. "We also have the Asian guy you described and at least two more, one woman and one man, but they look like computer nerds. Could be more but those two have been making periodic trips out to that SUV."

"That's ten total," Brin said. "Minimum. Not counting Jesse since he appears somewhat out of favor at the moment."

"Any sign our Asian friends are armed?" he asked.

It was something Sev had already assessed. "No outward sign of being armed. And if I were Cordero, I would have made sure they weren't carrying."

"Agreed." He slid back down the rock and picked up the laptop again. He hit reply to Mercy's email and began typing. *System offline. STAND BY.* He paused a moment, wondering what Mercy would make of this move. It would be the riskiest attack in the game but promised the largest reward. His finger fired off the email. Mercy's reply took a long, agonizing minute.

Please explain. Quickly.

Beck hammered out the next message. *I should have ACCESS*

SHORTLY. Believe I am close. All bank systems appear to be off-line. Ransomware attack? Russians? Chinese maybe? Nothing is working. If Chinese, could they suspect?

Brinley watched as he typed. "What are you doing?"

Beck looked at her. "Trying to even the odds a little."

CHAPTER 36

Mercy read the sheriff's reply with astonishment. Her neck was directly below the guillotine blade that was Marco Cordero. Didn't Beck understand that? *STAND BY*, it said. *ACCESS SHORTLY*. Did *Believe I am close* mean he was nearby? The short barrel of César's gun in her ear, she trembled, waiting for the explosion that would certainly follow. She would not hear it. Her cerebral cortex would be on the floor before it could register the sound and the fury of the bullet. She closed her eyes while César mumbled the words of the email.

"Well?" Marco Cordero shouted from across the big room. He did not like being made to feel vulnerable, and he could feel his blood getting hot. "What does this one say?"

César's eyes moved from the computer screen across the room to Cho, who was looking out the front window. "This Lisa person says the bank's systems are all offline, that it may be a ransomware attack, and that perhaps the Russians or Chinese have something to do with it."

Cho, listening intently, turned immediately, only to find César's gun now pointed at him. Mercy opened her eyes and turned slowly around, finally realizing what Beck was attempting. Cordero got up from his chair, rubbing his left shoulder which throbbed whenever his blood was up. He turned to Cho. "Explain."

Cho crossed his arms over his chest and glared at Mercy. "It's a trick. She's delaying."

César shook his head. "She's not doing anything. She *received* the message."

Cordero crossed the room and stood in front of the man from China. He studied his face like he had a hundred adversaries over the years, looking for signs of deceit. "Perhaps it is a delay, but her life hangs in the balance. She knows I will kill her unless that money comes back to me immediately. She has nothing to gain and everything to lose by attempting to trick me. Which means I have two questions for you. The first is *why*? If her associate in Europe, this Lisa, is telling the truth, she may have put a bullet in Mercy's brain. If she's lying to delay us, the result is the same. The only way I'm not going to kill her is if my money suddenly reappears."

Cho shifted his weight to his back leg. He had no weapon except for his body, Cordero's men having stripped it from him before they even got on Jesse Roy's plane. "*Why* is simple, as I said. The delay is in trying to divide us. Trust me, señor, I've been hunting this girl for years, and she deceives as well as any animal in the wild. What is your second question?"

"My second question is, how would the person sending us these emails know there are two parties here to divide, and that one of those parties is Chinese?" He pointed in Mercy's direction. "*This* girl knows you and your people are here, but no one else knows. Is that not correct?"

Cho's gaze flitted to Mercy and then back to Cordero. "I have no idea who knows we are here, but the Chinese government has not taken your money, sir. This is a ploy."

As he watched Cho, Cordero anxiously pulled at his mustache. Then he removed a pearl-handled Smith & Wesson .45 from the back of his waistband, one that Jesse Roy had brought him years ago. "Someone is going to tell me what has happened to my money, or I am going to start killing people."

He pointed the barrel first at Cho and then at Mercy and went back and forth between the two as if he were playing eeny meeny miny moe. Finally, he walked over to Mercy, dropping the muzzle on her forehead. He pulled back the hammer.

Mercy's words came fast, almost unintelligibly. "Last year I removed eighty-one million dollars from accounts the Chinese had set up, money they had hacked from the New York Federal Reserve."

Cordero took a step back, moving his gaze from Mercy to Cho. "Is this true?"

Cho was two moves ahead. He knew he could not stop what was going to happen next and moved in the drug lord's direction. He needed to be closer. "A pure fabrication, I can assure you. The girl is a—"

At the same moment, Nando came through the front door. "*Jefe*, we have company."

The heavy-duty Chevy pickup was almost all white but with a green stripe from front to back along both sides that bore the words FIRE and U.S. FOREST SERVICE in white block letters. It had a light bar on top along with two reels of red hose and other equipment designed to put out small fires. Marco Cordero watched the truck as it approached the ranch house, its flashing red and yellow lights visible even before the siren could be heard. The wait gave him time to pull his guards back inside the house and other outbuildings. It wasn't until it arrived when the shrill siren was finally silenced and a female exited the vehicle in the precise spot Shiloah had departed from the ranch forty minutes earlier. She was fit, with the build of a wrestler, and dressed in the khaki blouse and dark green uniform pants of the United States Forest Service.

Cordero met her in the driveway, waving neighborly. "Good afternoon," he said, noting the handgun strapped to her waist. "It looks like that fire up there is still growing."

Tuffy Scruggs took a quick look at the mountains behind the house. "Yes, sir. That's why I'm here. You the new owner?"

Cordero shook his head. "No. The place belongs to a friend. He's letting me relax out here for a few days."

Tuffy moved closer to him, hands on her hips. "Well, I'm afraid your visit will be cut short. We need to evacuate you. We don't yet have control of that fire, and it's already started coming down the hillside." She pointed up the slope. "As you can see. If the wind picks up even a little, it could be on you in no time."

Cordero placed a hand on his chin. "It's a shame, but I understand. My friends and I will pack our things and be out of here shortly."

Seeing no one else, Tuffy glanced toward the front windows of the house. "How many are you?"

"Just a handful," Cordero replied. "We'll be gone within the hour."

"I'd feel better if it was a half hour." Tuffy pointed toward the two planes, a few hundred yards away. "That's new. Your friend put in that airstrip?"

"A few months ago. I live in California, so it's much quicker than driving."

Tuffy looked up into the smoky sky. "Well, be careful flying out. You're bound to get some extra turbulence from the fire and all this smoke. And the sooner, the better."

"Will do, Officer, thank you."

Tuffy gestured for Cordero to follow as she walked toward the end of the drive where they could see around the east end of the house. "The BLM dropped a few of their smoke jumpers up there a while ago. They're cutting some preemptive fire lines on the lower slope there. See?" She pointed.

Cordero could make out two human figures kicking up some dust with their axes. "I do."

"They may come down and start digging one around your buildings here," Tuffy added. "They won't do any damage, but you might want to mention to the owner that they were here in case he sees some of the ground disturbed when he returns."

Cordero crossed his arms. "I'm sure he'll be grateful that you are looking out for his property."

"They might want to refill their water bottles as well at some point. It's also possible one of our aircraft will drop some fire retardant near the house. Hopefully, it won't come to that. If it does, it washes off any structure pretty easily." Tuffy turned back toward the truck. "All right then, sir, I'll let you get your people packed up. We have a few others in the area we have to call on. Have a good day, and be safe." She tipped her green Forest Service ball cap. "Please be quick. We'd hate for you to get stuck out here."

"We will," said Cordero with a friendly nod. He watched as the forest ranger drove west on the road that cut through the property and eventually turned north. Then he walked back into the house where Mercy and Cho were right where he had left them, under César's gun. Two of Cordero's other guards had theirs trained on Cho's team, all gathered in the great room of the house.

"That fire is coming down the mountain, and we have to evacuate," Cordero said, taking his pistol from César's other hand. "So, enough of this bullshit. Where is my money?" He glared at

Cho. "Do you have it? Have your computer hackers here taken it from me?"

Cho took a step toward him, only to be stopped by Cordero's rising gun. "Mr. Cordero, my government knows we are here, and that I have made a deal with you for Mercy Vaughn. We do not have your money. We have no interest in your money. You can believe me or not. But if anything happens to me or my team, you will have the Chinese government to answer to, and I can promise you that your troubles with Mr. Salazar will pale in comparison."

Cordero considered Cho's words for a few moments, the gun's barrel dropping slightly. "Has she given you what you need?"

Cho shifted his feet. The mission had changed during the night. Breaching Watcher was a priority, but considering what Mei Wu had already done over the last week, the Ministry of State Security had decided to seize an opportunity that might never be theirs again. A target had been selected, and Cho still needed her to take control of the drone. "The beginnings," he told Cordero. "We have the computer code we were seeking, but we need about fifteen more minutes."

"We're leaving now. And since we have to get out of this place, and I don't yet have my money, you will be coming with us to Caborca. Once we have resolved this issue, you will be free to go. Your people should pack up this stuff and get out of here. *Entiendes?*"

Cho exchanged nervous glances with his two agents. "I'm afraid that will not be possible. I need to return with my team."

Cordero ignored him, motioned César over and spoke quietly. Mercy, sensing a violent eruption of some kind, rose slowly out of her chair, looking for her exit. But then Nando walked into the room. "We have two people approaching the back of the house. They're carrying axes and packs."

"Firefighters," said Cordero. "They're trying to protect the buildings here. And they may want to fill up on water. Go outside, be friendly to them, and give them what they need. The faster they go, the faster we go. Take Rico here with you, and keep your guns out of sight."

Both men tucked their pistols behind their backs and covered them with their shirts. Much to Cho's delight, that left only Cordero, César, and Cordero's pilot, Santi, to cover his team and Mercy. When they had left the room, Cordero motioned to the computer equipment. "Shut it all down now," he said to Santi. He turned back to Cho. "When the firefighters leave, so do we."

CHAPTER 37

Nando and Rico did not immediately approach the two smoke jumpers as they backed slowly down through the junipers that lined the back of the immediate property. Instead, they watched from the large cedar deck built onto the back of the house and looked up at the mountain on fire, marveling at the orange flames leaping across the treetops less than a mile away. Not only could they see them clearly, they could *hear* the fire as it gorged on the fresh timber. From where they stood, it had the sound of a jet airplane. The smell of the smoke was so much stronger now, and it had drifted across the whole of the late-afternoon sky, turning it a beautiful orange-red. When his eyes finally settled on the firefighters, Nando was equally impressed with the weight they were carrying. Both had large, full backpacks riding on their shoulders, and the smaller one even carried a large chain saw.

"My God," Nando said. "It's a woman. *Ella es pequeña.*" *She's tiny.*

As the smoke jumpers stripped off their packs, the man on the right shouted some instructions. The two began moving away from each other. Reaching the west end of the property, the woman started cutting a fire line with her axe. Nando had never seen a wildfire up close and wondered how these people could expend so much energy under their heavy yellow fire suits in this heat. Every inch of their bodies was covered. *And how do they breathe through those scarves covering their mouths and noses? I would die!*

Moving away from Brinley, Beck ignited a drip torch and began spraying the flame in a straight line in the grass parallel to the trench she was digging. He stole quick glances over his shoulder to the deck at the rear of the house where two of Cordero's men were watching, being careful to keep his back to them as much as possible. Moments later, he saw them come down the steps and split up, the taller one moving toward him and the other walking in Brin's direction. Beck reached up with his right hand and quickly unzipped his jumpsuit from his neck to his navel. He shifted slightly, the drip torch in his left hand, spraying some of the brown natural grass with fire.

When the man was ten feet away, Beck made a slow turn with his torch, the flames on the ground reaching one to two feet in height. It had the desired effect. Cordero's man was watching the burning grass, not the wildland firefighter burning it. He didn't see Beck pull the short-barreled rifle from the inside of his jumpsuit.

"Not a sound," Beck said. "Do not move. Do not look away. If you do, I'll blow your heart right out of your chest." He set the drip torch on the ground and extinguished the flame with his gloved hand.

Nando's dark brown eyes grew big, and he froze, afraid even the slightest muscle twitch would cost him his life. He did not see Rico approaching the woman, did not witness her spin suddenly, swinging the heavy curved end of her axe into Rico's chest, did not watch him fall into some tall grass without a sound.

Beck had seen it all. "How many in the house?" he asked quietly.

Nando's nostrils flared. "Too many for you."

"Don't bet your life on it." Beck motioned Nando to his left with the end of the rifle, and they moved around the east side of the house. He saw the bulge in the small of Nando's back and snatched the 9mm Beretta.

Brinley caught up with them moments later, her Pulaski axe in hand. "You good?" she asked her brother.

"About ready for a nap." He dropped Nando's pistol into the deep side pocket of his jumpsuit, and raised his rifle with both hands, searching for any target that might be coming around the front. "That guy you hit still breathing?"

"I sincerely hope not. We can check on him later." She held up her Colt .380. "He was nice enough to return my gun."

Beck wheeled around, stabbing the butt of the Henry Axe sharply into the side of Nando's head. The cartel man dropped to his knees, dazed and ready to topple. "All yours, sis."

Brinley removed her helmet and the green shroud from around her face and looked down at Nando, the man who held the hot branding iron to her face in Jesse Roy's wine cellar. "Remember me?" She could see the instant recognition in his eyes, despite her still swollen cheeks. "Yeah, I'm not dead." She brought the handle of the Pulaski violently into Nando's groin, and he dropped with a loud grunt face down on the dirt. Brinley grabbed one of his ears, yanked hard, saw his lights were out. Then she zip-tied his ankles and wrists faster than a calf roper using a piggin' string.

"Feel better?" Beck asked.

She popped to her feet. "Getting there."

"Good. Get your helmet on and get back out there. Keep digging until the shooting starts." Brin took off at a trot, and in half a minute Sev could see her again through his scope cutting the fire line in the back of the house.

Beck pulled his radio from the clip on his waist, made sure it was on channel seven, and gave the rest of the team the update. "Uh, yeah, we're making good headway down here. Can I get a sitrep?"

Arshal's voice came first, low and ominous like thunder. "We're in position and ready to douse anything that flares up in your area, boss man. But you need to get moving, smoke is getting bad and could obscure vision shortly."

"Roger that," said Beck, rezipping his jumpsuit. "Here we go, everybody." He walked around the large two-story and right up to the front door.

Five minutes had elapsed since Nando and Rico had left the house. Cordero, his gun trained on the Chinese agent, waited impatiently for confirmation the firefighters had departed. He wanted to send Santi to the rear of the home to see what was taking so long but was afraid to have one more gun exit the room. Finally, he stepped close to Cho, pointing the .45 at his face. "We're going. Now."

It was the mistake the MSS agent had been hoping for. When you raise a gun to someone's head and are within arm's length of that person, you better be pulling the trigger. Cho's hands moved in a blur, and as he had been trained a dozen years earlier, his right forearm contacted Cordero's outer wrist, swatting it upward and across his body, while his left seized the barrel of the gun, pushing it in the opposite direction and twisting Cordero's wrist. White-hot pain ran like lightning through the cartel boss's fingers, causing him to release his hold on the pistol. Before his brain could register what happened, he found the Asian man now pointing the weapon at his chest.

Santi and César both moved too slowly, their guns having been trained on Cho's two subordinates. In the next second, Cho had moved behind Cordero, the semiautomatic pushed into the base of the man's neck.

"Tell them to set their weapons on the ground," he instructed. When Cordero said nothing, Cho shoved the muzzle into the man's right ear. "I have no wish to hurt you. Have them drop their weapons, and you may all leave."

"And the girl?" Cordero asked, his eyes flashing to Mercy, who had backed up to the rear wall of the living room. "I still don't have my money."

Cho rammed the gun into Cordero's eardrum. "I don't care about your money, you filthy little man."

Cordero saw no option. "Do as he says." Santi immediately squatted to the floor and carefully set his handgun on the large area rug he was standing on, where it was picked up by the Chinese woman. César, a man who had fought his way up from the street gangs of Tijuana, had killed and tortured his way through three decades of sleeping with one eye open, had not come this far only to surrender his gun in a standoff. He backed slowly away.

Cho's left arm circled tightly around his neck, Cordero spat, the anger flaring in his bulging eyes. "César."

But César would not comply. Step by careful step, he moved toward the front of the house, moving his snub-nosed .357 from Cho to the female Chinese agent and back to Cho. When he reached the dark oak double doors, he reached back with his free hand and found one of the brass knobs.

"Go, César," said Cho. "We won't stop you."

The big Mexican pulled, and the door opened slightly behind him. As he stepped to the side, his gun fell slightly. At that moment, Cho flung Cordero aside and fired. The bullet caught César in the right shoulder, but he had managed to squeeze off a round of his own, his bullet striking the rear wall of the room and sending everyone for cover.

Instead of diving behind furniture, Mercy sprinted to her left, hoping to make it to the kitchen and then the rear of the house where she had seen a glass door. Fast and with a huge wingspan, Daiyu caught her by the ankle, and both fell to the floor. The tussle prevented Cho from firing again, allowing César to open and back out through the front doors.

As soon as he was outside, César turned, only to see the face of the county sheriff inside some strange yellow suit. He was standing three feet away and pointing a short-barreled rifle at his chest. Blood already spreading through his blue polyester shirt, César struggled to raise the pistol. Beck shot him in the torso, the .410 load blasting Marco Cordero's number two back through the door with a three-inch-diameter hole in him. As he hit the floor of the entryway, more shots erupted from within the house, several contacting the double doors and causing Beck to jump backward. He spun the cocking handle on the Henry rifle with one hand, pulling the next round from the tube into the chamber. Tucked in front of one of the brick columns, Beck's head jerked up. The sound of four .50 caliber rounds from Sev's rifle were unmistakable as they tore through Jesse Roy's airplane. The Beechcraft actually hopped on the dirt as the bullets impacted. Cordero's plane was next. Nobody would be leaving the Grass Valley ranch by air today.

Three bad guys were down, something Beck felt pretty good about, but he wasn't overly optimistic. Despite there being nowhere for those remaining in the house to go, he didn't believe for a second they would hand over Mercy Vaughn and come out with their hands raised. He reached into the deep pockets of his smoke jumper suit and withdrew an M84 flashbang grenade. Then another. Designed to produce a flash of light that would render anyone in the vicinity blind for about five seconds, along with an afterimage that would impair vision even longer, it also created a detonation, the sheer volume of which was enough to disturb the fluid in the inner ear, causing a loss of balance. The only problem was the heat. The concussive blast was hot enough to ignite anything flammable and could maim someone close by. He would have to move fast. Beck held the first flashbang up in the air.

From two hundred yards away and prone in the dirt, Arshal spotted the grenade through the scope mounted on his .308 sniper rifle. "He's going in," he told the rest of the team over the radio. "Get ready."

It was quiet inside the house now. Beck pulled the pin on the first flashbang, and reaching around the column, threw it backward through the front doors. It detonated two seconds later, the one-hundred-and-seventy-decibel bang loud enough to rock him despite having a finger in each ear. A moment later, for good measure, he lobbed the second flashbang into the room through a blown-out window. Anyone within that space would be completely incapacitated now.

He charged through the entryway.

Inside the house, the man known as Dal Cho watched as César was launched backward through the doorway, bleeding from a second far larger wound than the one he had delivered. He returned fire, only catching a glimpse of the man in the fire suit before he jumped behind the brick column. His other eye caught Cordero flying down the long hallway. Cho snapped his fingers twice, drawing the attention of his two agents and motioning them to cover the front doors. Mercy, her formidable survival instincts finding a new gear, was able to kick free of Daiyu, and she bolted from the room as well.

Cho recognized the canister as it flew through the entryway and skittered across the wood floor. He knew what the result would be and that there was no time to get his people out. As he rounded the wall that led to the east side of the house, Cho clamped his eyes shut and covered his ears. The grenade went off. Cho never stopped. He was already in the dining room when the second one exploded.

Beck entered the big room into a cloud of smoke and heat, his Henry Axe in his right hand and his Glock in his left. Anything that had been on the walls or a shelf was now littering the floor, and what must have been a sofa was fully aflame. He heard a crunch to his right, someone stepping on a shattered computer monitor. A man, flabby and middle-aged, staggered by him toward the door and whatever freedom he could find beyond it. He had no weapon, so Beck made no attempt to stop him.

The room was large, easily thirty by fifty feet, and Beck scanned it for Mercy. Another man was on the floor, disoriented and holding his head. When Beck rolled him over, he saw an Asian face, but it was not the face he had seen outside Area 51 the day before. He moved to the wall opposite the front doors. No sign of Marco Cordero either.

That's when the flying spider came out of nowhere. Daiyu was a blur in the air, soaring over the flaming couch and catching Beck on his right side with both feet. The collision sent him crashing into the drywall. He managed to hang on to both guns, but before he could recover and point them in her direction, she was on him again, blood oozing from both her ears, raining blows to his vital areas like she was tenderizing a steak. The ridge of her right hand caught his jaw hinge below the right ear. Her left hand slammed into the side of his neck, concussing the vagus nerve and making him instantly dizzy. She jabbed a finger into his armpit, and Beck felt his arm go numb, causing him to drop the Glock and spin to his left. Then she hit him in the kidney, the blow angling upward into the ribs, standing him fully upright and paralyzing him in pain. Her hand grabbed for the rifle.

Marco Cordero was waiting for Mercy. He caught her as she rounded the corner into the kitchen, with its original 1970s cabinetry, red tiled floor, and yellowing walls. Seizing a handful of her hair, he flung her first into a corner cabinet and then into the old Kenmore refrigerator. She bounced off it, limp and bleeding. With both hands, Cordero reached out and pulled the refrigerator from the wall, opening a space barely wide enough for a body. He pulled Mercy from the floor by the throat, his grip a vise around her windpipe, and kicked her, half-conscious, through the small opening.

She felt herself falling, tumbling down wooden steps into complete darkness, where she had what she believed was her last thought. *This is how I die.* She landed on the tunnel's dirt floor, feeling blood trickling into her right eye. A second later Cordero had her by the collar. Above them, two loud explosions rocked the house, and dust fell like volcanic ash into the cold narrow passage. He knew the sound of flashbangs all too well. Cursing in Spanish, the cartel boss found the switch on the wall at the bottom of the steps and flipped it on. The tunnel flooded with light.

"Move," Cordero barked at her. "I want my money and you want to live, so move."

CHAPTER 38

When she heard the discharge of Beck's Henry Axe, Brinley moved behind a picket line of cypress trees laid out across the rear of the property. Sev came down the hill at a sprint, dropping to his knees behind an expansive chicken coop, his Barrett M82 braced against the structure for support. They both heard the flashbangs that followed, saw the intense light briefly flash through the rear windows, and expected to see some of Cordero's men or the Chinese running from the back of the house. What they witnessed instead was another light coming from sky, a white ball of fire and the roar of it tearing through the air before it collided a split second later with the second floor of the home. The explosion threw them like ragdolls off their feet as the heat of the immense fireball swept over them. Seconds later, they were up and running, Brinley entering what was left of the building from a gaping hole in the back and Sev continuing to the front, dropping the unwieldly rifle and pulling the SIG Sauer P226 from a side pocket in his jumpsuit.

The entire upper floor of the ranch house was blown away, only small portions of the exterior framing still intact and flaming bits of furniture landing everywhere. Most of the interior walls were likewise obliterated, engulfed in blue and orange flame, and the fire was already spreading to the badly damaged first floor of the house. As he came around the west side, Sev's eyes locked on the Black Hawk hovering in the sky a half mile to the south. The distraction lasted only a moment, as the two armed cartel men who had earlier dragged Jesse Roy back to the barn ran in front of him. Their eyes were locked on the deadly metal bird too, and they didn't see Sev until it was too late. His bullet ripped through the first man's chest just as his partner's shotgun was coming up to fire. Sev dove past him, catching the dead man as he fell and using his body as cover. His right arm rose up under the dead man's armpit, the SIG's trigger already moving. But the shotgun had found its target too, perhaps a split second faster. Sev felt the release of the trigger in the same microsecond the second man's head erupted like a popped water balloon.

Sev heard Arshal's voice through his earpiece. "You're welcome, Señor Velasco." He rolled to his feet and saw the old man two hundred yards out, holding the .308 high in the air, Tuffy, Charlie, and Johnny and Jimmy Green sprinting past him on either side toward the front of the house. "Beck," Sev shouted. "Where's Beck?"

Ten seconds later, Charlie and most of the Lincoln County Sheriff's Department entered the old house. There were huge sections of the ceiling between the two floors gone, and they found Brinley frantically tearing through a mound of drywall and ceiling truss in what was left of the large front room. Beck was at the bottom of the pile with a woman directly on top of him. Brinley peeled open one of his eyelids with a thumb. "He's breathing," she said. "Knocked out is all."

"How about her?" Sev asked, pointing to the bloodied body covering him. "Is that Mercy?"

The Jolly Greens, as strong as they were tall, worked quickly without a word passing between them. They grabbed opposite ends of the heavy beams and lifted them out of the way. Charlie bent down for a closer look and felt for a pulse. She had only seen Mercy's photo. "No, and no," she said. "Too tall. Somebody else. Very dead." Sev and Charlie grabbed Beck under each arm and hauled him outside, laying him in the dirt well beyond the semicircular drive and carefully removing his smoke jumper helmet. It took a minute, but Beck, his face blackened, coughed himself back to consciousness, spitting drywall dust and smoke from his throat and lungs. The first thing he saw when they raised him to a sitting position was the house almost fully engulfed in fire.

"She's still in there," he said, trying to get to his feet.

Brinley held him down, shaking her head. "If she is, she's dead now, Porter."

They watched as it began toppling over on itself, fire everywhere, black smoke rising from the burning wooden timbers and contents of the home.

"You did all you could, Beck," said Charlie. "Not your fault."

They helped him to his feet, dusting him off in the process. Arshal handed him some water, which he drank and spat out, and drank again, alternately coughing and gulping.

"You swallowed a ton of smoke, I'm guessing," Tuffy told him while patting his back hard between the shoulder blades. "We need to get you to the hospital."

Beck's brain started to clear, and he remembered now. "Check the back," he told them. "Mercy wasn't in the front of the house. Neither was Cordero or Dal Cho."

"We were covering the back when the house blew," Brinley said. "Nobody came out. Nobody could."

"The jalapeño and I took out the two guys coming out of the barn," Arshal added. "I saw a squirter going out the back side.

Looked like Jesse running for his life. I'll check the barn and then go see if I can get a bead on him."

One of the Greens had Cordero's pilot in cuffs on the ground and Beck recognized him as the guy who had run out the front door right before he lost his fight with the ninja woman. "We have two more in custody," he said, "one on the east side, one out back, along with this guy. Sev, bring one of the vehicles up and take them back to town. Johnny, Jimmy, you go with him. Split up the suspects, do what Sev tells you to do."

"Yes, Sheriff," the Twin Peaks answered in unison.

"Where's Shiloah?" asked Beck.

"On her way back to your station in Pioche," Charlie answered. "One of my guys has her."

While the three deputies set about collecting Marco Cordero's entourage, Tuffy and Charlie raised Beck to his feet. He was wobbling, still getting his sea legs. "Why did the house blow up?" Beck asked.

No one needed to answer. The answer was on the dirt landing strip next to what was left of Cordero's private jet. Two pilots sat side by side in the cockpit. Behind them, four men, armed to the teeth, spilled out of the Black Hawk looking for something to kill, Special Agent Maddox on their heels.

The special operators surrounded the burning house, at the ready in case any survivor came out. All Beck and his team could do was watch. They were looking for Mercy, and that confirmed everything in Beck's mind. Maddox tried entering a few times, but the heat and the fire were too much. With his own M4A1 rifle slung across his chest, he approached the Lincoln County sheriff's varsity team. He didn't appear pleased.

"What are you doing here, Sheriff?" He pointed to the blaze on the mountain. "You said you were going to fight a fire."

Instead of answering, Beck caught the OSI man by his tactical vest and flung him to the ground. When Maddox tried to raise his rifle, Beck stepped on it with his boot, pinning it to his chest. "You blew up a house with people in it!" he yelled. He bent down, putting all of his weight on Maddox. "Was she supposed to get killed? Was that part of it?"

Maddox wriggled out from under Beck's boot and raised himself to a sitting position. "I blew up a house with a *terrorist* in it. I received intel that Jesse Roy's plane was on the ground here. You told me he had her. That's why I'm here. Why are you here?"

Beck's eyes rolled back into his head. "And so you decided to kill her?"

"She had already hijacked two of our drones," Maddox shouted back, scrambling to his feet. "She used one of them trying to kill you yesterday. And she was in the middle of handing over—"

Beck bent down and seized the rifle from Maddox's hands, his face contorted in rage. He threw the M4A1 over his head. "Handing over what?"

Maddox recoiled. "I've said too much. I can't go into the rest. I'm sorry."

Beck took his Henry rifle from Brinley's hands and pointed it at the man's chest. "I don't believe you. You followed us because you expected I would find her."

"I did no such thing," he objected, climbing to his feet and holding up his hands in surrender. "You don't understand. That kid was imperiling the security of the United States. I had my orders." Maddox's face scrunched into a red ball. "And I had the authority."

"Uh-huh. Well, let me tell you what I think is really going on,

Maddox." He stepped closer, only inches from the agent's face. "You used her to smoke out the Chinese. You created a way—I'm not sure how—but you made it so the Chinese knew about her. You were betting they'd come for her. But why? Because she's also Chinese? Why go through all this trouble only to kill her?"

Maddox tried to look surprised, his voice overly frantic. "Are you telling me there are Chinese agents inside that house, Sheriff? Are you telling me she's working with the Chinese, that she's a foreign agent? When were you going to share this?"

Beck dumped some water over his head and looked again at the house engulfed in yellow flame and black smoke, creaking its final breaths in agony. "Jesus, Maddox, she was a kid."

Charlie and Tuffy flanked Beck, all watching the flames grow to their highest peak as the structure burned its way to the ground. "What do you want to do, boss?" Tuffy asked. "It will be a while before those flames go out and we can recover any bodies."

Beck looked at his second-in-command. She was right. He pulled out the radio Esther had given him, switched the channel. "Esther. Beck. I need another favor."

Two minutes later, an orange and white MD-87 swooped out of the smoke in the Patterson Pass fire and banked toward the burning wreckage. Both Beck's and Maddox's teams gathered at a safe distance and watched as the plane, a converted jetliner, bombed the target with precision, laying down a good two thousand pounds of the fire retardant and smothering the flames in seconds. When the smoke cleared, very little of the structure itself remained, a few wall studs, the foundation. Now there was only a mixture of black soot and pink slurry everywhere. And bodies. Everyone knew what was coming next, and nobody wanted to do it.

Beck looked up. The sky was turning to gray, fire smoke and the setting sun extinguishing what little color remained. His vision was already narrowing. It would be completely gone in another thirty minutes. He could barely make out Arshal returning from the barn.

"This is the stash house we've been looking for," Arshal said. "There's more drugs in there than I've ever seen."

Beck nodded. "Jesse?"

"Gone, like I said. But where's he gonna go on foot at night?"

"Not toward that fire," Tuffy said. "Lund is twenty-five miles, and it's even farther in the dark."

"You guys head up toward Lund, then," Beck said, looking toward the mountains to the east. "Charlie, we'll need some help with roadblocks on the 318 and up around Sawmill Peak. If we don't catch him by morning, we'll have to go up there after him."

"I'll set it up. You think he'll go up and over Ninemile?" she asked, referring to the mountain to the west.

"Hard to say. We won't catch him walking along the road, that's for sure. But he's got a long trip whichever way, and he's got no water or food, so there's no big hurry. I'll stay and handle the body recovery."

"No need, Sheriff," said Maddox, he and his men already moving toward the smoldering ruin. "We'll handle that."

Beck walked forward. "Like hell you will."

The kill squad turned in unison, all four rifles now trained on Beck and his deputies.

"You gonna shoot us, mister?" asked Beck, addressing the team leader as a civilian, knowing none of them still held a military rank. "This is my jurisdiction, and any bodies in that house belong to me."

The team leader was tall, chiseled from stone, had a thick, blond stubble lining his sharp jawline, and was clearly a man used to doing business the old-fashioned way. With a gun. Beck had seen him first in the station's parking lot and then later at the crash of the Daimler truck, his long, sandy hair now swirling in the wind. "With respect, Sheriff, your jurisdiction is the least of our concerns. That said, you seem like good people, and we would prefer not to have to use force against you."

"Well, I'm going in what's left of that structure to look for the body of a sixteen-year-old girl. I really don't see how shooting me in the back serves the greater interests of the United States. Do you?"

The unit's top man turned to Maddox. Beck could see the uncertainty on his face. More than anything, soldiers, even ex-soldiers, hate uncertainty.

"Don't listen to him, Jacobs," Maddox commanded. "You have your orders. Seal off that house. Nobody else goes in." Beck started toward the house. None of the squad reacted. Maddox positioned himself in front of Jacobs, screaming, "He is not to enter that structure! You will follow my orders!"

The elite killer turned his gaze to Beck and raised his rifle, his three subordinates covering Tuffy, Charlie, and Arshal. Suddenly, he swung the barrel left, where its tip found Maddox's chest. "We will not be following that particular order, sir. Our mission was to capture the person hijacking our RPAs before she could take down an airliner or something else. That person is dead now—you've seen to that—so our mission is complete. If you want to shoot the sheriff, you'll have to do that on your own, and I expect you'll meet some resistance. We're outta here."

The man named Jacobs raised a hand in the air and twirled it in a circle. "On me," he said. Relieved, the rest of the team lowered their guns and followed him toward the helicopter. Arshal raised his .308 and pointed it directly at Maddox's head.

"Jacobs!" Maddox yelled, but all four men continued on to the helicopter, its rotors still turning.

Beck stepped up next to the OSI agent. "Your ride is leaving,

Captain. It's a long walk back to your billet from here, wherever that really is." But Maddox didn't budge. They all watched as the helo lifted off, made an about-face, and headed south. As it was close to dark now, Beck removed the NVGs he had placed in his smoke jumper suit and pulled them over his head. He lowered the binocular tubes over his eyes and gave his team a thumbs-up as he saw the surroundings light up in green around him. "You guys get moving. Jesse's getting farther away by the minute." He walked over to Brinley, who was loading Cordero's pilot into Sev's Jeep. "Brin, you go with Sev back to the station. Shiloah will be there, and I'd feel a lot better if you were with her. Let her know we're looking for her dad."

"I don't want to leave you here alone."

He gave a slight shake of his head, the pain traveling all the way down his spine. "I'll be fine. Everybody else is already dead. I've got the night vision, and I've got Maddox here to keep me company. Send the EMS guys back with a truck to transport the bodies."

She wanted to stay with him, but now wasn't the time to argue. "What do I tell her about Mercy?"

Beck looked back at the house, the corners of his mouth turning down, imagining the horror he was about to find. "The truth. We're looking for her."

Maddox was now unarmed, so they dispersed as Beck had instructed. Beck started toward the house again. Looking back at Maddox, he said, "You don't want to be here when I come out with that girl's body."

"I need confirmation," Maddox answered. "I'll wait."

"It's your life. I'm happy beating it out of you."

Beck turned. He had seen a lot of bombed-out buildings in faraway places, homes and lives destroyed, burned to a crisp. That's what he was looking at now.

CHAPTER 39

When the missile hit the second story of the house, Dal Cho was already inside Marco Cordero's tunnel, following each lightbulb strung every twenty feet or so to the ceiling by wooden support beams. He had reached the kitchen perhaps thirty seconds behind Cordero and the girl, and when he saw the large refrigerator pulled away from the wall, he knew Cordero had provided himself a way out. Gun leveled in front of him, he stepped through the opening and down the stairs. It was nothing like Jesse Roy's wine cellar. It was a long trench burrowed beneath the home, too short for him to stand up straight and just wider than an average-size man. He felt the explosion before his brain registered the sound, and Cho had the fleeting thought that the house had been torn loose from its foundation, like in *The Wizard of Oz*. The concussion on his back launched him forward as if gravity had been suspended. He woke only moments later, on the tunnel floor, his face buried in dirt. Pulling himself to his feet, Cho looked up. There were several breaks in the ceiling and light and heat were pouring down onto him. *Fire*, he thought groggily.

The house is on fire. He stared at the flickers of light for several seconds before his mind began to refocus. *Move.*

He stepped over a few of the fallen support beams, stopped, and listened for anything moving. The echoes of footfalls entered his ears. They were running.

The fire was out, but the smoke was still thick in the home's shell. Beck tucked his mouth and nose in behind the high collars of his jumpsuit, doing his best to take short, shallow breaths. The pink slurry covered everything. He went immediately to the east side of the house to begin his search for bodies, figuring to make his way counterclockwise. He didn't need a door; the entire house was open. It was mostly dark inside, but his night goggles were illuminating both the fire retardant and the smoldering substances beneath it, all of it glowing in his eyes. The exterior east-side wall had largely blown apart, and what remained of the kitchen looked as if it had been hit by a tornado, the cabinets torn from their moorings on the walls; the appliances and countertops littering the ground in piles of various heights. Beck looked under each for Mercy's body.

And then he saw it. A hole in what was left of the drywall behind the fallen refrigerator, its contents spilled and ejected from the open door. At first he thought the opening must have been made by the explosion, but it was cut too perfectly, its lines too straight. He stared into the dim light coming from beyond the wall. It wasn't much, but it was enough for him to know there was something below. He climbed over the fridge and peeked into the darkness, the Henry Axe pointed directly in front of him. There were four steps to the bottom. When he reached the floor, he swept the tunnel with his eyes, straining to see through the particles of falling dust. Advancing slowly, Beck noted the passage was about six inches shorter than he was.

Looking down, he saw footprints in the dirt. Three sets, two large, one small. He took a beat to consider if he should go back, alert Maddox and the others, and try to determine where the tunnel came out from above. But Maddox had already tried killing Mercy once.

He stepped into the passage. It sloped downward and within fifty feet made a gradual turn to the north, all of it lit by LED bulbs strung by electrical wire along the top. Beck immediately realized where it must end.

He hadn't been there in twenty-five years.

The Horned Toad Mine had been out of operation for more than a decade, which made it perfect for Marco Cordero. Located about a mile northwest of the Grass Valley ranch he purchased the previous winter, it still had a number of equipment buildings standing, any of which could be used to store a vehicle, and it had a road that led to a highway that would eventually take you to Canada, if you were so inclined, or to Mexico if you preferred a warmer climate. For Cordero, it needed to get him to the nearest airfield.

He had always been lucky, had nine lives and then some it seemed, losing count of how many times he had walked away from a horrible death that claimed others. Bolting from the great room of the house when he did was another confirmation that the Almighty was not done with him. And he had Mercy Vaughn, which meant that he was going to get his fortune back. If she couldn't regain access to his accounts, he would make her steal it electronically from someone else. Maybe the damned Chinese. Yes, he was banged up, his left arm aching more by the minute thanks to the support beam that had landed on it after the larger explosion, but he had been broken before. He had spent more money having this godforsaken tomb of a tunnel secretly excavated than most people make in a lifetime. All he needed to do now was keep moving through it. Construction-wise, it was a near replica of the one under his home in Caborca, a few feet wide and maybe five feet tall. The going was slow, especially with the occasional smoke that had found its way off the eastern mountain, filtering down through the cylindrical air vents that rose twenty to thirty feet to the desert floor. At least they had light.

Sweating profusely, despite the cooler temperature of the subterranean shaft, Cordero kept a tight hold of Mercy with his good arm, marching her along the meandering dirt floor. Only a couple of minutes after leaving the house, he thought he heard footsteps behind him. Maybe an echo. Maybe not. From that point on, he smashed each successive lightbulb affixed to the ceiling supports, allowing him to still see ahead while leaving the section behind in complete darkness. If anyone was following, they would be feeling their way, and that would be a much longer walk. Cordero had been in the tunnel only once before, soon after it had been completed. The length of it, a miracle of excavation, made him vow to never enter it again, so intense was the claustrophobia and the effect it had on his breathing. But now, his heart racing faster than it ever had, he was glad he'd done the test run. In minutes he would be free.

Upon reaching the last intact lightbulb, Dal Cho silently cursed Cordero, vowing to put a bullet in the man's head. He was blind now, cramped and stooped over, with nothing to light the way. The darkness didn't slow him down, though. In fact, now unable to see the occasional air vents that led to the surface, Cho became so unnerved, he actually increased his pace, feeling the splintered wooden supports with his fingers. He smelled the smoky air from above worming its way into the tunnel, but not seeing those vents made him feel as if he were choking.

Somehow, the entire mission had come off the rails. The intelligence Beijing had sent him was faulty. There was no mention of a Mexican drug cartel's involvement with the girl, or of how much of an irritation the local sheriff might become. But that was intelligence work, and Cho's bosses at the Ministry of State Security would brook no excuses for failing to achieve the desired result. The Youth Center would not be destroyed, but at the very least Beijing now had the code they needed to exploit Watcher. And it would be a coup to bring Mei Wu home alive.

He couldn't believe how far the tunnel extended. With every turn, Cho was certain he had reached the end, only to be disappointed once more. The broken lightbulbs crunched under his hiking boots occasionally, but he couldn't worry about the sound. If Cordero made it out of here, he was sure to have a working vehicle waiting for him. And that would be the end of everything. He estimated he had already walked more than a kilometer when he heard Cordero screaming at Mei Wu.

"Get up the fucking ladder! Get up the fucking ladder!"

Cho saw light from around the bend ahead and lengthened his stride. He was close now, and he was confident Cordero had no weapon. Mei was shouting back, and the combination of her voice mixed with Cordero's gave Cho all the cover he needed.

Emerging into the light, he saw Cordero trying to push Mei up a cylindrical metal tube with one hand firmly on her waistband. The commotion allowed Cho to silently step up behind him. He would have preferred to drill a new tunnel through the man's skull with the .45 semiautomatic, but sound carries, especially in confined spaces. He chose instead a vicious elbow strike to the back of the neck.

Cordero crumpled, his brain literally shaken like a can of soda. Mercy felt him release his hold on her and instinctively looked down through the tube only to see Cho's face gazing up at her. She lifted her legs, tucking them under her butt, and began frantically climbing.

"Really?" Cho yelled. "I am the only one here trying to save you, and you are running away?" He grabbed the sides of the ladder and scaled the rungs two at a time, catching her just as she emerged through the opening into the Horned Toad Mine.

CHAPTER 40

Beck saw the body in the dirt at the base of the ladder and knew it was too small to be Cho. He rolled it carefully over with his boot. Up until now, he had only seen Marco Cordero through binoculars, but upon closer inspection, it was obvious this was the man responsible for a number of deaths in Lincoln County and, no doubt, a good portion of the western U.S. He was unconscious but breathing. Beck grabbed one of Cordero's arms, dragging him closer to the ladder that ran upward through a metal tube. There was no way he was going to haul the Mexican drug lord up with him, so he zip-tied him to the bottom rung.

"Don't run off," Beck said softly as he peered up through the tube. "Lots to talk about."

With the aid of his NVGs, Beck was sure he had made up some time. The only question now was how far behind he was. Discarding the smoke jumper suit he had been wearing since parachuting into the mountains hours earlier, he ascended the ladder quickly, estimating it rose some twenty-five feet to the surface. There was no sealed hatch at the top, only an old ceramic toilet that had already been pushed aside and which had been used to conceal the opening. It made sense coming up through an old latrine. Cordero had planned well for a last-resort escape. As he squeezed through the opening, he unclipped his radio and quietly updated his team.

"Well, kids, you'll never guess where I am," he whispered. The risk was minimal that Cho was on the other side of the wall listening. He would be trying to find a way out of the mine right now. The replies came to Beck's ear one after the other. They offered to turn around, but Beck assured them they were spread too thin already, and catching Jesse was as important as finding Mercy and Cho.

"Stay with the roadblocks you're setting up. The road out of the mine leads there anyway, so Cho will head that way if he can find whatever car Cordero has stashed here. I've got plenty of juice in my goggles, so I'll look around here and let you know what I find."

After signing off, Beck cracked the door on the mine's restroom. It opened in what was the administration building. The last time he had been here was the summer of his junior year in high school, when he and his girlfriend, Willa Benson, met Jesse and Cash for some late-night fun running around the open pit mine. Three months later, Cash would roll out to his right and throw a thirty-yard touchdown pass in a game against Battle Mountain but take a helmet to the base of his spine as he released the ball. The boy who already had offers to play college ball and get a fine education would spend the rest of his life in a battle with a much tougher opponent, a battle he lost because of Jesse Roy and Marco Cordero.

Beck adjusted the focus on his goggles, happy there was some light from the Patterson Pass fire flickering in the sky outside and filtering through the broken windows. That light was amplified now, and it helped illuminate what was probably scraps of metal and wood shelving and a few broken rolling chairs in glowing green. The magic eyes only improved his vision deficit, they didn't eliminate it. Like Cash's losing battle with pain, Beck could literally see his own disability slowly getting worse.

Smoke from the fire two miles away wafted into the room, but otherwise the air was still and quiet. Cho and Mercy were not in the building. As he reached for the doorknob that would take him outside, Beck heard an engine straining to start. It was trying hard to turn over, a vehicle whose battery had been idle for some time. Beck ran out of the administration building and to his left where the mine's former truck facility was located. Headlights flashed in Beck's eyes, temporarily overloading his goggles, the greenish glow blooming as the amplification plate was bombarded by all the photons pouring in. Beck tilted the binoculars up and over his eyes, reducing the glare of the headlights to two large tennis balls. The second the big engine kicked over and roared to life, a large SUV came roaring out of the garage straight at him. Beck dropped to one knee, bringing the Henry up to his shoulder, and fired at what he hoped was right between the lights.

He heard the first round of .410 shot scatter over the front of the vehicle, not overly hopeful any of it would penetrate into the engine, and then fired four more times in rapid succession as the SUV barreled directly toward him. One of the rounds shattered the right headlight, and Beck was able to both lower the lenses over his eyes again and dive out of the way just in time. As it passed, he could see a figure leaning out of the driver's window, the explosion of his handgun like lightning strikes of green in the darkness. The second round ricocheted off the ground, hitting the radio on Beck's left hip and knocking him over. Rolling into a crouch, he pulled the Glock from his thigh holster and fired six quick shots at the side and back of the vehicle, careful to keep his rounds away from the cab. There was no doubt in his mind that Mercy was inside.

The Chevy Suburban was moving fast, and as he ran toward it, Beck could hear the hissing of its punctured radiator. Then he saw the car fishtail on the hard gravel and heard the thumping of the tread coming off the left rear wheel. As it skidded to a stop, Cho leaned out the window and fired another quick burst. Caught out in the open, Beck cut across the back end of the gas-guzzler, sprinting to the old warehouse building. Cho wasn't firing blindly; his last round nicked the helix of Beck's left ear as he was rounding the far side of the metal hut. It stung, but Beck was confident the bullet had only grazed him. He reloaded both guns without looking, his eyes locked on Cho, who was pulling Mercy from the cab. As he turned to move around the backside of the building, the goggles caught the blur of a moving object right in front of his face. It struck him on the side of his head, and the green light suddenly faded to black.

He was out only for seconds. The NVGs were ripped from his head, and Beck heard them crunch beneath a boot several times. He was blind again, helpless. "Quiet, Sheriff," Maddox whispered, watching Cho run toward the road that led out of the mine. "I know you can't see it, but I'm pointing your Glock at your chest. Guns aren't really my thing, so please don't make me use it."

Beck could feel the blood trickling out of his hair and down his neck. "What are you doing, Maddox? She's right there. She's alive. I can get her back." He tried to get to his feet, but Maddox cocked the hammer on the Glock, and Beck heard it.

"Stay down," he said. "What we need to do is let her go."

"You knew she was alive, that she'd gotten out of the house. But how?"

Maddox peeked around the building to see that Cho and Mercy were still moving. "New Israeli tech. Pulse-based-through-wall-imaging. Don't ask me what the acronym is for that because

I don't know it. I could see her from the helo. Her and everyone else."

Beck shook his head. "You can't do this, Maddox. She's sixteen years old. She's not trained for whatever Homeland Security wet dream you're having right now."

"Do you know about Titan Rain, Beck?"

"Of course." He had heard the name "Titan Rain" when he was at the Army War College. It was the designation given to an ongoing series of coordinated attacks on computer systems in the United States and the United Kingdom and traced to China's state-sponsored hacking group. It was a cyberattack of immense scope and sophistication, patiently working its way into the systems of the FBI and NSA among others. The damage was almost incalculable.

"Then you know this is what we do now. Moves and counter-moves. We think like they do. Long term. We can play their game, and we can play it better. That's what this is."

"Mercy was a plant."

"She was a catalyst." Maddox squatted in the dirt next to Beck, kept the Glock on him. "Mercy, Jesse Roy, his daughter, even you, all carefully choreographed to bring the Chinese in, though we expected your part to be much less annoying. What you don't know about this girl could fill a book, but be assured she *is* trained and was a willing participant in all of it. Now it's time for you to take a step back. You're a hero now, Beck. You've got a load of drugs back there and a bunch of dead cartel guys. Enjoy it. Soak up the limelight. Hell, you could probably run for governor."

Beck felt the laceration on his temple with two fingers. "And Mercy?"

Maddox hesitated before answering. "I'm only telling you this because I've seen your file. You can appreciate how important this is to our country right now. Mercy goes with our Chinese friend. They melt into the dark night. And we let it play. We let it play so the Chinese think they've successfully hacked us again. She'll go to work for them but will be working for us the whole time."

If they don't kill her, Beck thought. But even as he did, he realized that Maddox was probably right. Mercy Vaughn was a chameleon. She could beat the "box," the polygraph the Chinese would wire her to. And with her talents, they would be looking for reasons to believe her. "And the Federal Reserve hack. Was that your idea too?"

"I wish," Maddox chuckled. "It was hers, and it was brilliant. And it was the first step in a plan that has taken two years to get us to this point today." He paused a moment. "You need to let this go, Beck. You're a lot smarter than I gave you credit for, but you almost screwed it all up. That was my fault. I should have given your service jacket more than a cursory review during our planning."

Beck sat up, putting his back against the metal building. "There's no way you could have planned all of this." When Maddox didn't respond, he added, "She changed her mind, didn't she? It's why she ran."

"She went a little off script. That's all. Was supposed to let Cho take her when she was on the road cleanup detail. Got too close to Roy's daughter, I guess. She's back on track now."

He could hear Maddox moving to his right, to the corner of the warehouse a few feet away. Probably looking to make sure Cho and Mercy were getting away. "So, the kill squad was window dressing."

Maddox grinned. "Sure, not that those silverbacks are aware of that, of course. We spared no expense in making it all look real. That was for your benefit mostly and all the other players in the cast. Everyone needed to believe Mercy was the genuine article." With a smirk on his face, he took another peek around the corner of the building to see how far Cho and Mercy had gotten. What he saw, however, was a fist catching him square on the jaw.

CHAPTER 41

Beck heard the commotion in front of him, felt Maddox stagger into him and then fall. *We're dead,* he told himself. It could only be Cho. He heard the man's steps in the dirt next to him, heard him pick up the Glock and rack the slide, and waited for the gunshot that would end his life. He saw Mercy's face, Pop's, Brin's, flash before his blind eyes.

"You just gonna lie there?" Jesse Roy asked.

The air that had been locked inside Beck's lungs exploded. "I can't see, Jesse. I can't see in the dark." Jesse didn't respond, and Beck realized his old friend must be contemplating killing him. He was unarmed and helpless after all. It would be easy.

"Well, you must feel pretty silly about now, then." Jesse reached down and grabbed Beck's hand, pulled him to his feet. "Didn't figure on running into you up here but overheard your conversation with Special Ed. You're after the girl, I take it?"

Beck nodded. "I am, but right now, I have no radio and no eyes. I'm gonna need your help."

It took only a moment for Jesse to respond. "Then we should

get going. That boy has her on the main road, but they're on foot, so we—"

"Can maybe get around them by heading around the south pit," Beck interjected. "I remember. Hand me my Henry. Should be lying around here somewhere."

Jesse found the rifle and placed it in Beck's hands. "I've seen these. Sold a few across the border. Nice gun. Won't do you much good if you can't see. It's darker than the inside of a coffin out here. Can hardly see myself."

They took off at a trot, moving south, Beck limping and holding on to Jesse Roy's right shoulder. "Thanks for not killing my sister," Beck said. "I appreciate that."

Jesse snorted. "That was a six-hundred-dollar bottle of Napa red, my friend, but what the hell, it was already open. She's okay, then?"

"She's okay," Beck said.

"She's the same scrappy fireball she was when she was a kid. Given the chance, she would have killed me."

"She might still."

"You remember the last time we were here?" Jesse asked after a minute. "Cash had that summer job with the mine and let you, me, and Willa in. We were drinking my old man's beer and driving as fast as we could up and down these haul roads in the middle of the fucking night."

Beck could see the memory clearly in his head, the four of them steaming up the ramp on the side of the pit that the ore trucks would drive, his truck tires barely gripping the loose earth. "Yeah, I remember we would run and jump from one bench to the next." It was like it was yesterday, Cash and Jesse in front of him, leaping out over the huge twenty-foot steps notched into the side of the pit, before landing hard on the flat dirt. "I remember Willa thought we would break our necks."

"God, that was fun," Jesse said. "I miss that time. I miss Cash." When Beck didn't respond, he added, "Imagine you'll be taking me to your jail after we're done here."

"If we both somehow manage to survive the next few minutes. You know I have to."

Jesse let out a small laugh. "Well, Helen Keller, don't count your chickens just yet."

"I think that was the county sheriff back there," Cho remarked in disbelief as he pulled Mercy along by the elbow. His hold on her was tight enough and all he could muster after taking the round to his shoulder. "How the hell did he find that tunnel so quickly?"

The road turned west, and it would eventually lead to the highway. If he could get to it, he could get to the next town. If he could do that, he could steal a cell phone and make his way out of this godforsaken desert.

His right shoulder was on fire, but the round had passed through the meaty muscle, and he had managed to stop the bleeding with Mercy's help. The girl seemed to be as good at first aid as she was with computers, and she seemed to be as anxious to get away from the authorities as he was.

"He came to see me in the Youth Center," she said. "I could see he was a very intelligent man. Good instincts. He suspected I hacked the drone. He did not say it at the time, but he suspected."

Cho didn't doubt it. The man correctly concluded he was Chinese and not Korean after a two-minute conversation. "Well, I know I hit him, so let's hope he's moving slower than we are." Cho turned, looking over his shoulder at the road behind them. It was pitch-black, except for the fire in the distance. He saw nothing.

He thought about his team back at the house, silently hoped they were dead, burned beyond recognition. It had been a missile, he was sure. He and the girl were both lucky to be alive, and he needed to make good use of that luck now, because the missile had been fired to kill them all, which meant that American intelligence had tracked Mercy Vaughn to the ranch house. And though he was confident there would be no way to detect the intrusion into Watcher, he worried they might be able to recover the flight console and piece together that they were setting up to destroy something consequential. Cho had one duty now. Get to somewhere he could contact his people and get Mei Wu home.

Brinley found a woozy Marco Cordero right where her brother had secured him, and that was pure karma in her mind. The drug lord had no idea who this tiny woman with a handgun was, but he promised her fifty thousand dollars if she would get him out of there. She complied without hesitation, pushing his head down with one hand while slicing with one quick stroke the nylon wrist strap with the switchblade knife she always carried. Cordero screamed, blood streaming from his wrist.

"Quit crying. I just nicked you." Brinley gave him a good ten seconds to wrap the wound then motioned with the muzzle of her gun. "Up the ladder there, Sparky."

A minute later they were walking the Horned Toad Mine, the light of the nearby Patterson Pass filtering into Brinley's NVGs and allowing her to see her sandy surroundings glow like a bioluminescent beach.

"Where are we going?" Cordero wheezed. "If you get me out of here, I will get you the money."

She had snagged an old broom off the wall in the building the tunnel ladder rose into and used it now to swat Cordero in the back of the head. "We'll know it when we see it," she said. "Keep moving."

They walked for only another minute before Brinley found what she was looking for. It was boarded up with old wooden slats and emblazoned with a sign that cautioned:

WARNING!

DANGEROUS MINE SHAFTS

DO NOT PASS BEYOND THIS POINT

It was a sign that Cordero couldn't read, let alone see in the dark.

"That's fine right there," she told him. "You can stop now. Walk toward me."

Cordero, his injured arm tucked tightly into his torso, turned in the dirt and walked to his left a few feet. "Please, señora. Can you help me out of here?"

"Stop there," she said, taking a moment to consider everything that had happened in the last few days. She moved to her left so that Cordero was between her and the mine shaft. "My brother is going to be furious with me."

"Your brother? Is he the sheriff? It doesn't matter," Cordero pleaded with his one good arm. "We can—"

Brinley kicked the king of the Caborca cartel squarely in the chest, launching him backward and down. He crashed through the wooden slats covering the shaft and fell for seconds until Brinley heard what sounded like a pebble hitting a pond. Then she took the broom and whisked away her tracks in the dirt.

Ten minutes after leaving the warehouse and a hog-tied Maddox, Beck and Jesse stood between the two massive holes carved out of the earth over decades by three different mining companies. All the gold to be found here had long ago been plucked from the hard ground, but the graveyard of rock and sand remained and probably would for centuries. Unlike the men who had made Nevada the largest gold producer in the country, there was no one who was going to strike it rich by filling in those holes, and no environmentalists were screaming for restoration of the site. Only wind and water and time would change it now.

"Tell me what happened," Beck whispered as they caught their breath. "How did it come to this?"

"Doesn't matter," Jesse said. "I got off the righteous path a long way back. Took too many shortcuts. The details are hardly important."

Beck stopped walking. "And Willa?"

"You were right about her. She hated all of it. The guns, the money, the drugs. Me too, I guess. Everything but Shiloah. I pushed her away, cheated on her, and was obvious about it so she'd divorce me. Thought it might keep her and the kid safe."

It was the kind of darkness Beck could see through. "She threatened to go to the authorities."

Jesse sniffled. "Tell me that son of a bitch Cordero blew up with that house."

Beck shook his head. "He's down in the tunnel, secured but alive."

"Don't let him live, Beck. Kill him, or better yet, let me do it. He killed Willa."

"Jesse!" Beck said a little too loudly. "Where are we?"

"The access road is up ahead of us. I don't think they could have made it this far yet coming from the north side. What do you want to do?"

"Give me the lay of the land," Beck answered.

"Jesus, what are you doing out here, Beck? You're going to get yourself killed for a girl you don't even know."

Beck looked in the direction of Jesse's voice, blackness swallowing his eyes. "That girl saved Shiloah's life today."

Jesse swallowed hard. "Yeah, she did. Okay, we're between the north and south pits. Access road is about sixty feet ahead, where it starts to curve around the south pit. You remember that?"

"I think so. Nothing but sand on either side, right?"

"Nothing but sand."

Beck reached out and put his hand on Jesse's arm. "Guide me over to the south pit and help me get down over the ledge. You take the pistol and get cover in the north pit. When they reach the point I can hear them right in front of me, I'll fire off a warning shot with the Henry. I might have winged him back by the warehouse, so we might be able to take him without a shot. He doesn't know I can't see."

"What's he packing?" asked Jesse.

"Handgun. Sounded like a .45. I counted ten shots back there, so he may have a few rounds left. Don't take any chances, though. If you have the shot, take it. He'll do the same, so don't give him a target."

"Got an idea," Jesse said.

Three minutes and change later, they heard footsteps on the road in front of them. Beck listened intently, confirmed it was two sets of shoes he was hearing, and with his left hand grabbed the base of a large sagebrush that had sunk its roots into the very edge of the south pit. With his right, he pulled back the hammer on the Henry Axe. Seconds later, he heard a shoe collide with the rocks Jesse had strung in a line across the narrow access road, heard them skitter across the blacktop. Beck pulled the trigger, and the .410 load split the night air.

He called out. "That's far enough, Cho. Drop the gun and let the girl go."

Dal Cho did nothing of the sort. Instead, he stared out into the black night. He could see almost nothing. With his arm around

Mercy's neck, he began slowly backing up, whispering, "Stay with me and stay quiet, or I'll kill you right here."

Beck could hear them retreating. "Where are you going?" he shouted. "I've already got people sealing off the way you came, and the rest of my team is coming in from the north. Nobody has to die here tonight. Release her and drop the gun. With any luck, the FBI will cut you a deal in exchange for your cooperation. You won't go home, but you might end up in a nice sunny place by the beach somewhere." His words weren't intended to move the Chinese spy to reason. That wasn't going to happen, but they might provide Jesse some cover.

As Beck made his plea, Jesse was crawling over the edge of the north pit. He could see the Asian man and the girl clearly, twenty feet ahead and backing toward him. But he had no shot. Cho had the much smaller girl directly in front of him. If he fired, the bullet might go directly through the target and into her. Jesse climbed to his feet, his boots dragging too loudly over the loose gravel.

Cho spun around, his eyes searching out the noise behind him. Jesse was already running when Cho fired. Beck was moving too, running toward the noise, his rifle left in the dirt. The bullet caught Jesse in the abdomen, causing him to drop the Glock, but his momentum carried him into the man who had fired it. The gun boomed again, the noise tearing through the desert air and Beck's ears like the shot from a cannon. At a dead run, he managed to hit them all, and for a moment they were wrapped together like a scrum in a rugby game. The pile of bodies kept moving, until it toppled over the rim of the north pit.

They slid and somersaulted down the steep grade, a distance of some fifteen feet, before hitting the first bench roughly at the same time. Beck hung on for dear life, hearing Jesse groan and knowing that Cho was between them. Somehow they landed as they had gone over, so the impact affected Beck the least. He was on top of the pile and had the others to cushion him. He heard Mercy cry out in pain from a few feet away and realized she had slipped Cho's grasp. As the rest of them rolled again, he could feel the training in Cho's muscles, his powerful arms and neck. And he could feel Jesse fall away.

Beck and Cho grappled, striking each other with short punches and kicks, the tactics Beck had been taught so many years ago and which he still practiced religiously. Cho maneuvered his way on top, but Beck pulled the man's neck down and into him, while pinning Cho's right arm under his own elbow. That left Cho with only his left arm to strike at Beck's face and head but with only short, almost harmless blows. And that meant Cho no longer held a gun. Beck worked his legs, waging their own war with Cho's for leverage, knowing that letting go was death. But without any ability to see and take the offensive, he could feel the sand running out. He had seconds left.

Cho squirmed, arching his back while pushing down and trying to straighten his arms. The sheriff was an adept fighter and extremely quick and strong. But Cho could feel the man's strength ebbing, swiping his right hand in search of the one he had freed. It was as if he couldn't see. With all his remaining might, Cho reached back with his right hand and brought it crashing down on the sheriff's face. It was enough. The blow stunned Beck, enough to reflexively unlock the viselike hold on his legs, and Cho pushed away, rolling off and to his right. He popped to his feet like the gymnast he once was, fast and sticking the landing.

Beck made it to his knees, looking frantically back and forth. Cho couldn't believe his luck. The sheriff seemed to be blind. Cho laughed, then charged. Two quick steps and his right leg flew in an arc toward Beck's head. Beck could see none of it. He heard only the sound made when propellant gases expand rapidly and cause a bullet to accelerate, the resultant pressure wave causing a boom of more than a hundred and fifty decibels.

The round ripped through Cho's chest from left to right. When he came down, he was, incredibly, still on his feet and teetering on the edge of the next descending wall. It took him a second to regain his balance, and despite the blood coming up through his mouth, he smiled. That's when Beck heard two more shots, heard Cho topple to his left, over the edge of the mine's next cut. Then behind him and much farther away, he heard something else hit the ground. "Jesse, is that you?"

"It's me, Sheriff," Mercy said after a moment, her voice low and mournful.

"Where is Cho?" Beck asked, his fists raised in front of his body.

Her answer was quiet, quivering now. "Below you."

"Can you see him?"

Her answer was not immediate, and Beck could hear her sliding in the dirt, maybe twenty feet away. "Yes . . . not moving."

"Are you hurt?" There was no answer. "Mercy!" he yelled. "Are you hurt?"

Her cry was almost inaudible now. "Yes . . . hurt."

Beck stayed on his hands and knees, feeling his way in the dirt as fast as he could toward her voice. "Keep talking, Mercy. I'm coming. I can't see in the dark, so I need you to keep talking."

"I . . . am . . . sorry," she squeaked in the black night.

"Jesse!" Beck yelled, the panic rising up in him like never before. He was disoriented, dizzy. "Jesse, can you help us?" But the air was still. "Mercy? Talk to me, Mercy. Where are you?"

He heard only his sister's voice shouting his name repeatedly.

CHAPTER 42

No aliens were freed on Alien Independence Day. The crowd that eventually gathered outside Area 51's back gate was far smaller than the event's organizers had hoped for, and as Beck and Arshal made their way through the throng of costumed, sign-carrying partygoers, Beck estimated that no more than six thousand crazies had made the pilgrimage. By Friday afternoon, most were already gone.

The rain helped. The clouds had swung up from Mexico and into Arizona, and instead of turning east as the monsoons normally do, they moved farther north. It pelted the alien aficionados so hard that a new conspiracy theory had developed: the government had seeded the clouds around the secret area in order to drive the truth-seekers away. The rain stopped around noon, but by that time only the real die-hards remained, all hoping that somebody else would be the first to climb the chain-link fence.

Arshal touched Beck on the arm and pointed. "Here comes trouble. Let me know if you want me to kill him."

Maddox was in a dark suit and sunglasses, and for that, the revelers surrounded him, deemed him to be one of the *Men in Black*. Maybe a very young Tommy Lee Jones, Beck mused.

Thirty-six hours earlier, Maddox had fumed all the way back to Pioche. Or so Beck had been told. Sev Velasco had retrieved and handcuffed the OSI agent from the Horned Toad Mine and had pretended not to understand English very well. The dawn was almost breaking when they finally arrived at the office, and Sev escorted Maddox to a cell in the detention center. It was noon before Beck, his right earlobe and hip stitched and bandaged, made his way over to the lockup. He wanted to tell Maddox he would be formally charged with trying to murder two law enforcement officers, that he knew it was he who had piloted and crashed the Reaper into his truck. But he knew a pipe dream when he saw one and knew he would never be able to prove it.

"You're done," Maddox said from his skinny bunk. "Impeding a federal agent, wrongful imprisonment. You're out of a job."

Beck nodded. "Well, it might be time for that, I guess. We might have to see which of us has more friends in the governor's office and the Pentagon. Right now, I'd bet on me. I made a few calls to my Air Force contacts. The OSI doesn't have a Special Agent Maddox in its ranks. Imagine my surprise."

"That changes nothing. The girl, Sheriff. Where is Mercy Vaughn?"

Beck dropped his head. "Right now, she's in our morgue. You got her killed, Maddox. The Chinese agent you wanted her to go home with shot her in the head before he died."

Maddox laughed. "And who killed him? You? You couldn't even see."

"No, I sure couldn't. That's a fact. But Jesse Roy could. And that cost Jesse his life as well, though I guess he had it coming. So, congratulations. I'm sure your parents would be very proud. Job well done." He unlocked the cell and opened the door.

Maddox got up and moved toward him. "Do you have any idea what you've done?"

"I think so. I failed Mercy. Do you have any idea what *you've* done?"

"I want to see the bodies. Hers and Cho's."

Beck was exhausted. He'd had enough of the man and wanted to be rid of him. "Fine," he said. "Autopsy will be done by Saturday. Come back then with a federal warrant and an identity I can verify. If that's not good enough, you can stay in this jail and wait."

He didn't wait, and now he was back a day earlier than Beck had told him to be, brandishing a federal subpoena. It looked official, though it did not identify Maddox's real name, so Beck left Arshal and the brothers Green to ensure the secret alien base remained in the hands of its military and intelligence overlords. Two hours later, after taking his sweet time driving the eighty miles back to Caliente, Beck walked Maddox into the small room that served as the morgue. Dr. Bishara, incensed by the interruption and cursing in Turkish, moved quickly to the stainless steel freezer with stacked cadaver compartments. It held up to six corpses, five of which were currently occupied. He opened the door to the middle locker on the left.

Maddox felt the blast of cold air and saw the bare feet and toe tag on the girl's body. He looked at Beck, who gestured to Bishara to pull the body out for closer examination. Bishara scowled. "Who is this fucking guy?"

"Hadji, please."

Bishara pulled the tray holding Mercy Vaughn's dead body all the way out. Maddox stepped up next to the head. He looked at Beck.

"Well, go on then," Beck said to him, turning away. "See what you've done."

Slowly, Maddox pulled back the white sheet covering the naked body. He got as far as the head, and not even all of that. The right side of Mercy's temple was destroyed, the blood dried and dark now, part of her brain extending through the cavity caused by Dal Cho's bullet. The rest of her face was devoid of pigment, her left eye lifeless and fixed open. Maddox turned from the body and covered his mouth to avoid retching.

"Don't you throw up in here, motherfucker," Bishara scolded him. "If you had waited a day, I could have autopsied her and cleaned her up." Gently, and with some reverence, he pulled the sheet back over her and slid her back into the freezer. Cho came next, and that was all Maddox needed to see.

Beck had already left the room. Maddox found him out in the parking lot, leaning against his truck for support. "Was it worth it?" Beck asked him. "Did her life mean anything to you?"

Maddox dropped his shades over his eyes, concealing them. "Her life meant more than you could possibly know, Sheriff. And she didn't need to die." There was a little catch in his throat now. "That wasn't part of the plan."

"She get you what you needed?"

Maddox raised both palms in the air. "I'm not at liberty to say. But she was aware of the risks. Know that."

Seething with disgust, Beck snorted and looked away. "Joan of Arc would have been proud."

"I'll send someone for the bodies," Maddox said. "We'll take care of it."

Beck's brows came together, the creases in his forehead deep and angry. "You'll do nothing of the sort, Agent Maddox, or whatever your real name is. You can have Dal Cho's body, but I will bury this girl. She deserves to have someone stand over her and say a few words. Now get the hell out of my county."

CHAPTER 43

To bury his two childhood friends, Beck wore his best suit. It was Sunday, July 13, nine days after it had all started. Cash Conrad went first, surrounded by an entire community who knew and loved the high school football standout who had struggled so long with pain and addiction. His parents asked Beck to deliver their son's eulogy.

"You were his oldest friend," Josie told him. His prepared remarks, bullet-pointed on notecards, never made it out of the pocket in his black suitcoat. What he had planned to say about old times and old friends suddenly seemed inappropriate as he faced the standing-room-only crowd fanning their hot faces inside the Elevate Life Church. Instead, Beck talked about failing those we love by not reminding them that their lives matter. Everyone in the church shared that sentiment.

Two hours later, with fewer than a dozen people present, Beck stood over the gravesite of the man responsible for Cash's death. He thought about what might have been. If he had stayed. If he had married Willa. None of it mattered. It was mud in the fire. There were no words he could offer, so he let the reverend do it.

Then Shiloah gripped his hand with hers, and Jesse's casket was lowered into the hot dry ground and covered in darkness.

There was no containing the story about the cattle rancher who ran drugs and guns with one of the largest Mexican cartels. Every news outlet in the southwest picked it up, especially since Marco Cordero and his escape tunnel made for exciting copy. What was omitted was any mention of how, after being secured to a steel ladder in a tunnel, the drug lord managed to escape, only to stumble into a deep mine shaft and die, or how a young Chinese hacker infiltrated the Chinese Communist Party's intelligence apparatus.

EPILOGUE

The following morning, they lowered another coffin. The day was mercifully cool and pleasant, and everyone listened as Dan Whiteside spoke about Mercy as if she had been a daughter. Shiloah cried a river, summoning tears that Beck was sure were for everything and everyone she had lost in her young life. They lowered the casket into the earth and that was that.

That night, the rain started again, and it continued off and on for three days, the longest period of rainfall in the last seven years. The precipitation, despite the accompanying lightning strikes, was sufficient to help extinguish the remaining wildfires in Lincoln County. Everybody was sick of all the water by then, primarily because people are creatures of habit, and in the desert lots of rain turns quickly into a different kind of disaster.

Charlie Blue Horse, a member of the Northern Paiute people, no longer lived where she had grown up, very close to where the Walker ran down to the Carson Valley Plain. She resided now with her mother and preteen daughter, Jules, in a small brick-faced house in downtown Reno, only blocks from where Beck had attended university. Her backyard was also small but had a lovely garden that Charlie and her mom obsessed over, especially the white spruce that attracted the crossbills, evening grosbeaks, and red-breasted nuthatches to feast on its light brown cones.

Beck hadn't seen Charlie in five weeks, and though he'd only known her for a few days, he missed her. "There's a job," she told him as they watched two of the nuthatches at work. "My boss is retiring."

"Wow, chief of investigations. You have a shot?"

"No," she said, turning to him with a grin. "But I think you do. They want someone from outside, someone with intelligence experience, someone who recently put a major dent in the state's drug problem."

Her suggestion stunned him. "Charlie, I'm losing my sight. I don't know how long it will be before it's totally gone, and I'm struggling to function with what I have left."

She reached up and kissed him softly on the mouth, something she'd been wanting to do since they met. "That has not been my experience. Think of it. You would have the entire division, Beck. You could take all the good you've done in Lincoln County and bring it to the State. You wouldn't need to be out in the field. Maybe on rare occasions, but you would have me and Columbo to help you. You have some special gifts, and we could use those."

Beck gazed across the yard at the dog, having no doubt he was up to the task. But there was Pop to consider and how managing a much bigger job from Carson City might impact his care. "Let's keep talking about it," he said. "I'd like to know more."

They sipped lemonade from red plastic cups, watching Columbo play catch with Brinley and the three girls. "She happy?" Beck asked.

"She's been absolutely miserable these last few days, knowing that she'd have to say goodbye to Shiloah until Thanksgiving break. I'm not confident she won't bolt from here in a few weeks when she's really missing her."

"She won't," said Beck. "She told me she loves it here. She loves having Jules as a little sister."

The ceremony in the judge's chambers a few blocks away had been short and sweet. Charlie Blue Horse was pronounced the legal guardian of a half-Paiute orphan teenager by the name of May Paya. To no one's amazement, all the documents were in order, impeccably forged by May herself and digitally inserted into the Social Security Administration's database, among others. A new identity, a fake past, and a longtime family friend and state police detective who agreed to become her guardian.

"I gave her a computer," Charlie said. "She wants to look for her real parents. Bad idea?"

He shook his head. "You gave her a life, Charlie. A home."

"You would have done the same if there wasn't a risk of someone there recognizing her."

May and Brinley walked over to them, and Beck touched the scar on May's right temple where the stitches had been only a week ago.

She smiled. "I hear you two kids are going to Burning Man together. How sweet is that?"

"I'll bring out the cake," Charlie said, blushing. Beck and May took a seat on the patio's wicker couch while Brinley pulled up a chair facing them.

"I see you really racked your brain coming up with a new name," Beck said.

May's eyes brightened. "Easier to remember. Same name, different spelling."

"And Mercy?" asked Brinley.

May giggled. "Laid to rest, I believe."

He nodded and motioned to Charlie's cozy home. "What do you think, May? Beats a dark freezer locker in the morgue, doesn't it?"

She laughed, shivering at the memory. "I was so cold in there. But how did you know he wouldn't touch me, that he wouldn't feel for a pulse or something?"

"I'd seen him react to a bunch of bloody cows on the highway," he answered. "I knew as soon as he saw you that he'd turn away."

May shook her head in amazement. "Brinley's movie people did such a good job on me. *I* was convinced I was dead."

Brinley grinned. It had taken two hours for the three special effects makeup artists to perfect the look of a gunshot victim who had bled out. "We were almost convinced ourselves."

May rose from her seat and wrapped her arms around Brinley. "You almost died because of me, Brinley. I am so sorry."

Brinley's face flushed with love and Beck could tell the display of affection had left his sister speechless. "You're both survivors," he said. "And you're both incredibly lucky to be alive."

May released Brinley from her bear hug and sat back down, closer to Beck this time. He set a hand gently on top of hers. "I'm sorry it took me so long to figure it all out. You really could have died."

"All of life is a dream walking," she answered. "All of death is a going home. I was only going home. I am sorry if I scared you." She looked up at him. "Shiloah said you had a very nice funeral for me."

Beck snorted. "All the finest people turned out."

"And Maddox? Was he there?"

"I'm sure he was watching from above. I could have sworn I heard a drone in the sky."

They all laughed at that. Then May looked up at Beck. "I

would have gone with him. With Cho. Once Shiloah was safe. It is what I was supposed to do. What I volunteered to do."

Charlie had returned with the cake, set it on the glass table nearby, and plopped down next to her ward. "I know *he* gets it," she said, pointing at Beck, "but help me understand that. What do you mean it's what you were supposed to do?"

May turned toward her new guardian. "I was the same age Jules is now, Charlie. My mother—the one who raised me—had done her best to disappear us, to hide us. We moved constantly to stay ahead of those that had sent us here. But they found us. I escaped death then, too, but my mother did not. I ran for some time by myself until I realized I did not want to run any longer. I wanted to make them pay for what they did to her, to us. She had taught me well. I ruined their hack of the Federal Reserve and then approached Maddox and the NSA with a deal. 'Put me in play,' I told them. 'I will bring their whole rotten house down.'"

Brinley whistled lightly. "My God, girl, I wouldn't want you coming after me."

May smiled. "Maddox arranged for me to be arrested and the court to place me at the Youth Center. It was all orchestrated. The drone. Jesse Roy. Some carefully placed information leaks. All of it."

Beck shook his head and looked into the late-afternoon sky, full of light and promise. "It's not your fight, May. It was never your fight. Perhaps it was your mother's, but it wasn't yours."

She considered his words for a moment. "I am a Uyghur. The fight is mine. But the point is moot, I suppose. Still, I did not anticipate some of what happened."

"You mean the cartel coming for you?"

"Oh no, I planned for that. That is why I moved all of Cordero's money. Maddox didn't see the cartel coming this far. Of course, he did not know I was falling in love with Shy and had changed my mind about leaving. I was supposed to let Cho take me when we were out on road cleanup. Maddox had told me he was in the area. That is why we arranged for me to be out there. But I could not leave her, not with her father and Cordero." She gazed into Beck's eyes. "Cordero killed her mother. Did you know that?"

Beck released a lungful of air, the vision of Marco Cordero falling through the dilapidated wooden frames loosely covering a deep shaft in the earth flashing across his brain. His gaze darted to his sister, but she looked away. "I suspected. Jesse confirmed it for me."

"You loved her once," May said. "Shiloah told me."

Beck considered her words for a moment. Knew they were true. He asked if they could talk about something else.

"Sure. What's on your mind?"

"I understand you have a new computer. But, May, you understand that you need to be very, very careful now. You have to fly under the radar. No high profile. No hacking. No one can find out who you really are."

She laughed. "Relax, Beck. I am not on the dark web. I am researching my past, trying to find it. Where I came from. Who I am."

Beck offered an apologetic tilt of the head.

May laughed. "And I am learning poker."

His eyebrows shot up. "Poker?"

Her head bobbed excitedly. "It is a fascinating game. I am going to win the World Series someday."

And the Chinese or Maddox will find you, and—

She saw the concern on his face. "I will be careful, Beck. Do not worry. Please."

Her smile warmed him the same way it had that first day they met, and he realized there was no point in arguing with her. She would do what she would do. "Speaking of games." He reached into the pocket of his blazer and removed a twenty-sided blue die. "I'm pretty sure this belongs to you."

She looked at the die in his hand, reached over and folded his fingers over it. "I want you to have it. I do not need it any longer. You would make a great D and D player, by the way." A tear made its way slowly down her cheek. "You risked everything to come after me, and I will never forget you or be able to repay you."

He put an arm around her, letting her head sink into his chest. "Not bad for a blind guy, I guess."

She hugged him as tightly as she could. "My good sheriff, you see better in the dark than anyone I know."

He didn't say anything, just squeezed her back.

ACKNOWLEDGMENTS

Like most authors, I write my novels in semisolitary confinement. At the outset, I know it will be a year or more until I get paroled and released back into the world, and all that time behind a closed door is, I suppose, one reason a lot of writers beg for an early release and never finish their book. I do my time counting the days (and the words), getting by with regular visits from my wife and the occasional correspondence from some loyal pen pals. It doesn't matter to them what I write; they are always willing to read and offer constructive feedback. So I say thanks to:

Steve Hampton (Lt. Col., USAF, Ret.) and Wayne Mason (Lt. Col., US Army, Ret.). You guys are forever sandbagging the parts of my stories that would otherwise leak the careless inconsistencies that make readers cringe and would make my editor second-guess his ability to recognize marketable talent. You may not fully appreciate that all my novels are written by the three of us. I can't imagine better friends.

Milan Njegomir and Ed Camhi, two college friends whose brains impressed me from the time we first shook hands. Our talks always remind me of the collected speeches of William F.

Buckley Jr. called *Let Us Talk of Many Things*. We have solved the world's problems many times and simply don't receive the credit we deserve. Your meticulous deconstruction of my writing warrants much more than my eternal gratitude.

Brett A. Wyrick (DO, FACOS, MPH, Major General, USAF, Ret.), for providing me an understanding of how emails and other communications work within the defense industry, and for being such a damned great friend for almost fifty years now. You're the best, buddy.

Jamie Woodard and Dr. William Gallus, Professor of Meteorology, Iowa State University. Your feedback always reminds me of Inigo Montoya's lesser-known mantra in *The Princess Bride:* "You keep using that word. I do not think it means what you think it means." Thanks for finding the things I can't and seeing the forest despite the trees. You are both first-stringers on Team Bruce.

Additionally, a number of people offered their unique experience and knowledge for this book:

Captain Adam (last name withheld, USAF) and John (Stazh) Borgos (MSgt., USAF, Ret.), for informing me on the workings of remotely piloted aircraft and their scary capabilities.

Stevee Topchi and Nicole Olgiate, for painting the picture of Mercy for me. You both are quality dudes, and I love you. And to Jared Judd for pinch-hitting and bringing your perspective to the story.

Amber Sandoval, Nevada State Trooper/DEA Task Force Officer, and Derek Fellig, North Las Vegas Police Department Detective/DEA Task Force Officer, for giving me the skinny on the war against fentanyl and the incredible men and women fighting it.

Daniel Porter, EVP, Cybersecurity, CyberGuard Compliance, LLP, for proofing my depictions of Mercy Vaughn, hacker extraordinaire. I don't believe I could sleep at night if I knew half of what you know.

Nicole Perlroth, for her amazing work *This Is How They Tell Me the World Ends* and for opening my eyes to the world of global cyberwarfare and zero days. Your book scared the hell out of me.

Kerry Lee, former sheriff of Lincoln County, Nevada, for generously sharing your stories and helping me make Porter Beck a character worth following.

Kristen Weber, editor and coach, for once again taking my novel to the next level. You got skills, girl!

Broader thanks must also be offered to:

Janet Reid, my uncensored and good-humored literary agent, whose gentle steerage of my writing career has helped me avoid the often hard to see icebergs while taking me places I had previously only imagined.

Keith Kahla, my editor at St. Martin's Press/Minotaur Books. Your redlines and suggestions always make the Porter Beck series a better read. I wish you had taught some of my writing classes!

Kelley Ragland, Sara Beth Haring, Hector DeJean, Grace Gay, and everyone at Macmillan Publishers who has touched my book in any way. It is a privilege working with you.

All my fellow authors that I've met along the way, be it virtually or in the flesh, you inspire me with your great stories and honor me with your friendship.

The bookstores, podcasters, reviewers, book clubs, and friends for lending me your venues and platforms to promote my work. Your unconditional support never ceases to amaze me.

And to Pam Borgos, my lifelong partner, wife, and greatest friend. Thanks for not letting any of this remarkable journey go to my head and for your patience and encouragement to chase this dream and do what I love most. You have always been the best part of us.

ABOUT THE AUTHOR

Pam Borgos

BRUCE BORGOS is the author of the Porter Beck Mystery series and two other novels. He lives in the Mohave Desert with Pam, his wife of forty years, and their golden retriever, Charlie Blue Horse. He has a lifelong obsession with words and stories and a fascination with how anyone can prefer white wine over red.

Visit his website at bruceborgos.com for more information on his books and wine recommendations.